# DEADLY REACH

## T.L. BECKER

ISBN-13: 9798992967012

Cover design by: T.L. Becker
Images: Canava Free Images; Typeface: KDP
Printed in the United States of America

# DEDICATION

To Mary, with thanks for your patience and kindness.

# DEADLY REACH

# CHAPTER ONE

## Day 1, 5:00 P.M., Islamabad

Gamir Halibid was a bundle of nerves as he looked out the window from the top floor of his building, which overlooked downtown Islamabad. His heart was beating well above its regular rate. At fifty-two years old, his black hair was beginning to silver at the temples. His rounded face nested in double chins atop his barrel chest.

He had moved from planning to action almost a week ago. Earlier this morning, he gave his second-in-command, Jahar P'Shari, the signal to proceed. Jahar used one of his burner phones to text the mercenary team leaders. The plan was officially underway, and it was too late to turn back. Jahar had transferred the money to offshore accounts, and special shipments were en route.

Gamir couldn't stop thinking about the plan. He expected news anytime from the other side of the world. The corner of his mouth lifted slightly; his brown eyes narrowed. He never liked being told to wait by anyone. Patience was not his best quality.

## Day 1, 8:00 A.M., Seventy miles south of St. Croix Island, US Virgin Islands

Mac Krieger held the helm wheel as the large sailboat crested a wave and plunged forward into a dark green trough. The boat shuddered each time the bow slammed into the water at the bottom of a wave, then rose to the top of the next in a smooth, repeating action. The large mainsail pulled the vintage cruiser through the rhythmic turbulence with ease. As the lone sailor on the large sailboat, Mac focused on the sea before him. He shot glances to the compass as he stood at the helm. He made minor adjustments to keep the boat on the north-by-northwest heading toward the US Virgin Island of St. Croix.

Three days into his vacation. Mac's unshaven face carried a light tan from the sunshine. His lips were chapped from the wind. His black hair

1

showed traces of bleaching from the daily saltwater swims. He wore lightweight blue cotton shorts with gray deck shoes, a gray t-shirt with a safety harness, and a dark blue windbreaker. The worn leather sailing gloves, borrowed from his father, were a last-minute addition to his gear.

The sailboat was forty-one feet from bow to stern. The boat's teak decking was worn smooth from years of sunshine and hours of human caress. The white hull gleamed in the morning sun as it moved through the green swells. Occasionally, a taller wave would break high on the bow, washing over the Antigua registration numbers and sending saltwater mist onto Mac's sunglasses.

Mac knew this boat well. The sailboat's name was *Mary's Baby*. At one time, it was his father's boat. His father had moored it for many years on Acton Cove, only a short distance from their home near the old city center of Annapolis. As a child, he could see the sailboat from his upstairs bedroom window. He loved to sail on it with his father.

At age eighteen, the US Naval Academy accepted Mac into fall enrollment, and a few months later, his father sold the boat, after twenty years of ownership, to benefit his personal retirement plans. The sailboat became the crown jewel of Jim Eberle's Antigua-based rental fleet. Mac had missed this boat for years. He had been trying to rent the boat, for a spring sail for each of the last two years, when the reservation finally came through.

This morning, the mainsail boom was tight to the centerline, the position known as a 'close reach.' The tall mast leaned almost fifteen degrees to starboard. Standing at the helm and leaning to his left to maintain balance on the tilted surface, Mac felt the wind in his hair and couldn't help but grin.

He felt a sense of teamwork between him and the vessel. They were once again united, working together in harmony. The wind pulled him toward a new island to explore, and he felt the excitement building in his chest as the hours passed. The next port he planned to make before sundown was somewhere beyond the horizon.

He lifted his sunglasses from his eyes and winced at the bright sunshine. The sun was never this bright outside his apartment in New York City. It was late spring in New York – cold and dreary. He dropped the shades back into place and smiled as he remembered what he had done as a boy when he was allowed to take the helm under the watchful eyes of his father. He lifted his arm and yelled into the wind, "Onward!"

## Day 1, 10:00 a.m., Mexico City

The stench of the city was overpowering as Katerina Batalle stepped off American Airlines flight 1459 at Mexico City's Aeropuerto International.

When she passed through the open door of the aging McDonnell Douglas MD-80, the smell of Mexico City hit her, causing an involuntary wince as she walked down the steps onto the tarmac. Pollution from the innumerable vehicles tended to hang in the city's air. The air pollution and the odor of nearby open sewers triggered her gag reflex. She was glad she wouldn't be spending too much time here.

She exited the customs area and entered the waiting crowd on the other side of the door. She studied the people, paying attention to the faces studying her, looking for hints of recognition. She knew the eyes to look for in a crowd. She had mastered that skill as a young girl growing up on the dirty streets of the tiny Spanish ocean city of Zarautz.

Katerina pushed through the crowd and walked to the taxi stand. Fifty pesos and a thirty-minute cab ride later, she walked into the lobby of the Tokyo Hotel in the city's Reforma District. Her first step on her new mission was complete.

## Day 1, 4:40 p.m., Twenty miles south of Point Udall, US Virgin Islands

Mac caught his balance as a large swell hit the boat. It had been a great day for sailing, but he still had a few hours before he could rest. Standing in the cockpit, he scanned the horizon for any ships on an intercept course, checked the autopilot settings, ducked under the boom, and descended the stairs to the boat's salon for a quick break to get a drink and check his satellite phone for messages.

He stepped off the bottom stair at the navigation center, walked past the tiny galley, and grabbed a beer from the refrigerator as he passed. He tilted his head under the bulkhead and stepped into the bedroom located under the cockpit. With his head stooped under the low ceiling, he found the waterproof bag he had put inside the small closet and threw it onto the bed. He sat next to it, twisted off the cap on the beer bottle, and took a long swig.

Mac pulled out the few personal items he kept in there: his passport and wallet, an extra pair of sunglasses, his United States Secret Service badge, his satellite smartphone, a 9 mm Glock pistol in a black leather holster, and a courtesy letter from the Organization of Eastern Caribbean States permitting him to carry his weapon in the region.

When he boarded the plane in New York, he was ready to go off the grid for a while. He felt he had managed it well for the last forty-eight hours, only checking his messages once or maybe twice. Supervisory Special Agents for the US Secret Service lived on their phones. For Mac, checking the messages only once or twice was almost the same as turning the phone off.

The display instantly updated when he pressed the button to awaken the sat phone. He didn't even have time to divert his eyes before he knew he had thirty-two unread emails, two text messages, and a few missed calls. His thumbs worked on the buttons, and he paged through the emails, most relating to the last presidential threat or Citibank fraud case the New York office was working on.

Then he read the text message from his boss, Special Agent in Charge (SAIC) Bill Michaels. The message read:

"Please call me. Re: Pakerisami."

"Interesting," Mac muttered under his breath.

He had to tap his long-term memory to recall the Pakerisami case. It had been almost five years. At the time, he was a newly hired rookie stationed in the Secret Service office in New York tasked to investigate financial fraud, an essential but little-known responsibility of the US Secret Service.

The key figure in this case was Helbol Pakerisami, an Egyptian émigré. Pakerisami had alerted the FBI about a possible terrorist in New York. The FBI passed the lead to the Secret Service to assist in the investigation, and it landed on the rookie's desk. There was not much to remember, Mac recalled.

The lead was cold. The suspected terrorist was never located or confirmed to be in New York. He had added the suspect's name to a National Security Agency watch list—end of story.

The boat hit another large swell; the "thump" resonated through the cabin, shaking Mac out of his recollection. He rubbed his chin. I'll call Bill this evening after I dock the sailboat and get something to eat. Mac returned the items and resealed the bag. He returned to the cockpit.

The winds were increasing. He saw white caps on several waves. He dropped his sunglasses over his eyes and saw the island ahead as a faint outline barely visible on the horizon. It was fifteen miles away. It would take another three hours to reach the port.

# CHAPTER TWO

## Day 1, 5:35 p.m., New York offices of the US Secret Service

"Damn it!" said the voice from the telephone. It was Don Jenson, Assistant Director of the US Secret Service. "Where the hell is Krieger?"

"I'm sorry, sir," said Bill Michaels, sitting at his desk in New York with the phone to his ear. "He's on vacation in the Caribbean on a sailboat. We've messaged him and tried his satellite phone, but he's yet to return contact."

"Well, what the hell good is a sat phone system if the agents don't call back?" Jensen growled.

In New York, Michaels sighed, "Sorry, sir. We'll keep trying."

"Thanks, Bill. The director wants to get Mac onto this case as soon as possible. You know he's not a patient man." Jenson's voice cooled noticeably.

"I understand the urgency, Don," said Michaels. "It's my fault. Mac is a workhorse agent. I told him to take a break from the phone and email. His vacation was long overdue, and I could tell he needed it. He's been planning this sailing adventure for almost two years."

"I can understand his reluctance to check messages." Jensen sighed. "Please try again, and let me know as soon as you make contact."

"Yes, sir, I'll call you as soon as it happens. I'm certain he'll check in by morning."

"Good, thanks, Bill." The phone went silent. Michaels momentarily leaned back in his chair, then reached forward and pressed a button on his phone. David Osrick, one of a handful of agents in the New York office, strolled in moments later:

"You need something, Bill?"

"Yeah, David, what time today did you send the last message to Krieger?" asked Michaels.

"Three-fifteen," Osrick said. "You want me to send another?"

"Yes, but this time, code it 'Urgent,' and tell him DC is involved. We need to get his attention."

5

"Okay, Bill. Anything else?"
"No, thanks for your help."

## Day 1, 5:40 p.m., New York office of the US Secret Service

Osrick left Michaels' office and went straight to the elevator. He rode the elevator two floors to the fifty-fifth floor and walked to the door marked 'COMMS.' A sign below the door read: 'US Government – Authorized Access Only.'

Osrick slid his badge through the card reader and waited for the click. About a second later, the door clicked open. Osrick entered the Communications Room for the New York office of the Secret Service. Mort Lasinski was the COMMS operation officer on duty for the afternoon-evening shift. Osrick walked over to Lasinski's desk, where the man was finishing a call to the Denver office.

"Thanks, Mike. I appreciate it. Are you going to make our fishing trip in June? That's great; I'll talk to you later. Okay, bye." Lasinski hung up the phone and looked at Osrick. "What's up?"

"Bill wants us to page Mac again," said Osrick. "Urgent, with the note 'DC now involved.'"

Lasinski nodded and turned in his chair to a computer terminal. He typed, and the screen changed to show Mac's full name and satellite phone number. Lasinski skipped his cursor several lines to the message area and typed:

*Urgent DC involved. Respond ASAP.*

Lasinski looked over his shoulder at Osrick, "Okay?"

Osrick glanced at the screen and gave a thumbs up, "Yeah. Send it."

## Day 1, 5:45 p.m., Mexico City

Crossing five time zones and passing through customs in four countries in two days using three false passports allowed Batalle to remain anonymous and move freely across the globe.

After she arrived at the hotel, she took a two-hour nap. She was tired, and her body was four time zones out of sync. But she was close to her next target.

She dialed the local phone number. The contact number activated an individual to provide support and supplies. She had been through this drill several times over the last year.

The man must have expected her to call. "Si," he stuttered nervously into the phone. "Do you need anything?"

"Yes," Katerina smiled on the other end. "You were told I would call today. Bring me my package and a current city map. I'm staying at the Tokyo Hotel, Room 505."

"Si, Señorita, it will be about an hour." She hung up the phone. The 'package' included a small but powerful Beretta .380 automatic. It was to be delivered with a screw-on suppressor, two eleven-round magazines, fifty rounds of hollow point ammo, and a concealable belly holster.

She picked up the phone, dialed room service, and ordered a plate of shrimp tempura rolls with a glass of white wine. She figured the food would arrive before the package from her Mexican contact.

## Day 2, 3:00 a.m. Washington, DC

### London, England – News Service

*A car bomb exploded as the vice-chairman of the Bank of England climbed into a limousine outside of her home in the heart of London at 6:00 a.m. this morning, killing the vice-chairman, her driver, and two of her security staff. The explosion is the first instance where a Bank of England official has been murdered in what appears to be a terrorist attack. Bank of England spokespersons were characteristically quiet about the incident and told the media the bank was assisting the London police in the ongoing investigation.*

### Frankfurt, Germany – Wire Services

*A European Central Bank official and his wife were killed, and over two dozen others were severely injured yesterday evening as they exited Deutsche Bank Park, home of the Eintracht Frankfurt Eagles soccer team. ECB board member Ernst Schneicher was gunned down by two motorcycle-riding gunmen using automatic weapons. Police are searching the scene for clues and interviewing witnesses.*

### Lisbon, Portugal – Wire Services

*Lisbon police are investigating a massive, early morning explosion at the headquarters of Portugal's largest banking conglomerate, Cesta Geral de Depósitos Bancos. The blast occurred at 2:00 a.m. local time, destroying much of the multi-story building in the distinctive central plaza. Adjacent buildings were severely damaged. The explosion was felt over ten miles away. At this time, at least three fatalities are known. Lisbon police are asking the public for leads. No groups have claimed responsibility.*

## Day 2, 7:10 a.m., St. Croix, US Virgin Islands

*'Mary's Baby'* rolled gently against the dock lines at Manny's Dock. Inside the sailboat, Mac was beginning to wake from the late night. He slid a leg slowly across the bed and struck something warm. The object moaned quietly and rolled into a ball. He smiled and opened his eyes while rolling onto his side.

He caught a blurry image of a head covered in long blond hair. He gently put his arm over the woman and pulled her close. The embrace received a warm reaction. He closed his eyes and tried to recall the prior evening's events.

Mac pulled into the marina at Gallows Bay at 7:30 p.m. The warm night darkness was beginning to envelop the city. He secured the lines at the dock and plugged the boat into shore power. He was hungry. After the sailboat was tied securely, Mac retrieved the only set of 'casual' clothes he had brought: black jeans, a white polo shirt, and a blue blazer.

His first stop was the dockmaster building to pay the mooring fees. When asked, the proprietor, Manny Steinman, suggested two or three restaurants near tourist hotels. Ten minutes later, Mac strolled along the street overlooking the bay, reading the menus in front of each business.

The *Mooring House* was a combination bar and restaurant next to several hotels. The people packed inside. Sitting at the bar, he ordered a beer and scanned the room while he waited for the bartender to give him a menu.

Looking across the room, he caught the glances of three women sitting together in a booth. They were glancing at him and talking to each other as they sipped on their drinks. The bartender delivered his beer and took his food order. As he drank the beer, he stole a look at the three women. They were looking elsewhere.

Mac finished his meal and was working on his second beer when a woman from the group walked over to where he sat. Mac was surprised. She was in her late twenties, maybe thirty, he guessed. Wearing blue jeans and a white blouse, a particular combination of clothing that Mac liked. She was petite and moved with a bounce in her step.

He looked at her as she took an empty seat at the bar beside him.

"Excuse me – I hope I'm not intruding." She raised her voice above the crowd noise. "Are you meeting anyone?"

Mac didn't hesitate. He raised his hand to signal the bartender, "I hoped I'd meet you when I saw you sitting with your friends. Would you like another beer?"

"Thank you. Beer is fine. By the way, my name is Rae. What's yours?"

"My friends call me Mac." He studied her face for a moment, and their eyes locked. He looked away when the bartender delivered the beers. He could tell she had spent a few hours in the sunshine during the last few days. She looked tanned, radiant, and beautiful.

"Do you live here? Work here? Are you from the islands?" she asked him. Rae wasn't afraid to get the conversation moving. She took a drink from the newly arrived beer. Then she turned and smiled at her friends.

"I wish I lived here," Mac said. "I work in New York. I'm a tourist. How about you? Where are you from? What brings you here?" Mac's social skills kicked in.

"Denver," Rae said. "I'm taking a little vacation from the snow. Are you staying at the resort?" She motioned across the street.

"Aboard my sailboat," Mac smiled. "I sailed into port about two hours ago." He wondered what her reaction would be. He watched as her eyes widened with the news.

"I thought I saw something different about you! That's why I came over." She began to barrage him with questions about sailing.

A beer later, they discussed each other's personal history. Rae was intrigued by Mac's job. The night became an enjoyable blur. They had a few more drinks and danced until almost midnight.

Mac met her friends Julie and Isabell. Later, the two of them wandered back to the marina. Rae wanted to see the sailboat. Mac's memory skipped forward to her quick inspection and comment about never making love on a sailboat. The next thing he knew, they were kissing, their clothes flying in all directions, and they landed entangled on the master stateroom bed.

Mac allowed himself a small smile, then drifted back to sleep as the sunlight began to creep down the wall toward the bed.

## Day 2, 8:00 a.m., Mexico City

Batalle was in a strolling mood. The morning of her second day in Mexico City was bright sunshine and the air was almost tolerable. She walked to the intersection of Chapultepec and Constituyentes avenues and into Chapultepec Park. The park is in the city's heart and is filled with sculptures, trees, and traffic. Many of Mexico City's financial institutions, foreign embassies, hotels, and modern buildings were along the avenue.

Katerina wandered at her own pace, stopping to browse the stores along the way. As she strolled the avenue, she evaluated landmarks and examined each building with the eyes of a specialist in civilian terrorism. She paused outside the BancaMex Tower, comparing it to the detailed photos she had studied before she began this trip.

*How did we miss this?* Katerina thought. *The first through fifth floors have blast-proof glass.* She would need to inspect the building firsthand this afternoon, looking at the structural design from the inside.

Her phone beeped. Stepping away from the street and pausing against a building, she looked at the brief message from her colleague Amir Abadai. It read: '*EU phase one complete. BR is almost ready but should go late today. We need MX to move up to tomorrow.*'

After reading the message, Katerina grimaced. *I'll need to talk with my contact tonight.*

# CHAPTER THREE

## Day 2, 8:45 a.m., St. Croix, US Virgin Islands

Mac awoke to a buzzing sound. It sounded like it was in the boat or out on the dock. He couldn't immediately place it. Then it stopped. He lifted his arm from around Rae's body and leaned to the side of the bed to look at his watch: *8:45 a.m.*

Strong sunlight streamed through the starboard portal. Mac listened to the water slapping gently against the hull and the halyards pinging against the aluminum mast in rhythm to the slight sway of the boat. The air in the cabin smelled of warm fiberglass, wood polish, clean sheets, and tropical salt water. It mixed well with the slight hint of Rae's perfume. Her breathing was regular as she slept.

Mac lay in bed watching the dust particles dance in the sunbeams streaming through the cabin windows. After ten minutes, he wondered if he could extricate his body from the bed and step into the shower without waking her. He slowly rolled away from Rae and sat up on the edge of the bed, stretching his arms.

"Where are you going?" Rae asked softly. "You stretch those arms like they're sore. I didn't break you, did I?"

Mac looked over his shoulder and laughed. "Thanks to you, I'm stretching after a great night's sleep." He watched as Rae moved her naked body out from under the sheet and across the bed. She came up behind him as he sat on the edge of the bed. She kissed his neck and wrapped her arms around him in a light hug.

"I want to let you know last night was special for me. I don't hop into bed with someone I've met for the first time." She kissed his neck. "I can't explain it, but I went with my heart and not my head. I hope that was the right thing to do."

Mac kissed her arm and twisted his upper body around to get one arm behind her and cradle her in his arms. He kissed her gently, "Maybe you're turned on by sailors?"

He grinned mischievously at Rae. She tried to scowl at him. They both

10

laughed.

"Seriously, Rae, I like you." Said Mac. "I'm not a one-night stand type of guy. Last night, something clicked. It seemed like the most natural thing to do."

"I don't think I could have stopped myself once I looked into your eyes." Rae purred in a soft voice. They gently kissed again. Mac admired the girl in his arms. Rae turned her head toward the bathroom and then looked back at him.

"The shower seems pretty small," said Rae. "Why don't you go first, and I'll follow in a few minutes? I may try to get a little more sleep."

Mac helped her back onto the bed and smiled as she pulled the sheets over her body. "There's barely enough room in the shower to turn around. You enjoy your nap." Mac said. He stood, walked three short steps to the shower, started the water, stepped in, and closed the door.

Across the boat, in the smaller cabin where Mac had put his duffel bag, His satellite phone buzzed, indicating an incoming call.

## Day 2, 9:00 a.m., New York Secret Service Office

"Try Krieger again in thirty minutes, sir?" David Osrick stood in the doorway of Bill Michael's office.

"What have you learned from the boat's owner?" Michaels asked.

"Mr. Eberly told me Mac's plans showed a northernmost destination at Gallows Bay, a small port in the US Virgin Islands. We're trying to call the local docks to see if anyone has seen him. Mr. Eberly is going to be there on business today. He told me he'd look for the boat at the docks."

"Good, let me know what you learn." Michaels stood and stretched. "I need a cup of coffee."

Osrick stepped away as Michaels moved toward the door. "I'll head back up to COMMS and keep working on reaching him."

"Thanks, David. We need to get him today and tell him to head to DC. The bank bombing in Lisbon last night and the murders of two key people in the European banking community are creating a buzz at the State Department.

DC thinks it could be linked to the Pakerisami case. Mac led the Pakerisami investigation. The director wants to talk with him about the case. Make arrangements for this Eberly fellow to pick up Mac's boat as soon as we locate him."

"Yes, sir," Osrick said. He pivoted and headed toward the stairs.

Michaels walked to the coffee pot and poured himself a cup full. As he added creamer, he muttered, "Sorry to cut your vacation short, Mac, but duty calls."

## Day 2, 9:30 a.m., St. Croix, US Virgin Islands

It was a full-time job to explain to Rae what each rope did on a sailboat. Even more challenging was explaining why one rope was called a 'line' and another was a 'sheet.' Mac smiled as he coiled a jib sheet and tidied up the cockpit. Rae was in the galley refilling their coffee cups. Mac didn't see Jim Eberly approaching along the dock.

Jim cleared his throat. Mac looked up at the noise and stopped smiling.

"Hi, Mac!" Eberly was always enthusiastic and smiling.

"Er, hello, Jim. What brings you to St. Croix?" Mac asked.

Rae popped her head up from the cabin, "Hi! Who's your friend?"

Mac did the introductions, "Rae, this is Jim Eberly. He owns the boat."

Jim shook Rae's hand and apologized to Mac. "I'm sorry, Mac. I was catching a flight from Antigua early this morning when I received a phone call from Mr. Osrick in New York."

Mac suddenly remembered. "Hold on, Jim. Let me grab my phone." He hopped down the stairs, scrambled into the aft cabin, and grabbed the blinking phone.

As he came up from the cabin clutching the phone, he nodded toward Eberly. "I was going to return a call last night," he said to Eberly. Then he smiled at Rae and said, "But I was a little busy."

"Well, I'm glad you've enjoyed these last few days because it sounds like your vacation will be cut short."

Mac looked dismayed as he dialed the New York number for Bill Michaels.

Bill Michaels answered, "Yes?"

"Bill, it's Mac Krieger."

"Mac! Thanks for the call. I'm sorry to interrupt your vacation. Am I your first call, or have you talked to David Osrick?"

"You're the first person I've called," Mac said. "Jim Eberly caught me at the dock in St. Croix." He sat down on the sailboat with the phone in his ear.

Rae disappeared below deck, and Jim Eberly wandered over to look at a couple of other boats tied up at the dock, which gave Mac some privacy.

"Mac, when you catch the news, you'll learn of several international financial institution attacks. Something happened in DC to flag the Pakerisami case, and the director is asking you to meet with him in person as soon as possible.

I'll send Osrick to meet you in Miami and brief you on the flight to DC. When can you be in Miami?"

Mac took a deep breath and said, "Bill, It took two years to set this up and get this boat."

"I know, Mac, and I'm sorry. Look, don't worry about the boat. DC has already authorized the office to pick up the tab for this trip, and you can reschedule your vacation when this crisis is over. The director has been all over me to find you. He wants you in DC for a briefing. Now, when can you get to Miami?"

Mac was wistful as he rubbed his chin and looked at the sailboat. "I'll catch a flight in two hours and be there this afternoon."

## Day 2, 3:00 p.m., Mexico City

Katerina Batalle strolled into the lobby of the BancaMex Tower, looking in every way like she belonged there. It was a short distance from her new hotel room at the Excelsior. At the elevators, she pressed the button to go up and turned to look around the lobby. The first floor was open-concept and supported by large granite pillars. Opposite the elevators were the bank's teller stations for walk-in customers.

She located the stairs leading up to the offices, down to the garage, and below, where the central vaults were. When her elevator arrived, she stepped away to allow passengers to exit and others to proceed ahead of her. She then walked to the next elevator bay and pressed the button again.

Turning one more time to the lobby, she reviewed the building's structural components and made her selection. When finished, she looked at her watch and walked away from the elevator bank, exiting through the glass doors and onto the street.

On the sidewalk, she walked around to the side of the building and located the delivery dock. She noted the loading dock's street address and returned to the park. She now had what she needed.

## Day 2, 3:05 p.m., Miami International Airport

Mac stepped off the jetway onto the tarmac and walked toward the airport entry door. His jaw was set, and his pace was fast. He was upset at the interruption of a vacation that took him almost two years to arrange.

He contacted the owner of his dad's old sailboat and managed to rent it for the week. It hurts to have to give it up. He was enjoying the time alone on the water. He would miss the sunshine, the sea, and the sailing.

He thought about Rae. Was there something there? It felt like a spark. There must be something. He left her standing outside her hotel, looking sad and self-conscious as the taxi pulled away to take him to the airport.

Mac reached into his pocket and pulled out the slip of paper with Rae's address and phone number in Denver. He wanted to see her again, so he folded the paper and placed it in his pocket for safekeeping.

Rae's last words when he dropped her off at the hotel on his way to the airport were, "Call me, please."

Mac had asked her if she could come to the islands when he rescheduled

13

his vacation. She smiled and told him she'd have to check schedules and let him know. Mac took a deep breath and smiled as he entered the Miami terminal.

"Mac!" David Osrick's yell echoed across the terminal. Mac looked up and spotted him. Mac changed direction and headed toward his colleague.

Osrick was younger than Mac. David was five years out of college, with an MBA from Wharton and a forensic accounting degree from NYU. Osrick was dressed in a fashionable suit. It fit his trim, athletic body quite well.

In New York, David blended into the business dress on Wall Street. But in Miami, he stood out. The dress was different in Miami. The city's influence from the Latin cultures was evident at the airport. Colorful, comfortable cotton shirts, chino pants, or shorts on the men and many women in tight skirts were the order of the day.

"I see you made it to Miami," Mac said. He smiled as he shook David's outstretched hand.

"Miami wasn't a problem," laughed David. "Getting out of Manhattan was far more dangerous!"

"How long have you been waiting?"

"I guess about an hour and a half." David started to reach for one of the two duffles Mac carried. Mac shook his head. He had them well-balanced.

"Our flight to DC leaves in an hour," said David. "It's a fifteen-minute walk to the 'B' concourse and a two-hour flight. There is plenty of time to brief you on recent intel. Sorry about the shortened vacation. I hope the few days you did get were fun."

Mac looked at David and grinned. "You know, David, these last three days were the best. I've got to do this again if I can set it up."

Osrick smiled, "I heard from Mr. Eberly that you had some company on the boat." His smile turned mischievous. "No wonder you didn't answer our messages! Here we thought you went on a sailing adventure!"

Mac grinned, "Let's get a beer on the way to our connecting flight. I'll tell you about the boat, the sailing, and a great little bar on St. Croix."

# CHAPTER FOUR

**Day 2, 4:30 p.m., São Paulo, Brazil**

Benício Ferreira needed an unwitting accomplice. He wanted a young girl or boy willing to do what he asked for a price. He stopped his rental '73 Ford Thunderbird under a bridge abutment along the highway. He walked about eighty-five yards to the first row of tumbledown favelas in Jardim Japao, a favela west of the international airport in São Paulo.

Ferreira walked around the cardboard, tin, and scrap wood shanties until he saw a man leaning against a wall in the shade. He was smoking a cigarette stub. The man was dirty and looked twenty years older than he was.

"What do you want?" The man said, stepping away from the building. "If you're looking for girls, I can help you find some. Beautiful girls cost you fifty dollars."

Ferreira looked at the man and said, "No, I need someone young for some business; a girl or a boy would be fine, but they must follow instructions."

"What do you want with a kid, man? I can get you some girls for twenty-five dollars apiece for the night. You will be a happy man."

"No, I need a kid to make a surprise delivery for me." Ferreira glanced at the man and looked around for someone to talk to.

When Ferreira looked away, the man responded. He didn't want to miss the chance to make some money. "Oh, drugs, man, why didn't you say so? I'll take your package myself for twenty dollars. Did I introduce myself? The name is Chi."

"No, I need a kid," Ferreira looked away and rubbed his chin. He looked back at the man. "I'll pay you fifty dollars to help me find a kid in this place, but the kid has to do what I ask. You understand?"

"Sure," Chi smiled and lifted his hands with his palms outward. "No problem, you come with me. I'll find a little shit for you. You stick with Chi, and I'll help you find somebody."

"Good. . . but don't take too much time. I'm in a hurry," Ferreira said.

15

He followed as Chi led him deeper into the favela. Glancing around at the other people looking out doors and windows as they passed, Ferreira adjusted the pistol concealed in the flat of his back as he walked. He knew that in this neighborhood, being armed was considered being careful. He hoped they got the message.

Ten minutes later, they stopped at a makeshift neighborhood school. The school was a few feet larger than a typical twelve-by-nine-foot home the children were used to.

The children turned to see who interrupted the class. They were learning to read from an eleven-year-old who might have had two years of actual school.

"Any of these look like the right type?" Chi asked. Ferreira scanned the thirty kids aged four to fourteen. He ignored the youngest and oldest. His gaze stopped at one girl who looked to be about twelve.

"What's your name?" Ferreira asked her.

"Antônia," the girl said. She smiled at the honor of being spoken to. She lowered her eyes down to her tattered dress and bare feet.

"Antônia," Ferreira repeated her name. "That's a nice name. Antônia, would you like to do a favor for me and make some money for yourself?"

Antônia eyed Ferreira with suspicion. "I'm no whore, señor." She said, The other children laughed. She glowered at them. They quieted.

Ferreira laughed with the children, "Antônia, I'm not asking you to do anything but deliver a package for me in downtown São Paulo this afternoon. Afterward, you can come back here and continue your schooling. I'll pay fifty dollars to do this, but you must come now."

When he mentioned the fifty-dollar payment for delivering a simple package, the other children began to push forward, hoping to be picked to make some easy money.

Ferreira watched Antônia as she looked at the other children. He guessed she might have declined the offer had the others kept quiet. But with the kids clamoring for the job, she seemed determined not to let the opportunity pass.

"I'll go with you. Can I change my dress?" She asked.

"No, it won't be necessary," said Ferreira. "You can buy a new dress with your money after you've delivered my package."

This comment made her smile. Antônia followed the two men down the path leading out of the favelas. When the men arrived where he had parked, Ferreira pointed to his car and told Antônia,

"Wait for me there." He then turned to Chi and motioned for them to walk to the nearest shaded side of a house.

Chi preceded Ferreira as they walked around the corner.

"Okay, man," Chi said, "you come back here if you need any more help. You ask for old Chi ..."

His next word was cut short as Benício Ferreira wrapped a guitar wire garrote around his throat and tightened it. The thin wire began separating the dark skin below his chin, cutting through his larynx and jugular vein.

Ferreira held him at arm's length to keep the blood spurting from Chi's neck from spraying on his clothes. He lowered him to the ground. He pulled the man's shirttail out and wiped his hands to remove the blood splatter.

Minutes later, Ferreira and Antônia were in the car, heading toward São Paulo's downtown. Ferreira was silent as he concentrated on the next steps he must take.

"What's your name?" Antônia asked, trying to make conversation.

"You can call me 'Jefe' if you wish," Ferreira said. He didn't intend to tell the girl too much about himself.

Ferreira swerved the car to miss a man on a bicycle. In the mirror, he watched as the man almost lost control. The bag in his basket didn't fare as well. It flew from the basket, spilling the contents from the man's trip to the local grocer. The right corner of Ferreira's mouth curled in an evil grin.

"You almost hit him!" exclaimed Antônia. She looked through the rear windshield to see the man struggling to stop the bicycle on the busy street.

"Shut up!" Ferreira growled. "If you want to earn the money, you better shut up and let me drive." Antônia studied her feet for the remainder of the drive. Ferreira's car slowed near the Metrô Conceição subway station.

He found a parking space a block from the entrance. He maneuvered the car into it and pulled ahead to bump the car in front of him, allowing more room to get into the trunk of his vehicle.

He peered into the rearview mirror before opening his door.

"Wait here while I get the package," Benício said in a low voice. He climbed out of the car and went to the trunk. Fitting his key into the lock, he glanced around for any onlookers. He opened the trunk and reached for a large, heavy package attached to a hand truck. Lifting the entire assembly out of the trunk, he balanced it on its wheels. He rolled the wheeled package around to the passenger side of the vehicle.

Opening the door, Ferreira began his instructions."Okay, this is the package I need you to deliver. You walk into the big building across the street and give this package to the man at the front desk. Do you understand? The front desk is where the security guards sit. It's a special surprise for my brother-in-law. You give the package to him and no one else. His name is Andre, and he works at the desk. Can you do this?"

Antônia nodded. Ferreira stepped aside and motioned for Antônia to take the package. She struggled with the cart for a moment.

"It's not too heavy for you, is it?" He asked her.

"No, I can do it," Antônia said.

"What is his name?" Ferreira tested.

"André."

He smiled at her. "I'll wait for you and pay you when you return to the car. Then I'll give you a ride home. Be careful crossing the street."

"Thank you, Jefe," Antônia mumbled. She took the package and pushed it a few feet. "I'll be right back."

He smiled as she walked away. When she was out of sight around the corner, he started his car and made a U-turn in the street. He headed in the general direction of Brasilia, about 600 miles straight north. He needed to get lost for a while.

The two thousand dollars he'd received from his commander would allow him to hole up for a week in Brasilia and head back to Costa Rica for the next step in his training.

He retrieved his phone, pulled up a saved number, and started counting back from 100.

## Day 2, 5:30 p.m., São Paulo, Brazil

As she walked up to the building, Antônia saw the name on the door: "Financeira Unibanco Holding SA." She knew from her teacher what a 'banco' was, although she had never been in one. She approached the large doors and waited for someone to open them. It didn't take long.

Once inside, she saw the large desk in the middle of the floor and followed several adults up to the desk. It was hectic, and Antônia felt a little scared to be alone. As the people in line at the desk found their directions and moved toward the elevators, Antônia smiled and got ready to deliver the package and say, "Happy Birthday" to the man André.

A gap opened in front of her. Antônia walked up to the desk, pulling the cart. She looked up at the large man peering down from across the desk. Opening her mouth to speak, she heard a small beep from inside the box. The building's entire first and second floors were engulfed in a brilliant flash.

It was the last light Antônia would see.

## Day 2, 8:14 p.m., Mexico City

The phone rang. Stirring the man from his chair, watching the telenovela. The middle-aged man swore under his breath and called out to his wife, "Maria! Telefono!" When he got no response, he realized Maria, busy bathing the youngest of their two children, couldn't hear his call over the running water in the bathroom.

"Chenga!" he exclaimed as the phone rang a third time. He jumped up and walked to the table in the entry. Exasperated, he picked it up and spoke in a low, stern voice:

"Bueno." The voice coming from the other end startled him. He sat down in a small chair.

"I need to talk to you tonight." It was Batalle speaking in English. He felt the color drain from his face.

"Si," he muttered. His voice cracked. "Do you want me to call you from another phone?"

"There is no point; I know who you are... Hector."

He closed his eyes. "Si," he murmured.

"Come to my hotel; I'm staying at the Excelsior Hotel now, the one by the US Embassy," Katerina said. "I'll meet you in the lobby bar. Can you be there at 9:00 p.m.?"

"No, Señora, that is our usual dinner time. My family will be worried if I leave now."

"I understand. 10:00 p.m. then."

"Si, how will I know you?"

"You won't. Take a seat near the windows; I'll find you."

He began to sweat. He reached under the small desk and pulled out a small concealed pistol. As he looked at the gun, the voice purred into his ear:

"Oh, and Hector, don't be stupid. I'm sure you want to see Maria, Miguel, and Juan again," She hissed. No trace of emotion in her voice.

Hector's jaw sagged. His hand loosened around the gun. It slipped in his grip.

"See you at 10:00 p.m. Please dress for dinner."

The phone line went dead. Hector cradled the receiver. He reached under the table and replaced the pistol.

## Day 2, 10:00 p.m., Excelsior Hotel, Mexico City

She approached the man in the ill-fitting suit sitting at a table near the window. He was alone and sweating. She approached him from behind and put her hand on his neck, the way a lover might touch.

She whispered in his ear. "Good evening, Hector; please listen to me. Look pleased to see me and smile during our conversation. I need some additional help from you and your network."

He jumped at her initial touch. He didn't move as she whispered in his ear. Upon being instructed to smile, he managed a weak grin.

He stumbled with his English, saying, "Hello, my sweet. It's good to see you." Katerina smirked. He couldn't fool anyone with the line, but at least he tried.

"Thank you, my lover. I've been waiting for you. Why did it take so long?" She sounded hurt.

Hector relaxed. "I'm sorry. My family delayed my leaving. You know how difficult it is to explain a late-night meeting."

"Oh, yes, I understand," Katerina lightened the mood. "Would you like something to eat?" She watched Hector's reaction.

"I've had little to eat since you called." He said.

The middle-aged, balding man and the beautiful young European woman drew no attention in the restaurant. As she looked around, she saw many other couples mismatched in age. She had hoped her restaurant selection would support the mentor/mistress appearance, and it looked as if she had guessed right.

"I need you to pick up and deliver a package for me. It must be delivered tomorrow," Batalle looked at Hector and smiled. "I'll give you more details, but let's eat first."

## Day 3, 6:00 a.m., Washington, DC

Mac pulled his suit from the case and checked that his belt, tie, and shoes were there. To his relief, they were. David Osrick had picked up the almost-always-packed suitcase from his apartment and sent it to the Ambassador Hotel before leaving Manhattan. The shoes were polished, and the white shirt with a maroon tie complemented the dark blue suit well. These were not Mac's usual street shoes, but a nice pair he kept for special days like today: a meeting with the director. After dressing, Mac headed downstairs to meet David for breakfast.

David caught him as he walked out of the elevator. "Did you see the news this morning?"

"No," Mac said, "I was too busy checking to see if my underwear was in my bag. What's in the news?"

David pulled Mac out of the elevator bank traffic and lowered his voice. "A downtown São Paulo bank was destroyed last night by a terrorist bomb. It was rush hour, near one of the subway lines. News reports say hundreds have been killed. The fires are still burning."

Mac was stunned. "What the hell is going on? First London, then Frankfurt, and Lisbon, now São Paulo?" He scratched his head. "Are they related? Are there any claims of responsibility?"

"No claims for Brazil that I know of." Said David.

"How is this related to the Pakerisami case?" Mac said as they walked toward the restaurant. "The Pakerisami investigation was five years ago, and the people involved are most likely in prison or dead."

Mac looked around for a waiter. Seeing the restaurant filling up with few seats, He changed his mind. "Let's get a cup of coffee to go. I need a few minutes in the file room to review the Pakerisami case before I see the director."

# CHAPTER FIVE

## Day 3, 7:30 a.m., Washington, DC

Mac walked into the official repository of the Secret Service files on the third floor. He found an open computer, logged in, and opened the file search window to locate the five-year-old case number US-00948769473-NY. Searching Pakerisami's name proved easy. In a matter of seconds, he scanned the document's history. Before the recent activity, an agent in the Washington office had accessed it once about two years ago. As he read the documents, the details came back to him.

A man named Helbol Pakerisami had tipped the FBI's New York office about a possible terrorist in the US. As usual, the FBI claimed to be understaffed and pushed the case to the interagency desk for follow-up. Mac had been assigned the case and interviewed Pakerisami.

Originally from Egypt, Helbol Pakerisami was a small, wiry man with a short beard, a pointed face, and skittish mannerisms. He constantly looked over his right shoulder. The skittishness may have been from his life on the harsh streets of Cairo or working the edges of legitimate business in New York.

Mac remembered the conversation. "Mr. Pakerisami, how long have you lived in the US?" Mac asked.

"Fifteen," Pakerisami spoke in heavily accented English. "I left Cairo at the age of twenty-five. I've been here fifteen years."

Mac followed with another question, "Why did you leave?"
"Mukhabarat" said Pakerisami.

Mac knew the name of the Egyptian agency responsible for state security. He pressed, "So tell me, who forced you to leave?"

Pakerisami sighed. "Ten years ago, I met a few of my business colleagues in Cairo. We were joined by the younger brother of my friend, Ahmed. He was an old friend, a good friend. His younger brother, Amir, had returned to Cairo to visit his ill mother.

We smoked the shisha and shared some tea. He was young, and he enjoyed talking. I think he tried to impress his older brother's friends.

21

Anyhow, during the conversation, he mentioned he was politically active.

"Agent Krieger, in case you don't know, an Arab in The West Bank who's 'politically active' usually means he's part of whoever is currently causing problems for Israel. It used to be Egypt, then the PLO. Now it's Hamas. You've heard of them?"

"Yes, of course," said Mac.

"It's simple. I contacted someone interested to know this young man's name."

Mac chanced a guess, "Am I to understand that you somehow flagged Israeli intelligence?"

"That's right," Pakerisami confirmed in a low whisper. "Now you know how I came to live in New York. Mukhabarat doesn't like people who talk to foreign intelligence agencies before they talk to Mukhabarat. I was young and lucky to escape. I came here with nothing."

"I understand," Mac leaned forward on the table. "So why did you call the FBI this time?"

"Two weeks ago, Ahmad reached out to me as an old friend," said Pakerisami. "We had a good talk. Then he told me his brother Amir was in New York City. Amir asked Ahmad to see if he knew anyone in New York who could help him, and unfortunately, I was the one to pick up the phone when Ahmed called."

"Has Amir called you?" "Not yet," Pakerisami whispered. "I'm hoping the FBI catches up with him before he catches up with me."

## Day 3, 8:45 a.m., Washington, DC

Mac checked his watch. It was time to go. He gathered his few notes and exited the library. On his way to the elevator, Mac noticed a discarded WASHINGTON POST newspaper hanging on the edge of a waste bin.

He picked it up to scan the headlines. On the front page, it screamed: BRAZIL TERRORIST ALERT! Little information was contained in the paragraphs below the headlines. Mac helped the newspaper into the trash bin.

He walked the rest of the way to the elevator and pressed the button. Exiting the elevator on the top floor of the building, he nodded to the security guards outside the elevators. They glanced at his credentials hanging from his neck and looked away. He pressed open the bulletproof glass doors into the foyer area outside the director's office.

Dennica Green, the director's assistant, recorded Mac's ID number and slid the logbook across the desk for him to sign. This wasn't Mac's first visit to the director's office in DC, but it wasn't a daily occurrence for a supervising agent in the New York office. In the last few years, he had maybe met the director in person almost ten times but never in a one-on-

one meeting until now.

After a moment, Dennica pressed the intercom to the director and said, "Sir, I've Supervisory Special Agent Mac Krieger here for your 9:00 a.m."

"Send him in," came the curt reply through the intercom. Mac walked to the door, opened it, and entered.

## Day 3, 9:00 a.m., Washington, DC

"Agent Krieger, please come in." Director Robert Fitzgerald said as he stood up and stepped around from behind his desk. He motioned Mac to sit at a glass-topped table near a window. "Let's sit over there. Would you like a cup of coffee?"

"Yes, sir," Mac said, "black for me."

Fitzgerald punched the intercom on his desk and requested coffee for both. "Mac, you've seen the details on the Brazil bombing?" Fitzgerald sat at the table across from Mac.

"No," Mac confessed. "I've been isolated on a sailboat for the last several days. I caught a headline and checked emails this morning."

"Right," Fitzgerald nodded. "We have been trying to reach you for the last two days. I'm sorry to cut your vacation short. Let me give you a high-level view."

He paused as a knock on the door preceded Dennica's entrance. She placed the two cups of coffee on the table and departed. Fitzgerald continued. "Yesterday at approximately 5:30 p.m., São Paulo time, a large explosion happened in the city's financial district. The explosion occurred at the Financeira Unibanco building. Preliminary casualties are over eighty dead and two hundred wounded. Many of the wounded are in critical condition. They expect the death toll to go higher. It looks like some form of a device, likely a large package bomb, detonated in or near the lobby. Details are weak. We hope to know more today."

Fitzgerald glanced at his notes. "Financeira Unibanco is the largest bank in Latin America, and this facility is also a significant depository location. Think of it as similar to our own Federal Banking System. They hold cash and gold deposits for other banks in Latin America and currency reserves for several countries.

"So now we're looking at the timing of the attacks in London, Frankfurt, Lisbon, and São Paulo. All attacks were on important financial institutions or key central bank figures. Mac, all the attacks happened without forewarnings or elevated chatter in the CIA's monitored channels. We don't know who may be behind this. While the US hasn't been hit, we've no reason to believe we'll be excluded any more than any other country. People in the financial world are on edge. They say this may be an attack to weaken the strength of key trade currencies and erode the strength of the US dollar. If we can't protect our banking institutions...."

He trailed off, then continued. "Russia and China both deny responsibility."

"Financial institutions aren't typical terrorist targets," said Mac. "Embassies, military bases, and civilian targets have been hit before by terrorists, but not financial institutions. Do we think this is a change in strategy for terrorism? Attacking financial institutions?"

"With all honesty, we don't know," Fitzgerald said. "But Wall Street is concerned, and the markets are on edge. I just got off the phone with the President."

"I reviewed the Pakerisami case notes this morning," Mac said. "It's been lying dead for several years. I know the NSA tried to track this suspected terrorist named Amir Abadai for almost six months after the interview, but nothing came of the tracking. He disappeared. We don't know if he was even in New York."

Fitzgerald leaned back and spun his chair to the side. He looked out the window onto the 16th Street Mall and said, "Within the National Intelligence branches, we're pulling on every thread we can find. There's not much to go on. A few days ago, I asked our analysts to refresh our trackers from the past ten years to see what we could find. Three days ago, we had a hit on your Abadai from the Pakerisami case. That's why I've asked you here."

"A tracking hit with Abadai?" Mac couldn't believe it. "That's news to me! Who is the analyst working on the track?"

"Andrea Douglas-Pfeiffer is her name. I think she's on the third floor. The tracker linked Abadai's passport to a crossing into Pakistan over a year ago. We found a few more passport crossings, including Germany and Japan, using several aliases we received from the Mossad in the last two days.

"About a year ago, he used one of his counterfeit passports to get into New York. The research is evolving as we get more details and learn more of his aliases."

"I'll connect with the analyst and get an active investigation moving in New York," Mac said.

Fitzgerald gazed at him. "Mac, since this case was initially transferred to the Secret Service and appeared to be a coordinated attack against financial institutions, we have the ball on Abadai. He's ours to track and find.

"I'd like you to lead on this for the Secret Service. You'll need to build a joint task force and interface with the FBI, CIA, and anyone else who can help. You're in New York. You know the FBI team there. I think John Riccardi from the New York office will be their point man."

Mac nodded and said, "I know him."

Fitzgerald continued, "You've met Pakerisami in person. Find him again. Maybe Abadai is talking to him. Let's find Abadai and see if he's involved with these bombings. The passport crossings may be a coincidence, but the dates are close enough to be curious. Frankly, Mac, this is one of the few leads in national intelligence. We must be all over it."

"I'll get right on it, sir," said Mac. Fitzgerald rose from his chair, signaling the conclusion of the meeting.

"I knew you would jump on this when you heard the details. I'll run point for you here in DC with the other agency directors. It will be a political shit-show with everyone wanting to lead and no one wanting to follow, but I'll have your back. Let me know if you need anything."

## Day 3, 9:35 a.m., Washington, DC

Mac walked from Fitzgerald's office toward the elevators for a trip down to the third floor to talk with Andrea Douglas-Pfeiffer. After a few quick inquiries, Mac found an empty desk covered in papers, file folders, and two large computer screens. The computer screens were still energized, but the user signed off. The screen saver showed a floating image of a US Secret Service badge.

Mac figured the woman was nearby. He walked down the hall to the break room and peered inside. A young woman was drawing a cup of coffee from an industrial-sized coffee maker.

"Excuse me," Mac said. "Are you Ms. Pfeiffer?" She wore a form-flattering sundress and remained focused on her coffee preparation.

Over her shoulder, she said, "Yes, I'll be with you in a moment." Finishing her refill, Andrea Douglas-Pfeiffer turned toward the door and said, "Hi, I'm Andrea. Who are you?"

"Sorry for the intrusion, Ms. Pfeiffer," said Mac. "I'm Mac Krieger from the New York office. The director gave me your name regarding a track you're working on. A man named Abadai?"

Andrea's face lit up. She smiled. "Nice to meet you, Agent Krieger. I recognize your name from the Pakerisami file. Follow me back to my cubicle. I'm happy to share what I'm doing."

She walked past him, and Mac's nose detected a slight whiff of lavender perfume.

"Please, call me Mac if that's okay with you; I've never been too formal."

"Great, Mac, I'm Andrea." He followed her as she headed to the cubicle where his search had started. He took a side chair adjacent to her desk. Andrea sat down and swirled both monitors toward Mac.

"Since tracking stopped on Mr. Abadai after the initial six months, it's been four and a half years since anyone has looked for him. In the past few years, he's been busy traveling. Israeli intelligence sent me their file on him. It's interesting. As of this morning, Abadai has now been linked to three other aliases through Israeli intelligence.

"We're now turning to the National Security Agency to use their tools to find others. He used pseudonyms and fake travel documents and bypassed US border security about eleven months ago. He's quite the globe-trotter, Pakistan, Italy, Germany, and more."

"How does the timing connect with the recent attacks in Brazil, Portugal, London, or Germany?" Mac asked.

"Close, but not exact," Andrea said, "but the timing has Abadai arriving in Germany three weeks before the assassination. We don't have any records linked to London or Lisbon, but traveling around Europe by car is easy. I think the landing in Germany may have been the connection to London and Lisbon. We don't have an exit from him out of the EU or any links to Brazil."

"Where else has he traveled?" Mac asked.

"We've data showing he traveled to Egypt, Argentina, Mexico, Costa Rica, and Pakistan over the last couple of years, but that's only with the three known identities we've found thus far."

"Any idea where he is now?" Mac asked.

"No," said Andrea. "I can tell you where he was six weeks ago, but I have nothing more recent than his arrival in Germany."

Mac frowned. "So, where do you go from here? And how can I help you?"

Andrea paused. "Abadai's trip to New York. I've not had the time to dig into it yet."

"I've got it," Mac said. "I'll have the New York office research this today. Have you called Interpol to see if they have anything to add?"

"Not yet; I'm not the special agent."

Mac laughed, "I'll call today and ask them to contact you about the data and details. Request whatever you need from them." He thought for a second, "Do you have a card with your mobile number?" Then he pulled out his card and gave it to Andrea. "Here are my mobile and office numbers. Feel free to call me if you find anything you think may be relevant to the case."

Andrea handed Mac her card. "When will you be updating the director?"

"I'm not sure. We didn't discuss a schedule."

"I can help," said Andrea. "Let's connect by phone at the end of each workday until we know a schedule. I'll prepare a brief for you. You'll have a report you can give to the director when asked. He's used to seeing them."

"Thanks, Andrea, you've been a great help," Mac smiled and offered his hand. "Please copy me on any communication to the director or the field offices. I know we can work well together."

"I think so." Andrea brightened. "Let me know next time you're in town. We can have a drink or dinner." She quickly added, "To stay aligned on our information."

"Sounds like a plan. I'll talk to you soon." Mac smiled at her as he walked out the door. He pulled out his phone in the hallway and dialed the New York office.

# CHAPTER SIX

### Day 3, 11:00 a.m., Mexico City

He watched her standing in line for a late morning latte as he sat at a table in the corner facing the door. After paying for her latte, she moved toward him.

Hector Perez Rodriguez was a middle-aged Mexican with two children, the youngest of whom was only three. He was a devoted husband and father. Hector loved his wife, but she didn't understand financial limitations and spent extravagantly on her children and herself. He needed extra money; like others, he was willing to compromise his ethics to earn money in any way he could.

After driving a taxi for many years in one of the world's most populous cities, Hector had been exposed to the city's good and evil and knew where to go for supplemental paid work. He was a reliable delivery driver for two black market organizations in Mexico City and a taxi driver.

His additional cash income, unknown to the tax authorities, had expanded over the past five years and was more than twenty times the average income of a typical Mexico City taxi driver today. Hector's taxi driving had always been at all hours. Any absence from the family was easy to explain.

He lived by his creed: Never loan money to family or friends. Never talk about where the money comes from. And never complain of needing more money. Take the package and the payment. Deliver it and disappear.

He watched the woman cross the room. He was almost sure the lady didn't work for one of his usual employers. She sat across from him.

"Hello, Hector. Did you bring it?"

"Si," Hector said. He knew he sounded tired but didn't care. "It's in the bag under the table. I've been here for two hours waiting for you. I've had enough coffee for today." He let his tone imply some irritation.

"You brought the package into the coffee shop? Why didn't you leave it in the car?" She asked.

"My job is delivery. I'm delivering the package to you. Now I'm done."

The woman smiled, but her face flushed with anger. She reminded him, "You're done when I say you're done."

Hector looked at her. The hotel restaurant the night before was her turf, but this cafe and life on the streets were his. He shot back at her, "Señorita, I don't know you. I don't know who you work for, and I don't want to know. I deliver what I'm told to deliver."

"I know you, Hector," her voice became cold. "I know what you've done since you began working your 'second job.' I know, even better than you, who you've worked for. You were selected for this job."

Hector looked into her eyes as she stared at him. He decided to change his approach.

"I understand, Señorita. Who pays me?"

"I do." She reached into her purse, pulled out an envelope, and slid it across the table to him.

"Instructions and payment are in the envelope. The payment isn't full until you finish the delivery and provide me with the keys." Hector swallowed and kept his eyes on her.

"The keys...?" began Hector.

"The instructions are in the envelope." She cut him off. "The details are to be executed, not discussed."

"Si, Señorita," said Hector, deflated. "Do you take the package with you?"

"No," the woman said, "you take the bag and follow the instructions. This must be completed today. Can I count on you, Hector?" Hector looked at her: the dark eyes, beautiful face, and strong will. He had no choice.

"Si, Señorita, you can be assured I will take care of it."

"Good, I'll see you after you make the delivery." She rose and walked out of the small cafe and onto the street, disappearing from his view.

Hector sat for a minute and stared at his cold coffee, thinking. He considered his work for the various crime organizations that utilized his services a natural progression of his life. His most challenging problem was managing the additional cash without giving it all to his wife or putting it somewhere the tax authorities could find it.

Over the past five years, he had used the extra cash to make home improvements. He started with the tiny house he had lived in for many years, using his additional income to make improvements. He sold it and retained the profit in his bank. It was an easy way to launder money. He was in his third home, much larger than the first or second homes. His wife loved decorating new homes, and as a bonus, his extended family now viewed him with ever-increasing respect.

Hector pulled a few pesos from his pocket and left it for the waitress. Then, he slid the heavy duffle bag out from under the table and carried it to the street. The weight of the bag made him grunt as he lifted it. Hector heaved the bag into the trunk of his taxi and climbed into the driver's seat.

Opening the paper, he began reading the instructions. As he read, the morning heat infiltrated his cab, and he began to sweat. He looked nervously around to make sure no one was watching him. After reading the letter, he fingered through the cash in the envelope. Determining he had enough to begin the next step, he put the envelope inside his jacket, started the car, and edged into traffic.

Hector drove from the Reforma district toward the northern part of the city, an area he knew well. Once outside the city's motor ring, he headed east toward the outer district of Jardines del Tepeyac. This area, north of the airport, was home to hundreds of run-down warehouses and junk yards. The crime syndicates that ruled the area paid the city's police force to look the other way.

Hector pulled into a junkyard he had often used to buy parts to keep his taxi roadworthy. Several other cars and taxis were also in the dirt parking lot. He walked in and waited for Domingo, the junkyard's owner, to greet him at the counter.

"Hello, can I help you?" Domingo sounded distracted.

Hector looked at him, "Do you remember me? I've been coming here for ten years to get parts."

"Yes, I'm sorry, Hector," Domingo said, pulling his glasses off and rubbing his eyes.

"It's been a busy morning, and I'm going through the motions, I guess."

"No problem," Hector looked around and whispered, "I have a special request for you. We need to keep it between ourselves. It pays well."

Domingo put his glasses back on and looked at him, "Something we need to keep quiet?"

"Yes," Hector said, "quiet, forgotten, and untraceable to either of us."

## Day 3, 2:00 p.m., Mexico City

Hector climbed into a twenty-year-old plumbing repair cargo truck. It ran well and had been signed over to Domingo's junkyard as a debt repayment. The plates were replaced with those of a similar truck that had totaled the week prior.

Sweating in the heat, Hector departed the junkyard and headed south toward the airport. The duffle bag he retrieved from his taxi's trunk sat on the passenger seat beside him. Near the airport's outskirts, Hector pulled off on a side street and again looked at the instructions from the woman.

Returning to his drive, he turned onto Calle 38, a street southeast of the airport. Hector parked in front of a small warehouse named Zona Freight. Zona picked up small freight packages from the airport's primary freight companies, such as DHL or Federal Express, and made the final delivery to the end customer. Zona had a small warehouse where the end customer could pick up packages.

He walked into the main office and handed a clerk the freight slip found in the envelope earlier in the morning. The man at the counter looked at it and entered the number into his computer. He gave the slip to a runner to take to the dock while Hector signed for the delivery.

Hector made up a new name and scribbled it onto the page. The counterman instructed him to drive his truck around to the dock side of the building and back up to the lower loading dock. The plastic-wrapped pallet was placed into the bed of the delivery truck.

The nine hundred pounds of weight caused the truck to sink about three inches. Every metal part squeaked as though in pain. Alarmed at the weight, Hector hoped the old truck would hold together until the delivery was complete.

Hector closed and checked the truck's doors when he was approached by one of Zona Freights' dock workers.

"One more box for you." The young man handed him the package. "Our instructions on this freight order were to load the pallet and give the driver this package."

"Okay, anything else?"

"That's it," said the young man. He then offered Hector the full instruction page, which Hector scanned. Handing it back to the young man,

Hector asked, "Are you interested in making some extra money today?" The young man looked at him and then around to see if anyone was watching.

"I'm always interested in making money, but I work here until my shift ends at 3:00 p.m. If you can wait, I could earn extra money after I finish."

Hector looked at his watch. "That's less than an hour from now, and I can wait. Where's a good place to get something to eat? I missed lunch."

"First, you tell me what it pays."

Hector smiled at the directness, "How does five hundred US sound?"

"It's about two weeks' worth of work. That sounds good!" The young man smiled. He directed Hector to a nearby café.

After parking, Hector transferred the duffle bag to the back of the truck, placed it alongside the pallet, and closed the door.

He had the small box with him, and when he returned to the truck cab, he opened it. He then withdrew additional instructions and two burner cell phones. After reading the instructions and following them to the letter, Hector turned on one cell phone and waited for it to indicate it had a signal. When finished, he slid it into his inside jacket pocket.

He picked up the other cell phone and reread the instructions. With the second phone, he texted the prescribed number he found in the instructions and hit send. A response was immediately returned: "X." Hector put the phone into his other pocket. After all was done, he walked into the cafe.

## Day 3, 3:10 p.m., Mexico City

Thirty minutes later, Hector finished his meal. As he sipped a cup of coffee, the young man showed up. No longer wearing his Zona Freight jacket, the young man looked like one of the city's millions of young, healthy men willing to do almost anything to create a future for himself. He walked up to Hector's table.

"Hola, what's the plan?"

"What's your name?" Hector looked at him. "I think I should know your name."

"Davos Garcia."

"Davos, I need you to drive this truck into the city to pick up my taxi," Hector said nonchalantly. "Afterward, I need you to take the truck to this address near Chapultepec and park it." He handed Davos a piece of paper with an address and continued, "Once you drop me off, I'll follow you to where you park the truck. After you lock up, I'll take you wherever you need."

Davos smiled, "This area in Chapultepec is a few miles from the bar where I sometimes meet my friends after work. After I deliver the truck, let's go our separate ways, and I'll catch another taxi to take me where I want to go."

"Sounds good." Hector pulled the phone he'd used to send the text from his pocket and handed it to Garcia. "Take this with you in case we get separated." He pulled two hundred fifty dollars from the envelope. "Here's fifty percent of what we agreed upon. You'll get the remainder when you give me the truck keys and cell phone at the end of our trip."

Davos took the phone and money and put them in his pocket. "The truck runs okay, right? I don't have to worry about it breaking down?"

"It's an old truck," Hector cautioned, "and it has a heavy load. Take it easy on the motor and brakes."

"Got it," Davos nodded. "Are you ready to go?"

"I am," Hector smiled. "This café was pretty good. Thanks for the suggestion."

They left the café and headed toward the truck. It was 3:30 p.m. when they were headed toward the address he had given Domingo's nephew to park his taxi. Twenty-five minutes later, as they approached the street, he was relieved to see his taxi parked neatly by the side of the road. Hector reached under the left front fender and found the keys on top of the tire where he had instructed the nephew to leave them. He popped open the door and climbed in. Starting it, he pulled out to follow the truck to the next location.

At 4:15 p.m., Hector followed the slow, lumbering cargo truck as it approached its destination. He watched as Davos found the entrance off a side street and parked the enclosed panel truck next to the loading dock. Hector turned on his emergency blinkers and double-parked behind the panel truck.

Seeing a taxi with flashers rhythmically blinking was common in Mexico City; no one gave it a second look. He waited while Davos climbed out of the truck, locked the door, and got into the taxi.

"Thanks for your help," Hector smiled at him. "I'm glad this delivery is done." He handed Davos another two hundred fifty, and Davos gave Hector the keys to the truck and the cell phone he'd carried.

"Give me a second, and let me confirm the delivery," Hector mumbled.

"No problem."

Hector saw he was counting his money and probably thinking about the fun he would have with his friends tonight. Opening the phone, Hector followed the final instructions, sending the delivery confirmation six-digit code to the number he had been given. He pressed 'send.'

The phone called another cell phone less than fifteen feet away. That phone was wired into a two-pound explosive block in the duffle bag alongside the 1,500-pound pallet of plastic explosive.

## Day 3, 4:20 p.m., Mexico City

The taxi and the cargo truck sat in the loading dock adjacent to the BancaMex Tower. The blast vaporized both men with an explosion of over nine hundred pounds of military-grade C4. The blast broke every window within one thousand yards.

The bank's security guard station, with its five occupants located under the overhanging building no more than ten yards from the truck, was unceremoniously cremated. On the main avenue, dozens of drivers almost had time to blink before the explosion demolished their cars.

Without supporting columns, the entire twelve floors of the tower buckled and collapsed into a pile of glass, steel, and concrete rubble. A large dust cloud immediately rose from the ruins.

More than a hundred lives stopped inside and outside the building. Many more would die within hours.

## Day 3, 4:18 p.m., Mexico City

As the smoke and dust plume rose from the destroyed building, a single United Airlines 757 began its ascent on its way to Panama City. Sitting in first class as the plane rose from Mexico City International Airport.

Katerina Batalle, traveling under another pseudonym, sipped an orange juice and looked out the window over the Central Mexico landscape. With her job completed in Mexico City, it was time to move on to her next assignment. She eased her first-class seat back and closed her eyes as the jet rose into the atmosphere.

# CHAPTER SEVEN

### Day 3, 6:10 p.m., New York

Mac stepped out of the shower and realized the ringing he had heard was coming from his cell phone. He picked up the phone and answered.

"Mac, can you hear me?" A woman's voice was on the line.

"Uh, yes, I can hear you; who is this?"

"Mac, it's Dennica from Director Fitzgerald's office. Can you please hold while I transfer you to the director?"

Mac looked at his watch, "Dennica, I'm sorry I didn't recognize your voice. Yes, of course, I'll hold on." About 20 seconds later, he heard the phone line go live and listened to what sounded like road noises before the director inhaled and began.

"Mac, sorry for the late call. Here's the situation: A major bank in Mexico City has been attacked by terrorists."

Mac blinked twice at the news and said, "I understand. I'll be at the office in twenty minutes."

"Thanks, Mac," Robert sounded tired. "We'll have all SAICs on an 8:00 p.m. secure conference call, and I want you there too for an update from the State Department. Talk to you soon." The line went dead.

### Day 3, 8:45 p.m., New York

Mac walked out of the conference room with Bill Michaels. The city was dark outside the windows of the office. He rubbed his unshaven face,

"It looks like we're starting the day about twelve hours earlier than usual."

Bill gave him a tired smile. "I can't tell you how many times I've been in the office overnight. I lost count."

Mac and Bill returned to Bill's office, overlooking Manhattan's Midtown district. Mac stopped to look out the window at the quiet darkness descending upon New York. Most of the adjacent buildings' lights were extinguished, except for the emergency lighting visible in stairwells or hallways.

The Empire State Building, a few blocks away, was displaying its evening art-deco red tower lighting.

Mac turned back toward Michaels and said, "Well, we're about ten hours until the rest of the agents arrive. When I called you this morning, I had no idea we would be in the office at 9:00 p.m."

Bill sat heavily in his chair and began, "I got hold of the full team, all twenty special agents and the five analysts and researchers, and told them to wrap up what they could and be ready to start a special project tomorrow morning."

"Thank you, Boss." Mac was genuinely appreciative. "

I asked David Osrick, who happened to come into the office late afternoon after you called, to connect with your DC researcher, Andy somebody. Sorry, I've forgotten the full name."

"Andrea Douglas-Pfeiffer," Mac said. "I think we'll be lucky to have her help with this."

Bill smiled wearily, "One of us needs to get some sleep. We need at least one fully awake supervisor, day and night."

Mac nodded. "I agree," he said, looking at Bill. "What do you want to do?"

Bill smiled at Mac and said, "I've been in your shoes. You'll need your sleep to keep up with the demands of the director's office. I'll take the overnight tonight and have one of the other supervisors take it tomorrow. I'll let you know if anything comes in."

Bill stood up and walked Mac to the door. Mac watched from outside Michaels's office as Bill looked at the old leather couch. He walked over to his closet, grabbed his pillow and blanket, and tossed them onto the couch. Bill slipped off his shoes, loosened his belt, and removed his tie. He settled onto the sofa, laid his head on the pillow, and lightly tossed the blanket over his torso.

On the way out, Mac picked up a few papers from his desk and headed home.

### Day 4, 1:00 p.m., New York

The offices of the New York branch of the Secret Service are located on three floors in downtown Manhattan on the fifty-third through fifty-fifth floors of a glass-encased building. After the 2001 attack on the Twin Towers of the World Trade Center, the office was moved from a building near Wall Street to this observatory location. It provides a good view of Midtown Manhattan, the downtown financial district, and the surrounding boroughs.

The building wasn't large, but it was tall. Each window on the three floors occupied by the Secret Service has a unique film inside the glass. When an electric charge is applied to the film, it darkens to reduce inbound sunlight and prevent eavesdropping. No other floors in the building use this film. From the outside of the building, the effect looks like a slightly darker band on the windows of these three floors, like a belt a little over halfway up the building.

Mac entered the office after joining Bill Michaels for a quick sandwich in a shop across the street. He found David Osrick coming out of a meeting and asked, "What is the latest count from Mexico City?" Mac walked to his office, and David followed.

Osrick shook his head, "Best estimate at this point is about a hundred killed and another three to five hundred injured. It's early on all the numbers. Local police and emergency teams are still working the scene. The Mexico police are estimating that over seven hundred pounds of C4 or equivalent were detonated. Based on the blast crater, the FBI's initial analysis is close to this estimate, too."

Mac stood up from his desk and turned toward the windows to look over Manhattan. "So the largest bank in Mexico is targeted. If we put this on the map, we would see São Paulo, Mexico City, and Lisbon—all banks, all bombed."

"Yes," David slowly nodded his head, "and don't forget about the assassinations in Frankfurt and London. The gentleman in Germany was a director for the European Central Bank, and the woman in London was the vice-chairman of the Bank of England."

Mac interjected. "Did I tell you the New York Federal Reserve chairman walked into the office this morning? We had an interesting discussion; what was his name again?" Mac paused and looked through his notes. He patted his breast pocket and pulled out a card. "His name was Jonathon Greenhouse. The chairman expressed his concern that the Frankfurt and London assassinations and the Lisbon bombing collectively were an attack on the European Central Bank and the Bank of London. The Mexico City bombing this morning and the São Paulo bombing have heightened his anxiety, and he raised the fear of an attack on the US. He wants to know what we're doing about it."

"Is it too early to make this type of connection?" Asked Osrick.

"To me, yes, but to someone watching banking stability worldwide, I guess not," Mac said. "You probably know Latin America doesn't have a central bank. However, the bombings in Brazil and Mexico were both on established and highly regarded national banks, according to Chairman Greenhouse. Maybe the chairman has something, maybe not. Who would benefit from attacks on banks or bankers?"

"I'm going to put another analyst on the banking angle. If we dig deep enough, we can find a lead," Osrick said as he walked out the door.

Mac sat at his desk and wrote notes. Moments later, his assistant, Natalie, popped her head around the door frame.

"Mac," she started to speak but waited for him to look up. When he looked up, she continued, "Per your request, I have all agents available gathered in the main conference room."

"Thank you, Natalie."

"Boss, I'm sorry about the short vacation. Per the director's orders, I'll arrange for the agency to cover the costs and reimburse you."

"Thanks, Nat," Mac looked up from his notes. "Can you also see if I can book a ten-day rental for next year about this time? Same boat, same itinerary, a couple of days more. Please use my card to book the deposit."

"You got it." Natalie smiled. "By the way, the sunshine you did get looks good on you."

Mac smiled, "I guess a little is better than nothing." Mac stood up and walked to the door.

Natalie quietly asked, "So, did you meet anyone?"

Mac caught the curious look in her eyes and smiled at her, "I did. Frankly, I don't know if anything will come from it, but I met someone nice. Unfortunately, everything hit the fan here as it was getting interesting. I may take a long weekend in Denver when this is over. Now excuse me, Nat. I need to meet with the team."

Natalie's eyes lit up with the news. She moved out of Mac's way.

## Day 4, 1:45 p.m., New York

Mac closed the meeting with the agents and analysts:

"All US Embassy locations and government buildings worldwide are running code orange. The military has moved to Def Con three. All intelligence and law enforcement agencies coordinate efforts through the National Security Director. We're setting up a joint task force. We've no reason to believe the US will remain untouched by whoever is behind these bombings. We must anticipate that an attack on the US will happen and make sure it doesn't. Our job today is to find Helbol Pakerisami and, if he's here, Amir Abadai. You all have your assignments. Let's get to work."

He walked from the front of the room and returned to his office as the agents and researchers departed. David Osrick walked a few steps behind him.

"Hey David, glad you're here," said Mac. "Come into my office and give me a more detailed background on Pakerisami and Abadai. I've seen a few emails from Andrea, but I'm hoping our team here has better details."

Taking a chair, Osrick began, "About eleven months ago, Abadai was on a flight to New York using one of his aliases. The flight originated in Cairo and landed at JFK. We checked the security camera footage from the airport and confirmed it was Abadai."

"Great," Mac leaned forward, "where did he go after the airport?"

"That's where our trail ended," Osrick said. "He grabbed a cab outside the airport and disappeared. We reviewed the security footage from the airport and checked with the cab company, but we didn't find much.

The FBI team hopes for another facial match from an outbound flight. But combing through a few million travelers out of JFK takes time. He possibly could have used some other airport. It's like trying to find a needle in a haystack. I don't give it much of a chance of success."

David paused for a few moments while he flipped pages in the folder. He then continued speaking. "We'll circulate Abadai's image from the airport and see if we can get any hits of where he stayed eleven months ago."

"Seems like a long shot," Mac said as he shifted in his chair. "What about locating Pakerisami and determining if he's involved?"

Mac watched Osrick close the folder he was reviewing and open another. Osrick started again. "Helbol Pakerisami lives in Queens. He owns a home on 87th Avenue. It's a predominantly Muslim area in the Jamaica neighborhood. He's been accepted into the community over the past five years. On a website for Dalees Salaam, a local community center, he's identified as a member of the governing board of elders. His tax returns and bank records are spotty, and he has little personal income. It's probably safe to say he's in cash ventures."

"Who's on him?" Mac asked.

"Yosali Tarik is working in the neighborhood," David said. "We're watching the mosque at the community center where we think he takes his daily prayers. We've had Tarik on the search for less than a day."

"Tarik's a good man. He should be able to track him down if he's still in the neighborhood," Mac said. "So, what are your next steps?"

"I will keep Tarik working in the area until we find Pakerisami or confirm he's no longer there. I have the other agents working on the transportation angle today and tomorrow. Planes, trains, and taxis."

Mac nodded at Osrick and watched him leave. He picked up the phone and dialed Andrea's number in DC.

# CHAPTER EIGHT

## Day 5, 9:00 a.m., London, England

Gamir Halibid was alone in his office, watching CNBC's breaking news updates on the bombings in Mexico City. Financial markets seemed unable to comprehend what was happening. Gamir smiled and said out loud, "They'll figure it out soon." He turned the TV off and returned to his expansive desk, and again, the thought occurred to him: *The Americans think they are untouchable.*

Gamir grew up in Islamabad. His grandfather had built a small business transporting and distributing fresh fruit and vegetables into many parts of the city. Gamir, his brothers, and his father also worked in the family business. But Gamir was a gifted linguist. By age twelve, he was fluent in English, French, and Urdu and could negotiate in all the street language variations around the city. He was also a prodigy at math, and from age fifteen, he managed the accounting side of the business for his father and grandfather.

By the time he was ready to enroll in university, Gamir had worked out an agreement with his father. If his father supported him in attending Oxford University, he would commit to returning to Islamabad to help run the family business.

Twenty-five years after returning to Islamabad, the Halibid family had built Pakistan's largest fresh produce distribution network. But it didn't stop there. Gamir used his contact and political skills to build South Asia's most significant private banking institution: South Asia International Bank, or SAIB, as it was commonly referred to.

Success for Gamir came with homes in several countries, including a spacious flat in London. He heard a knock on his office door. Without waiting for Gamir to respond, Gamir's London assistant, Emily, entered and escorted Lord Geoffrey Tanner, a wealthy manufacturing magnet, into Gamir's office for the day's first meeting.

## Day 5, 4:00 p.m., Fort Worth Alliance Airport

Katerina Batalle pulled her rental car into the parking lot outside the offices of Blue Ribbon Freight. The nondescript building was one of more than fifty freight-handling buildings surrounding the Fort Worth Alliance Airport, one of the busiest international freight hubs in the US. With a single phone call to a contact, she found a small company with a reputation among certain parties for helping to move freight across the world with limited documentation.

She was wearing a white blouse under a dark blue pantsuit. The dark sunglasses and pulled-back hair gave her the look of a busy executive as she exited the rental car and walked smartly into the building. Travis Harms, a senior manager, met her. He ushered her into his small, dusty office and offered her a seat.

"I'd rather stand," Katerina commented after looking at the dusty chairs. She saw a noticeable lack of organization in the office.

"No problem," Travis said, oblivious to the innuendo. "Let's see what I can find. There it is, yes, we've got a large package for you. A heavy pallet wrapped in plastic, about five feet tall. The freight instructions asked us to hold it here for someone to pick it up. We've had it in the warehouse for two days. I believe we told the broker there would be a pickup charge to cover the storage costs."

He looked at her, "I hope this isn't surprising."

She smiled slightly, "No, not a surprise. I was expecting some additional costs. How much?" "It's about two hundred for the storage and handling,"

"That's reasonable," She said. "Can we make it five hundred? And you can hold it for a truck to pick it up sometime next week?" She assumed he wouldn't report any storage or handling on this delivery.

Travis said, "Make it cash, and we'll be good."

"Done," she offered a smile and a handshake for the finalized business. Travis followed her out as they exited the building.

"When my truck comes to pick up the pallet, where do they pull up?" Katerina asked.

"The loading dock is right around the corner," Travis pointed in the direction. Pulling a business card out of his pocket, he continued, "I live a few minutes away. Have the driver call me, and I'll ensure it gets loaded onto the truck immediately, even after normal hours."

Katerina smiled at him, "That's great." She reached into her pocket, pulled out five crisp hundred-dollar bills, and gave them to him. "I know we agreed on five hundred, but for all the help you've given me and will give my driver, here's an extra tip." Travis's face lit up when he saw three extra bills added to the cash. She continued, "Let's say the extra money is for keeping this transaction quiet and off the books."

Travis smiled and raised an eyebrow, "Okay, for me." He turned his attention to the bills in his hand and walked back toward the building. He stuffed them into his pocket before opening the door.

She studied him as he walked back into the building. Her thoughts were simple: Do I walk back in there and kill him in his office chair? Or can I trust him to keep this quiet? Travis never looked back at her and walked purposefully into the building. She liked that. No second-thoughts. That's a good sign.

She opened the door of her car and climbed in. "Phase two begins," she murmured.

## Day 6, 7:30 a.m., New York

Helbol Pakerisami could feel something was wrong. He was always a bundle of nervous energy, but today, something felt different. He couldn't escape the itch. It triggered his subconscious and whispered to him that it was time to find a new, safer place to be.

It wasn't the first time he had this feeling. He credited the feeling with saving his life years ago in Egypt. That time, he suddenly, without full explanation, left on a freighter for Europe. He was carrying a backpack, a small bag of clothes, and whatever cash he could pull together. A few days later, the local police searched his apartment in Cairo. His relatives asked where he was.

His choice to leave without informing anyone saved his freedom and his life. Now approaching his early 40s, with pronounced wrinkles around his eyes, a permanently scraggly beard, and graying hair, Pakerisami was aging as he tried to live two lives simultaneously.

In the local Muslim community, Pakerisami was a trustworthy elder. He often attended community functions at Dalees Salaam Community Center and contributed monthly to the center, almost to the point of poverty. He successfully built a reputation as a wise and generous man, but it was a cover.

Pakerisami's other life was darker, more secretive, and well-established. Helbol Pakerisami's real work started many years ago as a teenager in Egypt. Over time, he became known as an 'enabler,' a middleman who could provide connections. He could use people's greed to twist arms and get things done.

He was comfortable paying bribes. He had no qualms about putting legitimate people into difficult situations for his advantage. Helbol knew how to make deals to do things that couldn't go through normal channels. Many years ago, he had set his morals aside and forgotten where he laid them.

Today, as he sat drinking a robust Turkish coffee at the local Muslim cafe, he could feel the hair on the back of his neck rise. He looked at his watch; it was a few minutes before 9:00 a.m. The table was near the back of the cafe, and he sat facing the door. He looked around the restaurant and saw nothing unusual. No one looked at him. He saw nothing different from previous days when he had sat in the same seat at the same table.

Pakerisami hunched his shoulders and stretched his neck to manage the slight chill he was experiencing as part of the feeling. He looked into the bottom of his coffee cup and reached his hand to grasp the carafe from the table. He gently refilled the small cup.

He nervously scratched at his hands and looked around the cafe again for anything out of place. Seeing nothing, he returned to his coffee and continued with his assessment. *If it's time to leave, I need to have a plan.* He didn't want to leave the US, so he considered his options. He required cover and places to go in the US where at least a small North African Muslim population existed and where he could easily blend in and be accepted.

Pakerisami signaled to the waiter to bring his check. He paid, rose from the table, and walked out of the cafe into the bright morning sunlight. The traffic on Jamaica Avenue was noisy this morning. Walking northeast, he headed toward the Dalees Salaam Community Center and Mosque. Turning the corner onto 187th, he saw several fellow faithful heading toward the mosque.

It wasn't time for 'Dhuhr' or noon prayers; however, the community center also had a daycare. At this time of day, it was common for many people to come and go from the center as they dropped off their children. The elders of the community center often met at 9:00 a.m. for an informal discussion.

## Day 6, 7:45 a.m., New York

Pakerisami didn't see the man standing in the bakery across the street. The sunlight reflection off the glass caused the large bakery window to act more like a one-way mirror. Easy to see out, almost impossible to see in.

Inside the bakery, watching Pakerisami and noting the time on his watch, was agent Yosali Tarik of the Secret Service. Most mornings, the bakery was a good location for a few hours. The couple running the shop served coffee to those neighbors who stopped by and purchased baked items.

After three days of watching for Pakerisami, the bakery location paid off today. Tarik saw him walking toward the mosque. Quickly picking up his box of pastries, Tarik said his goodbyes to the owners and left the store about 100 yards behind Pakerisami. Watching him walk into the mosque,

Tarik moved to the other side of the street. He pulled out his cell phone and called David Osrick.

"Osrick."

"David, this is Tarik. I've got eyes on Pakerisami. He surfaced and entered the Dalees Salaam Community Center and Mosque off of 187th. He is walking alone."

David was thrilled, "Finally, we got eyes on Pakerisami! Great job, Tarik! Keep an eye on his movements. I'm going to send Johnson and Marik for additional support. Confirm his daily activities, where he goes, and who he meets. You know the drill."

"Got it," said Tarik, "I don't want to spook him with a new face. I will keep out of his way and try to monitor him. Have Johnson and Marik stake out his house and call me when they get in position." "

Sounds good," Osrick said. "Let's be careful not to get the neighbors suspicious."

"Will do; I'll update you at the end of the day." Tarik ended the call and moved to the other end of the block to take up a new position to watch the mosque.

## Day 7, 8:25 a.m., Islamabad, Pakistan

Amir Abadai exited the crowded airport in Islamabad and hailed a taxi. The grit, smog, and noise of the airport in the southwestern part of the city slowly receded in the distance as the cab entered the central business district of Islamabad. He saw the foothills of the mountains in the distance and fondly remembered hiking in them. The mountain peaks were covered by a layer of clouds today. The vegetation was bright green in the parks they passed along the way. It was different from the deserts in Egypt and the West Bank.

Abadai's long hair was tied back, and he wore a kameez, a traditional Pakistani long tunic. Although he didn't speak Urdu, as most Pakistanis spoke English or French, he rarely had a problem. His taxi pulled up at the Crown Plaza Hotel. He walked in and checked into his reserved room. He was traveling under a Pakistani passport as 'Yusuf Ari,' a Pakistani citizen living in Singapore.

Abadai had changed over the fifteen years since he first left Egypt at age 17 and found his way to the West Bank, where he joined his brothers in the Palestinian Liberation Organization. In the five years he was in the West Bank, he was active in carrying out several actions with the net effect of killing multiple Israeli soldiers and citizens.

PLO leadership was impressed with the young rebel and suggested he travel to Libya for additional training. Eventually, he was selected to move to Pakistan to support the PLO's work in helping develop a terrorist network in Pakistan.

Ideologically and geographically, Pakistan was a prime target for the revolution. Large in land mass and located between India and Afghanistan, Pakistan is perpetually the underdog. India, Afghanistan, and Pakistan had warred for generations over religion, race, and political ideology. There was bad blood on every border.

Almost ten years later, the PLO was a distant memory for Amir. Abadai was an independent contractor for hire. Abadai checked his cell phone for messages. He noticed a new text simply stating: "Welcome Packet Delivered." Seeing this text, he smiled and pulled a small tip for the bellman.

Within minutes, a knock on his door occurred. Seeing a bellman through the keyhole, he opened the door and took the package. He expressed his thanks in a quiet voice.

Inside the package, he found a new burner phone with two new SIM cards and an easily concealable 9 mm pistol. Abadai removed the SIM card from his phone and crushed it under his heel on the bathroom tile floor. The old SIM card had his recent travels in GPS coordinates and texts recorded in its nonvolatile memory.

He opened one of the new SIM cards and placed it in his phone. After the phone recognized the network connection, a message came almost immediately: *"Ei Edriba Cafe, noon."*

## Day 7, 11:00 a.m., Islamabad, Pakistan

An hour later, Abadai exited the hotel and began walking in the opposite direction of his cafe meeting. Stopping in a roadside tobacco and news shop, he looked for any signs of a tail. Seeing nothing, he continued moving. He walked into a cafe and ordered a coffee. Taking the coffee outside, he sat at a table on the sidewalk and watched the road as he drank his coffee.

After a ten-minute pause, he stood up and began moving again, this time in a direction that would take him closer to the meeting cafe. He repeated the multiple stops and included a double back to look for surveillance as he proceeded to the meeting point.

Almost an hour after leaving the hotel, he arrived at his destination and entered Ei Edriba Cafe at noon. He ordered a coffee and took a table at the front of the cafe to watch the street again for several minutes. Seeing nothing to indicate someone following him, he picked up his coffee, walked to the back of the cafe, and sat beside a man.

"It's good to see you, Amir, my friend." Jahar P'Shari smiled at Abadai and offered his hand in friendship.

"It's good to see you as well, Jahar," Abadai said. "It's been a few months."

"Our benefactor is pleased with your progress. Impressed and pleased."

"Excellent news," Amir smiled. "We've more to do and need additional funds to expand our team and actions."

"Yes, I expected as much," said Jahar. He leaned forward. "I've been asked to review your progress in Central America with an onsite visit. I do hope you can accommodate me for a day or two."

Abadai was surprised, a look he tried hard to mask. "I can assure you the funds are being used appropriately."

"Please be certain I have no concerns." Said Jahar. "But our benefactor holds me accountable for the expenditure and wishes me to be more personally involved. I've no desire to travel to Central America, but in this instance, I have no choice."

"I understand," Amir said quietly. "When do you wish to meet?"

Jahar smiled, "I think we should be traveling soon. When can you depart earliest?"

Abadai considered his trip itinerary. It had taken him three days to travel to Pakistan through multiple stops, including an overnight stay in Dubai. To leave too fast could be a signal to intelligence agencies. He needed to wait a day or two before departing the country.

"Let's plan to meet in four days at the hacienda." He looked at this watch. "That would be on the 14th."

Jahar said, "Four days should work fine. Should I fly into San José?"

"Yes," said Abadai, "and then on to La Fortuna. Our pilot will pick you up and bring you to the hacienda."

"I'll work the trip into some other business I need to attend to," Jahar said.

"Very good," said Abadai. "I'll contact Katerina to join us." "I have one more thing for you," P'Shari said as he reached into his bag.

"Here's some additional funding for your travels." He slid the envelope across the table to Abadai. Amir picked it up. He could feel the weight of the cash and the edges of a few passports. Without looking inside, he slid the envelope into a pocket.

"Thank you. I appreciate the support," Amir said. "Whoever does these passports for you does excellent work."

"Thank you." P'Shari said, "These are for the identities we pulled together last time we met. I'll have new identities for Katerina when I see her in Central America."

Amir nodded to Jahar, then stood and purposefully walked out of the cafe into the bright midday sunshine. As he walked from the cafe, Abadai ignored the envelope in his jacket. He had always viewed money as a tool that helped him accomplish whatever was put before him. He didn't have a retirement plan and saw no reason to save money for the future. He didn't expect to live a long and healthy life. His personal view reflected what he knew from experience: Life would be short and brutal.

# CHAPTER NINE

## Day 7, 5:00 p.m., Dallas

Katerina Batalle entered the Renaissance Hotel on the outskirts of downtown Dallas after a late afternoon run in the heat and humidity. She paused outside the doors to catch her breath and drink from the water bottle that always accompanied her on her runs. As she rested, her phone blipped with a message. The message was designed to emulate spam text:

*"Hi, Karla. This is Monique from the Chicago Democratic Committee. Can we count on your vote for Deshawn Charles to become the next Chicago mayor? Please call me back at 312-675-8976 for more information and to sign up."*

Batalle recognized this spam as a signal to contact her colleague, Amir Abadai. She entered the building and went to her room, where she pulled the SIM card from her phone and replaced it with a new one. She dialed the number from the message but reversed the last seven digits of the phone number. The call was picked up almost immediately.

"Yes," came the response.

"Responding to your text," Katerina said.

The small phone speaker carried the voice of Amir Abadai: "I need you to be in Costa Rica for a visitor. Our visitor arrives four days from today. Try to be there in three days. Pause your activities for now."

She looked at her watch. "I'm on my way."

She ended the call and picked up the SIM card she had replaced. Using a small set of pliers from her suitcase, she crushed the old SIM card, put the pieces into the toilet, and flushed it away.

Batalle stripped naked and walked into the shower. It was an excellent place to organize her mind for the next few minutes and consider the reason for this request. Minutes later, she stepped out of the shower, dripping wet. She dried her hair and selected some clothes for travel.

She picked up the hotel phone and called the laundry service to return the clothes she had left with them earlier in the morning due to an unexpected change in plans.

Katerina dressed and put her suitcase on the bed to pack. A few minutes later, she heard a knock on the door; the maid brought her laundry. She took a perfume bottle, sprayed it heavily onto a washcloth, and began to wipe places in the room she had touched.

Katerina always added additional alcohol to her perfume bottles. It effectively wiped away fingerprints, and the perfume didn't linger too long in the room after she left. After tossing the washcloth and towels from the shower onto the bathroom floor, she turned on the exhaust fan to eliminate the smell. Then, she rolled her suitcase into the hallway and closed the door behind her.

## Day 8, 7:00 a.m., New York

Mac was rushing through his morning preparations in his apartment when his phone rang. He picked it up.

"This is Krieger." Mac used his formal, no-nonsense, special agent tone.

"Mac?" Said a female voice on the other end of the phone.

"Is this Mac Krieger?"

Mac immediately recognized the voice. "Rae?"

"Mac, I hope it's okay for me to call," Rae blurted. "I'd not heard from you, and I wanted to apologize if I said something wrong." Mac flushed.

"Oh, Rae, I'm sorry. I should have called you the first day I was back in New York." He tried to lighten the tone. "But I'm happy you reached out to me!"

"Mac, I was concerned I may have said something wrong when you dropped me off at the hotel. I hope you'll forgive me." Mac was embarrassed.

"I need to ask for your forgiveness! After the wonderful evening we shared, it's inexcusable for me not to have called you! It's been almost ten days! I hope you can forgive me!"

"Forgiven," Rae said. "Is this a good time? Can you talk?"

"This is a great time." Mac smiled as he sat at his breakfast counter.

"I'm glad you called. I feel like a complete idiot. I'm sorry."

"Don't apologize," Rae purred into the phone.

"I know you were pulled away, and I'm sure it was important. I wanted to hear your voice again."

"Your timing is perfect," Mac said. "I needed someone to take my mind off the bad things going on in the world."

"I wondered," Rae asked, "if you were interested in a second date?"

"Well, of course I am!" Mac said happily, "I'm disappointed I didn't call you sooner."

"Denver? New York? Sometime? Anytime? Do you have any suggestions?" she asked, her voice sounding like she was smiling.

49

"I would love to get together with you as soon as possible," Mac emphasized. "But right now, I'm sure I wouldn't be the best company. Rae, I want our next date to be memorable. Is there a time of day that is best for me to contact you? I want to talk more."

"You can text me anytime," Rae said. "Call before seven in the morning or after seven in the evening. Remember, it's mountain time, two hours different from New York."

"Mountain time," Mac smiled as he said it. "It sounds nice. Hey, we never talked about it, but in my imagination, I can see you teaching a yoga class—in the morning."

Rae laughed, "Pilates, three days a week. But why would you imagine what I do in my spare time?"

"Seriously?" Mac chuckled, "Have you ever looked at your legs? They're beautiful!"

Rae laughed. "Speaking of pilates, I've got to get to my class. Will I hear from you again?"

"Yes, you will, Rae. I promise," Mac said.

"I'll call soon. Thank you for making my day!"

"And you mine," Rae said. "Talk soon; bye, Mac."

"Bye," Mac said as the call ended. "I'm such an idiot."

Mac's voice was loud enough to reverberate through the small apartment. He immediately sent her a text: *Thank you for the call! It made my day! We will talk soon!*

After hearing the sound of the message, he picked up his credentials, gun, and a few items to mail and hustled out the door.

## Day 9, 3:26 p.m., Dallas

At Blue Ribbon Freight, a twenty-foot Salviano LTL Interstate Transport truck pulled to the warehouse loading dock. The driver climbed out of the cab and knocked on the door to the loading dock before trying the door handle. The door was unlocked. He turned the handle and entered the building carrying the bill of lading documents. Entering the same building Batalle was in two days before, he walked into the loading dock area and saw Travis Harms driving a forklift and moving a pallet near one of the freight doors.

Travis noticed the driver and motioned him to wait a moment while he moved the pallet into position. Turning off the forklift, Travis climbed off the rig and walked over.

"Afternoon, what's up?" Travis asked the man in a casual, conversational tone.

"I'm here to pick up a pallet you're holding. My boss gave me the paperwork and sent me over." He handed Travis the paperwork, and Travis looked it over.

"Come to the office and let me look up the pallet location. Do you want a cup of coffee?"

"Wouldn't refuse a quick cup."

"Follow me." Travis walked toward the office. Once inside, he motioned to a nearby dusty chair and the coffee pot.

"Help yourself and take a seat while I look this up." Travis sat behind his desk, keyed in the bill of lading number, and waited for the old computer to answer.

"Where is this pallet?" Travis mumbled under his breath as he looked at the bill of lading and tried the numbers again. When they didn't connect on the second attempt, Travis picked up the paperwork and mumbled to the driver, who had sat down, "Sit tight; I'll be right back."

The driver raised his cup of coffee toward Travis and nodded slightly, acknowledging he was okay waiting and drinking his coffee. Travis walked out of the office and directly back to where several pallets were set aside. These pallets were no longer in the system. He had intentionally removed them from the computer. Their audit tracing stopped when the pallet was delivered to Blue Ribbon Freight.

Legitimate cargo required some form of identification and a signature to pick them up. Usually, the freight company's name and the truck's DOT number were sufficient. Other packages became 'lost.' Travis would terminate the delivery at the warehouse for a few hundred dollars. These packages didn't have a clear destination. No records were kept of who picked up the freight or when.

Travis walked around the pallets and boxes, identified the right pallet from the paperwork, marked it with an X on the plastic wrapping, and returned to the office.

"Okay, I have the pallet and can bring it to the loading dock. Have you finished with your coffee?" Travis looked at the truck driver. The driver looked up from his coffee.

"Yup, ready to go." He left the office and started the engine on this truck, moving it around the building to the loading dock. Travis opened the freight door on the warehouse floor to see the truck backing up against the loading dock. The driver jumped out of the truck and climbed the steps to enter the warehouse. He lifted the truck's rear door. Several pallets were already inside.

Travis looked briefly inside the truck to ensure room, then walked to the forklift. He climbed into the seat and drove it over to the pallet he had marked with an 'X' moments earlier. A few minutes later, with the pallet loaded on the truck, Travis returned the paperwork to the driver, who wordlessly took it and closed the truck's roll-down door. Travis watched the driver pull out, and he closed the freight door without a second glance.

# CHAPTER TEN

**Day 10, 11:00 a.m., Costa Rica**

Amir Abadai climbed out of the small Cessna moments after landing on the graveled airstrip at the hacienda, a secluded 12,000-acre former vegetable plantation in the mountainous northern reaches of Costa Rica. He walked up to the main house, a short distance away from the end of the runway, while the pilot revved the engine and rolled the plane toward two aviation fuel tanks.

Jahar P'Shari's mysterious " benefactor " supported the purchase of the hacienda property two years ago. Negotiations on the property were swift, and Amir closed after P'Shari set up a Costa Rican bank account and wired funds from a bank in the Cayman Islands.

Only about five square miles of the hacienda were still active for farming. Abadai rented the farmable property to a nearby farmer. The rest of the property was a mostly untouched jungle. Birds, deer, wild boar, and many other animals roamed the land.

Driving access to the property from the nearest paved road was about five miles on a graveled road that connected several plantations. After reaching the unmarked entrance and encountering the gate, it was almost a mile from the graveled road to the main house.

The second major purchase was a used Cessna 172 airplane, purchased within days of the property acquisition. It was 200 miles over mountainous and sometimes impassable roads to La Fortuna, the nearest city with an airport. Many landowners in the area used light aircraft.

The third significant purchase was a used bulldozer. It was immediately used to expand the length of the existing runway. The dozer compacted the fertile earth and added a light gravel base. Runway lighting was installed for nighttime use.

Over the next two years, lots of changes happened. The main house was refurbished with a large kitchen, an expanded patio, and a pool area. Four new bunkhouses were built about five hundred yards from the main house, with two-person guest rooms for up to ten guests in each building. Another building was about 100 yards closer to the main house. It was designed to house guns, ammo, fishing rods, and other equipment under lock and key. Abadai called it the "outfitter building."

Several 'guests' began to arrive shortly after the guest bunkhouses were built. The 'guests' disappeared into the jungle with the bulldozer each morning and returned each night. Almost fifteen square miles of overgrown fields lay beyond the bunkhouses. A few small streams fed a river on the property's western border. The river flowed from the mountain foothills far off to the northwest of the property in Nicaragua.

Recently, electric gates with cameras were added at the front entrance, although traffic along the road outside the property was light. Abadai told Ernesto Garcia Secico when he hired him that the plantation would continue farming on tilled land. The remainder of the property would be turned into a hunting and fishing preserve. He hoped it would be more profitable than farming.

Ernesto was Abadai's overseer and pilot. He was local to the area and knew many of the hacienda owners. He had worked as a pilot for a nearby plantation for five years and was interested when Abadai approached him to come to work for him as a pilot and a land overseer.

A few months after the bulldozer started working in the jungle, staff members thought they heard gunshots coming from the north. Later that same day, Abadai pulled the employees together and told them several of the new guests were sighting in rifles at a gun range they'd built.

He explained they would soon open the hunting and fishing preserve to paying visitors. Abadai asked Ernesto to have a sign maker create an entrance sign for the property. The sign would read "Rancho Trevio Hunting and Fishing Preserve" with "Admission by Appointment Only" in smaller lettering below the main header. The sign was made and installed in two days.

## Day 10, 2:00 p.m., Costa Rica

Katerina Batalle, who had flown into La Fortuna after Abadai, was sitting in the passenger seat on the second round trip of the day. Abadai met the plane as it taxied up the runway. He walked out to the small Cessna to help her climb out of the airplane.

"Welcome back. It's good to see you again, Katerina!" Abadai was beaming.

"Good to be here." Abadai watched her lean over to Ernesto and say, "Thanks for the ride."

Amir and Katerina carried her small suitcases to the main house.

"Same room as before?" She asked. Amir nodded. She grabbed her luggage and walked down the hall. "I'll see you in thirty minutes," she said over her shoulder, "give me a chance to clean up."

Abadai watched her walk away, then turned and wandered into the kitchen to ask Anja, the full-time cook, to prepare some food for a late lunch. Thirty minutes later, in fresh clothes and with her hair tied back, Katerina walked onto the patio overlooking the pool and sat next to Amir.

He wore a Panama hat, sunglasses, light cargo pants, and a white polo shirt. He was drinking freshly squeezed juice and tending to his phone.

"Jahar texted me; he said he was departing the Cayman Islands on his way to Miami," Amir said, looking up from his phone at Katerina.

"I think tomorrow will be a good day for him to visit the hacienda; the weather looks like it'll hold."

From the kitchen, Anja approached with a fresh carafe of pineapple juice and a plate for Amir, a large croissant with chicken salad, lettuce, and a cup of fresh fruit. Katerina took one look and requested the same. Anja nodded, poured her a glass of juice, and told her she would return.

"The place looks good," Katerina looked around from her seat, "a lot different from six months ago."

Amir nodded as he paused to eat and dabbed a napkin on his mouth. "It has been a busy time." He looked around for Anja and continued in a low voice. "I've started using the new hires to build the training facilities in the jungle. By the way, I call them 'guests' in front of the staff."

Anja left the kitchen carrying Katerina's lunch, squelching the discussion. After eating, they rose and began walking back toward the bunkhouses. Several four-passenger all-terrain vehicles were sitting near the house, and Amir directed her to the passenger side of the first one.

Starting it up, Abadai drove toward the outfitting building.

"Our guests are working on the assault training buildings at the live fire range. I think everyone except Nasreen is doing that," Amir said as they pulled up to a one-story building.

"Nasreen is our armorer. He's a new staff member, and I'd like to introduce you to him." They climbed out of the vehicle and walked to the door. Abadai knocked and looked up at the camera located above the door. Momentarily, a man came to the door while wiping his oily hands.

Amir smiled at him, "Nasreen, this is Katerina." Nasreen nodded his head at her and opened the door. He was wearing a dirty work shirt with oil and sweat stains. His hands were filthy with machine oil, and his receding hairline was thin, long, and somewhat oily.

As they entered the building, Amir watched Katerina take in the first room, a typical hunting and fishing shop. Fly rods, waders, nets, hats, and mosquito netting were on one wall. Hunting rifles of various calibers with scopes were behind glass on another wall. A glass-topped table housed fishing flies, a few pistols of multiple calibers, knives, and other survival-type gear. There were racks of rain gear and rubber boots. The weapons and gear were new.

"This is interesting," Katerina said as she perused the room's contents. "It looks like a typical fishing or hunting shop to me."

Abadai smiled at her and signaled Nasreen to open the door to the next room. "Please follow me," he said.

Inside the room were the tools of the trade for someone who works with weapons. There were a couple of benches with gun mounts, a commercial-grade drill press beside a metal lathe, and reloading tools for creating specialized rounds against one wall. The room smelled of machine oil, gun-cleaning fluid, and sweat. Music came from a small speaker beside a video monitor. The monitor showed the feed from the camera outside the front door. Amir could see the all-terrain vehicle sitting outside.

Turning to another door, Amir motioned to Nasreen to open the door. "Nasreen takes care of everything in this building," Amir said. "I wanted you to see it before we drive to the backcountry. This building was added since you were last here."

Turning on the light in the enclosed room, Abadai opened the door wider and signaled Katerina to enter first. She walked into the brightly lit room and looked wall-to-wall. On each wall were dozens of military-grade weapons mounted floor to ceiling. Abadai waved his hand toward the first wall covered in rifles.

"This wall has weapons made in the US. AR15s in 5.56 mm, the common assault rifle. Long-range sniper rifles in 6.5 mm Creedmoor or .308 caliber, which, as you know, is the same as the 7.62 mm NATO round." Amir glanced at Katerina to see if she was following his quick explanation. Pointing to the next wall, Amir continued.

"Here we have weapons found in Europe and Russia. Austrian assault rifles in 5.56, 5.7, and 7.62 mm, along with a few Russian AK-47s in 5.45 mm." The wall where Abadai was pointing was covered with over fifty weapons, with the classic AK-47 being the most common. Amir continued.

"On this wall, we have several Chinese weapons, the 5.8 mm assault rifles. We also have a few Japanese rifles in 6.5 and 7.7 mm, although getting ammunition for these calibers has been difficult." Finally turning to the fourth wall, Abadai smiled.

"Here is where my heart is, though, our collection of pistols. We've everything from .45 caliber to 9 mm from almost every manufacturer on the planet. We also have .380 and .22 caliber semi-automatics with accurate silencers Nasreen makes right here for our close contact work." Amir watched Katerina examine the wall. Racks on the walls held over 150 pistols in various configurations, including a few Steyr and Uzi machine gun pistols.

"How did you…" She started to speak. Then stopped and stared.

"It wasn't difficult," Amir smiled at her. "Nasreen managed shipments from Taiwan, the US, and the UAE to pull this together. We've got extra magazines for almost everything and over 25,000 rounds of ammo. I'm also working on tactical gear, night vision goggles, and lightweight bulletproof vests, but I'm not sure where I'll put it all."

"Very impressive," Katerina said. "You have many I've never shot."

"You are invited to use the range," Amir said. "Tell Nasreen what you need, and he will have it ready for you to pick up. There's much more to show you. Shall we continue?" Once outside, Abadai and Batalle climbed into the all-terrain vehicle. He gunned the engine, and they disappeared down a road into the forest.

### Day 10, 6:00 p.m., Costa Rica

Later in the evening, they consumed a ceviche appetizer with fresh fish Ernesto had picked up earlier in La Fortuna, and both enjoyed a cold Imperial beer. Katerina shared some observations.

"You probably don't have to take the shooting range out to a thousand yards, but can you get a clear line of sight out to eight hundred?" She asked.

"I think we can do it at the current range," Amir said. "I'll ask Stevino to start working on a range extension."

Anja brought out the evening's main course: a rack of lamb with fresh vegetables for each of them. It would be the same meal they planned to serve to Jahar P'Shari on the first night of his visit. Seeing Anja bringing the lamb, Amir stood, walked to the small bar, and pulled a bottle of Opus One cabernet from behind.

"I thought we should taste the wine I'm going to serve tomorrow." Abadai picked up two glasses from the bar and returned them to the table.

"I had Ernesto pick up a case in La Fortuna yesterday."

Katerina smiled, "It should go well with the lamb."

# CHAPTER ELEVEN

## Day 11, 3:45 p.m., Costa Rica

At La Fortuna airport, a single-engine Cessna 208B fourteen-passenger plane was landing on the commercial side of the airport. Inside the connecting flight from San José, a large man with a two-day-growth gray beard and a wrinkled suit slowly put his book away and took off his reading glasses.

Jahar P'Shari was well-versed in the patience needed for commercial air travel. P'Shari's first stop on this trip was Hawaii, and it was quick. He met with the managing director of the Hawaiian Development Fund, where SAIB invested over 350 million dollars. The managing director was always pleased to meet with Jahar to review the funds' performance and current development programs.

This investment was legitimate, and the biannual meeting was simply SAIB's financial analyst auditing critical assets. The next stop was in the Cayman Islands at the offshore banking capital of Georgetown. This stop was a little more interesting to P'Shari, and he exercised extra caution. He flew to Miami and rented a hotel room in downtown Miami for the week.

Shortly after checking into the room, he hired an Uber driver to take him to Miami Executive Airport, where he chartered a flight using one of his false passports to the Cayman Islands. About two hours later, he walked into The Cayman Capital Bank to meet with his banker and review several private accounts. SAIB, with its various operating companies, held billions of dollars in dozens of locations around the world.

Actual currency and precious metal reserves were stored in lesser-known private places, such as the Turks and Caicos Islands, Jamaica, St.Thomas, and other island locations between South America and Florida. Most small island nations didn't require extensive records reporting to the local tax authorities or the global financial world, especially not from private depositories.

Gamir Halibid's favorite 'cash liberation opportunity' was the annual hurricane season in the Atlantic. Halibid's team monitored the storm's track as a hurricane approached an island location. If the two-day forecast was favorable for a strike on the island, a highly paid team of storm recovery personnel would work to secure the cash and gold from the SAIB facility and move it offshore and out of the storm's path.

The cash and gold were gone six hours before the storm destroyed the depository. The losses were covered by expensive insurance. The "liberated" cash was off the official books and squirreled away in particular banks that offered something highly costly and coveted: privacy.

The Cayman Capital Bank accounts Jahar visited contained over 800 million dollars in three currencies: US Dollars, Euros, and Japanese Yen. These accounts were the net result of the level four hurricane that hit St. Thomas Island in 2007 and destroyed the SAIB cash depository on the island.

Jahar P'Shari and the banker reviewed the holdings and the transactions on the accounts in close detail. He had authorized all of the disbursements from the accounts. A few were wire transfers into other private banks around the globe. Others were charges for the bank's costly personal services, such as facilitating the movement of large sums of cash to various locations worldwide. Any money fitting into a briefcase could be delivered to a person who matched a photo. No names and no questions asked.

Two wire transfers into Costa Rica were of particular interest to P'Shari. One for twenty-four million USD was transferred to an account at Banco de Costa Rica to facilitate property purchase, and the other for almost five million dollars to an operating account for Rancho Trevio, LLC. Jahar tapped his finger on the screen and looked at the personal banker.

"I will probably transfer additional funds into this account later this week. Can I call your cell?" He looked up at the banker.

"Of course. Please ensure you have your PIN ready, and we can do the full verification over the phone as we've done before."

"Very good," Jahar said. "I think we're done here."

## Day 11, 4:01 p.m., Costa Rica

After P'Shari's flight from San José rolled up to the gate at La Fortuna, he walked off the plane into the small terminal. Looking around the small terminal, he found signs in Spanish and English pointing him to the baggage claim and transportation at one end of the building. He saw a young man in a tiny corner of the baggage claim with a sign above him proclaiming "Terminal Two." Five minutes later, P'Shari walked into the private terminal on the other side of the runway.

Ernesto Secico sat near the service desk, paging through a Flying magazine, when P'Shari walked into the private terminal. He dropped the aviation magazine onto the side table. The motion and slight sound caught

Jahar's attention. Jahar leaned slightly to the left and looked at the man, "Rancho Trevio?" He asked.

Ernesto smiled and nodded at him, "Si Señor. I mean 'Yes.' I'm Ernesto, the pilot for the flight to Rancho Trevio."

"Pleased to meet you, Ernesto. My name is Jahar."

"Welcome to Costa Rica and La Fortuna," Ernesto said. "The flight to Rancho Trevio is a little over an hour long. Do you need to use the facilities before we leave?"

"Yes, I do," Jahar said.

"The door is over there, to the right. Would you like me to hold your bags?" Ernesto asked.

"Thank you, but no. I'll be right back."

Jahar entered the lavatory and took a few minutes to freshen up. He removed his coat, tie, and shirt, pulled a lightweight, breathable, short-sleeved shirt and a pair of light khaki pants from the small carry-on suitcase, and put them on. He exchanged his loafers for a pair of hiking shoes.

With clean socks, clean clothes, and a chance to wash his face and brush his teeth, Jahar felt considerably better. He folded his suit clothes and put them into the suitcase. He walked out of the lavatory and back into the waiting room at the private air terminal. Ernesto was coming in the door after making last-minute checks on the plane. He noticed Jahar was more comfortably dressed and smiled.

"Too warm for a suit?"

"Too warm," Jahar concurred. "Can I get a bottle of water for the trip?"

"I already have one in your seat," Ernesto said. "Are you ready?"

"Yes, of course; please lead on."

Ernesto approached the service desk and advised them he was ready to depart. "Follow me," he motioned to Jahar. Both men exited the building, Ernesto leading the way to the waiting Cessna.

On his way to the plane, Jahar glanced at a Diamond DA62, its beautiful twin engines and contoured body gleaming a dark blue in the sunshine. He paused and motioned to the airplane, "Too bad we're not taking this one."

Ernesto stopped, "Isn't it a beautiful plane? This is the first day I've seen that plane here. Sorry to disappoint you, but today, we get to ride our old Cessna 172."

"No worries," Jahar said. "It's good to know Amir isn't wasting our money. How much faster would our flight be if we could use a plane like this?"

Ernesto glanced at the new airplane. "I looked it up in the journal before you came in. I think it would almost cut the flying time in half."

"Something to think about for the future," P'Shari said. He put his bags into the Cessna and climbed into the passenger seat as Ernesto started the engine.

As they rolled onto the taxiway, Ernesto pointed to the large mountain directly in front of them, about twenty miles away, and said, "That's Arenal volcano, the most active volcano in Costa Rica. It is a tourist favorite but hasn't erupted in twelve years."

"Beautiful!" Said Jahar, smiling. "Maybe someday I'll be a tourist here and visit it."

"We fly west of it on our way to the hacienda. You'll get a good view of the crater out your window."

"Excellent, I look forward to that."

### Day 11, 5:25 p.m., Costa Rica

An hour later, the Cessna approached Rancho Trevio. Ernesto softly landed on the dirt runway and rolled to the end. He spun the plane around at the end of the gravel. When he shut down the engine, the passenger door was adjacent to the gate.

Abadai was waiting at the entrance. He heard the approaching plane from the main house, walked the short distance to the end of the runway, and waited for them to land. Amir smiled when he saw Jahar. Amir waved casually from behind the gate. He opened the gate latch and walked to the plane.

"Good afternoon, Jahar! Welcome to Costa Rica! I hope your trip has been good. We look forward to hosting you for a few days," said Amir.

"Yes, a good trip thus far," Jahar said. "Ernesto did an excellent job, and my other flights were fine."

"Excellent," Abadai said. "If you follow me, I'll take you to the house for refreshments, and we can start our evening activities."

Jahar took his bag from Ernesto. Amir and Jahar walked up to the house. Abadai showed P'Shari to his room. He walked into the kitchen to ask Anja to prepare coffee, tea, and fresh juice.

### Day 11, 5:50 p.m. Costa Rica

Abadai ran into Batalle as she walked out of her room. She was dressed and was towel-drying her hair.

"How was your day?" Amir asked.

"Not bad," Katerina pulled the towel through her hair. "Did Jahar make it in?"

"Yes," Amir confirmed. "He should be out in a few minutes. Anja's bringing some fresh juice and tea in a minute. Please join us."

"I'll be there in a couple of minutes," Katerina turned and returned to her room.

Abadai walked from the kitchen into the main living area of the plantation house. This area included a large living room with worn yet comfortable leather sofas and chairs, a large stone fireplace, and a large dining area suitable for ten with a massive chandelier over the table. The room was dwarfed by a wall of windows almost two stories high on the south side of the house, which led out to the veranda and pool area.

Off the main living room was an office with leather chairs around an enormous mahogany desk. Behind the desk were built-in bookshelves. The house had three large guest bedrooms. The floors were rust-colored terra cotta tile, and the ceiling was vaulted with large rough-hewn logs. Most homes in Costa Rica were the size of a single main living area.

Abadai took an armchair near the cold fireplace. Shortly after that, Anja brought out several carafes of drinks and set them on a serving tray on the left side of the fireplace. Above the tray was a painting of a stallion in an open field at sunset.

Anja asked if Amir wanted something to drink, and he accepted a small glass of iced tea. Moments later, Jahar P'Shari walked into the room. He looked around to get his bearings, then sat in a leather chair beside Abadai.

"Are we free to talk here?" Jahar asked.

"We do need to be careful," Amir said. "Anja, our cook; Ernesto, our pilot; and any farm workers or staff you may meet are only workers. We only tell them what they need to know." "Something to drink, Jahar?" asked Abadai.

He pointed to the drinks. "Hot or cold, whatever your pleasure." Jahar looked over at the drinks. He stood, walked over to the serving tray, and poured himself a small glass of juice. He took in the room and looked at the painting on the wall. He studied the large fireplace before returning to sit by Abadai.

Amir watched Jahar's movements and said, "This house was here when we bought the property. We've made a few improvements to expand the kitchen to feed our "guests." Most of the additional improvements are the bunkhouses and the training grounds to the north of the house. We did expand the runway, and we added lights for night landings. We also made some changes to make the fields more accessible to the farmers renting the land from us."

"I see," Jahar said, looking at the large room. "Was the furniture and artwork from the previous owners?" Amir nodded to Jahar and changed subjects.

"Did I tell you we discussed our plans for the undeveloped property with the local authorities? We told them we plan to open a hunting and fishing preserve for tourists. They seemed excited about potential tourism money flowing into the area. We will need additional investment to fence the entire property. I want to show you the property tomorrow and discuss it."

"I look forward to the tour of the property tomorrow."

Katerina's shoes clicked on the tile floors as she walked out of her room and into the main room. Amir looked up from Jahar and smiled at her. She was taller than both men, and her body was toned and athletic. Her caramel blond hair fell around her shoulders. She wore a white, long-sleeved blouse with black slacks and heels. In the fading afternoon light, she was striking. P'Shari and Abadai stood, but she waved them to sit down.

"Please, please, sit down." Looking at Abadai, she asked, "May I join you?"

Amir smiled at Katerina and waved her to join them in an adjacent seat.

"Something to drink?" He asked. He watched as she smiled at him. Her smile and her eyes were mesmerizing. Little wonder she was effective. Jahar smiled broadly at Katerina, showing several gold crowns.

"It's wonderful to meet you again, Katerina. I'm still an admirer."

"Thank you," she said. "I think you'll be pleased with the work Amir has been doing here."

Jahar's voice lowered to a whisper as he addressed them both, "I'm here to tell you that we appreciate your results in Europe and the Americas. I'm impressed with your ability to direct action in many areas of the globe."

Amir decided the location was too close to the kitchen for more conversation, and they should move. He said, "Thank you. We can do a lot with the right support. However, since we're all here, perhaps we should move outside. It's a more secure place to talk."

He looked at Katerina and asked, "Will you accompany Jahar to the pool? We've shade out there now, which may be better for our discussions. I'll confirm the dinner plans for tonight and join you in a moment."

"Of course," Katerina said. "Jahar, will you join me on the veranda?"

With Jahar in tow, they walked to a shaded table near the pool. Along the way, Katerina turned on the small fountain near the pool. The sound of falling water masked their conversation.

Abadai walked into the kitchen and spoke to Anja about the lamb chops planned for the evening meal and the particular wine to accompany them. He told her she could go home after the meal was served. Stopping at the wine cabinet on his way to the pool, he grabbed a locally produced Tinto Dulce and three glasses. He walked toward the broad glass doors leading to the pool.

Amir settled into a chair next to Katerina and across from Jahar. The late afternoon sun was dropping behind the tall trees west of the house. The temperature was comfortable, with a light breeze to keep mosquitoes away.

"We can talk more freely out here," said Amir, more relaxed as he set down the glasses and opened the wine. "I've asked Anja to leave early after dinner. We've all the privacy we need for this evening."

"I need clarification on a few items to explain them better to our benefactor," said Jahar.

Amir looked at Katerina and asked Jahar, "Anything, what would you like to know?"

"We're spending a lot on the mercenary personnel you are hiring. Some are here, and others seem to be waiting to come. I thought terrorists would be less expensive." Amir watched as Batalle leaned over the table to respond.

"Terrorists thrive where idealism, religion, or some cultural or ethnic situation is creating discrete 'sides' in a country or region. Terrorist organizations, on the other hand, recruit fanatics and train them poorly. They stoke their emotions, reinforce their beliefs that the other side is evil, and expect them to die as suicide bombers in various ways. They cost little because they are fanatics. Unfortunately, they are like unguided missiles; they often don't hit their target."

"That was a good explanation, Katerina," said Amir, as Jahar nodded in agreement. He continued, "Mercenaries are well-trained and experienced fighters. They don't 'take sides'. They are paid to execute the plan effectively and efficiently and extract themselves quietly from any situation. They practice extraction. Terrorists don't. Mercenaries have to be alive to collect their pay. Afterward, they continue to train and await their next assignment."

"I think I understand," said Jahar.

"To be brutally honest," said Amir, "I don't think we can find terrorists interested in attacking global financial institutions—unless perhaps the banks were in Israel."

Katerina smiled at Amir's comment and added, "We believe well-trained mercenaries are our best and perhaps our only option to achieve your objectives. And yes, mercenaries are more expensive."

"Thank you. Now I understand," Jahar nodded. "Don't worry about the cost. We have plenty of funds available. I don't have experience with mercenaries; I needed to ask."

The discussion turned to the recent successful operations in Latin America and Europe. Jahar expressed his satisfaction with the results.

Abadai added his thoughts. "You selected the banks in Brazil, Portugal, and Mexico, as well as the hits in Germany and the UK. These targets allowed us to exhibit what we like to call our 'deadly reach.' It's the ability to strike anywhere in the world from our base of operations here in Costa Rica.

"This training facility aims to create a professional organization capable of striking anywhere and simply disappearing. You may not be aware, but the Brazil and Portugal events used two new members of our mercenary team to conduct those bombings. Both men performed their roles well and returned safely."

Jahar looked from Amir to Katerina and shifted the subject. "I've seen some effects from these bombings in Europe and Latin America; it's destabilizing the Eurozone, and capital is moving as it seeks safety. Our deposits have increased nicely, but our most important target is the United States. We need to shake trust in the dollar. When one currency goes weak, the other gets stronger.

"The US dollar is the elephant in the room. Hell, they've owned the room! The dollar has been stable for too long. Your job is to make currency traders believe the US can be brought to its knees!"

Their discussion suddenly stopped as Anja approached to serve dinner. They returned to the topic when they watched Anja drive away at sunset.

Amir poured from the open wine bottle, "As you know," he began, "the US is the most difficult target. US security technology is integrated far better than the rest of the world. But we have a detailed plan. Shipments are on the way. Katerina and I will be in the US again next week. Our timing still looks good to what we committed to you a month ago. We can provide shipment details and discuss our current status with you." Amir paused.

"Perhaps you want to try Anja's dessert and nice port wine before we start?"

Jahar picked up his wine glass and leaned forward to casually touch it to both Katerina's and Amir's wine glasses. "You have my full attention," he smiled.

# CHAPTER TWELVE

**Day 12, 7:45 a.m., Dallas**

The call came to the Fort Worth emergency services operator at 7:45 a.m. on Monday.

"9-1-1, how can I help you?"

"Uh, yeah, my name is Charlie, er, Charles Templeton. I'm a truck driver. I'm at a freight company called 'Blue Ribbon Freight.' There's been an accident. I think there's a dead body over here. Can you send an officer over?"

"Stay on the line, please. Give me a minute to send an officer. Can you confirm the address?" the operator asked.

"Uh, yeah, let me see. The building number is one-oh-five above the door. I think the street name is Conroe. It's over here at the Fort Worth Alliance Airport,"

"Okay, I've looked up the company's name, and the address appears correct," said the operator. "I've sent the request to dispatch, and an officer should be responding along with fire and rescue teams. It shouldn't take long for an officer to get there, Charlie. It's Charlie, right?" the operator repeated.

"Yeah, Charlie Templeton,"

The operator kept him on the line, "Charlie, how do you know the victim is dead?"

"I don't know for certain," Charlie said, "but he's underneath an overturned forklift that appears to have fallen off the loading dock and trapped him under it. Based on what I saw from his skin color, he's been dead for a while. I didn't try to check for a pulse or anything. I don't know how to do that."

"Thank you for the description, Charlie. I have the phone number you are calling me from. Is this your cell phone? Let me confirm your contact information."

The operator continued getting the specifics as Charlie could hear the approaching sirens. The first officers on the scene confirmed the person under the forklift was dead and advised the fire and emergency services teams to turn off their sirens.

Charlie Templeton was asked several questions, and he showed the officers the bill of lading to pick up a pallet of one-half-inch bolts and nuts for a local machinery company. The police verified that the box of fasteners was inside the warehouse and told him to return in a day or two.

For the police on the scene, the case of an accidental death should have been completed soon after the accident team arrived, photographed the scene, and the body was taken away to the county morgue. However, in this instance, as the police entered the dusty and paper-strewn office to locate the names and contact information of the owners of the company, they were unable to turn up any contact information aside from the phone number for the building they were standing in.

The police recovered the wallet from the dead man. His name was Travis Harms. Reviewing his driver's license and motor vehicle data, they found no associated names or next of kin. An autopsy was ordered to determine the cause of death, although the police were pretty sure it was an accident.

### Day 12, 5:15 p.m. Costa Rica

When Katerina joined them, Amir and Jahar were beside the large stone fireplace in the living room. Amir had started a comfortable fire crackling in the hearth. Both men were holding a drink and talking in low voices.

Katerina smiled, "I think I detected a sparkle in your eye. In both of your eyes! Did you enjoy the sights today?" Jahar laughed, and Amir smiled broadly.

"I knew that when we invested in both of you, we were taking a serious step away from reliance on jihadists, terrorists, or other groups with their agenda. But this," Jahar smiled and extended his arms. "I never expected to see what you've shown me today."

"We're making good progress on the training facility. I hope you saw this on your tour."

"Oh yes," Jahar said to her. "I saw all the work both of you've been doing, and I'm as impressed with the work you've been doing to build a world-class training facility as I am with developing this as a legitimate hunting and fishing enterprise. This is the type of duplicative operation our benefactor loves." Jahar continued his praises as they walked to the patio and continued their lively discussion.

### Day 13, 6:15 a.m. Costa Rica

Early the following day, with the sun beginning to send rays of light through the trees, Ernesto loaded P'Shari's small suitcase into the Cessna.

Jahar was deep in thought. They buckled in for the flight after a few pleasantries between Jahar and Ernesto. Ernesto cleared the runway, rose to four thousand feet, and set the autopilot on for the flight to La Fortuna. He offered Jahar a cup of coffee from his thermos. Jahar gladly accepted but remained deep in thought.

*I need to talk with Gamir about the next steps. I'm impressed with their plan and the ease with which they made this look like a legitimate business venture.* Jahar looked across the plane to Ernesto and smiled. "This is a nice flight today."

"Yes," Ernesto confirmed, "the weather is beautiful for flying."

P'Shari smiled and looked out the passenger window at the green countryside passing below.

## Day 13, 7:15 a.m., Washington, DC

Andrea Douglas-Pfeiffer dropped the small paper bag containing her onion bagel on her desk. She set down her large coffee, with a bit of low-fat milk, from the downstairs commissary beside it. Her cubicle was small, an 'L-shaped' desk with a few file drawers. It was still a little early for Washington, DC. Outside, the morning rush was well underway. She liked the quiet and calm of the early morning in the office. She could think quietly, organize her thoughts, and plan her day.

If she turned the computer on immediately, she knew from experience that she would be drawn into the emails. There were many requests, each requiring her research and a well-reasoned and quick response. She waited until she finished the bagel and had several small sips of coffee before acknowledging it was time to start the day. As she took a deep breath and exhaled, she reached over to turn on the computer.

When Andrea touched the start button on her computer, her phone rang with a computerized "Tripp, Tripp." She looked up at the clock on the wall to check the time, reached over, and picked up the phone.

"Good morning, this is Andrea," she answered evenly.

"Good morning, Andrea." Mac sounded caffeinated and used to early mornings. He continued, "Sorry for the early call, but you mentioned the lab results on the explosive should be in today. I thought I'd call you to see if you've heard anything yet."

With the phone to her ear, Andrea smiled. "Well, good morning to you, Mac! You seem to be up early and raring to go this morning! I got into the office and have yet to turn on the computer. Give me a minute for it to boot up."

"Sorry for being early, Andrea; would you rather I call back?"

"No, no, no," Andrea said, "I finished my breakfast, and I've already powered up the computer. You've got about 60 seconds to wait for it to finish the boot-up sequence. So, Mac, while we wait, you've enough time to tell me how you like your coffee and what you usually eat for breakfast."

On the other end of the phone, Mac smiled and said, "That's a bit personal. Like the questions you ask on a first date?"

"Well, you know, Mac, sometimes we don't get second chances for a spare minute, which, by the way, you're down to about thirty seconds now."

Mac laughed, "Preferred coffee is Texas pecan medium roast, but this is my second or third cup, and the last two are government lowest bidder coffee from the pot in the hallway. I have no idea what brand it is."

"And breakfast?" encouraged Andrea.

"I'm old-fashioned," Mac said, "I love a good omelet with toast and hash browns from about any cafe where they keep my coffee topped off."

"I hear that," Andrea chimed in. "Let's have breakfast sometime. A cafe is best with a friend and a great conversation."

"Sounds like an invitation."

"Oh, it is," Andrea said, "once we get past this crisis. Okay, the computer's up, and I'm looking at my email." She scrolled, looking for her contact at the FBI test labs. "Here it is; let me open it up and look at the results. Mac, the lab confirms that the plastic explosives used in Mexico City and São Paulo have the same chemical signature. It's similar to a plastic explosive that surfaced in Afghanistan in 2015, but not exactly. The FBI doesn't know the manufacturing location of the explosive. It's not registered. It's probably one of the bad actors, countries like Iraq, Iran, North Korea, or some other country that doesn't play nicely."

"So Andrea, where do we go from here?" Mac asked. "We can't go after a source or manufacturing location."

"The terrorist is somehow transporting the explosive from where it was manufactured to the target countries," Andrea said. "Transportation takes sophistication and complexity to get the explosive into multiple ports undetected. Dogs cannot smell it without a tracing chemical and will walk right by a pallet of this material. It could be packaged multiple ways to avoid detection."

Andrea stopped talking momentarily, reaching across her desk, pulling a file, and opening it. "Mac, I need a moment to look something up." She paused for a few seconds before continuing, "Here it is. According to the FBI, the density of plastic explosives is similar to several other typical materials: asphalt shingles, bags of cement, or even the green clay imported for some tennis courts."

"I don't follow your logic here, Andrea," Mac sounded confused.

"To move material like this around the globe, it would have to be packaged as something resembling a commonly shipped material."

"Okay, now I'm following. You're saying we should look into

shipments of asphalt shingles, cement, or something with the same physical characteristics."

"That's what I'm thinking, Mac. The bombing in São Paulo required about forty pounds of plastic explosives inside the bank to bring that building down. But, the bombing of the Lisbon and Mexico City banks from the street required much, much more, maybe several hundred pounds of explosives to create the amount of damage. Large amounts require shipping and handling by a freight company unless the terrorists will somehow ship it across borders by themselves, which would be difficult and risky. It's easier to disguise it as something common."

"Andrea, this is helpful. I'll get my team looking into importers right away."

"Mac, before you go, at the most, this is perhaps a single pallet of material. You're not looking for shipping container loads of this stuff; we're looking for a single pallet weighing between 500 and 1,500 pounds —for example, a single pallet load of cement or a single pallet of tennis court clay. The more I think about it, it's a needle in a haystack. It's going to be difficult to find."

"Thanks, Andrea. You've been helpful. We're going to need some luck to find it. I'll ask the FBI if they have any ideas."

# CHAPTER THIRTEEN

**Day 14, 10:50 a.m., Dallas**

Melvin D'Angel sat at his desk looking out of the east-facing window in the Fort Worth Police station. He was the 'NG' or 'New Guy' with the detective badge. He spent his time dealing with lost kittens, elder walkaways, community outreach, and accidental deaths.

The phone on his belt chirped the "new email" tone he had recently programmed into it. Without pulling out his phone, he reached over, moved the mouse on his computer, and looked at the newly arrived email. It was from the police lab and contained the results from the tech team's work on the accidental death at Blue Ribbon Freight.

The techs found Travis Harms' fingerprints on the computer keyboard and desk. The equipment in the loading dock area showed that the freight company was primarily a one-person operation, with Travis's fingerprints on the hand trucks and forklifts. While reading the report's environmental section, Melvin was surprised to find the following sentences:

*"Incremental traces of guanidine nitrate were present in the air samples only. Guanidine nitrate is unusual as it is commonly used in explosives and requires additional transportation registration."*

He looked at the page and searched the internet for guanidine nitrate. A few minutes later, he called the department contact at the Dallas office of the Bureau of Alcohol, Tobacco, and Firearms.

"Doc Johnson," answered J. R. 'Doc' Johnson, a long-time ATF investigator and current liaison to the state police organizations in Texas.

"Doc, this is Melvin D'Angel, a detective in the Fort Worth Police Department. Can I ask you a few questions?"

"That's my role these days," Doc confirmed. "What can I help you with?"

"I'm working on an accidental death at the Alliance Airport, and the tech team came back with an air test. It captured guanidine nitrate at a trace level. I thought I'd call you to find out if this is a common find or something I should take to another level."

"Guanidine nitrate, you say?" Doc said, "That's interesting. We typically see it as a fuel for fireworks, but it's also used in different types of explosives. What was the name of the warehouse where you found this trace?"

"Blue Ribbon Freight."

"Hang on the line while I check our registrations database." Melvin could hear him typing.

"I'm finding nothing for Blue Ribbon. It would appear the company wasn't registered to import fireworks or explosives. Since it's an online process, our systems are current."

"Is it possible it's a false reading, or maybe something common in some other product?" Melvin asked.

"Very unlikely," Doc drawled over the phone. "It's rarely used in other materials because it's temperamental and can explode if mishandled in the pure form. It's used as an accelerant in plastic explosives. If the trace showed it, it was probably there. Say, can you hold the phone for a moment? I need to check on something."

Doc put the phone down before Melvin could reply. When he picked it up, he was already talking. "I remembered we received an alert from the FBI this morning, and I wanted to find a copy," Doc said.

"Okay," Melvin said, "what's it say?"

"I'm reading it now. The alert asks the ATF to report any indications that explosives may have traveled through a border to a unique phone number. Melvin, since this was a freight company where you found this, we should call this number."

"What do you need me to do?" Melvin sat back in his chair.

"Please stay on the line. I'll tie you in on a conference call, and we can jointly report the details to the FBI." Doc said. "It should only take a few minutes."

## Day 14, 4:00 p.m., New York

Mac sat down at his desk and looked at the paperwork growing like a fungus on his desk. He reminisced about two weeks ago when he was working on his suntan in the tropics. It was almost as if it never happened; it was too short to create long-term memories, and the short-term memories were already beginning to fade.

He owed Rae a follow-up call to let her know she was on his mind. He reached across his desk and jotted her name on a note. Below it, he wrote: *Call!* He folded up the note and put it in his shirt pocket.

The phone rang and jolted Mac.

It was Andrea, "Mac! We've got a possible lead."

Mac sparked out of his doldrums and said, "Tell me."

71

"ATF reported to the FBI an explosive compound called guanidine nitrate was found during an accidental death investigation at a Dallas freight company."

"Could it be an anomaly?" Mac asked. "How pervasive is this chemical compound? What was it again? Iodine nitrate?"

"Guanidine nitrate," Andrea corrected, "and, yes, Mac, this interests us. The compound is somewhat uncommon and usually linked to fireworks or explosives. The most important part you need to hear is that guanidine nitrate was also one of the trace elements found in Mexico City and Brazil. It's commonly used in plastic explosives."

"Who is the contact at ATF? What's the number?" Mac found a piece of paper and began writing.

"J. R. 'Doc' Johnson is the ATF contact," Andrea read from the email. "There is also a Fort Worth detective named D'Angel listed."

"Let's call this 'Doc' Johnson and the detective," Mac said. "Can you get permission for a quick trip to Dallas tomorrow?"

"I think all it takes is an email from you to your SAIC, and I'm on the next plane," Andrea said, sounding excited.

"I'm typing an email to my SAIC as we speak. Can you call Mr. Johnson at ATF? Let's have a conference call."

## Day 15, 10:00 a.m., Brooklyn Docks, New York

At the corner of 39th Street and First Avenue in the South Brooklyn Marine District, Helbol Pakerisami walked casually down the street looking for the freight offices of a small importer called "*Solvang Imports.*" He was concerned he would never find the warehouse he was looking for. Stopping in the middle of the block, he looked at the address on the paper in his hand. He glanced toward the building address in front of him. He slowly turned and looked across the street.

Across the street, in a somewhat dilapidated structure of gray stone and gray rusted corrugated steel, was the address "107." The company's name was on the door, but the lettering was too small to read from Pakerisami's location across the street. Helbol entered the street, dodging several cars and two large panel trucks. "*Solvang Imports*" was on the door.

He recalled the conversation with his friend Eliu, the import business owner.

"The name '*Solvang*' is Danish and means '*Sunny Field,*'" explained Eliu. "We use the name because an Arab name in New York often brings in only Arab business, and that's not enough business to be profitable."

Eliu was a Moroccan businessman who loved to trade and haggle. He had been operating the business for the last fifteen years and was slowly becoming one of the wealthier members of the Dalees Salaam Community

Center and Mosque neighborhood association. Helbol pushed open the door and walked into the offices.

## Day 15, 10:10 a.m., Brooklyn Docks, New York

One of the many other pedestrians on the street was Agent Yosali Tarik. Yosali noted the building's address in his small notebook. He moved across the street and casually walked past the address, registering the name on the glass door.

Tarik looked around the street for a good surveillance location and casually strolled until he stood behind stacked pallets outside a busy warehouse. From his new vantage point, he could observe the door coming out of Solvang Imports.

## Day 15, 9:50 a.m., Dallas

Mac and Andrea were in the rental car and departing Dallas-Fort Worth Airport after an early morning departure from JFK. It took them about thirty minutes to get to Blue Ribbon Freight. Melvin D'Angel and Doc Johnson were scheduled to meet them at the warehouse at 10:00 a.m.

They stopped at a drive-through and picked up four coffees and a few donuts to share with the investigators. They arrived at the warehouse ten minutes before the hour. Mac watched Andrea as she examined the sides of the building.

"I don't see any exterior cameras; that's interesting. I'll walk back to the entrance to see if I can see any cameras in the other buildings." Andrea said.

"Officer D'Angel's report said no cameras, but he didn't say if the police had checked adjacent buildings for cameras," Mac commented as he watched her walk away.

"I know," Andrea said, "that's why I'm looking."

"I was checking to see if you had read the report," Mac said wryly. "Since I didn't sleep, I had plenty of time to review it."

Andrea walked back the short drive to where Mac stood. She was wearing a dark brown pantsuit with a white blouse. She was petite, about five and a half feet tall, and wearing two-inch heels. Her brown hair was shoulder-length and pulled back to keep it under control. Mac picked up her coffee and handed it to her.

"Did you learn anything else from the reports you want to share with me?" Andrea said, feigning irritation. Mac laughed at her playful attitude and smiled.

"No, no, I'm not about to question your thoroughness. You've proven yourself. I wondered how you would handle a small dig from a partner."

"Partner? Okay, how did I do?" Andrea smiled at him.

"Perfect in every way," Mac said. They turned when they heard cars coming into the drive. Melvin D'Angel and Doc Johnson arrived at the same time. Mac watched as the two cars stopped and the drivers climbed out, almost in unison.

"You're early," Melvin said, looking at Mac and Andrea, "I stopped and picked up coffee down the street. Otherwise, I'd have been here five minutes ago."

"The plane was on time, and the traffic from the airport was moving," Mac said. "Let me introduce you to Andrea Douglas-Pfeiffer. I'm Mac Krieger."

"I'm glad you could get here fast," Melvin said as he shook their hands. "I'm Melvin, and, as you probably guessed, this is Doc Johnson."

Doc walked up to the other three. "Pleasure," he said. Doc was an older man of almost sixty-five, with longer-than-normal graying hair and a bushy salt-and-pepper mustache. He looked like an extra from a Hollywood western.

"It's great to get out of the office and back to an investigation," Doc drawled. "I'd never make it chained to a desk all day."

"I'll remove the police tape and walk you through the site," said Melvin. "I was here late yesterday afternoon. I'll try to point out what was in the police reports, and you can ask questions as we go. Sounds okay?"

"That sounds great, Melvin," Andrea volunteered. "Did you ask to look at the security camera on the building across the street?"

"You saw a camera? Which building?" Melvin looked embarrassed. "I looked yesterday, but I didn't see any."

"Yes, I saw one," Andrea confirmed. "Let's stop by and see if we can view the recording after we're done here."

Melvin agreed. "Thanks for finding it."

Andrea winked at Mac as he was holding the door. He shook his head and followed them into the warehouse.

### Day 15, 11:00 a.m., New York

Helbol Pakerisami's phone chirped with an incoming call. Looking down at the number, he didn't recognize it, but it wasn't uncommon for him to get calls from numbers he didn't recognize. The call was coming from a country code of "506." It was new to Pakerisami.

"Marhaba," Pakerisami answered. "Who is calling, please?"

"Marhaba," Abadai repeated, using the Arabic word for 'hello.' "Helbol, this is your friend. Can you talk privately?"

Pakerisami stood in the Solvang Imports office, looking directly at his friend Eliu Nasef.

"Can you hold on for one moment?" Not waiting for a response from

Abadai, Helbol looked at Eliu and asked, "Can I borrow a room for a private call?"

Eliu nodded and pointed to an office with a door and a small table across the hallway. Helbol moved into the room and closed the door.

"I...I...I can talk now," Helbol stammered into the phone. "It's been quite a while since we've spoken; I hope you're well." His voice was calm, but his actions were nervous. He looked around the room and finally sat in a chair.

"I know it's been a while, but I need your help," Abadai said. Helbol looked at his feet and felt his shoulders slump.

"What is it you need from me?"

"I need your help with a couple of shipments. One is small, a small box or two of stereo equipment. I've already sent it to your home," said Amir.

"The other is larger and heavier and requires a freight importer who can receive a pallet of material and help put it onto a truck."

"Where does the importer need to be located?" Helbol asked. He figured Abadai needed help in the Middle East or somewhere other than New York.

"It's a shipment to the United States and needs to be on the East Coast. New York would be best,"

Helbol paused momentarily, then asked, "It's a simple delivery and doesn't require any specific customs permissions?"

"Yes, that's correct; it has no special needs," Abadai sounded confident. "It's one pallet of modeling clay and weighs about two thousand pounds; it requires the proper loading and unloading equipment."

"Modeling clay?" Helbol asked. "Is it a good market for modeling clay in the US?"

"It's a special request from a contact of mine in New York," Abadai said. "I think it's a one-time import."

"Very good," Helbol said. He thought and added. "I have a friend in New York with a freight business. He mostly imports rugs out of North Africa. He's a good man. I think I can talk him into handling a pallet of modeling clay for you. Let me confirm with him. Can I send you a text to this phone?"

"It would be better if you called me," Abadai instructed.

"Okay, I'll call you back."

"Thank you, Helbol. I'll make sure you and your friend are well compensated for the time and trouble," Abadai said.

"That's what I hoped you would say," Pakerisami smiled. "Life in the United States can be expensive."

"Yes, I know," Abadai said. "You will be well compensated."

"Very good," Pakerisami said. "I'll call you back shortly to confirm."

He ended the call and walked out of the small office into Eliu's more expansive office, where he was smoking a cigarette. Eliu must have sensed his movement because he paused, held the cigarette away from his face, and lifted his eyes to Helbol as he entered the office. "Eliu, my friend," Helbol smiled, "I have a business proposition for you."

# CHAPTER FOURTEEN

## Day 16, 6:50 a.m., Costa Rica

The sky was blood-red as the sun rose over Rancho Trevio. Agricultural burning in Panama created the smoke, and the trade winds drifted north, creating colorful sunrises and sunsets. The picturesque scene was beautiful if you stood in one of the lettuce fields south of the main house and could look across acres of open fields at sunrise.

Approximately fifty migrant workers, most from El Salvador but a few from Guatemala and Nicaragua, were in the fields, working to remove anything that did not resemble a lettuce plant. They were eliminating weeds, not watching the rising sun.

The mercenaries began moving inside the bunkhouses as the appointed leaders woke the trainees for a morning run. The bunkhouses were surrounded by heavy tree cover, and the sun wouldn't penetrate for at least an hour. The energy inside the main house was a little more electric.

Katerina Batalle walked out of her quarters in her traveling clothes. She had three more changes of clothes in her carry-on bag. Her hair had magically changed from natural blond into dark brown with a streak of purple. She pulled it back in a low-maintenance ponytail. She wore lightweight khaki pants and a gray "Save the Planet" loose-fitting T-shirt.

To finish the look, a light-blue, long-sleeve fishing shirt was untucked and unbuttoned over the T-shirt. It was a bland, casual outfit that almost matched what she wore in her counterfeit passport from New Zealand, which was issued under the name Martha L. Beekman. The clothing did little to cover the athletic grace evident when she walked. She looked like a young woman on a mission to save the planet from too much pollution.

She saw Abadai sitting at the table reviewing his passports. He had allowed his mid-length beard to grow untrimmed for the past few weeks, and it was starting to look a little unkempt. He was wearing beige slacks with an off-white, long-sleeved shirt. Around his neck, a light brown tie was loosely knotted. His normally well-toned body was softer, and he had a small but noticeable belly courtesy of an upper bodysuit prosthetic purchased from a theater store in London. The outfit matched his Argentina passport. He was a newly hired university professor at the Universidad Tecnológica Nacional in Buenos Aires and even had the school ID. His long, black hair showed some slight gray at the temples, and he wore it in a classic man bun.

When Katerina approached the table, he stood up. They looked at each other professionally and critically. She indicated that he should turn around. She picked up his jacket and held it out for him to put on. Conceding, Abadai put the coat on and again turned around.

"Looks great on you, Amir. The body suit adds to the outfit and makes you look ten kilos heavier." Katerina said.

"Yes, it does." Amir agreed. He reached up and touched his slightly graying temples. "Thanks for the help with the hair. You're sure this will wash out easily?"

"It's designed for people who add color for a night and wash it out the next morning," Katerina explained. "It should wash out when you shower. Remember where the gray streaks are; you must reapply it after you shower."

"That's good to know," Amir said.

"Please sit. I'll have Anja bring in some breakfast," she said. Looking down at her clothes, she continued, "You didn't comment about my outfit. Do I need to change anything?"

"You've always had an eye for disguise," Amir complimented her. "There is nothing I can think of to change."

Anja walked into the room carrying a platter of breakfast bread, thinly sliced meat, and cheese. She set the platter down and returned to the kitchen, bringing another tray of juice, coffee, yogurt, and fresh fruit.

"What is your itinerary again?" Amir asked as he began selecting a few dried meats and cheese for his breakfast.

"La Fortuna, San José, and on to Miami," Katerina recited. "I'm staying one night in Miami and one night in Minneapolis. Three identities and tickets were purchased on three cards. These are all new identities and all new cards from Jahar."

"Mine's a little different," Amir said. "I'm traveling from La Fortuna to San José and onto Buenos Aires for the initial setup. I'm staying one night in Buenos Aires, changing identities again, and traveling the next day to Philadelphia. I'll be in Philadelphia for one or two nights before heading via train to New York. Depending upon how New York goes, I may or may not join you in San Francisco."

Katerina took a bite of bread. She chewed it thoughtfully. "The deliveries should arrive at their destinations within the next few days. Be quick to find your pawns and work your plan. We won't have much time to waste."

"I agree," Amir said.

They finished breakfast, rose from the table, picked up their bags, walked out the open patio doors down the steps, and headed for the airplane.

## Day 16, 7:00 a.m., Las Vegas

The enclosed panel truck with "Salviano LTL Interstate Transport" on the dirty door panel cruised down Interstate 15 with Las Vegas in the foreground. The driver turned on the blinker to exit at Sloan Avenue and rolled off the interstate to his next delivery. The sun was coming up in Nevada. The driver had packages to deliver in Nevada and a few pick-ups before he crossed into California on the final leg of his route.

Inside the truck were five or six pallets of materials and several dozen boxes of miscellaneous goods for delivery. Toward the front of the car was a single, dusty pallet marked "Modeling Clay." On the pallet were approximately thirty-six neatly stacked brown plastic bags, totaling almost 1,500 pounds. The stack was nearly six feet tall and carried no specific warnings on the outside.

## Day 16, 4:09 p.m., Washington, DC

Andrea was working at her desk when her cell phone blipped a short tone. She read the text message. Doc Johnson informed her that the security videos had been uploaded to the FBI evidentiary database. Andrea turned to her computer and logged in. Finding the link in the catalog search, she clicked and found three videos uploaded. Two videos were from the building Andrea had identified, and a third was from another camera on a building near the exit.

Andrea started with a video showing the building's driveway. She fast-forwarded the video until she saw police car lights approaching the building. This would have been the time when the police were called to the accidental death. The time was 08:18:01 on the video time record. Slowly backing up the video by about forty minutes, she watched as the truck driver who reported the accident pulled into the parking lot at 07:31:05 on the video time record. She scrolled slowly backward through the day on Sunday and found no activity moving into or out of the facility for the previous eighteen hours.

Finding herself at a time flag of 18:15:22 or 6:15 p.m., she paused momentarily and wrote a note summarizing her search and the time marker she was on. She slowly backed up the video to 15:48:12 or 3:48 p.m. and saw a truck leave the drive. Backing up more, she saw the truck enter the drive at Blue Ribbon Freight at 15:26:12.

It was a short-haul cargo truck with no markings on the sides. The vehicle plate was visible, and the white driver's door had some red lettering. Both were unreadable to Andrea. She marked the time code and the video ID and emailed the FBI video techs to see if they could use their video magic to extract anything from the grainy video.

Andrea continued her search and found two more trucks that had stopped at Blue Ribbon Freight the same day. She also sent those to the video techs. At 07:55:15, she saw Travis Harms arriving in his ten-year-old white Toyota Corolla to start his Saturday morning.

Satisfied she had accurately captured the traffic on the last day of Travis Harms' life at Blue Ribbon Freight, Andrea reviewed the previous week and captured three to four trucks daily. A few cars had visited the freight company in the week before the accidental death. She logged the time code for each of these vehicles and put them together into a complete request for the video techs at the FBI.

She called Mac at almost 3:00 p.m., went directly to his voicemail, and left a message: "Hi, Mac, it's Andrea. I've reviewed the videos and found several vehicles of interest. I've sent the details to the FBI video techs and asked them to process the images for greater clarity. We should hear back from them tonight or tomorrow. I'll call you as soon as I have something."

### Day 16, 9:00 p.m., Las Vegas

After almost eighteen hours of delivering boxes and pallets of materials to the Las Vegas casinos and other businesses, as well as picking up additional freight to transport to California, a large eighteen-wheeler with the markings 'Salviano LTL Interstate Transport' was beginning an overnight run. The trailer was at its weight limit. Most of the weight was from aluminum and copper sheeting picked up in Nevada. Near the back doors were several miscellaneous single pallets and several loose boxes. These were the last to be loaded and the first to be unloaded. A single pallet of Modeling Clay was included among these miscellaneous single pallets.

A fresh driver began the drive to Barstow, California, where the eighteen-wheeler would stop. The freight would be pulled off the truck and put onto smaller cargo trucks for deliveries within California, from San Francisco to Mexico. The smaller cargo trucks would take deliveries northwest up California State Route 58 to Bakersfield and then to San Francisco on Interstate 5. The passing traffic lit the road ahead as the driver pulled onto Interstate 15 and headed south at the Nevada 146 interchange. The driver worked through the gears of the Peterbilt tractor to bring the heavy trailer up to speed.

### Day 17, 8:15 a.m., New York

Mac's office phone was blinking when he walked into his office. It was the voicemail indicator. He removed his jacket and adjusted his gun in its holster. He reached over to pick up the phone, and with the receiver in hand, he was interrupted by David Osrick, who stepped into his office as if he'd been running.

"Mac!" David was breathless from running. He caught his boss in his office and not yet on the phone, "I need you for a moment." Mac hung up the phone and looked at David.

"Go on."

"Pakerisami visited a company on the docks, an importer called 'Solvang Imports' two days ago."

"Did he pick up or carry anything into the importer?" Mac asked.

"No, but it was the first time he had been at this location since we began tailing him," David said. "We looked up the registration, and it's an import/export company owned by a man named 'Eliu Nasef.' Records show the company imports rugs from North Africa."

"Is Tarik still tailing Pakerisami?" Mac looked out the window, thinking.

"Yes," David said.

"We need to find some way to identify Pakerisami's phone. We need to get a trace on it."

"I'll ask Tarik to ask a few people in the neighborhood for his number," David said, then asked, "What about the importer?"

"Yes, task another team to watch the importer, too; get some photos and ID anyone coming or going."

"We're on it, boss," David said. He strode out of Mac's office. Mac reached over and picked up his phone. He pressed the button to bring up his voicemail messages. The first one was from Andrea.

## Day 17, 12:30 p.m., Washington, DC

Andrea was finishing lunch at her desk when her computer beeped with an incoming email. At the same time, her phone rang. Reaching the phone and looking at the computer simultaneously, Andrea answered, "Douglas-Pfeiffer."

On the other end of the phone, the voice started slowly, "Um, yes, Ms. Pfeiffer, this is Kalama Cortez at FBI Intelligence. I wanted to tell you that I sent you the images you asked about yesterday. We did our best with our technology, and I hope the details are sufficient for your needs."

"Hold on. I'm opening the email now. Let me click on the images."

"Yes, ma'am, I'll hold," Cortez said quietly.

"Ms. Cortez," Andrea took charge. "I see from the images that we can't quite get the plate from the image on the truck in the driveway, but the side view of the truck, when it stopped at the stop sign, shows the lettering clearly. We've got a company name and phone number; even the smaller DOT numbers are legible."

"Yes, ma'am," Cortez confirmed. "We had more pixels to work with."

"This gives us something to go on," Andrea was pleased. "Thank you for the call."

"You're welcome. Call me if I can help again." Andrea hung up the phone, looked again at the image, and called Mac.

Mac picked up immediately, "Krieger."

"Mac, this is Andrea. We have an ID on the last truck to leave the freight facility in Dallas. The truck is owned by Salviano LTL Interstate Transport. I'm starting the research to find out the driver's name, the truck's location, and what's in it."

"That's good news, Andrea," Mac said excitedly, "call me when you've got more details. We need to find out what they picked up and where they dropped it off."

"As soon as I know." Andrea hung up the phone.

# CHAPTER FIFTEEN

### Day 18, 9:30 a.m., Philadelphia

The middle-aged, frumpy-looking man stood on the train platform in Philadelphia's 30th Street train station. He was dressed as a casual day commuter, holding a newspaper, a coffee, and a lightweight brown briefcase. He wore a gray suit with a white shirt and a dark red tie he purchased earlier in the day. His face had been softened with round, dark-framed glasses, and his hair was heavily grayed at the temples in a flowing hairstyle gathered in a grayed ponytail.

His normally swarthy facial appearance was lightened with makeup. Some liver spots were added to his hands to show his age. He was using a cane and slightly limping when he walked. His passport matched his appearance. Momentarily, a train arrived, and Amir Abadai climbed aboard with many others. The train departed for New York's Grand Central Terminal, a little over an hour away.

### Day 18, 11:00 a.m., Washington, DC

The security technician at the National Security Agency in Fort Meade, Maryland, was monitoring several computer screens when one screen blipped orange and brought up an image of a man exiting a train car in New York's Grand Central Terminal. The IBM supercomputer ran an algorithm that scanned thousands of images hourly and compared specific facial recognition bio-identifiers to identify individuals.

The distance between the eye sockets, the nose's length, even the mouth's width, or the length from the front of the chin to the bottom of the ear lobe were all biometric identifiers that were challenging to change without substantial surgery. The software was designed to see through changes in hair color or makeup to identify persons of interest accurately.

The system displayed an image of a man walking with a cane. The program zoomed into his face and analyzed the image. The algorithm determined it was seventy-eight percent probable that this person was Amir

Abadai, currently listed as code orange with the Secret Service, FBI, and CIA. The tech flagged the image and sent it to analysis, where an expert looked at the pictures and the technical results of the algorithm to determine if the image would be officially flagged and forwarded to the corresponding intelligence office.

Analysis was always busy. A code red image was reviewed within thirty minutes and was the highest priority for the analyst team. Statistically, the NSA was over ninety-nine percent on meeting this metric. This image was a code orange. The expectation was for a code orange image to be reviewed within two hours, but the statistics on meeting this goal were routinely missed, with averages closer to four hours.

At 12:45 p.m., an email from the NSA was on its way to David Osrick, the officer identified as the point of contact. David wouldn't see the email for another hour.

### Day 18, 8:45 a.m., San Francisco

Batalle's flight from Minneapolis landed early. She departed the plane and walked across the bridge into the San Francisco International Airport. She wore a red wig with large, dark-framed glasses and dressed in the well-tailored black pantsuit of a businesswoman on a mission. She carried a black valise and pulled a black rollaboard suitcase purchased at the Mall of America two days before. She strolled purposefully through the airport, heading for the taxi stand.

Under her blouse, a white elastic band with pockets held two other passports, each with a matching driver's license and credit card. The documents were securely held in place and surrounded by thin shielding sleeves to prevent the counterfeit passports from being accidentally activated by passport-reading machines at border crossings. She walked to the taxi stand and waited with the other business travelers. Within minutes, she was in a taxi and on her way to San Francisco.

### Day 18, 12:30 p.m., New York

Abadai exited a taxi near the Dalees Salaam Community Center and Mosque. Looking around at the people walking by, he noticed a mix of many ethnicities and a variety of styles of dress. People wore casual clothes like jeans or slacks and shirts with light coats, and business people dressed in suits. A small percentage of people wore traditional clothing from Northern African nations they had long ago called home.

Satisfied he could easily blend into the crowds, he used his cane to support himself as he walked down the sidewalk with a pronounced limp. Abadai slowly headed to a coffee shop a block from where the taxi had dropped him off. The coffee shop was filling, but he found a small table near the window. He opened the valise accompanying him on his train trip and pulled out a newspaper. He turned it to the crossword puzzle, pulled a pen, and placed it on the paper.

A waitress stopped at his table and idly asked him about the crossword puzzle and if he would like anything to drink. He ordered a cup of coffee. After the waitress walked away, he reached into his pocket, pulled out his burner phone, and turned it on. He dialed a number he had committed to memory before he left Costa Rica.

Several blocks away, Helbol Pakerisami's phone began ringing. He looked at the inbound number and pressed the button to answer the phone. "Hello?"

In the restaurant, with the phone to his ear, Abadai spoke quietly into the phone. "Helbol, this is your friend."

Helbol recognized the voice at once and quipped casually, "Good morning. We've got a good connection this morning."

"Yes, we do. It's a nice day in New York," Abadai said, looking at his crossword puzzle as he talked. "I hoped we could meet today; I've some business to discuss."

Pakerisami kept his voice calm and said, "I'm available today. Where would you like to meet?"

Abadai thought for a moment. "Let's go to late prayers together. I'll meet you there." He cut off the phone without waiting for Helbol to respond. The entire exchange had taken less than 30 seconds. He turned off his phone and returned it to his pocket.

The clock on the wall read 12:45 p.m. Prayers at Dalees Salaam Mosque for Asr, or 'late afternoon' prayers, would be at 4:43 p.m. He had some shopping to do before he met with Pakerisami. The thrift shop he had passed down the block looked like a good place to pick up what he needed. When the waitress returned, he ordered lunch.

## Day 18, 1:45 p.m., New York

"Oh no," muttered David Osrick, moments after seeing the code orange email from the NSA. "Oh shit!" He exclaimed as he read the email. He hurriedly printed off the notification and ran down the hall to Mac's office carrying the paper and dialing the number for Yosali Tarik. Mac was meeting with another agent, but the meeting broke up when Osrick rushed into the room. "Mac! Mac! We've got an image the NSA says is almost certain to be Amir Abadai; It appears he landed in New York this morning!"

Mac looked at David, "Who's on the phone?"

Looking at the phone in confusion, David put it to his ear. "Yosali, Are you there?"

"Yes, sir," Tarik said, "I picked up as you walked into Agent Krieger's office. Can you please repeat what you said?"

"I've got Agent Tarik on the phone," said David, continuing, "NSA's suspect video net triggered this morning on a man walking out of New York's Grand Central Terminal at 11:00 a.m. They captured an image of a man departing the terminal. Their algorithm gave a high probability that the man in the image is Amir Abadai."

"Let me see the image," Mac said. After studying the image for a moment, he looked up at Osrick. "The man is older and doesn't look like the other images I've seen of Abadai. If it's him, he's well-disguised." "Tarik, do you have eyes on Pakerisami?"

"Not currently," Tarik said, "I'm at the docks watching the import business he visited yesterday to see who else goes in and out. It's pretty quiet now. You want me to track down Pakerisami?"

"Immediately," Mac affirmed. "If this is Abadai, he'll probably reach out to Pakerisami. Tail Pakerisami and see if Abadai shows. Be careful. We need to assume Abadai is dangerous."

"I'm on it, boss," Tarik said.

## Day 18, 10:00 a.m., South San Francisco

Driving a rental car, Batalle pulled into a DHL facility off Interstate 101 and Railroad Avenue. Parking near the doors to the facility, she checked her makeup, climbed out of the dark blue Nissan Altima, and walked casually into the facility. She found a service counter and walked up to it.

"Can I help you?" The attendant, a twenty-something with his hair up in a bob on the back of his head, asked her when she approached.

"Yes, hello, I think you have a package for me," Katerina said. "My name is Stephanie Johnson. It should've arrived this week."

"One moment, please," the young man looked at his computer screen and typed in her name. "Let me check the package log. Yes, it appears we've two boxes. Can I see your identification?"

"Yes, of course," she said. She handed him her passport for Stephanie Johnson from Minnesota, which featured a photo of her with red hair, looking a few years younger.

"Thank you. Please give me a moment to track down the boxes. You are welcome to take a seat."

"Thank you." She looked around at the dusty seats in the DHL offices, and glancing down at her black pantsuit, she murmured under her breath, "I think I'll stand." The attendant brought out two medium-sized boxes three minutes later and asked her to sign for them.

"Hanoi Stereo Components?" The young man said, "I've never heard of them. They must sound pretty good if you ship them in from Vietnam."

"It's a surprise for my boyfriend," Katerina said, "he loves their stuff." She signed for the package and was back in her car within moments. She backed out of the parking space and rejoined the heavy traffic.

## Day 18, 2:15 p.m., New York

Mac Krieger and David Osrick were still in Mac's office looking at alternate pictures of Amir Abadai when Mac's office phone rang. Mac looked at the phone and punched the button: "Krieger, you're on speaker phone."

"Mac, it's Andrea. I've got some additional information for you."

"Hi, Andrea, please go ahead. David Osrick is in the room with us," Mac continued to study the pictures of Abadai.

"So here's what I've learned in the last thirty minutes," she said. "We have a video of Travis Harms arriving at work before 8:00 a.m. to start what turned out to be his last day. Several trucks drove into the freight company on Saturday, and all seemed to be routine pickups or drop-offs. The last one happened at 3:48 p.m."

"I contacted the trucking companies for the first two, and it appears both were freight drop-offs for small packages. The third and last truck of the day carried the markings 'Salviano LTL Interstate Transport.' We've enhanced images showing the truck with the Department of Transportation registration numbers on the side. I contacted the company and spoke with Mr. Eugene Mackey. He knew the truck. The records showed the truck was dispatched to pick up a pallet of material from Blue Ribbon Freight."

Andrea paused to catch her breath. Mac and David could tell she was getting excited. "So here's the interesting part: according to the company, the pallet of material they picked up was listed as 'Modeling Clay,' and the end destination was a freight facility in California."

"Modeling Clay," Mac said. "What is that?"

"It's sculpture clay," Andrea said, "so it's like fifteen hundred pounds of clay for sculpture artists."

"Remind me again why we care about Modeling Clay?" Mac asked. "Modeling Clay is the same weight and texture as plastic explosive!" Andrea said, sounding exasperated.

"I'm sorry, Andrea," Mac apologized. "You caught me in the middle of a meeting concerning Amir Abadai. We think he's in New York right now."

"Mac, I think we should be tracking this pallet of clay."

"Don't wait for me, Andrea! Get it going, and let me know what you find." Mac encouraged her. He then looked at David Osrick. "While you track that clay, we'll find Abadai."

# CHAPTER SIXTEEN

**Day 18, 3:00 p.m., New York**

Eliu Nasif stood inside his company's loading dock, watching two workers unload several thirteen-foot-long wooden shipping boxes of wool rugs from Tunisia. The rugs came off Eliu's truck with the 'Solvang Imports' markings on the side. The driver had picked up the freight from an ocean freighter earlier.

He saw a mixture of rugs in each box, and Eliu looked at the freight invoice and listed the various rug types. The rugs were highly anticipated. He had several rug dealers in New York awaiting these rugs, and a storm off the coast of Africa had delayed the shipment by almost a week.

Eliu wasn't prepared for the surprise of some additional freight now being unloaded. A large, heavily wrapped pallet of material slowly rolled off the truck with a hand-operated pallet mover. It was wheeled over to where Eliu stood.

The pallet was about five feet high. The truck driver walked over to Eliu and handed him the paperwork. He looked at the paperwork and then at the pallet. He walked cautiously around it and found a label partially covered in dust on the material.

He lifted his hand and slowly brushed to remove the dust from the plastic. The label on the pallet was printed: 'Modeling Clay.' The freight bill of lading also listed Modeling Clay as the material and his freight warehouse as the destination. The shipment appeared to have originated at the Port of Gwadar on the southwestern coast of Pakistan. The bill of lading instructed, "Hold for Pickup," and didn't have a phone number or other contact information.

Eliu wondered if this was related to Helbol Pakerisami's special request. He told his employee with the pallet mover to take it to a far corner of the warehouse and cover it with black plastic. He would deal with it later.

# Day 18, 4:30 p.m., New York

Helbol Pakerisami walked into Dalees Salaam Community Center and Mosque. He quietly acknowledged several community leaders as he proceeded through the foyer into the mosque. Outside the prayer hall, he removed his shoes and placed them on a shoe holder along the wall. He moved into the open prayer hall, or Musallā, finding an open mat near the middle of a large group of other men settling in for prayers.

Pakerisami lowered himself onto his hands and knees and bent slowly forward, touching his forehead to the mat. Pakerisami heard clothing rustling near his right ear and turned to see another patron join him. The man to his right had long, unkempt hair, a rough beard, and clothing that had seen better days. Pakerisami looked briefly at the man. Unconcerned, he began to pray along with the Imam.

"Helbol," the man next to him whispered. Pakerisami picked up his head and looked slowly to his right, straight into Amir Abadai's eyes. Pakerisami's eyes widened as he recognized Abadai in the wild-haired man beside him.

Seeing his change in attitude, Abadai moved his hand slightly downward, which was barely visible to anyone other than Pakerisami. Helbol averted his eyes back to the floor and continued his prayers.

As both men prayed with their foreheads touching the mat, Abadai turned his head toward Helbol and whispered, "You're being followed."

Helbol jerked in surprise as he registered Abadai's comments. He wanted to look around the room immediately but resisted the temptation and looked over at Abadai instead, blinking his eyes in acknowledgment.

Abadai continued, "Meet me tonight at 9:00 p.m. outside the Jamaica Transit Depot Building."

Pakerisami nodded. When prayers ended, Pakerisami stood up with the mass of other men and turned to where Amir had been beside him moments before. Abadai was gone.

Pakerisami exited the hall, looking around to see if he recognized someone following him. He knew many men his age but only a few younger men in the crowd. Most young men turned on their phones and checked their messages as soon as they departed the hall. Agent Yosali Tarik was simply another young man looking at his phone.

Although several men looked in Pakerisami's direction, he couldn't determine if they were looking at or past him and up the street behind him. Seeking a different perspective, Pakerisami crossed the street to the adjacent sidewalk and looked again at the dissipating group. He saw no indication of anyone following him.

Pakerisami walked up the corner of Jamaica Avenue and turned left, walking down the street to Emir's Turkish Coffee Shop, a cafe he often frequented. He hoped a coffee would settle his nerves. He entered the restaurant and sat at a table, looking toward the door. A waiter came by and took his order.

Pakerisami studied each person who entered or left the coffee shop. When his coffee arrived, he retrieved his cell phone from his pocket and put it on the table. He often used the cafe's Wi-Fi network to check his encrypted messages.

As Pakerisami looked at his phone, Agent Tarik slipped into the cafe. Pakerisami didn't see Tarik come in or sit down. Had he been watching closely, he would have seen Tarik take his phone out of his pocket and use the reflection from the phone's display like a mirror to glance Pakerisami's way.

Pakerisami's phone buzzed as Helbol received a new message. "*Two deliveries are coming to your home soon. Please hold these for me.*" The message came from a number he didn't recognize. Helbol figured it must be from Amir Abadai.

He picked up his coffee and began cursing himself. *You've had the chance to move on, and you ignored the warning signals*, he thought to himself. *Now you're helping Abadai to do something. What could this mean?* Pakerisami glanced at his phone again and thought, *I should have lost this phone a long time ago and made it harder for Abadai to find me. Now, how do I get out of this?*

Pakerisami sat back in his chair and looked up at the ceiling. He removed his small, round glasses and rubbed his eyes, his hands trembling slightly. He looked older than his forty-five years.

Taking a deep breath and exhaling, he looked around the cafe for anyone looking back at him. After scanning the cafe, he sighed, stood up, and walked to the restroom a few yards from his table. In his nervousness, he absent-mindedly left his phone alone on the table.

## Day 18, 4:45 p.m., New York

A few tables away, Yosali Tarik watched the Pakerisami's movement through his phone's reflection. He watched Pakerisami walk to the restroom and leave his phone on the table. Taking the risk of being identified by his target, Tarik rose from his table and walked to where Helbol's phone lay on the table.

Picking it up and popping out the SIM card, he expertly used his phone to snap a picture of the SIM card, including the small print of the ICCID identification. He returned the SIM card to the phone and replaced it in the approximate location. Tarik returned to his table and sat down. The entire action took less than thirty seconds. The cafe was busy, and with all the activity, no one noticed Tarik's bold move.

Seconds after Tarik returned to his seat, he watched Pakerisami return from the restroom and noticed his phone lying on the table. Pakerisami touched his left breast pocket and checked his pants pockets to determine if the phone on the table was his. Determining he didn't have his phone on his person, he looked around the cafe with wild eyes but found no one looking at him.

Tarik watched as Pakerisami rushed out onto the street and turned left. When Pakerisami disappeared, Tarik pressed the "send" key on his phone and texted David Osrick the photo of the ICCID from the SIM card. Tarik slid out of the chair and followed Pakerisami onto the street. As he left the cafe, he pressed the speed dial to David Osrick. He could hear Osrick's phone ringing in his earphones.

## Day 18 6:00 p.m., New York

"Great work, Yosali, this is the break we needed," said Osrick, "I'll call the boss and let him know." Throwing off his coat to a nearby chair, he called Mac, who was driving home.

"Krieger."

"Mac, it's David. Tarik somehow managed to get ahold of Pakerisami's cell phone and took a photo of the SIM card."

"Hang on, David. I'm pulling over. This is excellent news." Osrick waited for Mac to continue.

"Sorry for the delay, David," said Mac. "We've got to move on this now! Type up a request for a wiretap. We need to get to Judge Arminson tonight."

"Okay, boss, anything else?" Osrick smiled.

"No, I'm coming back in. I'll see you soon."

## Day 18, 4:30 p.m., San Francisco

Katerina stood in the Embassy Hotel lobby near the San Francisco International Airport. Under the cover of a business traveler from Minnesota, the hotel was convenient but undoubtedly different from the preference for Batalle. She was waiting for Abadai's scheduled call at 7:30 p.m. Eastern time. Her phone chirped, and she opened it, answering, "This is Stephanie," in a bright, midwestern accent. On the other end of the phone, Abadai was direct.

"Can you talk?"

"Give me a moment to find a quieter place," Batalle said, still in Stephanie's voice. She moved to a window chair farthest from the busy lobby and sat down. Returning to the phone, she spoke quietly, "Good evening, do you have a few minutes?"

"A few minutes, yes," Amir said.

"I've picked up my two smaller packages, and I'm awaiting delivery of the larger one from the freight forwarder. It should be here in the next day or two," Batalle updated him. She looked at her watch for the date, "I'm assuming our timing hasn't changed."

"No," Abadai confirmed, "the alignment must remain the same. Be ready in five days."

"I don't want to be here long enough for someone to remember me. I will spend a few nights in Las Vegas until the freight is ready to pick up."

"Just make sure you are ready," said Abadai. The call ended as abruptly as it began.

Katerina approached the concierge and asked when the next shuttle bus left for the airport. An hour later, she reclined in a first-class seat on United Airlines flight 1564, a one-way flight to Las Vegas that flies almost every hour, shuttling gamblers and business people from point to point. She told the hotel front desk clerk that an urgent meeting required her early departure.

Getting onto the flight was easy at the ticket counter. This particular flight was unique for United. Most gamblers walked up to the counter without reservation or luggage, and many paid for their tickets with cash. Her luck was getting a first-class seat. It was usually the first to be filled on this flight.

# CHAPTER SEVENTEEN

### Day 18, 9:00 p.m., New York

Pakerisami checked his watch as he strolled down the sidewalk and paused at Jamaica and 143rd Street. He stepped off the sidewalk and melded into a building pocket near a small storefront and waited, looking for anyone who appeared to be trying to follow him. No one was interested in a middle-aged North African man. He took a deep breath in the cool evening air and stepped away from the building, entering the light pedestrian traffic he had been navigating moments before. He continued his walk toward Sutphin Boulevard.

As he approached the boulevard, Pakerisami turned south on Sutphin and walked toward the Jamaica Transit Depot. Most of the pedestrians on Jamaica Avenue were also turning south on Sutphin, walking to catch a train or bus home at 9:00 p.m. With darkness closing in, many of the younger generation headed toward the downtown clubs or maybe the nearby casino to begin their fun evening.

The bus depot on the west side of the street had about six or seven buses parked in a large parking lot. The subway stairs were across the street. As Pakerisami walked toward the busy station, several large waste dumpsters appeared in the shadows, nestled against a warehouse wall. A few homeless people were loitering near the dumpsters, far enough from the buses. The transit cops didn't bother them, but they were close enough to ask for change from the pedestrians walking toward the station.

Pakerisami had a few dollars in his pocket and walked toward the five or six homeless people occupying the area near the dumpsters. As he encountered a homeless person, Pakerisami would pull out a couple of dollars and offer it to them, saying, "Allah provides to all. Please have a cup of coffee. It's on me." With each one, he gave the same message. After a minute and several dollars, he determined Abadai wasn't in this group and walked back toward the pedestrian sidewalk.

Walking past the parked buses, he continued south on Sutphin Boulevard. As he approached the station's main entrance, he saw three men

93

standing near the waste bins outside the doors. They were asking for money and were more persistent and daring. The transit police would walk toward them, and they would disperse. They would come back together near the doors when the police presence waned. Pakerisami walked straight toward this group of men and again offered blessings from Allah and a few dollars for coffee. Two men took the money and immediately entered the station to get coffee or something to eat, but the third didn't immediately leave. Amir Abadai quietly accepted the two dollars and stuffed them into his oversized coat. He motioned for Pakerisami to follow him to the edge of the building, where he leaned heavily at the corner and slowly sat down. Helbol followed and kneeled beside Abadai.

"Please pray for a homeless man." Said Amir.

Nodding his head with understanding, Pakerisami prayed, "Praise Allah and give hope to the homeless men and women."

Nearby, a man and woman passed by the men. Overhearing Pakerisami's words and the prayerful intent of both men, the woman commented, "That's nice."

After they left, Abadai asked, "Did you get my message?"

"Yes," Pakerisami confirmed, "but I've not yet received the packages you mentioned."

"Two packages will be at your home soon, maybe tomorrow. Has the shipment arrived at the freight company?"

"I've not been contacted by my friend yet," Pakerisami said.

"The freight will require a truck. When your friend notifies you of the shipment, tell him someone will pick it up soon. Are we clear?"

"Yes, clear," Helbol said. "Where do you need it delivered?"

"That's not your concern," Abadai said coolly.

Pakerisami was still holding Amir's hands. He asked, "You said someone is tracking me?"

"Yes, but I'll take care of him for you. Now it's time for you to go. One final prayer for a homeless man. Afterwards, you walk away like a good Muslim brother."

Pakerisami quietly recited a prayer for the homeless. He left Abadai with the final words, "Blessings to you, my brother." He then walked back the way he had come.

### Day 18, 9:10 p.m., New York

Abadai peeked from the dark shadows at the corner of the building and across the street. He could see the man looking hard at the shadows where Pakerisami had paused to pray with a homeless man. He seemed interested in Pakerisami and positioned himself to watch him leave the area. Abadai watched him turn away from the street and enter the lighted bus terminal.

He could see him pull a phone out of his pocket.

Abadai was up and running across the street toward the bus terminal when the man turned his back to him. In less than 15 seconds, he was inside and found the man checking his messages near the restroom entrance.

Walking up behind him and grasping him around the waist with one arm, Abadai unsheathed a ten-inch long flexible fillet knife from inside his jacket and expertly slid it between the fifth and fourth rib into the pericardium area above Tarik's heart. With a practiced quick jerk to the left, Abadai serrated Tarik's aorta and the superior vena cava of his heart.

Moving the knife above the top rib, he did the same type of movement and cut the man's windpipe, preventing him from expelling or inhaling air into his lungs. The man's heart continued to pump blood. It flowed directly into his pericardium.

Abadai's firm grip around his waist prevented the man from turning around. His eyes began to bulge as his first attempts at breathing failed. Although still standing but unable to speak, the man began to understand what had happened.

A woman walking by looked over at the two men. "Hey, is he okay?" She asked.

Abadai's body shielded the knife handle from her view. He casually said, "I think so; he told me he wasn't feeling well. I'm going to help him into the restroom."

The man began stumbling forward, and Abadai expertly used his walk to take him into the restroom. He led him to the first open stall. Quietly maneuvering and sitting him down, Abadai removed his knife and wiped it on the man's shirt. With life leaving the man's eyes, he looked at him and said, "You picked the wrong time to turn your back, my friend."

Closing the door to the stall and walking to the wash basin, Abadai washed his hands and looked into the mirror at the man's feet in the closed stall. Looking forward into the mirror as he washed his hands, he saw a dirty, homeless man in his reflection. He dried his hands and walked out of the restroom. He kept his head down and left the bus terminal. Abadai was intent on putting some distance between himself and the dead man in the bus station.

Abadai unhurriedly walked from the bus station to the train station across the street. Using his pre-purchased ticket, he walked to the first available train, which happened to be heading toward Manhattan, and climbed aboard. Three stops and five miles away, he departed at the massive Queens Station across the East River from Manhattan.

## Day 18, 11:00 p.m., New York

When his phone rang, Mac Krieger had opened his second beer at his apartment near High Bridge Park on Manhattan's Upper East Side. He left the office late but stopped for a forty-five-minute workout at the gym. He walked to his phone on the table and saw it was from The New York Police Department.

Mac answered: "Krieger."

"Is this Mac Krieger, special agent for the Secret Service in New York?" The male voice asked in a formal tone.

"Yes, it is, officer; what can I do for you?"

"Mr. Krieger, we have a detective on the line. Can you please hold?"

"Yes, of course," Mac said. Momentarily, a new voice came onto the line.

"Agent Krieger? This is Homicide Detective Teresa Gianatti of the 35th precinct."

"Yes, I'm Mac Krieger; please go ahead."

"Agent Krieger, we've got an officer of your agency found dead in the Jamaica Transit Depot about thirty minutes ago."

"Oh, my God!" Mac exclaimed. "Please let this be a mistake. What is the identification of the victim?"

"Yes, it appears to be a man named Tarik, Yosali Tarik." These words, spoken by someone who has seen a lot of death, were emotionless.

Mac was horrified, and it was evident in his voice. "Yosali Tarik is an agent of mine. He was working tonight!"

"Well, can you come to the county morgue to identify him?" The detective's voice was emotionless, "He should be at the morgue in about twenty minutes. They're loading him up now."

"Of course," Mac struggled to regain composure. "Can you tell me how he died? And where?"

"He was found in the restroom of the bus depot at the Jamaica Transit Station on Sutphin and 147th. We'll need to do an autopsy on the body to determine the cause of death, but there is significant blood and what looks like a knife wound to the back about where the heart is. Initial estimates by the EMTs say he's been here about two hours."

"Detective, will you be on the scene for a while?"

"Yes, I have to be here until the crime lab completes its investigation, which I'm guessing will take about an hour," Gianatti said.

"I will send one of my agents to meet with you on the scene. His name is David Osrick. He may be of assistance to your investigation."

"That's fine as long as he understands this is NYPD jurisdiction, and he can't interfere," the detective warned.

"He won't interfere," Mac growled. "I think he can help. I'll have him on his way in a few minutes."

"Good enough," the detective said. She abruptly cut the line short.

## Day 19, 7:30 a.m., New York

It was a clear, cool morning with few clouds on the horizon. Early morning streams of light in yellows and reds were now being overtaken by bright sunshine. Traffic in Manhattan was bumper-to-bumper and noisy.

The mood in the office of the New York Secret Service was anything but bright or happy. Mac heard people talking in low voices and someone crying. Everyone came to learn of the unexpected death of a fellow agent and friend.

Mac was on the phone in his office with DC human resources to ensure they were doing everything possible to support Tarik's family and his girlfriend. As Mac hung up the phone, David Osrick, looking weary from a long night, walked in and slowly sat down.

"Did you get any sleep last night?" Mac asked, concerned.

"None," David said, "and I'm not sure I'll get any tonight either. It is an awful situation. I'm feeling responsible for a good man's death last night."

"I know, David, but you know it's not your fault. I spent an hour at the morgue identifying Tarik and begging them to move a federal agent's murder to the front of the autopsy line. I don't know what we'll learn other than it was a knife wound to the back. The doctor told me that when they laid him on the stretcher, blood started pouring from his mouth and didn't stop until they reached the morgue. The EMTs said they had never seen anything like that before."

"Oh, sweet Jesus," David moaned and put his head in his hands. "I think I could have lived without knowing those details."

"I'm sorry, David," Mac said. "I wasn't thinking." Mac changed the subject. "Who's on Pakerisami?"

"Benson and Whillerby were on the case early this morning. They're watching his house as we speak." Osrick said as he looked up. Mac could see tears in his eyes.

Mac looked down at his list of phone calls to Tarik's next of kin. "Go home and get some rest, David. I don't want you in the office today. Take a little time to grieve."

"I'm going," said Osrick. "I'll be back tomorrow."

"I know you will," said Mac, sighing. "I hate this part of my job."

## Day 19, 10:00 a.m., New York

Helbol Pakerisami heard a knock at his front door. Dressed and drinking homemade Turkish coffee, he wondered who could be knocking at this time of day. Looking out the keyhole, Pakerisami adjusted his glasses, blinked his eyes, and peered again to see better who was outside. He could not see anyone.

Carefully opening the door and looking down to ensure his cat didn't try to escape, he noticed a package in front of it. Opening the door a little wider, he saw two packages on his doorstep. He stooped down, picked up both packages and looked at the addresses to ensure they were addressed to him. He carried the two boxes into his home and closed the door.

Pakerisami walked into his kitchen and set the packages on his small table. The return address on the delivery documentation was from 'Hanoi Stereo Components' of Vietnam and indicated they were shipped via air three days prior. Picking up his coffee cup, Helbol walked over to the sink and washed the coffee sludge out of his small cup. He reached for the coffee pot and poured another strong coffee. The extreme caffeine burst was beginning to have its intended effect. He picked up his phone and sent a message to the phone number for Amir Abadai: *'Packages [2] received.'*

## Day 19, 10:30 a.m., Washington, DC

Andrea sat at her desk in the same clothes she had worn the night before. She dialed Mac's office phone in New York.

"Krieger."

"Morning, Mac," Andrea was tired, and she could hear it in her voice. "It took the NSA longer than I thought, but I've got some information on Pakerisami's phone."

"Andrea, I forgot about it until you called." Mac's voice sounded strained. "We lost an agent last night, Yosali Tarik. He had been tailing Pakerisami for the past several days. We don't have any leads yet on the suspect, but we think it's related to this ongoing threat."

"I'm sorry, Mac. I heard some buzzing early this morning in the office. I wonder if it was related. Do you still want an update? Or should I call you later?" Andrea asked.

"Please, let's talk now," Mac said, "I need to focus on something else."

"The data from Pakerisami's phone shows it was a new phone set up about eight months ago."

"So we've eight months of data?" Mac sounded disappointed.

"The carrier records all phone numbers linked to a specific bill payer's address. We've got a good bit of data parsed together to give us a better picture. He's received calls from several states outside the tristate area, notably, from Florida, Texas, California, and Colorado." Andrea said.

"How about International calls?" Mac asked. "North Africa, primarily Egypt, followed by Gaza, Morocco, Syria and Tunisia. Outside North Africa, there have been some infrequent calls from several other locations, Singapore, Pakistan, Costa Rica, Panama, and Brazil. The calls from other parts of the world have been new in the last two to three years. The most recent international calls are from Costa Rica, twice."

"Do we have any text messages?" Mac asked, hopefully.

"Not yet; it's another report I'll analyze when it comes in. Don't hold out too much hope on this, though, Mac. Pakerisami has an encrypted messaging app. It's a data burst, and we can't read it."

"Good grief," Mac said, disappointment coming through clearly. "Call me if you find anything we can run with. I'll be here most of the day."

"Will do," Andrea said. "Maybe we'll get a break."

"Let's hope so. We know Abadai is in New York. It's probably not a tourist visit. I'd sure like to find him sooner rather than later." Mac paused and added, "I'd like to talk to him about Agent Tarik's death, too."

# CHAPTER EIGHTEEN

### Day 20, 7:00 a.m., Las Vegas

Katerina Batalle woke hungry in her hotel room at Bally's Resort and Casino on the Las Vegas strip. Getting out of bed and walking to the phone near the window, she called room service and ordered breakfast. Pulling the robe from the closet, she wrapped it around herself and sat at the small desk near the window. She called the hotel spa and reserved a half-day spa massage, steam, and soak treatment. A few minutes later, she heard a knock on the door and a muffled "room service." She got up from the chair and walked to the door.

### Day 20, 11:00 a.m., New York

At the freight office of Solvang Imports, Eliu Nasif was scratching his unkempt beard when one of his workers walked in and asked him in Arabic, "What do you want to do with the pallet delivered yesterday?"

Nasif said in English, "I need to make a call on it. I'll do it today." As an afterthought, he added, "Mohas, practice your English. I told your mother I would help you when I agreed you could work here."

"Okay, boss," Mohas taunted him. Shaking his head, Eliu picked up his phone, dialed the number for Helbol Pakerisami, and waited as it rang through.

"Pakerisami," Helbol answered.

"Helbol, this is Eliu. I've received a freight shipment that I believe is yours."

"Thank you, Eliu. I'll be by later today to talk to you about it."

"Very good," Nasif hung up the phone, muttering, "always better to talk in person."

### Day 20, 11:05 a.m., NSA Headquarters, Fort Meade, Maryland

The first phone call from the newly wiretapped number of Helbol

Pakerisami's mobile phone was triggered by Solvang Imports owner Eliu Nasif. The nine-second exchange was captured and recorded. As a high-priority message of possible national security consequence, an email and text message were sent immediately to the analyst on duty, notifying a call was recorded.

At the end of the call, the computer flagged the recording, uploaded it to a cloud network, and analyzed the call electronically, looking for any of the thousand different words in multiple languages that would trigger immediate escalation.

Finding none in this message, the computer's simple AI wrote an email within seconds detailing the target phone number and ID of the person owning the phone and the name and address of the person making the call. The email included a full transcript of the phone call. The email was sent to Andrea Douglas-Pfeiffer, David Osrick, and ten other Intelligence Joint Task Force people within seconds.

The wiretap didn't capture the encrypted data file sent over the Internet via Pakerisami's Wi-Fi network. This encrypted exchange, sent by Pakerisami to Abadai, said, *"Your package has arrived at the docks. Where do you want it delivered and when?"*

## Day 20, 12:00 p.m., New York

Amir Abadai was blending in with the homeless population in the city. His clothes were dirty and worn, and he appeared to be much older than he was. He copied the other homeless men and imitated their 'lost' expressions and off-balance movements.

He limped slowly toward a restaurant with indoor and outdoor seating. The owner had placed a few charging transformers on a relatively wide windowsill near the corner of the building. They were popular with the shelter residents, several of whom had government-supplied cell phones. Every once in a while, the local police would stop by, asking anyone standing there if they'd seen a missing teenager from another state.

Abadai plugged his phone into an available charger and turned it on. He waited for it to connect to the restaurant's Wi-Fi signal. Once connected, he opened his messaging app and checked his messages. Two messages appeared on his screen, one from Pakerisami and the other from Batalle.

Abadai read Pakerisami's message first and grunted, "Good." He replied: *"I will schedule a pickup. Did you receive any other shipments?"* Pakerisami was online and wrote: *"Yes, I have two boxes."* Abadai wrote: *"Take the boxes to the warehouse today and put them on the pallet. Tell your friend to leave the warehouse door unlocked tonight."* Helbol wrote: *"He will not leave it unlocked, but I will get you the door code."* Amir texted: *"Good, I will have a driver pick up the pallet the day after tomorrow. He will ask for a pallet of modeling clay for 'Zeitz Studio.'"*

Abadai ended the encrypted exchange and looked up from his phone. He was one of many looking at their phones while they charged them. Returning to his phone, he brought up the message from Katerina. It read, *"Waiting for date and timing."* The message had been delivered the previous evening.

Abadai typed, *"Get your driver and pick up the package. Plan for Thursday at 10:00 a.m., your time."*

Abadai turned off his phone and looked up again. No one was watching him with any particular interest. He walked down the sidewalk and away from the cafe with his limping gait.

## Day 21, 3:00 p.m., Solvang Imports, New York

Helbol Pakerisami left his small, weathered house on 108th Street almost an hour ago. He was carrying a light shopping bag with sharp corners of a box jutting out through the fabric. After several trains and a bus ride, he walked to the front door of Solvang Imports and pressed the button.

He was surprised when Eliu Nasif walked the short hallway to open the door for him. The two greeted each other, and Pakerisami entered, carrying his bag. Nasif locked the door and walked behind Pakerisami down the hallway. He invited him to take a seat in his cramped and cluttered office.

"So this pallet," Nasif began as he settled behind his desk, "it's pretty large and heavy. What are you going to do with it?"

"It will be picked up the day after tomorrow," Pakerisami said after opening his phone and reviewing the message from Abadai again. "A truck driver from Zeitz Studio will call to collect the package."

"Very good," Nasif was pleased. "Who will pay for my time and storage?"

"I'll guarantee your payment if that's acceptable to you."

"Also, good; may I offer you a coffee?" Nasif asked.

"I would be delighted," Pakerisami said, "I didn't have time to stop on my way, and the weather here at the docks is considerably cooler than Jamaica Avenue." He was quiet for a few moments and watched as Nasif stood and moved to pour the coffee.

"I do have one request," Pakerisami said. "I need to place these two boxes on top of the pallet in the warehouse. They need to be picked up at the same time as the pallet. Can I do it while you make coffee?"

"Certainly," Nasif said. "The pallet is easy to find in my warehouse. It's to your left as you enter the warehouse. In the far corner."

"Thank you, this won't take long."

Helbol picked up his bag with the two boxes and turned the corner toward the warehouse. Reaching the warehouse door, he pulled the handle, but the door wouldn't move. It was locked with an electronic lock. Pakerisami looked at the lock and walked back to Nasif's office.

"Eliu, what is the code to get into the warehouse?" Helbol stuck his head around the corner of the door.

Turning slightly from pouring coffee into two cups, Nasif raised his voice. "Ah yes, the code is '3601,' a combination of the avenue and the street. It works on the front door, too."

"Thank you. I'll be right back." Helbol smiled to himself, pleased to have the door code Abadai wanted.

Pakerisami entered the mid-sized warehouse and stopped. He waited momentarily to adjust his eyes to the dimly illuminated space. The delivery doors were closed, and the windows high up on the walls created shafts of light swirling with dust particles as a few warehouse workers shuffled paper-wrapped rugs of all shapes and sizes onto double pallets marked for the various retailers in the New York area.

With his eyes adjusted, Pakerisami noticed a single pallet of material near a wall. Walking around the edges of the busy workers unloading and loading rugs, Pakerisami made his way over to the pallet and looked at it. He could see the material was Modeling Clay. He placed the bag on top of the pallet. A supervisor approached him as he was looking at the pallet with the bag on top of it.

"Is it your freight?" The warehouse supervisor pointed to the material.

"Yes, a truck will pick it up in two days. I put a couple of boxes on top of it to be picked up with the pallet. Can you please make sure they stay with the pallet?"

"Shouldn't be a problem. Anything valuable in the boxes?" The supervisor looked back at his workers.

"Nothing I know of," Helbol said, "but if it would help, I'll gladly give you twenty dollars to ensure they're not touched." Helbol reached into his wallet and handed the supervisor a folded twenty-dollar bill. The supervisor looked back at his workers and turned toward Helbol.

"I'll do my best to keep the youngsters away until it's picked up." He reached out, took the twenty-dollar bill, and put it into his pocket. He returned to his crew, who were trying to move a large rug. He yelled harshly at two young men as they stood by as their fellow workers struggled with the heavy carpet. The men jumped at his words and scrambled to help the other workers.

Pakerisami paused before departing the warehouse and opened his phone. He sent a message to Abadai containing the four digits of the security code for the warehouse doors.

At the door, he paused and looked one last time at the pallet sitting innocently near the south wall of the warehouse. He slowly turned back to the door and disappeared into the hallway.

## Day 21, 5:45 p.m., New York

Mac stood at the coffee maker, pouring his third cup of coffee and discussing the results of the day's surveillance of Helbol Pakerisami with David Osrick. His tie loosened, his white shirt wrinkled, and his sleeves rolled up to his elbows. His government-issued 9 mm Glock semi-automatic pistol nested on his hip, and a Secret Service badge on a lanyard hung from his neck with his ID and access credentials.

Mac was at his tenth or eleventh meeting of the day, not including two hours of calls to collect information from his teams, align with the FBI and the Joint Task Force, and update the higher-ups in Washington. Mac asked Osrick, "So, into Solvang with the packages, but nothing is coming out?"

"That's right," Osrick said. "He left the boxes there, or they were taken to someone there. It's a warehouse and freight forwarder; it's difficult to know what was in the boxes or where they went."

"Let's not wait any longer, David. Get the search warrant request to the judge first thing tomorrow morning. Coordinate with NYPD and the FBI for an early raid the day after tomorrow."

"I think we should pick up Pakerisami simultaneously and question him," David said. "I'll take care of the warrant and coordinate with the FBI on Pakerisami."

Mac nodded his agreement and said, "I need to call Fitzgerald and let him know what we're doing,"

## Day 21, 6:00 p.m., Las Vegas

Batalle walked through the exterior doors of the hotel and casino, looking much younger than she did when she checked in. She wore newly purchased 'grunge' clothing that looked like it dated from the 1980s. Her hair was black, and she was sporting a bright purple streak from the talented stylist in the hotel.

Outside the hotel entrance, she waited patiently in line for a taxi and directed the driver to take her to the airport. She was intent on catching the next hourly flight to San Francisco. It was time to get to work.

# CHAPTER NINETEEN

**Day 22, 7:30 a.m., New York**

Due to the rain outside, Amir Abadai spent a little more time in the Sisters of Holy Grace homeless shelter. As he lay on the cot and watched the activity, he counted almost three dozen homeless people, either refugees or nomads.

He focused on a young man who didn't fit the homeless category. Unlike others in the shelter, his clothes were not dirty, ill-sized, or torn. He carried a backpack in good condition and a small suitcase. His shoes were newer and the right size for his feet. Abadai rolled to his feet while keeping his eyes on the young man. The young man had packed his backpack and stood to put it on, appearing ready to leave, when the sound of rain on the windows increased. Abadai watched the young man sigh and put his suitcase and backpack on the cot. Then, he wandered over to the food line for breakfast.

Abadai followed him through the food line. The young man walked to a nearby table and sat down with his tray. Abadai sat down at the same table.

"You don't look like you've spent much time in places like this," Abadai said. The young man stopped eating and looked at Abadai. A moment or two passed as the young man considered whether to ignore the conversation attempt or respond to it.

The young man said, "Yeah, I don't know what I'm doing here. But I've got no place to go. Here I am."

"Where are you from? Detroit, Philadelphia?" Abadai threw out a couple of names.

"Atlanta, I'm trying to make some money to return home. My mom doesn't know I'm sleeping in a shelter. I don't want her to worry about me, at least not yet."

"Figured out a job yet?" Abadai asked.

"Not yet, but I've gotten some help from the sisters, and I think I'll find something soon." Said the young man.

"I may know of a job. If you're interested," Abadai said. "It involves picking up and delivering a single load of material."

"What day?" The young man said with some interest. "Tomorrow," Abadai replied. "I'm told it pays one thousand cash for a day's work. It seems like a lot to me, but I'm not a truck driver in New York."

"A thousand for a day's work?" The young man was incredulous. "That's crazy; no one pays that much. What's the cargo, drugs? I'm not going to risk my life for a thousand bucks."

"No," Abadai said quietly, "it's not drugs. It's a type of clay sculptor's use, and it's going to an art studio in downtown Manhattan. The owners order it maybe once a year." The young man looked at Abadai, somewhat bewildered.

"Why are you telling me this? Why don't you take the delivery job?"

"I lost my driver's license. I can't rent a delivery truck, and I don't have experience moving heavy material around," Abadai said. "The owners asked me if I knew someone, and I told them I'd try to help. I'd forgotten about it until I saw you this morning."

"So what do you want for giving me a job lead?"

"Ten percent," Abadai said, "one hundred dollars from the one thousand you'll be paid for the delivery job."

"That sounds fair to me," the young man said. "I'll take nine hundred and return to Atlanta with cash in my wallet."

Abadai smiled. "It's a deal. I'll talk to the studio owner today." Looking outside, he saw that the rain was ending.

He turned to the young man and asked, "So, what's your name?"

"You can call me Donny."

"See you tonight, Donny," Abadai smiled at him. Then he got up from the table, dropped his tray into a dirty dishes bin, and headed toward the door.

## Day 22, 6:55 a.m., San Francisco

Batalle sat in her rental car about three hundred feet south of the Mission Workforce Community Job Center on Capp Street in San Francisco, watching the young men in the street waiting for the small building to open at 7:00 a.m.

She was focused on one young man holding back from joining the line and appeared to be contemplating his next decision. He wore blue jeans, old boots, and a dirty long-sleeve shirt. He carried a small bag.

It was apparent to her that he was in the country illegally, had slept in the streets for the last few days or perhaps even a week, and hoped to make some money to buy food. The decision he was contemplating, she surmised, was whether or not to put his name on the sheet.

Batalle put her car in drive, rolled it forward, and stopped beside the young man. She rolled down her passenger window. "Hola, ¿Buscas empleo?" (Hello; Are you looking for work?)

"Si," the young man said, "¿Tienes trabajo?" (Yes, you have a job?).

"¿Hablar Inglés? ¿Puedes conducir?" (Speak English? Can you drive?).

"Yes, I speak a little English, and yes, I can drive."

"Very good," Batalle said, "how about a delivery truck? Can you drive one of those? I need someone to pick up a pallet of material and deliver it to an address."

"Yes, I can drive a truck, no problem; I drove a truck in El Salvador before I came here."

"Good," Batalle smiled at him. "Why don't you get in with me, and I'll take you to breakfast? I'll pay you for a week's work, and you'll only need to work two days."

"You'll pay me for a week of work?" The young man looked hard at her. He was suspicious of easy money.

"I'll give you enough for a cheap hotel and food for the week," Batalle said. "What's your name?"

"Juan Carlos," said the young man.

"Please get in, Juan Carlos," she said. "I know of a nice cafe not too far from here." She watched as Juan Carlos looked at the men waiting to enter the Job Center.

He scratched his week-old beard and asked, "Why didn't you go through the Job Center to find someone?"

She smiled conspiratorially at him. "Like you, I didn't want to register my name with anyone." Juan Carlos opened the door and climbed into the passenger seat.

## Day 22, 7:30 a.m., San Francisco

After Katerina Batalle watched Juan Carlos consume two breakfasts, they left the restaurant. She drove to a Ryder truck rental location, renting a 20-foot cargo truck for the week. After she signed the paperwork, she gave Juan Carlos the keys and asked him to follow her to a nearby Walmart parking lot.

She gave him the address of the freight company holding the pallet and a city map. Then she called the freight facility and told them Juan Carlos was picking up the material. She confirmed the loading dock to use and gave them her credit card to pay the freight and storage fees.

On the map, she circled their parking lot and the freight company's location in Oakland. They agreed to meet in the parking lot after he collected the material. She watched him drive away.

## Day 22, 11:15 a.m., San Francisco

Batalle looked at her watch and slowly tapped her foot. Sitting in the Walmart parking lot for the last hour stretched her patience. She didn't want to call his cell phone because she didn't want to leave an electronic trace, so she waited. Ten minutes later, almost an hour after their meeting, Juan Carlos turned the rented truck into the parking lot and pulled up next to her rental car.

"Sorry for being late," Juan Carlos apologized. "It took longer than I expected at the freight offices to free up a pallet mover to load it."

"Open the back, and let me look at it. I want to make sure everything is correct," said Katerina. He walked to the back of the truck with her and opened the doors. The pallet of material was centered in the enclosed cargo bay.

"Very good," Batalle confirmed. "I've found a place to park the truck not too far from here; why don't you follow me to the location, and we'll pull into the garage together." Juan Carlos nodded. They both returned to their vehicles, and Batalle drove about three miles to a mall with parking. He followed her closely.

Entering the oversized parking ramp, they parked on the third floor. Juan Carlos entered the passenger side of her car.

"The keys and the ticket, please," Batalle said. He handed over the keys with the parking garage ticket, and she used the key fob to ensure the truck's doors were locked. She put the keys and ticket in her pocket, pulled out three hundred dollar bills, and gave them to Juan Carlos, who smiled and nodded his thanks.

"I'll confirm the delivery; it should be tomorrow," she said. "Keep your phone charged, and I'll notify you. I'll pay you five hundred dollars for your work at the end of the day."

"I feel lucky to have met you," Juan Carlos smiled at her. "I was getting tired and hungry after my trip to San Francisco. Maybe this trip was a good decision after all." Batalle put on her sunglasses, exited the ramp, and peered ahead into the bright late morning sunshine as she drove toward downtown San Francisco.

# CHAPTER TWENTY

## Day 23, 2:30 a.m., New York

Abadai slowly stood next to his cot in the darkness of the homeless shelter. He heard the homeless snoring and coughing. A few were murmuring in their sleep. He picked up his bag and walked into the shelter bathroom. He set the bag on the sink counter and changed his clothes. Inside the bag, he had a dark-colored outfit of a loose-fitting, long-sleeve shirt, a pair of used jeans, a soft, lightweight jacket, socks, and black shoes. It had taken him two thrift stores to find the correct sizes.

He covered his head with a wide-brim black floppy hat and added a pair of thin black leather gloves to his jeans pocket. He had cash and IDs in a body wrap around his waist, underneath the "spare tire" body wrap he had been wearing since Costa Rica. He put the small packet of tools he had purchased the day before in his coat. Over the black clothes, he added a lighter-weight tan overcoat. He walked out of the shelter, trying to be as quiet as possible.

On the street, he searched for an empty cab at 3:00 a.m. in the cool, dark New York morning. After a few blocks, he found a sleeping driver, woke him up, and asked if the driver could take him to Brooklyn. The driver asked where in Brooklyn.

Abadai pulled out two hundred dollars and asked him if it was enough to ensure fewer questions.

The driver nodded, "Okay, we're off the clock. Two bills to take you anywhere in Brooklyn."

Abadai climbed into the cab and said, "I want to go to First Avenue, by the docks, around 38th Street."

The cab driver looked at him, "Are you sure? There's nothing down there at this time of night except warehouses and maybe a few dock workers. You could get stabbed down there."

"I'm sure," Abadai growled. "Let's go."

"No problem," said the driver, "but I'm dropping and running from that part of town. You'll need to find another way back."

After thirty-five minutes of navigating to 38th and First Avenue, Abadai instructed the cab driver to pull over. He gave him an extra hundred-dollar bill to forget the night and exited the cab. The street was poorly lit and vacant.

Abadai ditched the tan overcoat in the nearest dumpster and walked down the street, looking like a dark shadow on the pavement. The cloud cover was heavy, with only a little moonlight occasionally filtering through the heavy clouds.

Amir walked to the front door of Solvang Imports and punched "3601" into the keypad. The door unlocked, and within seconds, Abadai was off the street. He felt better inside the dark building, away from the unblinking eyes of security cameras.

He waited a minute for his eyes to adjust to the limited light, which allowed him to proceed down the short hallway without bumping into the walls. He could hear the soft murmur of the light wind outside and the occasional rattle of a loose sheet of corrugated steel on the roof.

Abadai reached the warehouse door. He listened. It was quiet. He pressed "3601" into the keypad. The click of the door lock was startling in the silent warehouse. He opened the door and stepped inside.

Inside the dark warehouse, Abadai saw the dark outlines of dozens of rugs, most wrapped in heavy paper, all in various states of unpacking or repacking. He breathed in the new wool rugs and the stale smell of Arabic tobacco, which brought back a long-ago memory of his uncle and mother. Pushing aside the old memories, he walked around the warehouse's perimeter and up to the almost six-foot pallet covered in black plastic. He removed the covering and stepped back.

The thirty-six bags of explosives were packed in an orderly manner on the pallet. Through the shrink wrap, Abadai could read the label identifying the bags as "Modeling Clay." He looked at the top of the pallet and smiled. He reached up and pulled off the bag containing two boxes of stereo components, carrying them over to a small workbench with a light. Turning on the light and adjusting his gloves, Abadai opened the shipping boxes and pulled out two Anthem stereo receivers.

Abadai set the two units on the bench and pulled out his tool kit. He flipped over the first receiver and removed the six screws attaching the top and sides of the case to the chassis. Flipping the unit back over, he removed the receiver housing. He found what he was looking for as he looked at the amplifier components.

A gold-colored case marked 'High Voltage, No User-Serviceable Parts' was attached to the motherboard with one-inch standoffs. The label showed a stick figure being zapped by touching a high-voltage wire. The box connected to the motherboard with a multi-conductor flat cable.

Abadai pulled out another screwdriver and deftly removed the box from its mounting. He then returned the case to the unit, sealed it, and set it aside. Repeating the same operation with the second unit, he retrieved a similar box from the second receiver and put it on the bench beside the first.

Abadai used his tool kit to remove the top from each small box. He found a small circuit board encased in black epoxy inside the first box. One side of the block contained three small wires in three different colors. An LED was encased on the other side. The other items in the box were a small lithium-ion battery, several short wires with clips, and a three-foot-long piece of almost invisible wire about the thickness of a human hair.

In the second box was a tiny cellular phone with a number attached to it and a small metal tube-like container with two red wires coming out of it. Abadai pulled out his phone and added the number to his contacts as "NY1." He put the small paper in his mouth and swallowed it.

Abadai picked up the cell phone and turned on the power to check the battery. The battery was fully charged, and the connection was good, even inside the warehouse. He turned the phone off. The phone was modified and had two wires coming out of it.

He found himself sweating in the cool warehouse. Picking up the three small components, Abadai walked over to the plastic explosives pallet and placed them on top. He looked at his watch and noted it was almost 4:00 a.m. He returned to the bench and moved a chair closer to the pallet. He scrambled to the top.

Once on top of the pallet, Abadai pulled out his small lock-blade knife and made about a two-foot cut in the plastic on the top of the pallet. Reaching under the plastic, he lifted out the first package of plastic explosives, a forty-pound bag. Enough to take out five armored tanks. Below the top layer was a gap in the bag stack, enabling a small "pocket" for the phone, battery, and box to sit. Abadai placed pieces of the trigger into the pocket. He cut a small opening in one package of plastic explosives and inserted the blasting cap into the material as far as his fingers could push it.

"Allah Akbar," Abadai muttered under his breath as he slid the lithium-ion battery into a small battery holder on the black block. The LED on the box began blinking yellow as the battery charged the large capacitor in the block. If this trigger had a faulty electrical component, connecting the block to the blasting cap could result in an unplanned explosion.

He was sweating as he connected the wires from the black epoxy block to the blasting cap. The connection went smoothly, and Abadai watched as the LED on top of the black epoxy block changed colors from yellow to green. He exhaled.

Abadai connected the three-foot-long ultrathin wire to the small white wire from the phone's case—an external antenna wire. He then connected the final two wires from the cell phone to the black block. He lifted the plastic wrap and pushed the fine wire under it, rendering it invisible.

To complete the preparation, he mumbled another prayer and pressed the power button on his phone. The phone lit up and acquired a signal, and nothing happened. Abadai let out his breath and moved the top block of plastic explosive over the components, sealing them in. He crawled slowly off the top of the pallet, feeling exhausted. Looking at his watch, it was 4:45 a.m.

Abadai departed Solvang Imports into the darkness. Over several blocks, parts of the shipping boxes were deposited in five street trash bins. He carried the two stereo receivers with him for almost a mile before finding an unlocked car where he could leave them. He found a taxi near a bus depot and had it drop him two blocks from the shelter.

## Day 23, 3:00 a.m., San Francisco

Batalle pulled alongside the parking garage in San Francisco and parked out of the line of sight of two security cameras on the side of the building. She walked up the steps and casually strolled over to the rental truck. Within thirty minutes, she had installed the cell phone-activated trigger into the plastic explosive inside the cargo truck. She left the truck in the parking garage and drove away in her rental car. Back at her hotel, she entered her room and removed her black coat, hat, and gloves. Picking up her phone, she sent an encrypted text to Abadai: *"Package has been prepared and is ready. 10:00 a.m. today."*

# CHAPTER TWENTY-ONE

**Day 23, 7:30 a.m., New York**

Mac Krieger and David Osrick stood outside Solvang Imports with ten FBI agents and five NYPD SWAT members when Mac signaled the team to "go." Several FBI agents took off at a trot, with weapons drawn, down an adjacent alley and around to the rear door and loading docks. The rear team leader gave a short verbal burst over the radio: they were in position.

"We're going in now," Mac said into his radio, nodding to the assembled team outside the building to approach the door and press the button. The only people in the building were Eliu Nasif and his warehouse supervisor, Walid. They were brewing a pot of strong Turkish coffee. Nasif heard the entry door buzzer and assumed some warehouse crew members were arriving a few minutes early.

Mac looked through the glass and saw Eliu Nasif walk to the door. Eliu looked outside at almost a dozen officers, including the FBI, Secret Service, and NYPD, all dressed for special operations and heavily armed. Wide-eyed, he nodded to the men outside and slowly raised his arms to be visible through the glass.

The FBI agents at the door indicated that Nasif should open the door and let them in. He slowly complied, and once the door was open, Eliu was pulled outside, searched for weapons, and held by Osrick against the wall.

"How many people are inside?" asked Osrick.

"It's only me and Walid, my warehouse supervisor," Nasif said. Osrick raised one finger to Krieger, who prodded the FBI team to enter the building.

The FBI agents entered the door and declared, "FBI!" A crash from the small break room was heard in response as Walid dropped the coffee carafe. He looked around the edge of the door, his eyes wide. The agents stormed through the front door and cleared the offices and break room. Walid was escorted outside to join his boss.

Mac and an FBI agent approached the warehouse door and tried to open it. It was locked. The agent lifted his rifle butt and prepared to break the glass separating the offices from the warehouse when Mac growled, "Hold up."

The agent stopped and waited. Mac yelled back toward the front door: "Ask them what the code is for the warehouse door." He heard a brief murmur at the front door.

An agent looked around the corner, "Try 3601."

The agent, who was about to bash in the door, reached up to the button access pad and pressed the buttons with a gloved hand. The door clicked open. The team entered the warehouse. It was dark inside. One agent walked over to the door near the loading dock. Before opening it, he spoke into his radio, "Opening the rear door."

"Roger." Came the reply.

The agent pushed open the door, and a bell rang somewhere inside the warehouse. Two agents, guns at the ready, entered through the open door.

Mac looked around for a light switch, found it, and turned it on. Light flooded the warehouse as the large sodium vapor lamps flickered high above. The rising dust from the open doors and the men's movement created a slight haze in the warehouse.

The warehouse was filled with rugs of every shape and color. Mac saw large steel warehouse racks impressively stacked with rolled rugs. Several pallets of materials were also on the floor and in the racks. The team spread out into the warehouse to search for possible bomb material.

Nasif and Walid were moved into the small conference room and told to sit at the table. David Osrick controlled their cell phones nearby. Nasif was reading the search warrant signed by a federal judge the evening before.

Two NYPD patrolmen guarded the front door outside the building, and others watched the back. A couple of patrol cars were in front of the building. Once the team was inside, they turned the patrol car light bars on. The NYPD set up a roadblock, blocking access to the area.

There were a few shouts inside the building before the SWAT team leader approached Mac and said, "We think we may have something." Together, they walked to a dark warehouse corner, where a material pallet sat quietly.

Mac looked at the pallet. It was eight layers high, or about six feet. In several languages, each package labeled the material "Modeling Clay." Mac pulled his camera out and snapped a picture of the pallet on his cell phone.

"Okay, guys, back away. Don't make radio or cell phone calls from this side of the street. I think this is what we're looking for," said Mac. "Let's clear the warehouse. Don't touch anything; get out of the building immediately. I'm calling in a bomb squad."

He walked back through the door leading into the office area, stopped at the break room, and asked Nasif if he had made any phone calls or sent any text messages this morning from the warehouse. Nasif shook his head to indicate he had not used his phone. Mac told Osrick and the other agents to exit the building. Nasif and Walid were handcuffed and led outside to a patrol car.

Stepping outside, Mac walked to the far side of the street. He dialed the Joint Task Force hotline to request an immediate response from a bomb squad and then asked the NYPD to clear buildings for two blocks in all directions. The federal agents and police moved away from the building as they waited for the bomb squad's arrival. Nasif and Walid, sitting in the squad car, were driven three blocks away from the building. Mac sent Andrea a photo of the material.

### Day 23, 8:25 a.m., New York

The NYPD bomb squad arrived at Solvang Imports and took one look at the pallet of material. The supervisor told Mac as he stood outside, "If it's a plastic explosive, you need to clear at least six blocks in all directions."

"When will you know if this is a plastic explosive?"

"I'll do a quick chemical test of the air and a small piece of the material on the pallet and see if we pick up specific chemicals," the sergeant said. "Should take about fifteen minutes."

"I'll wait for your results before we dislocate any more people," Mac decided. "If you can confirm, we'll move to get people out of the area."

Mac's phone rang, it was Andrea.

"Krieger." "Do you know if it's a plastic explosive?" She asked. "The director is asking everyone."

"I'll know in about fifteen minutes."

"Mac, I can't help thinking this isn't the same material pallet that landed in Texas and was headed for California. Do you think there are two threats, one on each coast?"

"I don't know, Andrea. Can you follow up with the trucking company to find out where the Texas material is?"

"On it," Andrea hung up the phone.

Ten minutes later, Mac was back on the phone with the director: "Yes, sir. The bomb squad says it is a plastic explosive. They backed away until we could clear a six-block radius. The NYPD is working on it now. We don't know if it has a trigger embedded, and we won't know until about 9:00 a.m. when the bomb techs get into it. I've spoken with the FBI, and they're on the way to pick up Pakerisami for an interview."

### Day 23, 8:45 a.m., New York

On the street, about eight blocks from Solvang Imports, a large Ryder truck sat behind a roadblock with several other delivery trucks and several dozen cars. Inside the Ryder truck, Donny McBride looked at all the police lights and activity and shook his head.

"Well, shit," Donny said, upset. "There goes my quick money." He didn't own a cell phone and couldn't reach Abadai. They'd agreed this morning that before he headed to the truck rental company, he would pick up the pallet of material and be at the address Abadai provided him by 1:00 p.m.

"I don't think I'll be there by one o'clock," Donny moaned in his slow, Georgia drawl. "I hope whoever signs for this delivery can take it late."

## Day 23, 8:30 a.m., Queens, New York

Helbol Pakerisami was cleaning up his breakfast dishes while listening to music by an Egyptian artist who recreated some classical Arabic music using mostly steel drums and a synthesizer to recreate the sounds of the Darbuka and Qanun. The music reminded him of home.

He heard a knock at his door, which startled him. He turned off the music and walked to the front door. Looking out, he saw two men in suits and sunglasses. He furrowed his brow and opened the door slowly.

"Y-Yes?" Pakerisami stuttered.

"Helbol Pakerisami?" The lead agent asked.

"Yes, I'm Pakerisami,"

The agent held his badge, "FBI, you're to come with us."

"What?"

"Mr. Pakerisami, we would like to interview you downtown. We've been permitted to arrest you if you resist. I hope you'll come with us." The FBI agent smiled and worked not to sound threatening all the time with his hand on his gun.

"We want to ask you some questions," the second agent said. "It shouldn't take too long, and we'll bring you back here when we're done."

Helbol considered his options. "If you can bring me back, how long will it take?"

"Just a couple of hours," the lead agent said. "Let me get a jacket," Pakerisami decided, "and I'll come with you."

The agents held open the door and observed Pakerisami pulling his jacket from the coat closet near the front door and collecting his keys and wallet from the nearby table.

"Did you leave any items turned on?" One of the agents asked. "Are there any animals in the house?" Pakerisami looked around.

"No, everything's turned off. I have a cat who can take care of herself. Let's go. I have things I need to do today."

## Day 23, 9:30 a.m., Sisters of Holy Grace Homeless Shelter, Brooklyn, New York

Today was Amir Abadai's last day in New York. His plans included limping toward the train station and catching a late morning train to Boston. He soon would begin his multi-country travel itinerary, eventually returning to Costa Rica. He planned to be well on his way to Boston before the bomb he had armed overnight went off in Manhattan.

As he exited the shelter and limped toward the small restaurant with the phone charging stations, he recalled his conversation with Jahar P'Shari ten days ago when they sat outside and ate dinner at Rancho Trevio.

*"Why the Federal Reserve Bank? There are many more targets in New York which would have a bigger impact,"* Amir said. *"We could hit the subway and cripple the travel arteries. We could have mass casualties if we hit a stadium during an athletic event. We could even go after the Statue of Liberty if we wanted."* Jahar smiled and lifted his wine glass. Amir added a few ounces of the cabernet they were drinking. *"We've discussed this,"* Jahar's choice of words implied he and Gamir Halibid, chairman of SAIB, had discussed the targets.

*"Removing this volume of gold and cash from the world market, even if the United States can recover the gold and replace the cash, impacts the value of all other secure depositories worldwide and increases the demand for available currency. Due to the US currency market disruption, I expect the demand for our banking services to increase to double. That's the first reason."* Jahar paused, sipped his wine, and continued, *"The dollar, pound, euro, and yen control almost eighty percent of the world's international trade transactions. These central banks hold deposits backing their currencies in circulation. One little shake to the historical stability will cause trillions of dollars to move to other currencies worldwide. People will move money if they think its value will be more secure. That's reason number two.*

*"The final reason is that the location is critical to the technology infrastructure in New York City. The buried fiber optic lines below the building will shut down the New York Stock Exchange for days, maybe weeks. The subway lines below the street will be impacted for months. New York's Wall Street will never be the same. This is the right target."*

*"That's brilliant,"* Abadai recalled telling Jahar as he limped down the sunny street in Queens. He opened his phone and sent an encrypted message to Batalle, typing: *"10:00 a.m. local time."* He recalled the contact labeled "NY1" on his phone to ensure he had the phone number ready to send. He closed the phone, put it back in his jacket, and continued slowly limping toward the train station.

# CHAPTER TWENTY-TWO

### Day 23, 10:00 a.m., FBI Offices, New York

Pakerisami sat quietly in an empty, gray interrogation room in the FBI office in downtown Manhattan. His coffee was cold. He wasn't handcuffed to the table. The room was locked, and he was sure he was being watched through the one-way glass as he sat alone. Unbeknownst to Pakerisami, the FBI teams waited for several Joint Task Force members, primarily Mac Krieger and John 'JR' Riccardi, to return to the Manhattan office before beginning an interrogation.

Pakerisami fidgeted with his fingers. He cleaned his nails and looked for anything to occupy his time while waiting for someone to enter the room. Looking at his watch, he decided he would give them thirty minutes more before he would demand to be released. Taking a deep breath, he looked at his shoes for the ninth or tenth time since the FBI agents brought him into the interrogation room. He drank the tasteless coffee given to him when he arrived. He quietly cursed his indecision to leave New York.

### Day 23, 10:05 a.m., FBI Offices, New York

A buzzer sounded, and the door to the interrogation room clicked. The door opened, and Mac Krieger walked in wearing black tactical cargo slacks and a long-sleeved black shirt. Over the shirt, he wore a light jacket in dark blue with bold white letters across the back spelling out 'US SECRET SERVICE.' Mac was accompanied by FBI agent John Riccardi, who was dressed similarly but with an FBI windbreaker. Both men briskly walked toward Pakerisami and sat across from him.

"Mr. Pakerisami, I'm Mac Krieger from the Secret Service, and this is Agent Riccardi from the FBI. Do you remember talking to me several years ago?" Pakerisami looked at Mac and tilted his head slightly as he focused on the man.

He nodded slowly, "Yes, Agent Krieger, I remember talking to you, but it was long ago."

"About five years ago, I interviewed you in New York as part of a case we worked on. We talked about a contact of yours named Amir Abadai, whom you identified as a potential terrorist."

When Abadai's name was mentioned, Pakerisami looked away and became more nervous. Krieger glanced at Riccardi to see if he had noticed. "I don't know Amir Abadai," Pakerisami said as he shifted in his chair.

"Mr. Pakerisami, your name came up this morning when we interviewed Mr. Eliu Nasif. Do you know Mr. Nasif?"

"Yes, I know Mr. Nasif," Pakerisami brightened, "he attends the same mosque as I do."

"And you know he owns an import business," Mac led Pakerisami forward.

"Yes, he owns a business importing rugs from North Africa. I've visited him at his business once or twice."

"We found a pallet of material at his business this morning," Mac was leaning toward him, "and he identified you as owning this material. What can you tell me about this material?"

Pakerisami took a moment to consider his options. He looked from Krieger to Riccardi, lowered his eyes, took a deep breath, and decided he needed to try to save himself.

"The pallet of material isn't mine; it belongs to Amir Abadai. He contacted me a week or more ago and told me he needed me to arrange for an importer to accept a shipment. I contacted my friend Mr. Nasif, and he agreed to receive the shipment at the docks and bring it to his warehouse." Krieger and Riccardi listened.

Mac asked, "Do you know what the material is?"

"Abadai told me it's sculpture clay. I assumed Abadai was using my contacts to get some business done. I help people get things done. I usually don't ask too many questions."

"Why did Abadai bring it into New York?" Mac asked.

"I don't know why he imported a shipment of clay to New York, but he can be persuasive when he surprises you and asks you to do something for him. I hadn't seen him for many years, but then I saw him praying next to me in the mosque. It was quite a surprise."

Mac asked, "What do you know of this modeling clay? Do you know where it comes from? Are there any other details?"

"No, I don't know where it comes from or anything about it other than it's heavy and needs a truck to pick it up. Abadai asked me if Nasif had a truck to move it. I said he did. But then Abadai decided to hire a truck to move the material. As far as I know, the material is still in Nasif's warehouse and hasn't been picked up yet."

"How does Abadai contact you?" Mac took the interrogation in a different direction.

"He calls my mobile phone. Usually, it's a number I don't recognize. Sometimes, he sends messages to me using a common messaging app. Many community members use these messaging apps because they don't like the idea of the government spying on them." Looking up from his hands at the two agents, Helbol added, "No offense."

"None was taken," Mac said. "So this pallet of modeling clay, would you be surprised to learn the material is plastic explosive? Not only that, but enough plastic explosive to destroy a square block of downtown New York?"

Pakerisami's eyes widened at the news, and he gasped for a breath. Catching his breath, he sputtered, "Abadai had two boxes delivered to my home. The boxes came from a stereo shop in Vietnam. They were a little heavy. He asked me to deliver them to the warehouse and put them on the pallet. I did it yesterday."

"We know, we were following you yesterday." Pakerisami leaned back in his chair and ran his hands across the thin hair on the top of his head. He looked at the ceiling. "I swear, I didn't know the material was dangerous. I would never have agreed to help him. I have no idea what he was planning to do with it."

"I seem to remember from the first time we talked that you were willing to accept certain illegal activities, but you don't agree with terrorism or the death of innocents. Sound familiar?" Mac was throwing Pakerisami a lifeline and was curious about how he would react.

Pakerisami almost jumped out of his chair. "Yes, Yes! This is right. I disagree with terrorism, and I don't want to be associated with terrorism!"

"Well, Mr. Pakerisami," Krieger glared at him, "it seems you're guilty of 'aiding and abetting' a terrorist. You're looking at many years in prison for what you've done to help Amir Abadai."

Helbol cupped his face in his hands and sat with his elbows on the table before him. "I didn't know! I didn't know!" Helbol whimpered. "He asked for my help, and that's what I do. I helped him." He looked at Krieger and Riccardi and blurted out: "What can I do? How can I fix this?"

Krieger and Riccardi looked at each other. JR growled, "Help us find Amir Abadai."

"I don't know where he is," Helbol leaned back in his chair dejectedly, "I don't even know if he is still in New York. The last time I saw him, he looked like he was living on the street."

"When did you see him last?" Mac probed.

"Near the Jamaica train station, in Queens. He was begging for money with homeless people by the train station."

"When was this meeting?" Mac's face turned hard and serious.

"I don't know, five or six days ago." Pakerisami looked at Mac. "It wasn't much of a meeting. He told me to expect some packages and asked if the freight shipment had arrived."

"Anything else? Did he tell you anything else?" Mac asked.

"No, nothing else," Pakerisami said.

"Did you know one of my agents was killed in the bus station across the street that same night?"

"No! Oh no! I'm sorry, but I had no involvement in any killing." Pakerisami blurted.

Krieger and Riccardi looked at each other. Riccardi growled at Pakerisami again, "If we find out you had prior knowledge of a plot to kill a government agent. I'll see to it personally that you go away for life."

"I didn't know anything!" Pakerisami begged. "I'm a simple man; I'm not a threat to anyone."

Mac softened his tone slightly. "Helbol, even if you are simply a middleman, if you can't help us, we can't help you."

Helbol's face brightened. He looked at Mac, "Do you know where the woman is?"

"Woman?" Mac looked at Pakerisami and over to Riccardi.

"What woman?" Pakerisami sat back in his chair and looked at the two men.

"There is a woman who is working with Abadai. What will you do for me if I tell you about her?"

"It depends upon what you tell us," Mac warned. "Helping stop a terrorist organization from blowing up a city could help you with federal prosecutors."

"I need something in writing from your government prosecutors to provide me immunity from any charges I may face related to Amir Abadai." Pakerisami played his hand.

Agent Riccardi snorted, "You've no chance at any immunity in this case, you sick dog. You helped bring a weapon of mass destruction into New York City."

Pakerisami took a deep breath and found a little backbone. He shot back at the agent from the FBI. "I helped import what I believed was modeling clay. I had no idea it was anything other than modeling clay. Both of you," he looked over at the one-way window, "and your cameras captured my surprise when I learned it was a plastic explosive. I know what Abadai told me. He is the real terrorist you want to catch. Maybe I can help you catch Abadai or the woman. I don't know. But I do know I need immunity if I help you."

Agent Riccardi inhaled deeply, getting ready to launch into Pakerisami when Mac reached over and touched his arm. "Mr. Pakerisami, please excuse Agent Riccardi and me for a few minutes. We need to step outside."

## Day 23, 10:30 a.m., FBI Offices, New York

With Riccardi still glaring at Pakerisami, Krieger signaled for the door to be opened. As they stepped outside and closed the door, Krieger looked at Riccardi and said, "You know he's within his rights to ask for immunity if he can help us. Our case against him is circumstantial unless there is some evidence he ordered the materials to be shipped to New York.

"All we've now is his name and address on the shipping manifest of the materials from Vietnam. He doesn't know anything about the boxes or Tarik's death. I would speculate we won't find anything on Pakerisami other than acting as a middleman for Abadai."

"Little twerp," muttered Riccardi. "The little twerp pisses me off. We trailed him to the importer's warehouse carrying the two boxes. Nasif corroborates that he was there yesterday, looked at the pallet, and put the boxes on top of the pallet. He admits to meeting with and helping a suspected terrorist named Amir Abadai. He should go away for a long time."

"I agree with you, JR," Mac said, "but we also want to catch Abadai and whoever is the money behind this. From what we can prove, Pakerisami is a logistics flunky. If he can help us find the other shipment in California, give us another name of a terrorist, or even help us find Abadai, it could save innocent lives.

Let's contact DC and let them discuss this with the US Attorney General's office. I'll tell Pakerisami we're considering his request." Mac looked at John to see if he agreed with the suggestion; after a moment, Riccardi nodded and apologized.

"Sorry, I came on too strong in there; I agree; let's keep the bigger picture in mind. This guy is not the mastermind."

"I'm glad you agree, JR. Let's meet back here in twenty minutes." Mac approached the interrogation door as Riccardi turned and walked down the hall to find the first available phone. Mac walked into the interrogation room and advised Helbol Pakerisami that they were considering his request.

"Do you want anything to eat or drink? This could take an hour or more."

"I don't know if Abadai is still in the US, but I want to help you find him," Pakerisami sounded sincere. "Yes, I'll take something while I'm waiting."

"I'll see what I can do," Mac said, leaving the room.

## Day 23, 10:45 a.m., New York

The air in the borough of Queens was warm, and the skies were sunny as Abadai limped toward the train station. Dressed in his thrift shop clothes with a short, graying beard and hair in disarray, he looked the part of the homeless street dweller. People would see him coming and avert their eyes, hoping not to be approached for a few dollars. He carried a backpack over one shoulder. He had pulled it out of a trash bin almost a week ago. His gaze was cast downward to avoid cameras, and he continued at a pace fast enough to move through a block every ninety seconds.

Near 30th Avenue and Vernon Boulevard, Abadai stopped at a small park opening up to the East River. Along with dog walkers and a few runners in the late morning hour, he was another homeless person limping toward a bench. He stopped, sat down, and put his backpack on the bench. Lifting his view, he looked toward the river with Roosevelt Island in the middle. Across the river was the skyline of Manhattan.

The view was impressive. Abadai knew the address he had given Donny to drive the truck, but from this vantage point, he was unsure if he could see the buildings that wouldn't be standing once the explosion happened. He envisioned the dust cloud rising from the blast and wondered how high and expansive the cloud would be. He smiled.

Abadai looked at his watch and picked up his backpack. He needed to keep moving, so he limped at his improvised pace, returning to the main road. On 21st Street, he headed south toward the Long Island Railroad train station. The train to Boston would take him out of Queens and away from New York before the blast shut down the city. Limping slowly down the street, he stopped suddenly and was bumped into by a man behind him. The man moved away from Abadai.

Abadai stopped because Donny was directly in front of him and coming toward him on the sidewalk. Donny's hands were in his pockets. He appeared sad and somewhat lost. Abadai crossed between several people to step in front of him. Donny jumped backward when his path was suddenly blocked.

"Oh," Donny's face changed, "it's you!"

"What are you doing here?" Abadai whispered, "You should be in a truck on your delivery run!"

"I was," Donny drawled. "I picked up the truck and drove to the import company address. I saw police everywhere when I got there. They had everything blocked off. I didn't get within six blocks of the building." Abadai pulled Donny from the sidewalk's center toward the building they were standing alongside.

"Tell me again," he said, holding him tightly. "What happened?"

"I rented the truck," Donny was defensive. "I have the paperwork here if you want to see it." He handed the rental paperwork to Abadai. "I was in the warehouse district before 9:00 a.m., but I was stopped by a police roadblock about six blocks from the warehouse. The police told me it would be closed most of the day and suggested I return tomorrow. I don't own a cell phone and couldn't reach you for additional instructions. I waited to see if the road would open. I returned the truck a few minutes ago. I walked back to the shelter to find you."

Abadai thought and looked up and down the street. "Did the police question you?"

"No, an officer told me and the other drivers waiting for their loads to leave the area," Donny sounded more than a little upset. He'd have to spend another night in New York.

"Could you see anything from where you were stopped? Any idea what was causing the traffic delay?" Abadai relaxed his grip.

"I did see a truck marked 'Bomb Unit' go past me and into the area. After waiting over two hours and the police continually telling the drivers to leave the area, I thought I better get out. I'm sorry the delivery will be delayed. What do you want to do? We can try again tomorrow. Do you want your money back?"

"Give me a moment, Donny," Abadai looked concerned. "Give me a minute to think. Why don't you wait for me outside the truck rental office?"

"Yes, sir," Donny said. He turned around and began walking back in the other direction.

Abadai's heart was racing. He waited for Donny to get a few feet up the street away from him before pulling out his cell phone. Checking for messages, he found none. He dialed the number for Pakerisami. The phone rang several times and went unanswered. He opened his encrypted messaging app and typed a message to Pakerisami: "*Are you okay?*"

### Day 23, 11:06 a.m., New York

Pakerisami was sitting by himself in the interview room when his phone rang. He pulled the phone out of his pocket and looked at the incoming call. He knew it was Abadai. Looking around, He tried to remain calm, but his fingers shook as he pressed the button to ignore the call. A few seconds later, his phone chirped. This time, it was a message from Abadai: "*Are you okay?*" Pakerisami didn't respond to the message. He didn't want to do anything to incriminate him in Abadai's actions.

### Day 23, 11:08 a.m., New York

Abadai needed to think clearly about the situation and his next steps. If Pakerisami were in police custody, he would probably immediately rat on him. Abadai decided it was no use waiting. He opened his phone and found the number for "NY1." He pressed the call button and looked south along the river, expecting to see a rising cloud or even hear an explosion. He heard nothing, so he pressed the call button again.

Looking up from the phone, he saw Donny standing outside the truck rental office, looking the other way. He took off his light coat and tossed it into the nearest trash can. Abadai tied his shoes tighter. He snapped the phone in half with his hands and pulled out the knife he had used to kill the Secret Service Agent a few days before. Leaning down near the street's curb, he casually flipped the phone, the knife, and the rental paperwork into the stormwater drain, hearing the blade and the phone chassis clank several feet below street level.

Abadai stood and started running. He was thirty feet past Donny when he heard Donny say, "Hey!"

## Day 23, 11:12 a.m., New York

Abadai was two blocks away and still running in a dead sprint when Donny lost sight of him. Donny's mouth was agape as he watched the man he knew as an older man with a limp run like a Georgia Bulldog running back.

Donny reached into his pocket and pulled out the money Abadai had given him. He looked again at where Abadai had disappeared. Stuffing the money into his pocket, Donny decided that catching a bus back to Georgia was his priority. He started walking toward the bus terminal.

# CHAPTER TWENTY-THREE

### Day 23, 11:15 a.m., New York

Mac stood outside the interview room when his phone chirped. Opening it, he found a text from Andrea: *Mac, please call me.* Mac was waiting for Agent Riccardi to return from his call to the FBI director. Not seeing Riccardi, Mac decided to call Andrea. She picked up on the first ring.

"Mac! Thanks for calling."

"I've only a minute." Mac was quick to reply.

"Okay, first, the plastic explosive is a chemical match to the trace amounts we found in the Texas warehouse," said Andrea.

"Thanks, Andrea; that connection will help with the Attorney General."

"One more thing, Mac, our tracking on the pallet from Texas shows it was delivered to an Oakland warehouse and picked up yesterday by a man driving a rental truck. It's not the same shipment."

Krieger's phone beeped. He looked at it and said, "Andrea, Abadai figured out we got the explosive and tried to detonate it. The bomb squad texted me to tell me it received a call a few minutes ago. Had we not found the bomb, it would have exploded here in New York!"

"Oh my God, Mac, we don't know when the bomb in California is going to be detonated, but if it's been picked up, we should assume it's been armed!"

"Andrea, I've got to go. I need to talk with the director. We need to get the teams in San Francisco looking for a rental truck and warn the city."

Mac hung up the phone and called Fitzgerald, updating him on the latest news and verifying the second threat on the West Coast. He dialed the Joint Task Force number and started a barrage of calls to FBI and Secret Service offices on the West Coast.

Riccardi returned with a thumbs-up signal. The Attorney General's office had agreed to immunity for Pakerisami if he could help them capture Abadai or prevent a bombing in the US.

"What are the strings?" Mac asked.

"Just that he fully works with us, and his cooperation leads to the arrest

126

of Abadai and any accomplices," Riccardi said. "It's a good deal."

"And if he helps, but it doesn't lead to an arrest?"

"The AG reserves the right to charge him for aiding and abetting a terrorist activity and whatever else they can come up with," Riccardi smiled at Mac.

Mac flexed his facial muscles as he set his jaw. "That sounds good to me. Let's go talk to Pakerisami."

## Day 23, 11:25 a.m., New York

Abadai was two blocks from the train station and still running hard. He blew past a traffic cop directing traffic.

"Hey! Stop!" The cop called out to the man in baggy clothes, running what looked to be a personal marathon. Abadai raced through the intersection in long strides, dodging cars and people. The cop blew her whistle, but she didn't step in the man's direction, knowing she couldn't catch him on her best day. After running another block, Amir slowed down and looked back to see if anyone was chasing him.

He began walking to cool down. Still wearing his backpack, he sweated profusely. He needed to be calm when he entered the train station, so he breathed deeply and slowly walked toward it, less than a block away.

Abadai noted the time on the giant clock inside the Long Island Railroad station. It was mounted above the sign pointing to the train platforms above and the subway platforms below. *Thirty minutes*, he thought, *cutting it close*. He headed toward the restrooms halfway down the building toward the clock. Walking into the bathroom, he moved to the farthest empty stall against a wall and closed the door.

After removing his backpack and setting it down, he breathed in the cool air and finished the water. He removed his dirty pants, sweat-soaked shirt, and fake bodysuit. He opened the stall door and looked out. He walked to the sink, wearing his undershorts, and turned the water on. Wetting several paper towels, he wiped down his face, chest, arms, and legs with the makeshift sponge bath.

Walking to his backpack, he returned with a battery-operated beard trimmer and removed all but a mustache and a soul patch below his lower lip. Holding his hair, he began cutting at it, reducing the overall length from almost six inches to two inches.

Pulling clothes out of the backpack, he dressed. He wore a light blue shirt, dark chocolate pants, and leather slip-on shoes. He unfolded a dark blue lightweight wool jacket and put it on. Last but not least, he put on a pair of round-framed eyeglasses.

When Abadai walked out of the restroom, it was 12:15 p.m. He stopped at several waste baskets and dropped in everything he was carrying.

Stopping at a traveler's kiosk, he made his selections and approached the cashier with a small leather valise and a paperback book. It was 12:25 p.m. He headed for the ticket counter at a fast pace.

"I'd like a ticket to Boston on the 1:00 p.m. train." Abadai smiled at the woman behind the ticker counter.

Glancing at the man and checking the time on her computer, she said, "You'll have to run to catch the train. Do you have any luggage?"

He lifted his newly purchased valise and said, "It's a quick trip for me." He raised his other hand, holding his credit card and ID.

"Thank you, Mr. Tolenz." The agent looked at his ID. She ran the charge through Abadai's credit card, which matched the Roberto Tolenz from Queens ID he had given her. The charge was approved. Ticket in hand, Abadai headed toward the train platform ten minutes before the train departed.

Passing through security, he found the platform almost empty. The other passengers had already boarded. The train car where he was assigned general seating was three or four train cars away. With a final check of his ticket by the agent hollering, "All Aboard, for Boston!" Abadai boarded at 12:55 p.m. The doors closed. The train began the slow departure from the station.

## Day 23, 9:55 a.m., San Francisco

Juan Carlos was driving the cargo truck to the address Katerina provided. He was instructed to drive it to 101 Market Street and park it in the parking garage at the address close to the street side. But this was downtown San Francisco, with many parking garages. He began circling several blocks near the address.

Many buildings were in the downtown Embarcadero area, including several massive skyscrapers. He looked at his watch. He needed to catch up to his scheduled delivery time. A bead of sweat broke out on his face. Traffic was heavy; people were in their usual hurry to get from one place to the next. Everyone was willing to step into the street in front of him. "Worse than San Salvador," he hollered out loud.

## Day 23, 9:56 a.m., San Francisco

Twenty miles south at San Francisco International Airport, Batalle was boarding her flight for Mexico City. The flight was running twenty minutes late, and Batalle was determined to get into the air and away from San Francisco before the Federal Aviation Administration shut down the air routes in the US.

Katerina expected a federal response if bombings occurred at the same time on both coasts. She looked at her watch and thought, *It's almost 1:00 p.m. in New York, and Abadai's explosion should happen soon.* She pulled out her cell phone and keyed in the number of the phone detonator in the rental truck. Katerina's finger hesitated over the call button, and she hit cancel as the line to board the plane moved forward.

She boarded and was settling into her seat when the pilot's announcement came through:

*"Ladies and Gentlemen, this is your captain speaking. We're expecting a quick loading and departure to Mexico City. If everyone could please find their seat and settle as soon as possible, we want to roll back from the gate to make our departure window. Currently, we have a couple of planes in front of us. I'll try to make up time in the air to get you to Mexico City on schedule."*

Batalle looked out the window. She saw nothing but the plane at the gate next to her. "Come on, come on," she said quietly but urgently. The passenger next to her glanced over, indicating he had heard her. He folded down his reading material. She closed her eyes and took a deep breath. Her cheeks puffed out as she exhaled.

"Nervous flyer?" the man asked, slowly lowering his papers into his lap. He looked with kind eyes toward the tall young lady with purple hair, a black leather jacket, torn jeans, and noticeable tattoos sitting next to him.

"Oh nah," Batalle said in her best valley girl accent, "I want to get moving, and could somebody turn on the air conditioning?" She spun the purple hair of the wig in her finger as she drew out the vowels and looked up at the man.

The passenger beside her smiled politely. "I think we'll be in the air soon." After the interchange, he picked up his papers and adjusted his glasses to return to reading. She picked up her phone and checked the screen. She didn't find any messages from Abadai, which didn't give her a good feeling.

## Day 23, 10:01 a.m., San Francisco

Juan Carlos was making his second circle of the address in downtown San Francisco when he saw a car pull into a parking garage. He pulled in behind the car and looked at the entrance to the parking garage, trying to estimate if the cargo truck would fit into the garage. He rolled forward as the car in front of him entered. He opened his door, stepped a few steps away, and looked at the truck's height versus the entrance's. It didn't look like it would fit. While Juan Carlos looked, a young man emerged from the booth inside.

"Oh man, I'm glad you stopped." The young man said excitedly. "The last guy who tried to pull a cargo truck as big as this into the garage got stuck."

"This is where I was told to drive it."

The young man looked at him and said, "It won't fit in the garage. It's too tall. You'll have to take it somewhere else."

"Where else?" Juan Carlos looked confused, "Where could I park?"

"Why don't you go down the street? It's less than a block." The young attendant pointed in a direction. "The name of the lot is 'Joe's Parking.' It's a small lot with surface parking. They don't have any height restrictions."

"Just down the street?" Juan Carlos asked.

"Yes, I'll help you back up and point you in the right direction. It's down the street between the Bank of America and Fed buildings. There are usually parking spots available."

The attendant helped Juan Carlos reverse the truck and turn it around. He stepped out into traffic, holding his hand to allow the truck to enter the street. Juan Carlos waved to the attendant as he turned onto the street. He looked at his watch. It was 10:05 a.m., and he was late.

## Day 23, 10:05 a.m., San Francisco

Katerina Batalle's plane was next in line for the departure. Sitting by the window, she watched the plane before her go through last-minute flight surface checks as the jet engines accelerated. The pilots released the brakes, and the big plane started lumbering forward. She watched the jet engines flare with the boost of fuel. Simultaneously, she heard the engines on her plane accelerate and urge the heavy jet forward. She pulled out her phone, planning on triggering the bomb as soon as the plane had cleared the ground.

A flight attendant walking past her seat saw her phone and admonished, "Please make sure your phone is in airplane mode."

Katerina watched the attendant continue to the forward galley and take a jump seat. The attendant pulled on a seatbelt and chatted with the other attendants. Katerina scowled and slid her phone to the side of her seat, out of view of anyone, including the flight attendant. The plane lined up on the runway. She could feel the engines accelerating and fighting against the braked wheels. The pilot released the brakes, and everyone on the plane felt the giant aircraft lunge forward down the runway.

Looking out the window, she watched the wings respond to the slight unevenness on the runway as the wing tips bobbed up and down with every lump in the pavement. The plane's speed increased, and the wings lifted into the air. She looked out the window and watched the ground fall away, and then the runway ended, and the bay began. Katerina waited until the plane had turned west over San Francisco Bay before she reached for her phone. Keeping her phone alongside her leg, she entered the ten digits she had memorized a day before. Then she pressed the call button.

# CHAPTER TWENTY-FOUR

## Day 23, 10:18 a.m., San Francisco

Juan Carlos stopped at the entrance to Joe's Parking. He was talking to the parking attendant and asking about a place to park when they both heard a faint chirp. It lasted one-tenth of a second. The truck, with its pallet containing over 1,200 pounds of Pakistani-made plastic explosive, instantly turned into millions of sharp pieces of scrap metal moving in every direction at several thousand miles per hour.

The explosion's shock wave collapsed the lungs of anyone standing along the street within three blocks who didn't have a wall or other immovable object in front of them. Chunks of concrete and metal landed seven to ten blocks away, damaging cars, buildings, and homes and taking many lives as they landed.

Cars near the blast were flattened against buildings before they crumbled. Many cars became gas-fueled fire starters, creating hundreds of fires and adding to the noise, dust, and smoke. At ground zero, a hole measured over one hundred feet across descended deep into the ground as if creating a path to hell itself. The demon hole sparked, smoked, and steamed. Screams could be heard far below in the destroyed subway platforms.

The dust cloud rose to over ten thousand feet and expanded outward. The dust was carried by the sea breezes coming onshore from the west, and the cloud began to move slowly east over San Francisco Bay. It kept rising as it moved toward the docks and downtown area of Oakland. As the cloud lifted, the heavier particles fell, covering the city's heart in fine, concrete dust. Smoke from fires followed almost instantly at the explosion site, turning the gray cloud of caustic dust into a gray and black cloud of death.

The explosion in downtown San Francisco leveled every earthquake-proof building within a three-block area, including dozens of businesses, restaurants, and over two hundred condominiums. The Hyatt and Four Seasons hotels, as well as over two dozen smaller hotels, were destroyed. The San Francisco Ferry Building and the surrounding docks along

131

Embarcadero appeared to submerge halfway into the bay.

Most of the San Francisco Federal Bank building was an unrecognizable stone and twisted steel pile. The headquarters of Pacific Gas and Electric and the One Market Center building, home to Bank of America, were ninety percent destroyed. Over fifty tech startups' headquarters were in the surrounding buildings, and almost all suffered catastrophic damage. The Google building and the Salesforce building, nearly three blocks from the blast, were severely damaged.

Five primary subway lines were linked below the street at the point of detonation, from thirty feet to almost fifty feet below the street level. The explosion collapsed the subsurface infrastructure onto two trains, one departing Embarcadero Station and another slowing as it reached the station. Electrical, water, and wastewater lines were severed instantly. The power, lights, water, and almost everything stopped in downtown San Francisco at 10:18 a.m. Juan Carlos, the parking attendant, and nearly fifty other people in the immediate area would never be positively identified.

## Day 23, 10:19 a.m., San Francisco

Katerina looked out the window near her seat on the aircraft's right side. She saw little as the plane banked. Her view was to the north. San Francisco was visible out the other side of the aircraft. Passengers on the other side of the aisle began murmuring as they looked out their windows toward downtown.

As the plane pulled out of the turn, she looked across the plane to the far side windows and saw a vast, dark cloud of smoke and dust rising from ground level.

The aircraft moved west and away from San Francisco, effortlessly flying over the Golden Gate Bridge before turning south over the vast Pacific Ocean. Batalle calculated that the plane would be over Mexico in an hour and headed south toward Mexico City. She sat back in her chair amid the noise and chaos engulfing the plane's passengers and put on her headphones. She began listening to her Valley Girl playlist. She wanted to be vaguely recalled as a twenty-something without a care.

Passengers across the plane started asking questions, and several pressed their buttons to call the flight attendants. More people were turning in their seats to see out the windows toward downtown San Francisco. The dust and smoke clouds grew more prominent over the downtown area. The flight attendants asked several people, who stood in their seats to gain a better view, to please sit down and put their seat belts back on.

One minute later, the pilot came on the public address system:

*"Ladies and Gentlemen, many of you on the aircraft's left side can see the dust and smoke over downtown San Francisco. At this time, we don't*

*know what has caused it."* There was a brief pause when the pilot, unknown to the passengers, responded to a San Francisco Air Traffic Control request.

Moments later, the pilot came back on:

*"Ladies and Gentlemen, per the new regulations put in by the FAA after 9-11, we're not allowed to leave US airspace at the moment. The tower has put us into a holding pattern circling the city of San Francisco at about thirty miles. We don't know how long we'll be in this holding pattern before continuing our flight to Mexico City; however, we may need to return to San Francisco and refuel if we're close to our fuel safety margins for our trip."*

The pilot continued,

*"Ladies and Gentlemen, the FAA has asked us to return to San Francisco and land. They'll take a while to fit us into the landing order. We'll ask all of you to remain seated with your seatbelts fastened. If you need assistance, please press the button, and one of our flight attendants will approach you. I'll let you know more when I have more information."*

The pilot's voice went quiet, and the entire plane was silent. Then, as if someone had signaled "go," the passengers erupted into an instantaneous cacophony of voices, some loud and others quiet. Hundreds of questions were asked at once without expecting an answer but feeling they needed to say something to anyone. Everyone suddenly felt small and vulnerable.

Batalle's eyes were closed, and she was rolling her head in time to the music. She had heard every word the pilot spoke. With effort, she kept her eyes closed and bobbed her head to the music, even as she felt her hands clench and stomach tighten. *Return to the airport? New FAA rules after 9-11? I'm going to need a new plan*, Katerina mused to herself. The last thought stuck in her mind. *A new plan!*

She stopped bobbing her head, opened her eyes, and looked up at the people on the plane, who were talking to one another or no one. Slowly, she removed her headphones and looked around again.

Katerina looked at the man sitting beside her and waited until his eyes returned to hers before asking, "So, is something wrong?"

"You must have missed the pilot's announcement," the man smiled at her. "We're going back to San Francisco. Something happened, but we don't know what. The pilot mentioned we'll be landing in thirty minutes or so."

"Well, I gotta pee," said the purple-haired terrorist, unbuckling her seat belt unceremoniously and standing. She stepped across the man's legs next to her before he could even move his papers, and she was in the aisle of the plane and walking toward the restrooms in the back of the aircraft.

The man tried to say, "They said to stay in your seat..." His voice trailed off, and the girl was gone before he could finish the sentence.

Walking back to the restrooms, Katerina pretended she didn't hear the flight attendant say, 'Please return to your seat!' With her long strides, she was to the restroom and into it. The door locked before the flight attendant could repeat her admonishment.

Within moments, Katerina heard a knock on the lavatory door, and the flight attendant scolded, "Miss, we need you to return to your seat. We'll be landing soon."

"I had to go," she said through the door. "I'll be out in a minute."

"Please hurry." The flight attendant hurried off to talk with another anxious flyer who had pushed the call button. Batalle looked at herself in the mirror and held tightly onto the sink. Taking a deep breath, she worked to control the slight shaking she saw in her hands. *Relax, girl*, she thought as she looked at the woman in the mirror. *You've had many close calls. You'll be fine.*

## Day 23, 1:40 p.m., New York

Mac stood outside the interview room checking his phone for an email from the Justice Department when it rang in his hand. He looked at the Washington, DC number and answered immediately.

"Mac Krieger."

"Mac, this is Robert," began Director Fitzgerald.

"Are you near a television?"

"No, sir, we're interrogating Helbol Pakerisami. I'm in the FBI office."

"Find a TV, Mac," Fitzgerald was uncharacteristically quiet. "San Francisco has been bombed."

Mac's jaw dropped, "Do you think it's the truckload out of Texas?"

"It's the only possible shipment we're aware of."

"I'm on my way to find a TV," Mac began walking toward some office cubicles. "Sir?"

"Yes, Mac?" "We need to ground everything, all types of transport," Mac said. "Abadai is on the run. His plan in New York was disrupted, and we had a chance to catch him. If San Francisco is linked to Abadai, we must stop all travel to catch these people."

"The FAA has halted all flights. Outbound flights will return to departure airports, and all inbound flights will land. All other air traffic has been stopped," Fitzgerald said calmly. "Now, I don't know about trains or buses. I'll talk to the joint chiefs. We've got a meeting in ten minutes."

"Thank you, sir. We must throw a net now. We can't wait. This is likely related to the other bombings around the world."

"I'll talk with you in thirty minutes after I meet with the joint chiefs and the president." Fitzgerald ended the call.

Mac walked a few more paces, looking for a TV. He reversed course and headed toward the Joint Task Force bullpen, a large conference room in the middle of the building. Inside the conference room, he found twenty people standing in front of a large television display. CNN was broadcasting from the rooftop of a building a couple of miles east of downtown San Francisco, showing images of the destruction and death.

When Mac entered, the room was silent. The harried reporter on camera was covered in dust, her usual perfectly coiffed hair was messy, and her voice cracked as she tried to describe the damage to her city.

"I don't have words for the destruction," she said as the camera panned to the bomb blast area. "Everything is gone: buildings, people, cars, everything." Her voice started breaking, "Who would do something like this? All these innocent people were going about their day. The children... "

She stopped as the camera panned the scene. She attempted to regain her composure before continuing. "We've emergency services coming into the area for the dead and wounded, and I see San Francisco utility trucks turning off gas, water, and electricity. There are dozens of fires in every direction and not enough fire trucks for all of them." She started coughing, and the studio cut back to the main newsroom. Two noticeably worried-looking news commentators took over the dialog.

Mac turned away and cleared his throat, "Ahem, folks, if I could have your attention, I spoke with Director Fitzgerald before he walked into a joint chiefs briefing with the president. The next few hours will be critical for all of us. We need to catch the people responsible, wherever they may be. We need to start by catching Amir Abadai."

## Day 23, 1:50 p.m., Somewhere between New York and Boston

Abadai was resting from his run across New York's Brooklyn borough. His head was resting against his seat. His eyes were closed, and his heart rate had slowed to a resting pulse. In his quiet state, he felt, rather than heard, the train coupling suddenly reverse as the engineer applied the brakes. The slowing momentum was almost unnoticeable, but it was there.

Opening his eyes, he rolled his head forward and looked out the window. Seeing trees and open fields, it seemed odd that a nonstop train would begin slowing this far from Boston. He glanced at his watch and looked around at the other passengers.

A voice broke through the silence on the sound system:

*"Ladies and Gentlemen, we've been asked by traffic control to stop the train and to stand by for further instructions. You'll note that we're slowing down now. Currently, we're about sixty miles from Boston. There will be no services where we stop, and all passengers will remain on the train. We'll provide additional information when possible. I appreciate your patience."*

A service attendant entered the car. Abadai stood and leaned toward the man.

"Can you tell me what's happening?"

"I know little, sir. We've not been briefed yet." The young male attendant, maybe twenty-two years old, looked at Abadai. "It's all over social media, in any case. People are saying there's been a bombing in San Francisco. Maybe this is related."

"I don't have a social media account," Abadai said. He wanted more information, "Can you tell me what happened in San Francisco?"

"I'm sorry, but I've got to walk through the next six cars to ensure everyone is seated and no one fell when we started slowing. I'd suggest you ask one of your neighbors."

Abadai sat back down and waited. He knew several other passengers in the car had overheard the attendant's comments. Phones were popping up all over the vehicle. People began gasping, and more than one person exclaimed, "Oh my god! Did you see this?"

Abadai glanced at a phone displayed between two passengers and saw the dust and smoke cloud enveloping central San Francisco. *Katerina was successful.* He thought.

Ten minutes later, the train stopped. A few houses were visible in the distance. They were on the outskirts of New Haven, approximately five miles from the nearest station. Abadai was restless. He expected some form of communication from the public address system and looked for another attendant.

The PA system came alive, and a voice carried clearly over the system: *"Ladies and Gentlemen, We're told of an explosion in San Francisco about an hour ago, and it's believed to be the work of terrorists. If you were old enough to remember September 11, 2001, when terrorists attacked the Twin Towers of the World Trade Center, you may understand what is happening now. All air flights, all buses, and all trains have been requested to stop and return all passengers to their departing destination."*

An overall gasp could be heard in the train car where Abadai sat. The speaker continued: *"This is a change in our procedures implemented at the request of the 9-11 Commission to protect the population and assist authorities in finding and capturing the terrorists. I'm sorry, but we'll be returning to New York shortly. Your travel will be rebooked when it is authorized. At this time, we don't have a timeline."*

The gasp on board the train became a groan as travel plans for hundreds of travelers were disrupted. Abadai's gut tightened up as his pulse began to quicken. He knew by now that he was probably on the radar of more than one US law enforcement agency. He guessed he was the prime suspect in the failed bombing attempt in New York.

# CHAPTER TWENTY-FIVE

## Day 23, 11:05 a.m., San Francisco International Airport

The direct flight from San Francisco to Mexico City stayed in San Francisco airspace during the first hour of its flight time. Air controllers, following the new protocols, put all flights in the air into holding patterns. Batalle's plane was scheduled to remain in the holding pattern for the next hour.

Katerina's brain triggered question after question: *What happens when we land? Will everyone be subject to interrogation? Will I even be stopped? How will I get out of the airport? Where will I go? How do I get to Mexico? Do I have another set of identification? What have I used in San Francisco? What do I have that's new?*

Batalle, the girl with the purple hair and headphones on, played the millennial girl without a care in the world. Sitting beside her, the professorial-looking older man tried to make small talk, but she ignored him and appeared to anyone around her as someone lost in her world. She let the music droning in her headphones block conversations as she considered her options.

## Day 23, 2:15 p.m., New York

Mac bustled out of the interview room, cell phone to his ear. "David? I met with Pakerisami. He told us Abadai was living on the streets or maybe in homeless shelters. Abadai had long hair and a beard when Pakerisami saw him five days ago. Can you please get the NYPD and maybe the FBI to run around the best picture of Abadai with a beard and see if we get something?"

Mac hung up the phone. He dialed Andrea's office in DC and got her voicemail. "Andrea, this is Mac. Pakerisami has confirmed that Abadai was working with a female. This person may be responsible for San Francisco. Pakerisami didn't have a name or any other details about the woman. It's not much to go on, but can you run with it and see what you can find?"

Mac ended the call and turned as Riccardi exited the interview room.

"JR, what do you think?" Mac nodded toward the door.

"I think he's an Egyptian scumbag who moved to the US to be a scumbag here." Riccardi's voice growled. "I'd like to see him in prison if you want my opinion."

"I'm with you," Mac agreed. "I've asked Osrick to connect with your team and NYPD to see if we can track down where Abadai stayed in New York."

Mac's phone pinged. It was a text message from David Osrick: "*NSA pinged on a visual ID for Abadai in New York. Call me!*"

"Riccardi! Join me for a call in your office. David Osrick has been working with the NSA to try to locate Abadai. He's got something!"

They hurried to Riccardi's office. Mac speed-dialed David on his cell phone and turned on the speaker.

"Mac!" David said.

"David, I'm here with agent Riccardi. Please go ahead."

"The NSA computers pinged on a man likely to be Abadai at two locations. One was caught on a traffic camera in New York as he ran across the street, and a second was taken at the Long Island Train Station as he boarded a train bound for Boston at 1:00 p.m. today.

"The running photo was a little blurry but showed a pretty wild-looking man dressed like a homeless person. In the second photo, he had changed his looks before getting onto the train. He removed his beard and cut his hair. In both photos, his eyes and nose both flagged above eighty-five percent. The one from the train is pretty clear, and he looks like Abadai."

Riccardi and Mac looked at each other. "David, can you please text me the photos? I want to confirm them with Pakerisami." Mac asked.

"I'm sending them now." Mac could hear David's keyboard clicking.

Riccardi broke in next, "Great work, David. Do you know the train number for the 1:00 p.m. train to Boston?"

"I used to take it all the time to visit an old girlfriend in Boston," he said. "It's Amtrak 431. It leaves at 1:00 p.m. and arrives at 3:30 p.m."

"Amtrak 431," repeated Riccardi. He looked at Mac and said, "I'll take this." Mac nodded. Riccardi ran down the hall as Mac thanked David.

Mac's phone pinged again, and he looked at it. The message contained the photos from Osrick. He enlarged the pictures to see the face with the overlaid biometric measurements from the NSA computers. The first one was grainy and had a low resolution but was visible, while the second photo was clear and crisp.

Mac walked back into the interview room. Pakerisami looked up when Mac entered. "Mr. Pakerisami," Mac looked at his phone. "Can you please look at a couple of photographs and see if the person in them is Amir Abadai?"

"Yes, I'll look." Helbol wiped his hands on a napkin before touching the phone. "This one is difficult to make out." Pakerisami looked at the running image. "But I recognize the shirt he's wearing. I saw it on him at the mosque. I think it's him."

"How about the second image?" Mac scrolled the image on the phone to show a more precise face-on shot of a well-dressed and coiffed man. Helbol studied the image.

"He's good at disguises, I see." Helbol looked again at the picture and zoomed into his eyes. "Yes, this is Abadai. It's hard to forget his eyes."

"Thanks for confirming." Mac grabbed the phone and turned to leave.

"Are you going to catch him?" Pakerisami asked.

"I've no doubt," Mac said as he left the room, letting the door slam shut.

## Day 23, 2:45 p.m., Washington, DC

The Washington headquarters for the Secret Service was in a flurry. Every agent was pulled from vacation and was in the office or already tasked and running. The bomb found in New York and the devastating explosion in San Francisco put everyone on high alert. The Secret Service covered all valuable assets in and around the DC area.

The president and half the cabinet were aboard Air Force One, cruising 40,000 feet above North Dakota, about 5,000 feet above commercial altitudes. But then again, most commercial aircraft in the sky are not accompanied by F-15s ready for a fight. The other half of the cabinet and most of the Senate were on their way to Raven Rock Mountain Complex in Pennsylvania, an underground city designed to withstand a nuclear attack.

Andrea called Daniel Whitefeather, her colleague at the NSA. A native Florida Seminole with a Ph.D. in computer science, Whitefeather was known for tracking digital signatures using specially designed HPE Cray computers in Fort Meade. His powerful algorithms were used to classify billions of images, texts, and spoken words daily. Andrea left a voicemail. *"Daniel, this is Andrea Douglas-Pfeiffer from the Secret Service. We have a lead on a possible suspect in the San Francisco bombing. There is no name or image, but I need your help to look for patterns in the data to see if we can track her down. Daniel, I don't know anyone else who could do this; please call me back. Thanks."* She hung up the phone, a little discouraged by the lack of anything she had to work with or share with Daniel.

Less than two minutes later, Daniel called back."Hello, Andrea. I'm returning your call. What can I do for you?" Daniel said.

"Thanks for calling me back," Andrea said brightly. "As I said in my message, we have a lead that the perpetrator of the San Francisco bombing is a female. We've no description and no details with which to work.

Frankly, I need a little help."

"Tell me a little more," Daniel encouraged. "I need some ideas on how we can proceed with this."

"Well, we have a male perp identified for an attempted bombing in New York. According to a source, this man is working with a woman who may also be the terrorist responsible for the San Francisco bombing. We've identified a shipment of what is now known as a plastic explosive that matches the chemical makeup of the plastic explosive found in New York.

"The shipment of this material arrived in Texas and was transported overland to California. We think this could be the material used for the bomb in San Francisco. It stands to reason this terrorist probably has been in California more than once in the last year, maybe more than once in the last month."

"Wait, wait," Daniel muttered, "thanks for allowing me to think through this problem. We believe this person isn't a resident of California and may not be a homegrown terrorist, right? Why is that?"

Andrea looked up from her phone, pushing her glasses to consider the question. She said, "We know the man in New York is Egyptian in heritage and travels globally. We don't know where he calls home, but we believe he traveled here recently. His burner phone has a Costa Rican area code and number, but that may not mean anything.

"I guess I'm assuming his colleague in San Francisco is also a globe-trotting terrorist and not someone he employed at the last minute to execute one of the largest terrorist attacks in history."

"Okay, hold on as I write down some thoughts." Daniel let the silence build for almost two minutes, and Andrea finally couldn't stand it any longer.

"Are you still there, Daniel?" "Yes, yes, I'm here," Daniel sounded distracted. "I've got some ideas on how to program the computers to track her down. First, let's assume she flew into California from somewhere and has come several times to set up this event. If I program the computer to look at arrivals and departure images from all the major airports in California and reduce the timing to a month or two…"

Daniel was silent momentarily, then began again. "If we can eliminate obvious male characteristics such as male pattern baldness, beards or estimated weights, or perhaps even dress characteristics, we may be down to a usable comparison table the computer can scan." He faded away again as he worked through the coding process to get the massively large computer systems to do this one crucial task. "Okay, Andrea, I'm looking for facial recognition matches through California airports with immigration control. I want anyone who has flown into or out of San Francisco at least twice in the last thirty days. I'll find all the matches for females and run them through the passport and immigration database to match faces to names.

"My director has prioritized whatever is needed to support a terrorist manhunt or help locate survivors. This should be up and running in less than an hour. Give me a little time, and I should be able to give you an estimate of how long it will take to get through the full thirty days."

"Daniel, you're a treasure! I appreciate your help!" Andrea's voice was emphatic.

"Can you tell it to my wife and five kids? Seriously, I get no respect at home." Daniel joked.

"Anytime," Andrea said with sincerity. "Talk to you soon, I hope."

Andrea put down her phone after the call and texted Mac to let him know the NSA was helping in the hunt for the mysterious woman in California.

## Day 23, 3:00 p.m., New York

Viewers tuning into CNN's fourth hour of live coverage of the bombing in San Francisco were startled when the anchor broke into a live report from San Francisco with the following information: *"Ladies and Gentlemen, we've new information coming out of Turkmenistan of all places. Here, a group we've never heard of before, the "Turkmenistan Freedom Fighters," has taken credit for the bombing in San Francisco. CNN received an email from this organization in the last fifteen minutes. "The US Embassy in Ashgabat couldn't confirm the organization's existence. We were told we must talk to the State Department in Washington. We've sent a request to the Turkmenistan government for a comment but have not received a response. Again, here is the late-breaking news..."*

The announcer droned on to repeat the breaking news. News organizations worldwide would repeat the report for the next twelve hours.

# CHAPTER TWENTY-SIX

### Day 23, 3:30 p.m., New York

Mac Krieger and John Riccardi boarded the helicopter at the top of the FBI building in New York and headed northeast toward Boston. Almost fifty miles away and twenty minutes by flight was Amtrak 431. The train sat still on the tracks about five miles outside of Milford, Connecticut, as the Amtrak rail controllers reversed trains coming out of New York on the busy Northeast Rail Corridor. The train had been sitting still for the past seventy minutes but was beginning to reverse direction slowly. The train was destined back to Long Island Station.

Krieger, Riccardi, and five FBI Special Operations team members were headed on an intercept route with the train. Amir Abadai's photo had been shared with the train's rail service team. They confirmed he was currently on board the train in car number twenty-one. It was agreed the train would slow to almost a stop through Stamford, Connecticut, where the FBI team would jump onto the train. The Amtrak team onboard was told to stay clear of the man and to call the FBI if he made any attempts to leave the train.

### Day 23, 3:45 p.m., Milford, Connecticut

After sitting for over an hour listening to the other passengers' updates on the bombing and the near-relentless details shared through the public address system about the upcoming reversal of the train back to New York, Amir Abadai could no longer stand it. Picking up his valise, he casually walked to the car's rear and entered the handicap-accessible bathroom.

Abadai's options were limited. If he tried to leave the train through the doors, alarms would sound, and the emergency stop would be triggered. Without triggering any alarms, the best exit would be through a window. The two bathrooms at the end of the car were side by side, and the larger wheelchair-accessible bathroom contained a small window about six feet off the floor and about eighteen inches wide by twelve inches tall. The window wasn't intended for ventilation but to add natural light to the small room.

Abadai removed his coat and ran some water in the sink while he waited for the train to begin the trek back toward New York. As the train started moving, he dipped his coat into the sink, allowing it to soak up some water. Removing the coat and turning off the sink, he reached down and triggered the toilet flush. He immediately placed his coat on the glass and forcefully punched his fist through it.

Abadai waited momentarily to see if anyone heard the noise of the glass shattering over the sound of the water rushing into the toilet tank. There were no immediate inquiries at the door. He used his coat to protect his hands as he removed the remaining glass shards from the window and tossed them out into the light breeze blowing in through the now-open window. He placed his coat over the edge of the window frame and pulled himself up to look out.

Bringing his head back inside the small compartment, he grabbed his valise and tossed it out the window. Abadai was hanging by his hands outside the train a few moments later. He looked down at the ground, which was beginning to move under him faster. Looking up, he saw a brush pile fast approaching. He coiled his feet under him and launched himself off the side of the car. He landed tucked into a roll, stopping behind the brush pile.

Once the train had passed, he brushed the dirt from his clothes. He began his hike back to where he had thrown his valise. Picking it up, he walked the tracks south toward the Saugatuck River and the village of Westport. As he approached the bridge crossing the river, he looked across and saw a small bar on the riverfront. The building was almost under the I-95 turnpike. Thinking it may be an excellent place to pick up a ride somewhere, Abadai trekked along the tracks and was pleased to find an easily accessible bike path across the bridge.

## Day 23, 4:20 p.m., Stamford, Connecticut

As the New York-bound train slowed to less than five miles per hour rolling through the small train station at Stamford, Connecticut, three of the FBI special operations team members scrambled aboard car number eighteen. A few moments later, the other two, along with agents Krieger and Riccardi, scrambled aboard car number twenty-three. The teams radioed each other and immediately began moving toward each other with weapons drawn and pictures of Abadai at the ready. They reached car number twenty-one, the target car.

The agents burst through each end of the passenger car simultaneously and received wild looks and muffled screams from the passengers. Many were shaken at the exposed firearms and attempted to hide in their seats.

"FBI, FBI!" The agents hollered, brandishing their badges for all to see.

"We're looking for this man," Krieger said to a young lady who looked uncomfortable in her seat. Have you seen him? Please look at the picture!"

"He sat over there." She pointed toward a seat about two rows away from her.

"He's in the bathroom!" yelled a teenager who saw the picture Mac was showing. "I saw him go in, but the dude hasn't come out yet!" The two teams converged on the toilet. Not waiting for a command, the leader of the Special Operations team nodded, and the team member nearest the door slammed it hard with the butt of his rifle. The door flew open.

The first commando dropped to his knee, and the second covered the toilet area with his AR-15.

"There's no one here, and the window's been broken," reported the first commando. Krieger and Riccardi approached the bathroom.

"Let me in there; I need to look." Mac elbowed his way inside. The FBI team cleared out of the way and took up positions at both ends of the car. Mac stepped into the small restroom and looked at the open window. "Could he have made it out through the small window?" He looked at Riccardi, who looked in the doorway.

"I couldn't do it," Riccardi quipped, "but I'm not as young as I used to be." He turned to the people nearest the toilet. "Who of you saw this man go into the toilet?" He held out the picture of Abadai. Three people all raised their hands.

"How long ago?"

"He went in there about fifteen minutes ago," said the teenager with a green tattoo on his face and wearing a black hoodie. "I knocked on the door a few minutes ago because I needed to use the bathroom, but he didn't answer. He never came out."

Mac looked at Riccardi. "We've missed him. But he can't be far away. Let's get off this train and track him down."

Riccardi shook his head. "I'm going to have the teams search the entire train first. I want to make sure we know he's not on this train. I'll call in a search for Stamford, Westport, and Norwalk and get an APB to local police and sheriff's teams. Maybe we can find him since he's on foot."

## Day 23, 4:30 p.m., Westport, Connecticut

Abadai brushed the dirt from his clothes again as he approached the Black Duck Bar and Grill on the shore of the Saugatuck River. The place was hopping on a late afternoon, filling the parking lots. About two dozen semi-trucks with trailers were in the most distant parking lot, with closer lots filled with cars and pickup trucks.

Country music blared from inside the building, changing the volume

Amir could hear as he approached whenever the door opened. He walked into the bar from the parking lot and stepped aside to allow his eyes to adjust. The bar inside was busy, and most booths were packed. The large, U-shaped bar had two busy bartenders.

Abadai looked at the bar and found an empty seat next to an older man wearing a "Peterbilt" cap. The man had a month's growth of gray-brown beard and wore a blue and white checkered western shirt covering a gray t-shirt. He sat beside the man and waited for the bartender to stop by for an order.

"What would you like?" The bartender leaned over the bar towards Abadai.

"Sam Adams for me and whatever this gentleman wants," Abadai gave a friendly gesture toward the man in the ball cap.

"What? Wait a minute, who are you?" The man was surprised.

"No offense, sir; I wanted to offer to buy a drink for one of the men who keep this country running."

"That's nice of you, but I must get on the road in a few minutes. I've had my meal and a beer. I'm good." The old trucker said.

"I respect that." Abadai turned to the bartender and amended his request, "Can you please get my friend here a glass of water when you bring me my beer?"

The bartender nodded.

Abadai turned to the truck driver and asked, "Where's home?"

"Georgia," the driver said warily, "Peachtree City, Georgia."

Abadai smiled, "I've been to Georgia, but never Peachtree. Is it near Atlanta?"

"Just south of Atlanta, almost a suburb." The trucker watched as the bartender brought him his water.

"Where are you headed now?" Abadai asked.

"Baltimore is the last stop. I'll get back to Peachtree and take a few days off." The trucker said, slowly warming up to Abadai.

"I'm from Miami, and I'm headed back that way. I've got a problem, though." Abadai left the sentence hanging.

"What sort of problem?"

"I need a ride," Abadai confessed. "I have a funeral to attend for my grandmother in Miami in three days. The government shut down commercial travel. I walked over here from the train station. I needed a few minutes to work up the courage to call my mother in Miami and tell her I'll have to miss the funeral."

"This disaster in San Francisco is terrible, and I hope they catch the bastards responsible. It's no wonder the government has shut public transportation down. Sorry to hear that." The trucker's words were sincere.

"Would you consider letting me ride to Baltimore or even Atlanta with you?" Abadai asked. "I could pay my way. If you're open to that, I'll buy your meals or help pay for fuel."

"I don't know." The truck driver drawled slowly, "Company policy and all that."

"I hoped you were the company and you made the policy," Abadai said, sounding disappointed. "Maybe I missed my guess."

The trucker thoughtfully lifted the water glass to his lips and took a long drink. As he put the water down and wiped the droplets from his beard, he said, "Well, I'm the owner, and I make the rules. I'll let you ride with me to Atlanta, and you can buy the meals. Once we get to Atlanta, I'll drop you at a truck stop to pick up another rig going south to Miami. Many trucks are running to Florida. Finding a ride won't be difficult."

"Deal," Abadai smiled and offered his hand. "Let me get your check and some takeout to go, and we can leave whenever you're ready. By the way, what's your name?"

"Bob is the name, Bob Gray." The driver shook his hand. "We'll get to Atlanta late tomorrow; it's about sixteen hours away. The trailer drop-off and pickup in Baltimore should be pretty quick. It's at the same location."

"I'm Franchesco Altuna," Abadai lied easily, "but my friends call me Freddy. A pleasure to meet you."

"Nice to meet you, Freddy. Get your food, and I'll meet you outside in ten minutes. Make sure you hit the head before we leave. I don't care to make many bathroom stops."

"I hear you," Abadai confirmed, reaching for a takeout menu. "No bathroom stops between here and Baltimore."

## Day 23, 12:15 p.m., San Francisco International Airport

Katerina Batalle was determined to be one of the first off the plane. She carried a small bag with two outfits and a makeup kit. When the plane finally rolled to a stop and was fully depressurized, the door was opened. She walked up the ramp. She was disappointed to learn she would have to pass through immigration and passport control to exit the airport.

After departing the plane, she took almost seven minutes to reach the immigration and passport control area. There, she walked directly to an available passport control agent.

"Good evening, what was your flight number?" the passport control agent said, rambling his standard greeting.

"The one to Mexico City, American Airlines," Batalle mumbled as she looked for her travel documents. She was traveling under the name Micca Rhodan; in her cover, she was the daughter of California tech parents. "We turned around, I guess. I don't know the flight number. Do you need it?" She spoke in her best valley-girl-with-the-purple-hair voice. It was a combination of boredom, impatience, and bother.

"It's been a long day for everyone, Miss... Rhodan," The agent looked at her passport and swiped it. "You'll be on your way soon."

"It's awful that someone would do something like this terrorist thing."

"Yes, it is, young lady." The agent said while waiting for her passport to clear. "We should be done here in a moment. I'm waiting for the passport reader to register."

"Anything wrong?" she feigned concern.

"I don't think so," mumbled the agent. "The readers have been a little slow all afternoon. We're lucky the explosion didn't remove our fiber optic link."

"I suppose that would be bad." She stared at a wall, looking bored out of her mind.

"Okay, there we go, Miss Rhodan. You're cleared to go," the immigration control agent said, happy to see her leave. He added, "Good luck completing your trip."

"Thank you. I guess I'll find a way back to Cupertino." The agent nodded slightly at her departure and looked up for his next passenger.

# CHAPTER TWENTY-SEVEN

### Day 23, 9:15 p.m., NSA Headquarters, Fort Meade, Maryland

Daniel Whitefeather took off his glasses and rubbed his eyes. It had been a long day. A few hours earlier, when his wife saw the news about San Francisco, she knew she might not see him for days and texted him to remind him to take his blood pressure medicine. He stood at his raised desk with six monitors surrounding him. Three of the monitors analyzed the performance of the supercomputers as the system processed millions of video images. The other three monitors ran Daniel's queries to locate a specific female bombing suspect using the world's largest database of video, audio, and written information.

The facial recognition algorithm Daniel helped develop for several years isolated individuals' faces in the video and saved pictures of each individual. A tiny bit of code that Daniel liked to call the DNA of the image was added to the digital image file that was saved. This code carried the original file name, camera location, individual biometric data, and date and time details. The supercomputer stored the images from the video in a vast database and a copy of the DNA data in another. When asked about the process, Daniel smiled and said his ancestors were good at tracking their prey.

The most crucial part of the search process was knowing what to exclude. A successful query didn't take weeks or months to provide tangible results. Daniel looked at his watch: 9:25 p.m. Time to refill his coffee mug.

### Day 24, 2:30 a.m., Fayetteville, North Carolina

Abadai's ten-hour drive with the Bob Gray was quiet and uneventful, with sparse conversation. When Gray refueled at the truck stop in Fayetteville, North Carolina, Abadai remained behind to pick up another ride. He went inside to get something to eat at the small restaurant. While nursing his coffee and waiting for the blue plate special, he overheard a brief news report from the small TV behind the counter.

*"The FBI informed the media moments ago. They are looking for two persons of interest related to the bombing in San Francisco. One of these people, a man from Egypt, is believed to be on the East Coast, looking to exit the country. If you see this man, he's considered armed and dangerous, and you should not approach him. Instead, call the FBI at the following number..."*

Abadai tried to look at his cup of coffee. He knew he needed to remain calm and not react or draw attention to himself. He felt exposed. He picked up the spoon to stir his coffee and noticed his hand was trembling. He put the spoon down and slowly turned in his seat, preparing to leave, when the waitress slid his meal toward him. At about the same time, a large, bearded, hairy man sat in the chair beside him.

"Hey dude, is this seat taken?" The mountain of a man asked Abadai in a low, calm voice. The voice was much smoother in vocal tenor than expected from such a large person.

"Ah, yeah, it's available. Please have a seat." Abadai moved his coffee and reached across the counter to slide the plate of meatloaf, mashed potatoes, and green beans with a little brown bread roll under his chin. He picked up his fork. Looking at Abadai's plate, the large man exclaimed,

"Oh, man, that looks good!" The man looked up at the waitress who was approaching. "Hey, ma'am, can I get me one of these plates and a cold Coors Light with a glass of water?" She nodded and turned toward the kitchen, writing on her small pad.

The man stood with his long legs on either side of the stool. He shucked off his jacket and laid it over an empty adjacent stool. He was big, at least six and a half feet tall, and wide enough to block the overhead light above Abadai when he stood. Hair poured out from under his hat. Abadai judged him to be maybe two hundred and fifty pounds or more. The man's massive shoulders and muscled arms stretched his shirt to the maximum.

"You driving?" Abadai asked, taking advantage of ten hours of light conversation and learning the correct language for truck stops from a veteran driver. The man took a long sip from the beer on the counter. He looked over the glass and down at the average-sized man sitting beside him. The large man continued drinking, and when he had finished the beer, he slowly put the glass on the counter.

He cleared his throat and said quietly, "Yep, I'm headed to Atlanta for a drop-off in the middle of the night. I'll head south to Orlando after the drop. Why do you ask?"

"I'm hitching rides to Miami," Abadai said casually. "I started in DC, and I'm working my way south."

"Interesting way to travel," the large man said, shifting his stool. "I'll bet you wind up in some out-of-the-way places at all hours... like this place." A smile crossed his face as he emphasized the last few words. His steaming plate of hot food arrived.

"Yes," Abadai confirmed, "this isn't as big as other truck stops, but it's busy."

"So tell me. Why are you traveling south now? What's your story?" Sensing an opportunity for another ride to get him closer to his destination, Abadai's mind thought fast. "I was in New York for the past few weeks," he began, "and the job opportunity didn't work out for me. After three weeks, I was getting tired of New York. I was ready to head south where people seem to be more welcoming."

"Well, I can understand not wanting to stick around the big city," the big man said. "What was your job opportunity?"

"I'm a civil engineer specializing in bridge inspections," Abadai easily lied, "I was offered a job with the New York Roads and Bridges Authority. I took the job and came up to start work. But the job was less than I was promised. Less pay, less responsibility. Although I'm a bridge specialist, they wanted me to start in traffic analysis, something I did years ago. So, after two weeks, I was done. I'm heading back to Miami to set up my consulting company."

Abadai thought it sounded like a convincing story. He hoped the big man sitting next to him would agree.

"Well, that's a better story than I was expecting. Where did you go to school?"

"Miami, my parents emigrated from Egypt to Miami before I was born. I grew up there and went to university."

"Ah," the man smiled, "I thought, with that accent, you were born outside the USA." The big man swallowed a mouthful of meatloaf. "The University of Miami is pretty good; I've always liked watching the Dolphins play football."

"They usually put together a pretty good team," Abadai said hastily.

"They do. By the way, the name here is Jake, Jake Tapper. I'm taking off in about twenty minutes. You can hitch a ride with me if you want to. I can have you in Orlando by 10:00 a.m. You can catch some sleep as I drive if you want. I mostly do short runs. The sleeper doesn't get much use. It may be dusty, but you're welcome to use it."

"That sounds great to me," Abadai smiled. "I could use some sleep. I hope you let me pick up your meal." He reached for Jake's bill on the counter.

"That sounds fair," Jake said, picking up his coat and hat. "I'm going to take a quick shower and call my wife. How about I meet you here in fifteen to twenty minutes?"

Abadai smiled and nodded his head, "I'll be here." Jake gathered his coat and walked purposefully toward the driver's shower area.

Abadai watched him go and put a couple of bills on the counter to cover the cost of his meal and Jake's. He walked over to the newspaper rack, opened the paper to the sports section, and found a story about a new coach for the Miami Dolphins. The new coach was a Miami native who, fifteen years before, had been a quarterback for the University of Miami Hurricanes.

Abadai shook his head slowly and looked around. He put the newspaper back into the bin. He thought: *Either Mr. Tapper baited me on the 'Dolphins' comment, or it was a mistake. Either way, it's best to leave immediately.*

He picked up his bag and walked out the door, heading toward two trucks refueling. A few minutes later, he climbed into one of them. The driver climbed into the truck and rolled out of the truck stop. The truck entered the highway, heading south.

Standing inside the truck stop, Jake Tapper held his cell phone to his ear and repeated his location to the FBI call center.

## Day 24, 3:00 a.m., New York FBI Offices

John Riccardi was exhausted and sleeping on a foldout cot in a spare conference room when his cell phone rang, waking him up.

"Riccardi."

"Agent Riccardi, this is Savanna from the DC call center. I've received a call from a man in Fayetteville, North Carolina, who thinks he met your search target, Amir Abadai. Would you like to hear the recording?"

"I most certainly would," Riccardi was suddenly awake as he rolled upright on the cot's edge.

"One moment, please," Savanna calmly spoke into the phone, "recording is beginning now."

The noise on the line changed slightly, and Riccardi knew the recording was playing. Savanna's voice came on the line, *"FBI, how can I help you?"*

The man on the other end cleared his throat and began in his smooth, baritone voice, *"Yes, hello. My name is Jake Tapper, and I'm calling from the East Gate Truck Stop at the intersection of I-95 and Highway 13 in Fayetteville, North Carolina. I'm a truck driver, and I think I may have met a man you're looking to capture..."*

Riccardi listened intently to the recording and the exchange between Savanna and Jake as she gathered his details. Once he had Tapper's phone number, he hung up, stuck his head out of the conference room door, and hollered toward a couple of agents working overnight in the office. Riccardi was putting his shirt back on when the agents entered the room.

"I think we may have a hit on Abadai in North Carolina." Said Riccardi. "Let's get to a conference room where I can call the man who reported the contact. Jensen, call logistics and get us on the next plane to Charlotte. Baker, call the Charlotte office and get them to send four agents to this location. Then, contact the Fayetteville PD to ask for their help."

Two minutes later, Riccardi and four other agents gathered around a speaker phone as Riccardi dialed the number for Jake Tapper.

"Hello, this is Jake," came the quick response when Tapper picked up the phone.

"Hello, Mr. Tapper. My name is John Riccardi. I'm the supervisory special agent for the New York office of the FBI. I heard your report to our call center, and I hoped you'd have a couple of minutes to talk directly to me."

"Yes, of course," Jake was calm. "Please go ahead."

"Is the man you met still in the building?"

"I'm unsure; I can't see him from my location. I told him I was showering and calling my wife and would reconnect with him in twenty minutes. I have another six or seven minutes before I need to meet him again."

"Can you give me a description?" Riccardi continued.

"Dark hair, a dark complexion, and a noticeable accent. Thirty-five to maybe forty, and solidly built. He's about six feet tall. He seemed quite intelligent and was comfortable telling lies to me. He looked for a ride to Florida, Miami specifically."

"How do you know he was telling lies?"

"He told me he was from Miami and had gone to university. But when I mentioned the university's sports team as the Dolphins, he didn't correct me."

"Should have known it was the Hurricanes," Riccardi admired. "Smooth trip up."

"I served in Iraq with the 82nd Airborne," Tapper said. "After three years of interrogating Kurds and Iraqis, I think I can tell when I'm being told a story. This guy is smooth. But he assumed I was another truck-driving hick."

"Jake, I'm sending you a picture of the man on your cell phone. Please review it and let me know if it's the same guy."

"Okay, I'm receiving the picture now..." narrated Jake into the phone, "Interesting, that's a lot of hair. It's shorter now, more normal. But, yes, it looks like the guy I was talking to."

"Okay, Jake," Riccardi instructed, "whatever you do, don't let him in your truck. He's dangerous. We've four agents on their way to your location. I think the earliest they can be there is around an hour. Can you wait?"

"Sure, but what do I tell him if he's still waiting for me?"

"Find any good reason you can to justify the delay. Don't let him get in your truck. If he's not there when you go back out, give me a call. Please wait for the agents to show up and answer their questions. We will take it from there. We appreciate your help, Jake."

## Day 24, 3:10 a.m., Fayetteville, North Carolina

Tapper hung up the pay phone, stepped into the restroom, washed his face, and combed his hair and beard. He dried his hands and walked back into the restaurant. He looked around for Abadai. Not seeing him, Tapper checked inside the building and stepped outside. He returned, checked the restrooms, and looked throughout the retail area. Abadai wasn't to be found. Tapper pulled out his phone and pressed the 'callback' button for Riccardi's phone.

# CHAPTER TWENTY-EIGHT

**Day 24, 7:00 a.m., New York**

In his apartment, Mac listened to the news, most of it detailing the rising death toll in San Francisco. At the end of the update, Mac leaned forward when the newscaster announced the nationwide search for Abadai:

*"Federal authorities, specifically the FBI, are searching for this man, recently in New York, who may be linked to the bombing in San Francisco and possibly other bombings and killings around the world. We have a couple of images of the man who can easily disguise himself. His name is Amir Abadai, a native of Egypt. He's probably traveling under an assumed name. Please consider him armed and dangerous. If you see him, call the FBI at the following…"*

Mac turned off the TV as they gave out the contact details for people to call. He clipped his gun holster onto his belt. As he poured a travel mug of coffee, his phone chirped. The text was from Andrea Douglas-Pfeiffer: *"Mac, call me when you can."* He put his coffee on the kitchen counter, pulled up Andrea's contact information, and called her.

"Morning, Mac!" came her bright voice. "Sorry for the early morning call, but I wanted to let you know the NSA has been computing on our female San Francisco bomber all night. Daniel texted me and asked for a quick meeting at 8:00 a.m. Will you be available?"

"I'll be there. Can you set up the video call and email me the link?" Mac asked.

"I'll have it for you before you get to your office," Andrea said. "I'll talk to you at eight."

Mac ended the call, grabbed his coat, picked up his keys and coffee, and left his apartment.

## Day 24, 7:00 a.m., Atlanta, Georgia

In Georgia, Donny McBride sat in the basement of his mother's home, watching television and eating a bowl of cereal. When the picture of

Abadai came on, Donny's eyes became larger and larger as he listened to the announcer's request to find the fugitive. As the announcer began to repeat the FBI's phone number, Donny spilled his cereal and scrambled for a pen to write down the number.

## Day 24, 8:00 a.m., New York

Mac walked into the office as his phone began to ring. He answered.

"Hi, Andrea, I'm logged in now, getting your email…I'll be online with you in a moment." He hung up the phone, pressed the video conference link on his computer, and was soon looking at Andrea Douglas-Pfeiffer and Daniel Whitefeather.

"Hi, everyone; sorry I'm late. Daniel, it's nice to meet you." Daniel and Andrea waved and greeted Mac.

"Agent Krieger, may I call you Mac?" Daniel asked. Mac nodded.

"Mac, in response to Andrea's request for help finding potential leads for your San Francisco bomber, I used the systems here at NSA to run image capture and identification queries on any female passengers traversing through any of the nine California international airports."

"Go on, I'm with you," Mac confirmed.

"The algorithm came up with approximately 3.2 million women who passed through the airports at least twice in the last thirty days."

"That's a lot to comb through," Mac sounded disheartened.

"Well, it gets better. The image algorithm uses biomarkers to create individual tags for the people in each image. We capture lots of images as people pass through immigration and have their passports scanned. This allows us to attach names to faces without re-analyzing the image."

"You can take an image from a video camera and link it to a passport; that's impressive," Mac said.

Daniel explained, "Of the three point two million individuals, one biometric marker was the same for two women. Both passed through San Francisco International Airport over the last thirty days."

"Please explain," Mac looked perplexed, "why would there be a duplicate biomarker?"

"This is the interesting part, Mac. A duplicate biomarker indicates that two women have identical facial biometrics but different names and passports. Here, let me show you these two people." Daniel's fingers moved across his keyboard, and he shared his desktop with Mac and Andrea.

Daniel pulled up an image of each woman standing in the immigration control line and the passport photos for each woman. He arranged them side by side. Stephanie Johnson was a redhead with large glasses and dressed in business attire. The other was Micca Rhodan, who had long black hair with a purple streak and wore clothes that reminded Mac of grunge fashion. She had tattoos on her arms, what appeared to be a stud through her lip, and one on her nose.

"These women don't look similar to me at all," Mac said doubtfully. "Are you sure your biomarkers are right?"

"It's the glasses," Daniel said. "The glasses for Miss Johnson are large and tend to distort the facial features. The computer can remove the glasses, reconstruct the face, and remeasure. These two women are the same person. Let me show you another image which helps me be certain."

Daniel clicked on another image from the video camera behind the rental car counter. When Stephanie Johnson stopped and pulled down her glasses to read a map in front of her, Daniel pulled the image from the rental car and Micca Rhodan's passport photo and cropped both images to show the eyes, nose, and mouth. Daniel transposed the image of Stephanie over the image of Micca. They matched.

"Amazing!"Mac shouted. "It's the same person!"

"Yes, sir, they are. I also had Homeland Security deep-check the passports; they determined both were counterfeit. The first one arrived on a flight from Minnesota using the name Stephanie Johnson, from Woodbury, Minnesota," Daniel explained. "She left after two days in San Francisco and flew to Las Vegas.

"Then, two days later, this Micca Rhodan from Cupertino, California, flies into San Francisco from Las Vegas, spends a couple of days in San Francisco, and it appears she was on a flight from San Francisco to Mexico City departing the airport a few minutes before the bomb exploded. The flight returned to San Francisco. She may still be in the area."

"Amazing work, Daniel, thank you!" Mac said. He shifted his eyes to the image of Andrea on the video call. "Andrea, will you please prepare a briefing to share with the director? We need to get an all-points on this person as soon as possible."

"I'll have it to the director in thirty minutes," Andrea said. "Daniel is sending me the details and images now. I'll also ask Homeland Security to run a passport control scan against these images to see if we can find how she entered the country, assuming she's not a homegrown terrorist."

"I can do it faster than Homeland Security," Daniel interrupted. "It's quick work for the supercomputers here but will take Homeland weeks to complete. Give me an hour or two, and I'll see what I can find. We've got a great start with these two images. It shouldn't take long to see if there are others if we only check passport swipes and biomarkers."

"Thank you, Daniel," Mac agreed. "Anything additional makes a stronger case for the APB. I will sign off now and update the FBI team on the details. It appears we've got two manhunts underway."

Mac pressed the on-screen button to end his participation in the call. He picked up the phone and called Director Robert Fitzgerald. Fitzgerald picked up immediately.

"Sir, sorry for the early call," Mac said.

"I've been in here since 7:00 a.m.," Fitzgerald said. "I think I'm on my third cup of coffee, and this is the fourth call. The first one was from the President."

"I've got some news I thought you would want to hear. We may have identified the woman in San Francisco responsible for the bombing." Mac said.

"Is she in custody?" Fitzgerald asked.

"No, sir, not yet," Mac said. "Andrea will come to your office with an APB request for your signature. We can blanket the media in San Francisco and smoke her out. Daniel Whitefeather at the NSA came through for us."

"It's good to hear of the collaboration and the results. Thanks for the call, Mac. I needed some good news. Is there anything new on Abadai?"

"The FBI is tracking a possible sighting in Fayetteville; it appears he is heading for Florida," Mac said.

"Keep me in the loop. Talk soon." The director ended the call.

Mac called Riccardi, who was traveling to North Carolina, directing the FBI search for Abadai.

"Riccardi," answered JR. Mac could tell from his breathing that he was walking.

"JR, this is Mac," Krieger said, "anything new to share?"

"The security cam over the pumps shows our guy meeting up with a trucker as he filled his truck," Riccardi informed. "The camera resolution is poor, but we're looking for a dark-colored Kenworth pulling an unmarked trailer. Our tech guys are analyzing the truck's plate. I've alerted all highway patrol and sheriff offices in a six-state area to be on the lookout for this rig, but we're about six or seven hours late. They could be almost anywhere."

"JR, please let me know when you find him," Mac said. "Let me tell you what's going on with San Francisco. We've got a possible identification of a female suspect in the San Francisco bombing. It was developed this morning in collaboration with the NSA. I've got an APB heading to my director's desk, but it'll also need the signatures of the FBI and DOJ. Can you put in a call to your director?"

"I'll call him next," Riccardi confirmed. "You're going for a 'Person of Interest APB'?"

"That's correct," Mac continued, "we don't have any data linking this person to the bombing, but she's been traveling into and out of San Francisco using false passports. Her timing with the bombing is suspicious."

"I'll pass it along to the director; he'll be happy to hear it."

"Thanks, JR; talk soon." Mac ended the call.

As Mac put his phone down, David Osrick knocked on his door. Mac waved him in. He leaned against Mac's desk.

"The FBI received a call about thirty minutes ago from a man named Donny McBride in Atlanta," David said. "McBride recognized Abadai from the pictures released to the news media. He told the FBI he was with Abadai in a homeless shelter in New York last week. The name of the homeless shelter was 'The Sisters of Holy Grace' in Brooklyn. The FBI in Atlanta is picking him up and getting a statement from him within the next hour."

"Send a team to the homeless shelter and see if anyone remembers Abadai or can tell us about his time there."

"We're already on it; Berkofsky and White are on their way now. They have photos of Abadai. We should know more by 10:00 a.m."

"Thanks, David. We've got a lead on a 'person of interest' in San Francisco."

"I overheard the call with Riccardi."

"You're up to speed," Mac smiled. "The FBI is scaling up for the East Coast search for Abadai. We need to jump on the West Coast and find this mystery woman. I'm requesting a dozen seats on one of the federal assistance charter flights later tonight to initiate a hunt. I'd like you to pull together a ten-man team from here. Can you jump on this and have everyone ready by 5:00 p.m. tonight?"

"Consider it done, Mac." David's voice was solemn. "The agents have been asking what they can do to help San Francisco ever since the bombing. I know I'll have plenty of volunteers."

"Good; make sure everyone brings their gear; we don't know what to expect in San Francisco when we get there."

## Day 24, 9:00 a.m., Redwood City, California

The hair dryer's sound was louder than the small television in the hotel room where Batalle had stayed since her return to San Francisco last night. The hotel was old, and every part of it was worn out. She had taken a cab from the airport and decided to lay low until she could arrange transportation south into Mexico.

The cab driver looked surprised when she asked about inexpensive hotels in South San Francisco. However, he jumped on Highway 101 southbound and pulled off at Pennsylvania Avenue in Redwood City at a two-star hotel called Redwood Inn. The hotel was classic 70s retro, with a "vacancy" sign illuminated most of the time.

As the taxi driver pulled up, he looked at her in the mirror. "It's not much to look at, but the sheets are clean. My wife is the housekeeper and says the people running it are okay." He smiled at her. "I think you'll be safe here."

"Thank you." Batalle smiled at him as she handed him the fare with a respectable tip. "You're kind to think of me."

"You remind me of my niece. She was a good girl who ran with the wrong people in Mexico. I've not seen her in five years. I pray she's alive and well and hope to see her again someday."

"I hope you do," Katerina added, "the world can be dangerous."

"I pray for her every day."

"I will, too. Thank you for the ride." She popped open the door and stepped into the hotel lobby.

After an uneventful night in the hotel, Batalle was watching TV reporters discussing all aspects of the bomb blast with various experts. They gave minute-by-minute updates on the emergency response crews engaged in the hunt for survivors. Talking heads were revisiting the death toll and the number of buildings destroyed in the downtown area.

She had turned off the hair dryer when she heard the words from the TV, *"This woman is a person of interest."* The hair dryer clattered to the floor, and Batalle bolted from the small bathroom to the bedroom to watch as images of her played across the television screen. The announcer's voice came back into her consciousness, and she heard:

*"This woman, who is shown wearing two different disguises as she passes through San Francisco International Airport, is wanted by the FBI for questioning. She may be a person of interest linked to the bombing. If you've any news on this woman, please call..."*

Batalle tuned out the announcer, picked up her items, and returned them to her case and backpack. Moments later, she was out the door, out of the hotel parking area, and onto the street. She hailed a cab and was gone.

The cab dropped her off at a bus station in Redwood City. Never having seen this bus station before, Batalle knew she was taking a risk. She didn't know where cameras were placed in the building and, therefore, was unsure of the best way to avoid them.

Instinctively, she pulled the thin hood of her windbreaker over her head and intentionally kept her face toward the ground as she strode into the building. Glancing around, she identified the women's restrooms and walked toward them. She didn't stop until she was safely locked into a toilet and could pause to assess her situation.

*"Keep it together, make some changes, stay strong,"* she murmured. Her only unused identity was that of Adrianne McCallister of Cork, Ireland. She was a beautiful redheaded Irish woman about ten years older than Batalle. She was tanned and looked relaxed in the passport photo.

Almost an hour and a half after Batalle entered the bus terminal bathroom, Adrianne McCallister of Cork, Ireland, walked out. The previous two passports were torn and flushed down the toilet in small pieces. The makeup case was gone. She was in her last change of clothes and had a backpack. It was time to move fast. At the bus station, she was able to get a cab.

Once settled in the cab, Batalle asked, "Do you know where an internet cafe is?"

"Yeah, I know one; it's about five minutes away." The driver confirmed.

"Please take me there."

Batalle ordered a coffee and a small breakfast roll inside the small internet cafe and paid for her connection. She was directed to an open computer, where she put her coffee on the table and rested her backpack under the desk. She was facing the door with her back to a wall.

Batalle opened the Tor browser and, from memory, typed the address for her online cryptocurrency vault. Once logged into her crypto wallet, she reviewed the account balance and requested an exchange of fifty percent of one Bitcoin into US dollars. After verifying the request, she approved the site and transaction fees and was provided with the address of the nearest Bitcoin ATM. She was assured of sufficient funds in the ATM to pay the total amount, almost $18,000 in cash. She restarted the computer and checked to ensure the history of her actions was not on the computer before getting up and leaving the cafe. She walked outside and hailed a cab.

# CHAPTER TWENTY-NINE

## Day 24, 5:00 p.m., New York

Mac, David, and a select team of agents milled about the tactical room in the Secret Service parking garage below their offices. The room stored weapons and assault gear. Long weapons, mostly AR15s, were piled on the large table in the center of the room, along with tactical vests, ceramic armor plates, and ammo packs.

Government-issued black duffle bags containing clothing, boots, and additional weapons were under the table. The team members were talking to one another in the room, making it difficult to make out any single conversation. Some pulled on black tactical gloves to stretch them out, while others double-checked ammo packs or oiled their weapon.

Mac walked away from his pile of equipment and up to the front of the room. He yelled, "Listen up!". The room quieted as attention spun toward the sound.

"Thanks for your attention. It looks like everyone got the memo on preparation. First of all, thank you. I appreciate each of you volunteering for this mission. It means a lot to me. We have an opportunity to track down the woman who may be responsible for the bombing, and I need everyone to be ready once we land to put in long hours again to find this woman."

He heard several excited shouts of "Hell yeah!" "We can do this!" Several other exclamations filled the room until Mac put his hand up again.

"FBI Agent Riccardi is leading the East Coast search for Abadai, and I'll be leading the West Coast search for this mystery woman. We call her 'Micca Rhodan' until we find her real name. We will join with FBI teams from California in this pursuit."

Mac looked at David Osrick and asked, "David, any new updates?"

"About two hours ago, the FBI received a call. A clerk at a hotel in Redwood City saw the images on television and called the hotline. Last night, a woman fitting her description checked in and supposedly was still in the room. Redwood PD responded with tactical teams and took the door

161

down. She was long gone, and the room was clean. There are no fingerprints, but we may have a DNA sample from a couple of strands of hair found on the bed. We expect she's aware we're looking for her and is now on the run. She seems good at changing her appearance and identity. We've got the teams at NSA mocking up some images with different-colored hair, which may be helpful. We should have it when we land in San Francisco."

As David finished, Mac looked around at the faces of agents he knew well. Many were years-long friends.

"David, thanks for the update. I want to suggest that everyone try to get some sleep tonight on the transport to San Francisco. Let's get rolling." He walked to the table, picked up his AR-15 and duffle bag, and left the conference room. Outside, two vans were waiting to take the team to Stewart Air National Guard base to catch a military transport. The plane was carrying supplies and personnel to help secure San Francisco.

## Day 24, 8:00 p.m., Redwood City

Katerina Batalle was frustrated. She had been negotiating on a red 2007 Toyota Camry with 145,000 miles and sun-scorched paint for thirty minutes. The test drive with Charo, the owner and salesman of the small used car lot, was quick but not thorough. She smelled something in the car and wasn't sure if it was an old spill buried deep in the fabric upholstery or Charo's unique mix of aftershave, cigarette smoke, and sweat.

"It's a good little car. Miles are not bad for a car of this age. It'll last you a long time. $7,000 is the price, and I'll replace the tires with newer ones," Charo said as he lit another cigarette. Katerina could tell he loved to haggle.

"It's a piece of crap, Charo," Katerina grumbled. "I'll give you $3,000 and drive it off the lot. I don't want you to replace the tires or do anything to the car. Let's make the deal. You can go home, and I can get on my way."

"Oh, I couldn't let this car go for that price! That's $4,000 less than I can get for this car tomorrow. No, I can't do that; it's bad business. Tell you what, Miss, what was your name again?"

"I didn't give you my name, and you know it. Stop stalling, and let's get this done. I'll give you another $500. Let's make it $3,500. But that's all I'm going to give. Am I wasting my time?" Batalle was impatient, but she was waiting for the question she knew would be coming from Charo. He was a classic dirtbag, the likes of which she had dealt with her entire life.

Charo stepped away from the small trailer he used to store tires and spare parts. It also doubled as his office. He opened his hands to her.

"I'm doing the best I can, young lady. I need to make a small profit on

162

the cars I sell. I'm sure you understand."

She waved off his outstretched hands and made her play. "I have $3,500 on me. It's my final offer."

Charo smiled. He took a short step toward her. "Now we're getting somewhere. I think the best I can go is $4,500. We're $1,000 apart in price." Charo said softly, "Perhaps we should discuss cash and in-kind payment options."

She couldn't help but smirk at him. She had expected this when she saw the used car lot in this part of South San Francisco.

"Why, Charo, what could you be suggesting?" She asked.

"I think we could work out a suitable agreement if you join me in my office. What do you say?" Charo involuntarily ran his hand over his stringy hair.

"Are you suggesting what I think you're suggesting?" Katerina said in a quiet, hesitant voice. "Would you be willing to trade for my cash and perhaps a little fun between you and me?"

Charo broke into a broad smile. "Oh yes! I can make you a good deal. Will you follow me into my office? I'll turn the air conditioner on to make it more comfortable for you." Charo pointed to the small trailer and encouraged her to move in the general direction.

"You first, I'll follow you." Charo jumped at her suggestion. He turned around and walked up the two steps into the trailer. She followed a couple of steps behind him, and once inside, she slowly closed the door while looking at Charo, who was motioning for her to close it.

"You mentioned the air conditioner?" Batalle removed her light jacket, and Charo saw her toned arms and body for the first time.

He turned and walked a few steps to the AC unit. "Let me turn this on..."

Charo's voice was cut short as Batalle approached him from behind and wrapped the guitar string garrote around his throat. She tightened it. Charo straightened with surprise, but his movement only helped her gain better leverage. He tried to get his fingers under the string, but because it was thin and already cutting deeply into his skin, his hands came away bloody. Charo tried to reach behind him and grasp at her, but she was more than his equal physically and overpowered his groping hands.

Charo's knees buckled as the wire crushed his windpipe, and his breathing stopped. He passed out on the floor. Batalle kept the wire cutting into his throat until the blood started to pour from the severed carotid artery. As his heart pumped its last crucial efforts to get blood to his brain, she finally released the garrote and unwound it from his neck. She wiped the blood from the thin wire, and her hands on his shirt wound the killing tool into a small coil and put it into her bag.

She didn't see the Toyota's car keys on the desk. Sighing, she reached into Charo's pocket to search for the keys. Her first recovery was a condom package. She looked derisively at the dead body of Charo and tossed the condom foil onto the floor. On the second attempt, She retrieved the car key. She walked around the small desk, opened the file drawer, and looked for the title papers. Finding the document, she folded it and put it in her pocket.

She found a drawer with several 'Temporary Transit' papers printed out with the name 'Charo's Used Cars' already filled in. Batalle grabbed several of them and a black marker and filled in the buyer's information. She found a small greasy rag and cleaned any fingerprints off the door handle and any other place she touched. She used the rag to open the door and looked into the setting sun. There was no movement in the small parking lot and little traffic on the street.

Batalle strolled out of the building and closed the door quietly behind her. She walked down the two steps to the faded red car with the bald tires and climbed behind the wheel. The car started, and she rolled it slowly off the lot onto the side street. She took the turn onto El Camino Real, heading south, accelerated, and disappeared with the fading daylight.

## Day 25, 12:30 a.m., Travis Air Force Base, Fairfield, California

After landing at Travis Air Force Base, The team walked off the C-17 Globemaster military transport plane. The base was hosting military assistance flights because of its proximity to San Francisco.

John Edward Walker, a San Francisco Special Agent for the FBI, met Mac. He walked from the flight operations center onto the tarmac. The two shook hands.

After brief introductions, Walker said, "I've got five vehicles for you and your team in the parking lot. I've assigned agents from my team to act as liaisons and drivers for your team."

"I appreciate your help, John. How are you and your family doing?"

"I think we're all in shock," Walker said. "My wife's driving the kids back to her family in Wisconsin until things settle down here."

"Let's walk out to the parking lot and have a meeting. We won't have to waste time in the morning with another one," Mac said. "It's late. I've got a team to take the night shift. The other team can get some rest for tomorrow."

Walker nodded at Mac as the conversation was overrun with noise from a departing transport. He pointed toward the FBO and led Mac and his team through the small building to the parking lot, where six black Chevrolet Suburbans were waiting in a nearby row.

They were not the typical clean, shiny, black vehicles the Secret Service or FBI commonly used. They were dirty. Covered in gritty dust from asphalt, concrete, and every other material consumed in the explosion. In the hours following the blast, the sea breeze from the ocean pushed the cloud east by southeast and blanketed the downtown area and many surrounding cities. While the explosion was felt as far away as San José, the fallout impacted the neighborhoods southeast of San Francisco with gritty powder one to three inches deep.

Mac addressed the group in the parking lot. "We will go twenty-four hours a day until we catch her. I want teams one, two, and three to go with Agent Walker. He's coordinated accommodations for you. Get some sleep. Your tour begins at 6:00 a.m. I'll lead the night shift. We start with the last place this woman, currently known as 'Micca Rhodan,' was seen."

Mac looked at the assembled team and continued. "We've notified the Border Patrol to be looking out for this woman. We don't know much about her, but we should assume she'll do almost anything to save herself. Please take care when approaching any suspect and rely on overwhelming force should a situation escalate. Agent Walker, anything to add?"

"Only one thing," Walker said. "San Francisco is hurting right now. Tensions are high, and people are on edge. Be careful, and please try to be compassionate and understanding. De-escalate any situations as fast as you can. The people need to begin the healing process."

"Thank you. That was well said," said Mac. "Now, let's get rolling."

The agents loaded their equipment into the vehicles while Krieger and Walker discussed the timing of the update for the FBI and Secret Service brass. When the equipment and the men were loaded, Krieger climbed in the first truck and nodded at the driver.

# CHAPTER THIRTY

## Day 25, 6:00 a.m., thirty miles north of Jacksonville, Florida

A lonely stretch of Interstate 95 north of Jacksonville was the chosen site of FBI Special Agent John Riccardi's roadblock. It was a stretch of an interstate roadway, elevated twenty feet above wet swamplands. The FBI and the local State Patrol knew that miles-long stretches of elevated roadway were ideal for car-by-car searches.

Between midnight and 5:00 a.m., Riccardi had been on the phone with the FBI director, the governors of both Georgia and Florida, the State Highway Patrol for each state, and the Nassau County Sheriff's office. Getting permission to block a critical north-south traffic artery had taken hours.

Riccardi and his team were in the cabin of a hastily chartered Gulfstream IV jet headed toward Jacksonville Executive Airport when the approval finally came through. The FBI was granted a three-hour window to capture the fugitive Amir Abadai.

With the sun slowly rising, Riccardi and his team stood on the elevated roadway one mile north of the only exit on this five-mile stretch of I-95. A Florida State Patrol helicopter had dropped off the FBI team and began slowly circling about two miles away over the wetlands.

Florida Highway Patrol cruisers, with lights flashing, placed orange cones to force southbound traffic to slowly migrate to the edges of the roadway, where two lines of cars could be searched. State Patrol officers processed each vehicle in seconds. Even though traffic was light at this time of the morning, it was less than five minutes before traffic was backed up for over a mile.

## Day 25, 6:00 a.m., forty miles north of Jacksonville, Florida

Ten miles to the north, Amir Abadai was driving the Kenworth. The truck's owner and driver, who had picked him up in Fayetteville, was dead and slumped over in the passenger seat. He had bled out six hours ago

166

when Abadai's patience was thinning. The tanks on the big rig were about half full and would get Abadai far into Florida, if not to Miami. The trailer in the back was almost empty, holding a few boxes of machined parts that missed their delivery in Georgia.

Abadai wore the driver's "Caterpillar" hat and his denim jacket, which had a well-soaked blood spot on the right sleeve near the elbow. He would need to get rid of the truck soon. Abadai had ignored two weigh stations, one in South Carolina and another when he entered Georgia. He hoped the weigh stations were understaffed and wouldn't pursue him. He didn't know the FBI had been trailing him for hours.

Enhanced video footage from the truck stop in Fayetteville identified the truck Abadai had climbed into following his brief encounter with Jake Tapper. The FBI was able to locate the truck and find a cell phone number for Benjamin Wooten, the rig's owner. They tracked the truck's movement using 'find my phone' technology. Mr. Wooten's ex-wife had identified her husband's habit of stopping at strip clubs on the outskirts of cities along his delivery routes using this same application.

Abadai knew about phone tracking technology but didn't know that Wooten owned a cell phone. It was stuffed into one of the many pockets inside the sleeper cab, with the sound turned off. After his divorce, Wooten found that he had little need for a cell phone and rarely used it. Out of habit, he kept the phone on the charger in the sleeper.

The FBI had been tracking the truck for the past twenty-four hours as Wooten made deliveries in Georgia and slowly worked his way south toward Florida. The FBI didn't know Ben Wooten was dead and slumped in the passenger seat.

The truck passed the last exit in Georgia before the Florida roadblock. After it drove by, two unmarked Florida Highway Patrol units moved onto the highway behind the truck and moved along with traffic, keeping the big rig in front of them. At the three-mile point before the roadblock, Abadai began to see tail lights slowing traffic in the distance.

He eased off the accelerator. Moments later, traffic was at a standstill, almost a mile ahead. The bright flashing red and blue lights of the police units were more visible in the semi-darkness than the slowly rising sun.

Abadai looked at the traffic backing up behind him and noticed, for the first time, two black Ford Explorers about ten cars back. Both vehicles looked to have the push-bumpers most police departments used, but he couldn't be sure with the headlights flaring in his eyes. The dark vehicles were side by side in the two lanes, and one allowed a car to change lanes in front of it. The trucks had identical headlights and driving light configurations. Seeing them sitting side by side was unsettling for Abadai.

The traffic moved forward a car length or two at a time. Abadai pulled the big rig fifty feet forward and stopped. He repeated this slow roll forward, checking the side mirrors to study the traffic behind him each time. The black vehicles stayed two hundred feet back and never separated more than a few feet.

Abadai's eye caught the flashing red light on a helicopter as it moved slowly from south to north about a mile from his driver's window. "Traffic helicopter or police?" he wondered. After a few minutes, he could see his surroundings a little better. The sun was climbing higher in the eastern sky. He didn't like what he saw.

He was on an elevated roadway, almost tree-top height. He saw treetops off to the right, some with Spanish moss. Looking beyond, he saw bulrushes, ferns, and other swamp plants surrounded by water. The other side of the road was the same, with what appeared to be miles and miles of wetland.

Amir thought he was about ten miles from Jacksonville. He didn't like what he saw. He didn't know how many miles of swamp lay around him. The distance from the elevated roadway to the water below was about twenty feet. He knew he could make the jump if he could land in deep water and let the water slow his fall. But it was a dangerous height to land on any form of solid ground. A broken bone was possible from such a height.

Abadai was experienced. He had trained in African deserts and South Asian jungles. He led attacks on Israeli settlements using small boats and entering unseen from the Mediterranean Sea. He had learned to live off the land in many environments and survived. What would he do in a North American swamp?

He leaned over to the passenger side of the vehicle and grabbed the dead leg of Ben Wooten. It was difficult for Abadai to move. Rigor mortis had begun to set into the limbs. He pushed the body against the door of the cab and pulled both legs up. Abadai looked at the boots Ben Wooten was wearing and decided they were better than the light shoes he had on his feet. He untied the boots and transferred them to his feet.

He was less than a mile from the source of the congestion. The police were detaining drivers and letting them pass. He knew it was a roadblock, and he was trapped. Almost a hundred cars were in front of him, and even more were behind.

A modern tank would have had difficulty moving through the line of cars to force an escape. A three-foot-high reinforced concrete wall on either side of the roadway was a formidable blockade. Abadai reasoned that the big rig could break through the wall with enough speed, but there was no way he could get enough room to get it up to speed. It didn't take long to decide he would need to jump over the wall and take his chances in the swamp.

He rifled through every storage area in the tractor cab he could reach and came away with a five-inch folding knife Wooten kept in the side door pocket. He slid it into his pants pocket. Searching the center console area, he found a small pistol with five rounds in the magazine. The gun was a small Czech-made .380 semi-auto. He checked the empty chamber and jacked the slide to put a round into it. He put the gun in his jacket pocket.

With little else in the cab to take, Abadai moved the truck forward to close the small gap between it and the car in front of it. He set the parking brake. Looking out a final time at the traffic block in front of him and seeing the helicopter again at almost a mile east of his position, he opened his driver-side door and slid down to the roadway.

He walked directly to the side wall along the truck's passenger side and peered over the edge. Below, he saw tree limbs, muddy water, grass, weeds, and several areas that had "don't jump here" indications. Directly below the roadway were several large rocks appearing to have been used as fill for the roadway piling. Abadai estimated he needed to jump about ten to twelve feet from the roadway to avoid the rocks. Who knew what lay hidden below the surface of the water?

Abadai looked up when the car in front of his truck moved forward another car length. It was time. He backed up to the center of the two-lane highway and sprinted toward the wall. He leaped onto the wall with one foot and pushed off the wall with the same leg while thrusting the other leg forward.

The leap carried him ten feet into the void before he plummeted down and out of sight. As he jumped, he heard gasps in the surrounding cars from the other drivers. They watched in amazement when the crazy truck driver, with a suicide wish, flung himself from the bridge. The two unmarked State Patrol vehicles immediately lit up their lights when they saw someone fly off the roadway into the swamp.

## Day 25, 6:01 a.m., Jacksonville, Florida Wetlands Preserve

Abadai tried to get his legs back under him as he fell through the air. In the quick, twenty-foot fall, he was partially successful. He landed hard in the water. It was about ten inches deep but had an additional six inches of mud under it. The landing on one leg forced it up into his chest, knocking the air out of his lungs while forcing his face into his knee. The blunt impact caused him to fall backward into the water as if he had been kicked in the chest.

He was stunned by the blow to his face. His head went underwater. It took a few seconds to flail his way to a sitting position. He knew his jaw was broken and some of his teeth damaged. Bleeding profusely from his mouth and his nose, he did a quick check for any other broken bones and found a painful and stretched ligament in the leg he had landed upon. He forced himself to stand slowly and looked at the raised roadway. He could hear car doors slamming and people talking and saw two or three people looking over the highway's barrier. They were pointing at him.

He gathered himself and turned away from the road toward the darkest part of the swamp. The heavy swamp thicket in the semi-darkness enveloped the wet and muddy man, and in seconds, he was gone from sight.

## Day 25, 6:02 a.m., Jacksonville, Florida Wetlands Preserve

Two Florida Highway Patrol officers arrived at the jump site moments later and peered over the barrier. One of the men triggered his shoulder microphone and radioed the details to the roadblock team.

When the call came in, Agent Riccardi was talking to the Jacksonville Area Highway Patrol supervisor at the roadblock. Both men listened intently to the radio. Riccardi looked up at the flashing lights less than half a mile away and started running toward them.

Arriving at the jump site, he spoke with the witnesses who had witnessed the jumper hurl himself into the swamp. Meanwhile, one of the highway patrolmen opened the door to the Kenworth and saw the dead body in the passenger compartment. He called Riccardi, who stepped over to take a look.

Riccardi picked up his handheld radio and called for the helicopter to come to his position. He told the State Patrol supervisor to remove the roadblock, contact emergency services and a medical coroner, and bring the investigative unit to the truck's position. Traffic was routed around the truck within five minutes, and emergency services were en route.

The two highway patrol officers stepped out and temporarily stopped traffic long enough for the helicopter to touch down. Riccardi climbed onboard, and the bird lifted off. Once in the aircraft, he had the pilot rise to 500 feet and hover over the area where Abadai had jumped. From altitude, Riccardi saw the flashing lights of emergency services, still three miles or more away, fast approaching from the south.

Riccardi got on his radio. "Abadai is running. He's in the middle of the swamp. I'm over his jump position. We don't see any movement now, but we must assume he's moving away from our position." Riccardi put on his headset to speak with the helicopter pilot. "Are there any roads he can reach?"

The pilot shook his head, "The nearest road is about five miles in any direction. He's pretty much in the middle of the swamp. But it's not easy for the sheriff to get in there either. We need an airboat and some tracking dogs from Jacksonville to track him. It'll take a while to get those resources here."

"Shit!" Riccardi sputtered. He was back into his radio to his FBI team: "Pilot says the nearest roads are five miles in almost any direction. I want Reno to work with the State Highway Patrol to get units on each surrounding road. Sevilla, please work with the sheriff's office to get an airboat and some hounds in here to track him. We know where he landed and where he went from the roadway; maybe they can pick up a trail. Pasko, you take charge of the investigation of the truck." Riccardi Looked at the pilot again, "How much time do we have before you need to refuel?"

The pilot looked at his gauges, "We're good for about twenty minutes."

Riccardi keyed his mic again and advised the team, "I'll be in the helicopter doing an area search for the next twenty minutes. Maybe by being up here, we can slow Abadai down and keep him from outrunning us. Sevilla, get airboats up here as fast as possible.

Riccardi signed off and told the pilot he wanted to fly in slowly expanding circles starting from where they were. As they started moving and looked hard at the swamp below them, Riccardi looked at his watch; it indicated the current time was a minute or two before 7:00 a.m. Eastern time. He pulled out his phone and dialed his director to give him an update.

# CHAPTER THIRTY-ONE

## Day 25, 4:30 a.m., Redwood City

It was dark in Redwood City at 4:00 a.m. The lights from the black Chevrolet Suburban illuminated the roadway as Mac and his team were pulling out of the Redwood Inn parking lot. Batalle had departed the room a little less than eighteen hours earlier. The Redwood City police searched the room and found several hair strands in the bathroom.

Mac took possession of the evidence and sent the samples to the FBI lab for DNA testing. They would run the DNA through CODIS, the Combined DNA Index System, which the FBI and others use to match criminal DNA. If this woman's DNA had been mapped in the US or several other countries' criminal DNA databases, it could provide a link to track her down.

Mac's team and the FBI agents working with them were heading back to the San José FBI Office. The trip to the San José office took them through the fringe of the fallout radius. Even though it was early, the roads were still busy, with crews working to remove dust and debris.

The dust was microscopic particles, not dissimilar from volcanic ash. It was everywhere, giving the landscape a muted gray patina and making the morning seem even darker. The wind moved some dust around as cars passed the roads slowly. The dust caused by the explosion had gone up into the atmosphere, spread out in a mushroom-type cloud, and fallen back to Earth almost immediately.

When disturbed by wind or traffic, the dust was strangely light. It would lift into the air and blossom into a cloud of some size, drift, and resettle. It was gray and gritty to the touch, creating havoc on the lungs if inhaled. Water effectively washed it out of the eyes, but nothing could be done for the lungs. Hospitals were full of patients with lungs full of dust and slowly dying. News organizations discussed the significant health toll doctors were expressing for future years.

Mac and his crew arrived at the San José office minutes before 6:00 a.m. John Edward Walker had arranged sleeping cots for them in one of the

172

conference rooms. Mac was walking through the office door when Riccardi called him.

"Krieger," Mac yawned as he answered the phone.

"Mac, I'm calling you from Florida. We don't have Abadai yet, but we should within the next few hours. I'm calling you from Jacksonville Executive Airport as we refuel the helicopter.

"Helicopter? What happened, JR?"

"He jumped from an elevated roadway into some swampy wetlands north of Jacksonville, Florida, about two hours ago. We've got the area surrounded by the State Patrol and county Sheriff's teams. We're getting two airboats and some dogs brought in. I don't know how far he can travel or how fast he can run in this area. It's about twenty-five square miles of wetlands and pretty nasty. I wouldn't want to be on the ground there."

"Let me know when you catch him," Mac said. "We're getting started here in California. We were at the motel where our target had stayed the previous night. We're about a day behind her. We need another lead."

"Good hunting," Riccardi said.

"Same to you," Mac shot back. He closed the connection and headed for the conference room to wake the next crew and get them moving.

## Day 25, 9:00 a.m., Jacksonville, Florida Wetlands Preserve

Abadai was moving slowly west. He was staying under tree canopies where he was shielded from the helicopters. The State Highway Patrol helicopter would pass overhead close to his location every few minutes. He knew they'd not spotted him because the aircraft continually flew in ever-widening circles. He knew he needed to find an escape path out of the wetland area. His boots were full of water, and his clothes were soaked through. Before sunrise, the wetlands seemed quiet and calm. With the sun up and well into the morning sky, the realities of his situation began to sink in.

As the sun rose over Florida, the heat and humidity blossomed. Abadai wore a denim jacket, a long-sleeved shirt, cotton pants, and boots. When he jumped, he lost the hat he had taken from the dead truck driver. He could feel the heat and humidity move into his clothes, and sweat poured out of his body with every movement. He jumped without water to drink, and he knew dehydration was a distinct possibility as the warm day wore on.

With the sun climbing in the sky, the swamp came alive minute by minute. First were the mosquitoes. Millions were focused on a new source of heat and carbon dioxide, and Abadai's skin was less protected than most animals in the swamp. The mosquitoes began there.

They attacked. Abadai flailed, trying to keep the bugs at bay. Failing that, he hiked his coat over his head to protect his head and eyes. The mosquitoes were not discouraged. They attacked his hands, lower back, and abdomen, where his sweat-soaked shirt clung to his body. He could feel the hundreds of bites as the mosquitoes attacked him mercilessly. He trudged forward through the water. He could feel his skin swelling.

Slowly, the rest of the swamp began moving. Large and small insects were on the trees and scampering across the ground. They were in every bush Abadai pushed through. A giant twelve-inch centipede in camouflage surprised him when it suddenly moved on a tree root he was about to grab as he crossed a small bog. Reaching for a handhold near another tree, he disturbed a five-foot-long black snake, a poisonous Water Moccasin, which moved slowly away from him and into the water.

As mid-morning approached, the mosquitoes took a break from reducing Abadai's hemoglobin levels. He stopped under a tree to shield himself from the police helicopter as it passed overhead. When he looked up into the tree's canopy, searching for the aircraft, he saw a twelve-foot python snake moving slowly toward a bird's nest on a stout branch. The python stopped its forward motion and moved its large head toward Abadai. The snake looked at the mosquito-swollen man. Abadai wasted no time backing away from the python. He headed west through the reeds, thorns, and vines.

Three hours into his escape, he had made some progress, but not much. Abadai judged his location to be almost three miles from the interstate. He was making slow progress west. His idea to jump from the roadway wasn't well considered, but what other options did he have? Take a hostage with a small caliber gun? Allow himself to be taken into custody and sentenced to consecutive life terms in a federal prison? Take his own life? None of the options were better than risking his life on his survival skills in a swamp.

A new sound caught Abadai's ear. The sound was piercing in the morning air and made him immediately stop in his tracks. The bawl of two bloodhounds pulling against their leashes on a scent trail carried strongly through the heat and humidity of the morning. The sound sent a shiver through his sweating body. The dogs, trained since the Middle Ages to track animals and people, were on his trail, and they knew it. He wasn't expecting dogs.

The dogs sounded far away, at least a mile southeast of his position. He could hear them bawl when they caught his scent and go quiet when they lost it, but judging the distance between them was difficult. The insistent barking and bawling of the hounds were among the most frightening sounds he had ever heard.

### Day 25, 6:35 a.m., San José, California

The day crew was running the show now, but Mac couldn't close his eyes. He was struggling to sleep. Many thoughts were going through his mind: the late-night flight to California and the disappointing visit to the hotel where the woman had slipped away from them. The eerie images from their drive to the edge of San Francisco. The clouds of gritty dust stirred up by the vehicle tires as they rolled across the roads. The dust would bloom upward as the car stirred it and settle somewhere in the darkness as they drove toward the city.

He knew he would never forget the gap in the lights of downtown San Francisco, where the buildings were destroyed and power disrupted. Who could sleep when hundreds, maybe thousands of lives have been lost? Who does this? Who would do this? Why? The questions kept running through Mac's head. Eventually, he drifted into an exhausted sleep.

## Day 25, 10:15 a.m., Jacksonville Florida Wetlands Preserve

Keeping to the trees had helped Abadai remain hidden in the swamp, but it also left a pretty clear scent trail for the bloodhounds. He would need more time in the water to slow the dogs. Water was everywhere, but the deepest water was in open areas with no canopy to protect his location from the helicopter search teams. Two helicopters circled in the skies above the swamp, constantly causing him to hide under the tree canopy.

In the distance, he could hear what sounded like an airplane, but it was at ground level as he was. Abadai surmised it was an airboat. He had never studied airboats or ridden in one of them. He didn't know how fast they moved or their maneuverability in the swamp. He did know he disliked the sound of the airboat about as much as he disliked the baying bloodhounds. He picked up his pace. He needed to take risks to see another sunrise as a free man.

## Day 25, 10:16 a.m., Jacksonville Florida Wetlands Preserve

Riccardi was overhead in one of the helicopters, wondering if they'd lost Abadai. JR was snacking on an egg sandwich and drinking a cup of coffee he picked up in the airport lounge while the helicopter was refueling. His eyes never left the swamp below him as he looked for movement. He could see the interstate in the distance and one of the airboats below him. The helicopter stayed at five hundred feet above the canopy. Riccardi knew the bloodhounds were somewhere on the ground, but they were invisible to him.

## Day 25, 10:17 a.m., Jacksonville, Florida Wetlands Preserve

Abadai needed to cross a large piece of open water and hopefully throw off the dogs. The helicopter nearest to him was moving slowly away. He broke out of the overhead canopy and sloshed through high brush to the edge of an open water area. Looking across to the other side, he could see more high brush and trees. The open water was about seventy-five yards across. Not a great distance for a good swimmer, but it was not insignificant in full clothes and heavy boots.

Abadai crouched and listened to the hounds' baying. They were getting closer to him. If the handlers let go of the hounds, they'd be on him. He stood and waded into the open water, trying to maintain his balance. The water soon reached his waist, and he moved slowly forward.

## Day 25, 10:20 a.m., Jacksonville Florida Wetlands Preserve

The pilot in Riccardi's helicopter was the first to see the ripple waves caused by the man in the water.

"Agent, we've got movement at eight o'clock."

"Swing around. I need to see him." Riccardi demanded. The pilot spun the aircraft, and Riccardi spotted the man slowly wading, almost chest-deep, into the water.

"Move us over him and move up another couple hundred feet," Switching his radio to the joint operations frequency, Riccardi hollered, "Agents! We've sighted a man in the water moving west. Watch where our helicopter hovers! Everyone, please start moving toward our location."

Confirmations from the teams on the ground and in the airboat came as the teams began to change directions to converge on the area.

The man in the water looked up and saw the helicopter as he took another step and plunged into the water over his head. He started to swim toward the other bank in an uneven, thrashing stroke. From above, it looked like he fixed his eyes on the far shore and fully committed to the swimming sprint. He threw his arms forward and tried to kick hard with the boots on his feet. His clothes restricted his body's ability to glide through the water and slowed his progress.

In the helicopter above, Riccardi watched the struggling swimmer. The pilot keyed his mic.

"Agent, his splashing is drawing some attention." Riccardi was surprised by the pilot's comment, but it caused him to break his focus on the swimmer and to look more broadly at the water body below him.

About thirty yards south of Abadai, a giant nine-foot alligator was moving toward the struggling swimmer. Slowly moving its tail, the alligator glided under the water and made no track on the surface. The animal was visible to Riccardi and the pilot but invisible to Abadai. Another smaller alligator, maybe five feet long, was moving toward Abadai from the east. It was coming slowly in behind him and was getting closer.

"I'd rather take him into custody than recover a body," Riccardi shouted to the pilot. "What can we do?"

"Not much from here," the pilot said. "This helicopter isn't a Huey with open doors, and we don't have appropriate weapons to take out gators."

"What's the chance they will leave him alone?"

"The little one will probably determine he's too big to attack and back off. The big guy, well, that's another story. The big boy is probably nine or ten feet long and king of the swamp. I've seen big gators take down full-size deer crossing smaller water puddles than this one. I'd say he's at risk of an attack."

"What if I shot at the gator with my weapon?" Riccardi asked.

"Probably wouldn't stop him unless you had a direct hit. Your pistol may not penetrate his thick hide after it hits the water first."

Riccardi keyed the radio to the ground teams. "This is Riccardi. We've got a large alligator tracking him now. Can we get an airboat into this area? If we don't, we may not have a live suspect to interrogate."

In the airboat moving through the swamp toward the hovering helicopter, Sevilla picked up his radio and said over the loud noise of the engine and propeller. "I'm in the airboat, and we're working toward your location. I think we should be under you in two minutes."

### Day 25, 10:27 a.m., Jacksonville, Florida Wetlands Preserve

In the water, Abadai was swimming toward the far shore. He was about fifteen yards from it when he tried to kick his right leg and found it stuck. It felt like it was in a vice. The five-foot gator had reached Abadai first and clamped onto his trailing leg. The bite was brief. The alligator decided the meal was more than he could handle. He let go and moved back a few feet.

Abadai looked toward his suddenly free leg. Then he noticed the two eyes barely above the water's surface as the small alligator looked at him from a few feet away. His eyes widened as he realized it was an alligator in the water with him. He turned toward the close shore and thrashed hard toward it. He was within seconds of reaching the bank.

Suddenly, he was no longer within an arm's length of shore but was being pulled slowly away. It took a second for Abadai to realize he could no longer feel his legs. The same vice-like pressure from before was surrounding his hips. He flailed with his arms to swim toward the weeds on shore, but the shore moved farther away. He tried to turn his body and found he had no control. He felt with his hands on his waist and found the hard, scaly skin and ragged teeth of the alligator whose massive jaws clamped around his midsection. The alligator slowly dragged Abadai toward deeper water. He tried to take a breath of air. Abadai looked up at the hovering helicopter as his face disappeared under the murky water.

## Day 25, 10:28 a.m., Jacksonville, Florida Wetlands Preserve

From the helicopter, the pilot and Riccardi watched in awe as the nine-foot alligator pulled Amir Abadai out into the middle of the water and carried him down into the deepest part of the swamp. With several flips of the gator's powerful tail, Riccardi saw Abadai's body being flung around like a rag doll as the gator rolled and rolled. The death roll lasted about thirty seconds until the body in the gator's teeth stopped resisting, and all muscle activity ceased. The gator settled onto the bottom of the small wetlands lake with the body in its jaws and didn't move. Amir Abadai was dead.

The airboat containing Agent Sevilla entered the open water. The boat slowly coasted over where the gator held the body at the bottom.

Riccardi keyed the radio he was holding, "Team, we're now in a recovery operation. The suspect is dead. He didn't make it through the lake. Pull back the dogs and get another airboat to Sevilla's position. We probably need divers to recover the body. There are gators in the lake. Let the local authorities handle the recovery since they know what they're doing. Sevilla, stay through the recovery process."

Riccardi signaled the pilot to return to base and pulled out his cell phone. He had calls to make. The first needed to be Mac Krieger.

# CHAPTER THIRTY-TWO

### Day 25, 8:06 a.m., San José, California

Mac's phone rang less than two hours after he fell into a deep sleep. It was a little after 8:00 a.m. in San José. He answered his phone on the third or fourth ring.

"Mac, it's Riccardi. It's over. We're in a 'bag and tag' operation now. Abadai is dead. We still have to recover the body to make sure it's him, but we'll have that done shortly. It was quite the chase. I'll give him credit for that, but it's over."

Waking up, Mac stuttered, "Huh? What?... What do you mean by 'recover the body'?"

"A fucking alligator got him! It was the most violent thing I've ever seen. I may have nightmares of alligators after this. Man, they're ruthless killers."

"Okay, wait a minute, let me get this straight, JR. You let an alligator bring him down? And you still have to recover the body? Shit! We need to interrogate him and find out who was behind these bombings! You know, who was paying for it, who provided the explosive."

Mac slowed and grew silent for a second, then said, "Well, damn it!"

"I know it's not the outcome we wanted," Riccardi said, "and the alligator isn't on my team either. This outcome was a surprise to everyone but the locals in Florida. The sheriff told me, after the fact, he expected Abadai's death would be by snakebite or an alligator. He said, 'There's a reason people don't live in swamps.'"

Mac rubbed his head and replied, "Abadai was a terrorist and got what he deserved. It ties up one end but takes us from two chances to get an interrogation to one. Now, we need to capture this woman alive." Mac looked down at his feet as he sat on the edge of the portable bed. "Let's get the body for verification and see if a dead Amir Abadai can give us any more information on the source of the explosive or the money behind the attacks. You update your side, and I'll update mine. I'll give you a call after I catch up with my team. It'll be in about an hour. I need to let my overnight team get a few more hours of sleep before I wake them."

"The FBI director wants the press conference in two hours," Riccardi added. "I'll mention the Secret Service support in the briefing. Talk to you soon."

Mac was wide awake. He reached over the side of his cot and pulled on his pants. He put on his shirt from the night before. He looked at his watch and knew it was nearing lunchtime in Washington, DC. He pulled out his phone and dialed the director's office in DC. Dennica Green picked up.

"Hi, Dennica, it's Mac Krieger. Is Director Fitzgerald in?"

In her calm, professional voice, Dennica said, "Hello, Agent Krieger. It's good to hear your voice. Director Fitzgerald is attending a luncheon with the Security Council. I'd recommend you email or text him if you have urgent news. He usually will try to respond at the next available break."

"Thanks, Dennica. I'll text him right now. Can you put me through to Andrea Douglas-Pfeiffer?"

"Please hold, Mac, I am transferring you now." The line clicked, and in seconds, Andrea's phone began ringing on the other end.

"Andrea Douglas-Pfeiffer," she answered in a sunny voice.

"Andrea, it's Mac, calling you from San José."

"Hi, Mac, it's early out there. How can I help you?"

"Amir Abadai is dead," Mac said. "According to Riccardi, whose team is on-site. They still need to recover the body."

"That's good news, isn't it Mac?"

"Not good," Mac sounded frustrated. "I wanted him alive. We needed to interrogate him and find out who was behind these attacks. I find it hard to believe Abadai had the resources to fund these attacks himself. It seems like there should be a bigger organization."

"It sounds like you need to catch this woman," Andrea said. "How can I help you do that?"

"We have the APBs out on her in California and along the border, but I'm worried about the border. If she gets into Arizona or New Mexico, there are many places where she could get across. Can you do some research for me? Can you find out whatever you can on how people cross into Mexico from the US? Where are the most common areas for going south? Are there people out there who specialize in getting others into Mexico?"

"I'm on it, Mac!" Andrea said. "I've got a few ideas about where to start. I'll get back to you in a couple of hours." Andrea clicked off, and Mac pulled his phone buds out of his ear. He started texting Director Fitzgerald but stopped when he looked around the room at his sleeping team. He got up from his cot and left the conference room, looking for a cup of coffee to help him finish the text.

## Day 25, 9:00 a.m., Manzanita, California

The faded red Toyota Camry pulled away from the small filling station called "Mountain View Market and Gas" outside Pine Valley and turned east toward Old Highway 80. Batalle sipped coffee as she drove away from the gas station. She went about a mile down the road before finding a pull-off. She had driven almost 600 miles overnight and was still in California. Stopping the car, she put down her coffee, pulled a map of California and Arizona, and studied the highway. The highway she was on was south of the primary traffic artery of Interstate 8 and ran parallel to the US-Mexico border.

As she sat, with the car idling on the side of the road, she studied where the highway routed. "Jacumba Hot Springs," Batalle mumbled out loud. "It will have to work." She folded the map. The road ahead was visible, and she placed the map in the passenger seat. Almost two hours later, after following the highway in and out of the shadow of Interstate 8, the road finally wound south toward the border and Jacumba. She was in the high desert, coming out of the Laguna Mountains. The area was barren. Scrub brush and a few ranch buildings scattered every ten to twenty miles.

As she drove along the highway west of Jacumba, she got her first glimpse of Mexico off in the distance. Batalle frowned and inhaled a whistle through her teeth when she saw the newly built border wall. It was an impressive barrier. Twenty feet tall, it cast a long, dark shadow on the landscape. She slowed the vehicle to a stop alongside the road and stared at the wall, continuing in a straight line as far as she could see. She took another look at the border wall and whispered under her breath, "How the hell will I get into Mexico?"

## Day 25, 12:00 p.m., San José

Mac and his team were moving fast on Interstate 101, heading south toward Redwood City. Twenty minutes ago, he had received a call from FBI dispatch about a suspicious death at a used car dealership on El Camino Real in Redwood City. Mac joined his daylight team by catching a ride with John Edward Walker, who was itching to get involved.

As Walker and Krieger rolled south from San José with lights flashing, David Osrick, running fifteen minutes ahead, and the five other team members arrived in two black Chevrolet Suburbans at Charo's Used Cars. Two Redwood City police black and whites, an emergency services vehicle, and an unmarked detective's car were already there. The six vehicles took up all the remaining space in the small corner lot not already taken by the small inventory of used vehicles.

Cops circled the property looking for evidence when a detective stepped out of the trailer Charo had once called an office. Osrick and a couple of the agents with him approached the detective.

"Who are you?" The detective looked at the agents. "We're a combination of FBI and Secret Service," Osrick said, pulling out his badge. "You must be Detective Corino?"

"Yeah, but how do you know who I am?" "The Redwood PD shared the details with us about thirty minutes ago," Osrick said. "We're looking for leads on a woman who may be responsible for the bombing in San Francisco. We understand this murder looks unusual. Can you fill us in?"

Corino looked at his feet. "Let me make a quick call to understand how I'm supposed to proceed." Corino pulled out his phone and stepped away. Moments later, he was back.

"Okay, we're good. I've been told to help you in any way I can. The short story is about a dead man inside the trailer. He's been strangled with something thin, like a piano wire, or maybe even smaller, like a guitar string. The head was almost decapitated, and the carotid artery was cut before he died. Half of the floor is covered in blood. It's a mess. We've not found the murder weapon, but we did find a footprint in the blood. We're unsure whose footprint it is now, but it appears to be a woman's shoe based on the size."

"Who found him?" Osrick asked.

"His girlfriend did. He didn't come home last night. She came by to check on him and opened the door."

"Is it her print?"

"No, we don't think so. She doesn't have the same shoe size."

"Anything missing?"

"The girlfriend told me of a nice red Toyota she wanted Charo to buy. It's no longer on the lot. We looked for any papers on a sale and found nothing. There's some blood on the drawer holding the titles, and the title for the car isn't in the drawer," Corino said, "but that's not a guarantee of much at this point. He may have sold it in the last day or two."

"It's a possible lead," David said to another agent, who nodded in agreement. "Do you have any details on the make, model, year, color, or VIN?"

The detective paused momentarily, then said, "Wait a minute. The girlfriend showed me a picture of the car from her phone. I'll get it for you." He walked over to one of the patrol cruisers, opened the back door, and spoke to a round-faced Latino woman sitting quietly inside. She handed him her phone. Corino brought the phone back to Osrick and his team. They looked at the phone, and one of his team members spoke up.

"That's a Toyota Camry," the agent said, "'06 or maybe '07. I used to have one."

"You sure?" Osrick asked. "Yes, sir, I'm sure," the agent confirmed, looking again at the picture. As this exchange occurred, Krieger and

Walker pulled up at the curb, jumped out, and walked up to the group. David was quiet as Mac nodded toward Corino.

"Detective, I'm Agent Krieger, and this is Agent Walker." Mac turned to Osrick, "David, what have you learned?" Osrick ran through the facts.

"Can we see the body?" Mac asked.

"The investigation is still ongoing," Corino said. "The crime scene van isn't here yet. I can't let you into the crime scene. I'll let you look in the door, but you can't enter."

The group approached the door to the trailer, and the detective stepped off to the hinge side and pushed it open. Osrick, Krieger, and Walker looked in at the body and the obvious signs of a struggle. After about three minutes of quiet interchange, the three federal agents stepped back down the steps, and Corino pulled the door closed. They returned to the front of the Suburban and stood in a circle.

"Pretty gruesome," Walker observed. "Do you think this is our suspect?"

"I think it may be," Mac said.

Osrick looked at Corino and said, "Detective, when was the last time you saw someone's head almost cut off with a guitar string? Have you ever heard of one in San Francisco?"

"Not in the last twenty years," Corino said. "At least not since I've been on the force."

"It makes me think it's her," Mac said. "It's a silent, quiet kill, something an assassin would do. It's not something your average bad guy with no training could do. Thugs use guns or maybe knives to do the deed. This shows preparation and training. I think it may be her."

"I'll update the APB to include the car," Osrick said. "She has about a twelve, to fourteen-hour lead on us."

"David, can you call the California Highway Patrol and the Border Patrol and get them looking for the car?" Mac asked.

Turning toward the detective, David offered his hand. "Thank you, Detective Corino. I'll let you know if we find the car or suspect. We appreciate your help." Corino nodded and turned back to his murder investigation.

"If she has a car, she's running," Osrick told the group. "Most likely, she's running south toward Mexico. She would probably guess we've got an APB with her photo out to the Border Patrol and law enforcement. She will try to bypass the main border crossings."

"David, I think a small team should catch a flight to San Diego. Will you lead it? Head toward the San Ysidro border crossing, make sure your team talks to each agent on the border, and review the video of the cars going south into Mexico, looking for this Toyota Camry," Mac said.

"I'm on it, boss." Osrick nodded at Mac. "We'll leave one team here in the Bay Area chasing any new leads." David watched as Mac turned to John Edward Walker.

"Agent Walker, I think I'll head south to LA. Could you help me pick up my gear and maybe drop me off at the airport?"

"Let's go," Walker said. Then he added, "If it's okay with you, I'd like to join you for the next few days on the hunt for the woman."

Osrick climbed into the passenger side of the Suburban. Glancing at his driver, he twirled his finger, indicating it was time to go. He watched as Mac and Walker headed toward Walker's Chevrolet Suburban. As they pulled out of the small dealership, the Redwood City crime scene van arrived to process the scene.

# CHAPTER THIRTY-THREE

## Day 25, 1:00 p.m., Jacumba Hot Springs, California

Batalle pulled into Jacumba Hotel at about 1:00 p.m. Painted white, sun-bleached, and sandblasted to an ugly ochre, the worn and dilapidated building from the 1960s had six cars parked outside. It looked like a roadside motor lodge that hadn't seen a new coat of paint in two decades.

Katerina didn't care. She was tired and wanted a quick shower and a short nap. Three hours later, she walked out of her room. Her clothes were clean, heavily wrinkled, and only partially dry. She had slept on her wet hair. She needed something to eat and drink and to keep moving. She didn't leave anything in the room.

Outside the hotel, the afternoon's heat was approaching ninety degrees, and a south wind blew about five miles per hour. When a car drove by, it created dust whirlwinds in its wake. The sky was clear, blue, and almost cloudless. Batalle looked up at the sky, winced, and shielded her eyes from the sun as she exited her room. She lowered her hand and looked up and down the street. To her right, she spied a small cafe about a half-block away. It looked as old and worn as the hotel. A red neon sign declared, 'OPEN.'

She walked to the cafe and went in. A petite Hispanic lady behind the counter greeted her by pointing to a table and asking her to sit down. Within a minute, the counter lady walked over with a glass of water and a menu and set it in front of her.

"Welcome," the waitress seemed unhurried. "Special today is turkey with mashed potatoes. What would you like to drink?"

Batalle looked at the woman, "Can I still get breakfast?"

"Sure, we make breakfast all day. Do you want coffee?"

"No, I need to hydrate. Can I get another glass of water, and can you make me an omelet with ham and onions?"

"Certainly," the waitress scribbled on her notepad, "skillet potatoes or hash browns?"

"Skillet potatoes sound good."

185

"Toast?"

"How about wheat toast?" Katerina hadn't eaten a good meal for a while.

"We've homemade brown bread that's quite good."

"Homemade would be great, thank you." Katerina smiled.

"Should be up in a few minutes," advised the waitress. "Let me know if you need anything else."

## Day 25, 4:30 p.m., Ontario, California

When the call came into Walker's phone, Krieger and Walker were on Highway 60, southeast of Riverside.

Walker turned on the speaker phone, "Walker."

"Agent Walker, this is Captain Torres from the Border Patrol."

"Hello, Captain Torres. You're the speaker. Agent Krieger is in the car with me."

"Perfect," the Captain said. "I was told to contact Agent Krieger, but I was only given your phone number."

"No problem, Captain, this is Mac Krieger," interrupted Mac. "What's happened?"

"We're not sure, sir," Torres hesitated. "One of our rookies near Jacumba contacted us a few minutes ago and told us she received the updated APB and may have seen a car earlier today matching the description."

"Tell us more," Mac encouraged.

"Yes, sir," Torres said. "Like I said, she's a rookie. She didn't check her search list for updates for hours. But she did call when she saw the APB and reported seeing a faded red Toyota with temporary plates."

"Mac, we're about three hours from Jacumba," interjected Walker.

"Captain, do you have anyone near Jacumba who could cruise the area looking for a red Toyota Camry?"

"I've got the same agent heading there now," Torres said. "She should reach the town in about thirty minutes."

"Thanks, Captain; give her this number, and please have her call us directly if she sees the vehicle," Mac then cautioned. "Don't have her attempt to intercept the vehicle or apprehend the driver. This woman is a killer, and I don't want to risk your agent's life."

"Yes, sir," Torres said. "I'll do that. I assume you're headed toward Jacumba?"

"As we speak, Captain. Agent Walker will probably try to set a land speed record."

## Day 25, 5:00 p.m., Jacumba Hot Springs

Batalle had finished her late afternoon breakfast and paid her bill. She was finishing her third glass of water. She hoped to find someone in Jacumba to help her, but she was surprised to find it was the person sent out to bus her table. He didn't speak English, was quietly doing his job, and didn't even try to start a conversation. He checked the window and door to see who was stopping outside the cafe. She was surprised when he suddenly stopped his work and stared out the window.

Batalle glanced over her right shoulder and looked out the window. A dark green Border Patrol truck rolled slowly past the cafe. The officer in the truck, wearing dark glasses, looked away from the cafe toward the hotel. She watched as the truck slowly continued moving through town and turned onto the highway, heading out of town.

As her face returned to the cafe, the young man was nowhere to be seen. Inside the kitchen, she could hear some quiet voices. Then, a door was opened and closed somewhere in the back. The waitress reappeared behind the breakfast counter with a full carafe of coffee and began refilling the coffee cups of the few patrons sitting at the counter.

Batalle picked up her belongings and left the cafe on Main Street. She found an alleyway leading to the rear of the cafe. She walked around the building and saw the young man smoking a cigarette near the garbage bin.

In Spanish, Batalle asked the young man, "Are you on break until the Border Patrol leaves the area?"

"Yes," nodded the young man, "the Border Patrol, INS, local cops, anyone carrying a badge. I have an agreement with the owners. I can take a break whenever one of them shows up. I'll work later into the night to cover the lost time."

"Where are you from?"

"Tamaulipas," said the young man, "along the Gulf of Mexico."

"How long have you been in the US?"

"This time, about three months. The last time I was in the US, I worked in construction in Texas for four years. I went home to see my mother for a few months, but getting back into the United States took longer, and it was impossible through Texas. That's why I'm here in California. I'm lucky to have a job and a place to sleep." The young man nodded in the direction of the cafe's back door.

Katerina nodded at him. "I'm looking to get into Mexico, but not through the normal border crossings. Do you know someone who might help me?" The young man looked her up and down.

He smiled at her. "You must be in trouble, yes?"

"Can you help me? Yes, or no?" Batalle demanded.

"What's in it for me?" The young man said.

"One thousand dollars if you help me find someone to take me into Mexico today."

"Today? You must be on the run from something or someone. Let me see the money," the young man said, standing upright and trying to look menacing. He took a couple of steps toward Batalle and stopped.

She laughed at his change of attitude. "What, you think you could steal it from me? Good luck if you want to try it. And no, you don't get to see the money. Either you help me, or I leave, simple as that."

The young man stepped back to the barrel he had sat on previously. He looked at her. "I could introduce you to the man who helped me. He lives in the area. He knows people."

Batalle looked at the young man. "Contact him now, set up a meeting. When he shows up, and I'm satisfied he can and will help me, I'll give you your money."

"Give me a few minutes to call and set it up. Let's meet back here in thirty minutes." The young man snuffed his cigarette in the dirt with the toe of his boot and walked toward the cafe's back door. He disappeared inside and left her standing alone.

Katerina looked up and down the empty alley and agreed it was as good a place as any to meet. She walked around the building to the main street. Not far away was a small Tractor Supply store. It had a few trucks parked outside. She walked toward it.

Thirty minutes later, Batalle exited the store looking much different. She was wearing new tan-colored hiking pants with new hiking boots and carrying a desert camouflage military-style backpack. Her old clothes were stuffed into a trash can in the ladies' room.

She was a few minutes late getting back to the cafe. Two men were standing outside the building. One was on the phone, standing beside a newer Ford F-250 crew-cab pickup truck. The young man who worked in the cafe tapped the other man, a few years older, on the elbow and pointed in the direction of Batalle as she approached the two men.

She asked the young man, "Is this the man?" The young man nodded. The slightly older man, Caucasian and maybe thirty, hung up and looked at her.

"Diego tells me you want to get into Mexico undetected." The man spoke in English.

"That's right," she confirmed, "can you help me?"

"It's expensive and dangerous. Can you afford to pay?"

"How much?" Katerina asked.

"Ten thousand in cash. Five thousand now, three thousand when I get you to the border and show you where to cross."

"That's eight thousand dollars," Katerina said.

"I'll arrange a pickup for you on the other side. The other two thousand will be paid to my colleague on the other side to get you to Chihuahua. After you're on the bus, you're on your own."

"What do I call you?" She looked at him.

"No real names. I don't want to know yours. You can call me Pedro, I'll call you 'Joda.'"

"Joda," Batalle laughed when she heard the Spanish word for 'Pain in the ass.' "When do we leave?"

"Stay here for ten minutes while I go gas up my truck. Find your cash. You can pay me when I return. And be ready to go. If all goes well, you'll be across tomorrow night." Pedro climbed back into his pickup truck and roared off.

Katerina and Diego watched him leave. She pulled out one thousand dollars and gave it to Diego. He smiled and put the roll of money into his pocket. "I have to go back inside and work," Diego said in Spanish.

"Go ahead," Batalle said as she counted out an additional five thousand in cash. The eighteen thousand she had pulled out of her crypto account was dwindling, but she had no choice. This could be her only chance at getting into Mexico.

Ten minutes later, Pedro drove into the alley. He looked at her. "Is the Border Patrol looking for you?"

"Possibly," Katerina said. "Why?"

"Two BP trucks are in town, and it looks like a couple of other unmarked cars are also there."

"They may not be after me. Could be after someone else."

"Right," Pedro smirked at her. "This is the first time I've seen this many cops in this little town, and it coincides with your desire to cross into Mexico."

"Can we get going?" Katerina asked.

"Get in the backseat and sit on the floor; keep your head below the windows. There's a blanket back there in case we get stopped. You go under it. Understand?"

"That's the best you have? A blanket?" Batalle looked incredulous, "I thought I was working with a pro."

"You are," Pedro hissed. "I didn't know you could pass as a Caucasian until I met you. We will head to my place and pick up some camping gear. We're going 'camping' near the border if anyone asks. But I don't want anyone to see you in Jacumba or at my home. Shut up and hunker down. We will move you to the front seat in about an hour." She did as told and sat on the rear seat compartment floor in the truck.

"Hand the five grand over when you get settled," Pedro growled over his shoulder. Batalle gave Pedro the money. He put the truck into gear and rolled forward through the alley. At the end of the street, he turned and drove down the block and onto the main street, moving past the cafe and the hotel on his way to the highway. She watched him as he paid little attention to the two Border Patrol trucks and the black Chevrolet Suburban stopped in the parking lot. Later, he told her they were particularly interested in an older red Camry sedan in the parking lot.

# CHAPTER THIRTY-FOUR

### Day 25, 7:00 p.m., Jacumba Hot Springs

Krieger and Walker bagged two red hairs from the pillow on the bed and secured them as evidence. With the help of the Border Patrol agents, they slipped a Slim Jim inside the door and had it open in seconds.

The car was clean, except for another red hair found on the driver's headrest and a used coffee cup. Looking for DNA or fingerprints, Mac bagged both items and dropped off the evidence at the Federal Express office in Calexico.

On his return to Jacumba Hot Springs, he unknowingly met the truck carrying Katerina and Pedro, driving in the opposite direction on their way to Tucson.

### Day 25, 8:35 p.m., Near Rio Rico, Arizona

Katerina was enjoying the ride along Interstate 8. After the quick stop at Pedro's small home outside of Jacumba, she stayed low in the back seat of the large pickup truck until they were about to get onto the Interstate south of Desert Tower. Once in the front seat, they appeared to all interested parties as a couple on their way to Arizona for a camping weekend.

They stopped at a small cafe on the outskirts of Tucson for a late dinner and then headed south toward Nogales. At Rio Rico, they turned off the interstate and followed a lonely highway west for ten miles until they reached White Rock Campground. Pedro set up the tent as the sun was setting.

As she watched Pedro set up the tent, she looked around the campground. Most campers were couples or young families escaping their suburban lives for a few days. Kids were laughing, and adults were relaxing. The campground was small and packed. It advertised a short half-mile walk to Pena Blanca Lake. She saw swimsuits and towels drying in the other campsites.

After the tent was up and the sleeping bags tossed in, Pedro set up a light inside the tent and motioned for Katerina to crawl into the tent. She carried her backpack into the tent and rolled out a sleeping bag on the floor. She stretched out on the bag and waited for Pedro to do the same.

"So, what's the plan?" Batalle watched him crawl across his sleeping bag and collapse onto his back.

"Tonight, you'll hear Border Patrol trucks on the road every thirty minutes. This is an active crossing area, and they watch this campground closely."

"You brought me into the heart of Border Patrol country?" Katerina's temper flared.

"Everything on the border is 'Border Patrol country,'" Pedro shot back at her. "Relax, you're in good hands. If you remember, when we checked in, I told them we were going to Ruby tomorrow. It's an old Ghost Town about twenty miles from here. I also told them that if we had time, we could hike into the Buffalo Soldiers Graves. They're about ten miles south of Ruby on an old forest service road. That's our activity plan for tomorrow, as far as the Forest Service knows. And you can be assured that if the Forest Service knows the plan, the Border Patrol will also know the plan."

"So we're telling the Park Service and the Border Patrol what we plan to see tomorrow, but somehow, I get across to Mexico?"

Pedro reached into his pack and pulled out a map of the area, which he spread on the tent floor between them. "We're here, see? Ruby is over here, about twenty miles to the west. To the south of Ruby is the Buffalo Soldiers' grave site," Pedro pointed at the locations on the map.

"I see the map and the terrain. What happens after we get to these places?"

"I'll tell you when we get there. The less you know, the better."

"Tell me what happens once I get into Mexico." Katerina probed for more information. "Who is your contact on the other side of the fence?"

"Miguelito is his first name. He's a close friend of mine. Migo and I grew up together in Jacumba and went to grade school together."

"How did he wind up in Mexico?"

"His father and mother were deported. They were in the US illegally, and INS finally caught up with them after fifteen years of working as migrant farmers in California and Arizona."

Pedro turned off the lamp and continued his story. "Migo could have stayed in the US since he was born here, but he decided to go to Mexico with his parents. He and I've been working together for almost five years, moving people from Mexico into the US. It's illegal, but it pays well."

Pedro whispered to her in the dark tent. "Look, I know it's frustrating for you without all the details, but you've got to trust me. I've done this before, and I can get you across. It would be best if you got some sleep. We want to be moving early in the morning."

## Day 26, 6:00 a.m., Rio Rico, Arizona

The light behind the park's namesake rock, directly east of the campground, began to glow in the early morning. They were up and moving. Katerina shivered and pulled her jacket around her. The desert surprised her with its early morning chill. Pedro finished packing the tent while she watched a coffee pot on a small backpacking stove for signs of boiling. Two mugs were standing by, ready for use.

"How did you sleep?" Pedro whispered.

"Good," Katerina said, her voice in a low whisper. "The ground was hard, but the sleeping bag was warm."

"We should be out of here soon. How's the coffee coming?"

"Almost ready, a couple more minutes," Katerina was watching the pot boil.

She looked up toward the sky, where the sun would be coming up in about fifteen minutes. "Do you like living in a desert?" "It's beautiful in its way."

"I think I'm more comfortable in a city where it's easy to disappear or blend in." Katerina was being honest. "This seems more dangerous to me than in the middle of a million people."

"Pour a cup of coffee for me," Pedro said. "It's time to get going. We'll wake up a few campers when we start the truck, but it can't be helped."

She poured two large mugs of coffee and poured the rest of the pot into a thermos bottle. Pedro broke down the small stove while the coffee cooled. He put it into the back of the pickup. The last thing to go into the truck were the two small camping chairs they were sitting on. When everything was packed, Katerina handed him his coffee, and they climbed into the truck.

The quiet of the early morning was broken when the truck started up noisily. Rolling forward slowly with the lights off, Pedro moved the truck out of the camping area as quietly as possible. He sped up when he reached the mile-long acccss road. They approached the Park Service building at the entrance; a Park Service Intern was at the window.

Disheveled and sleepy, she was missing her leisurely mornings in the dorm at Arizona State University. She smiled as they pulled up. "Getting an early start?" The intern asked.

"Yeah," Pedro said. "We're headed up toward Ruby. I want to show her the Ghost Town."

"Good to get an early start. It's not far, but the road is quite rough. You two have a good day."

Pedro nodded his thanks and rolled the truck slowly away from the gate.

Coming out of the park entrance, he turned onto Highway 39. As the pickup truck reached speed on the highway, Batalle's next question caught Pedro by surprise.

"Do you have a gun?"

## Day 26, 8:00 a.m., San Diego, California

The hair samples Mac had collected from the used car lot, the car, and the hotel room had arrived in DC overnight and had already been tested. They matched at a DNA level. The FBI was running a trace against several million records in CODIS.

Somehow, the woman had disappeared from the hotel. No one at the hotel could provide any information about where she could have gone. The clerk at the Tractor Supply store thought she may have been in the store and purchased some items. However, the clerk's recollections could have been better. The woman at the cafe said a nice redheaded woman had a late breakfast there, but she couldn't identify her from Mac's pictures. No one else at the cafe had seen her.

"She's got to be heading for Mexico," Mac told Walker as they sat in the FBI's San Diego field office. "I think she was in Jacumba because she's looking for a way to cross into Mexico."

## Day 26, 9:30 a.m., Ruby, Arizona

Katerina's bright red hair was tied up tight and pulled under her hat as she walked through the ghost town of Ruby, Arizona. They paid an entry fee to visit this far-flung, little-known ghost town well-preserved by the desert air almost one hundred years after being deserted early in the twentieth century after the mine nearby shut down.

Pedro explained to Katerina that his truck's license plate was recorded at the Forest Service campground they'd used last night, and he knew it was also recorded when they stopped to visit Ruby. The two locations could be confirmed if they were stopped by the US Border Patrol today. Pedro's cover story was simple. They were camping and sightseeing over the weekend.

"How long do we hang out here?" Batalle looked around at the other visitors and the Park Service employees. "I'm feeling exposed."

"Long enough for the people here to know we stopped," Pedro tried to calm her nerves. "We stay until about noon. After that, we head to the Buffalo Soldiers' Grave site. It should take about two hours."

"And after the Buffalo Soldiers site?" Katerina asked.

"After we get settled at the Buffalo Soldiers Grave Site, I'll tell you the rest of the plan. Be patient."

"I'll be patient when I'm in central Mexico," growled Batalle, "and away from here."

## Day 26, 11:20 a.m., Ruby, Arizona

A couple of hours later, they were making lunch on the tailgate of Pedro's truck when a Border Patrol officer pulled up and stopped next to them. Batalle, seeing the agent pull up in the car, put her head down and focused on making the meat and cheese sandwiches Pedro had instructed her to make. Two sandwiches were already made, but she was about to make several more for future meals when the Border Patrol agent stepped out of the vehicle.

"Afternoon," the officer nodded to Pedro as he climbed out of the Border Patrol vehicle.

"Afternoon, Officer," Pedro said coolly. "How's your day today?"

"Pretty good. I'm making some routine stops. Can I ask you a few questions?"

"Sure," Pedro said, "what can we answer for you?" "I see you're from California by your plates. What brings you to Arizona?" The agent asked.

"We're camping for a couple of nights and exploring some sites in the area," Pedro said. "We stayed last night at White Rock Campground, and today, we're visiting this place and, hopefully, the Buffalo Soldiers' grave site south of here."

"Okay," the agent wrote Pedro's license plate number in a small notebook. "The road down to the grave site is rough, but I'd guess your 4x4 should be able to make it. Where are you heading after you visit the grave site?"

"We're heading back to California. I think we'll stay in a hotel with a shower tonight." Pedro nodded toward Katerina when he mentioned the hotel and shower.

The agent smiled. "I'll let the other agents know you will be on the road to the grave site. We patrol this area often because of illegal crossings."

"I'd appreciate that," Pedro looked at the agent. "I expect we'll be out of the area well before sunset."

"That sounds good. If you encounter anyone walking on the road, don't stop; keep moving. If you see a large group, turn around and leave the area. It's better to be safe."

"I understand. It's the same situation when camping near the border in California. We'll be careful."

"Very good," the Border Patrol Agent said as he closed his notebook. "Well, I'll leave you two to your lunch." The agent walked back to his truck and climbed in. He started the engine, rolled forward to another vehicle, and underwent the same interview process.

"Are we good?" Katerina whispered after she was confident the agent was busy with the next car.

"Perfect," Pedro said, "just where we want to be."

## Day 26, 1:50 p.m., Ruby, Arizona

Two hours later, Katerina and Pedro were about a mile from the border, having navigated the rough track. The narrow road was surrounded by dense scrub brush and small, thorny cedar trees. Pedro pointed to a small parking area and a narrow foot trail to the left side of the dirt road.

"That's the trail to the Buffalo Soldiers' grave site. We're going to park here for an hour." Pedro pulled the truck into the dusty parking area and stopped. He turned off the engine. "Get your backpack ready, with all your gear, water, and food. Don't forget your hat."

"I'm ready," Katerina said, looking at the sagebrush and trees. "Are we heading toward the grave sites?"

"No, we're about a mile away from another trail. Right now, we walk down the gravesite trail and wait for the Border Patrol to pass us. They will probably stop and check my plates against their list. Hopefully, it's a quick check, and they'll leave."

Pedro reached under his seat, pulled a Smith & Wesson M&P 9 mm pistol out, and checked the chamber for a round. She watched him put the gun inside his belt and pull his shirt over it to conceal it. He opened his door and climbed out. He pulled a small pack out of the truck, put it on his back, locked his vehicle, and led her onto the trail toward the gravesites.

They walked down the rough trail for about 100 yards. Pedro stepped off the trail and ventured into the scrub brush. He climbed a small rock outcropping, which gave him a view of the road and the parking area. He motioned for Katerina to climb up. They sat on a rock in the shade and waited.

Twenty minutes later, a green Border Patrol truck came slowly over the rough road and approached Pedro's truck in the parking area. The patrol truck stopped. The driver could see the other trucks' license plates. Less than a minute later, the Border Patrol truck slowly began to drive away. Katerina and Pedro sighed in relief, not realizing they were holding their breath.

When the truck cleared the top of the hill and was no longer visible, Pedro led Katerina back onto the trail and toward his pickup. Once on the road, they walked briskly south.

"Walk fast, but keep your eyes looking for any movement on the road ahead," Pedro advised. "We've about a mile to go, and we don't want anyone to see us on the road."

Katerina nodded at him and looked forward. Pedro glanced at the road behind them. Fifteen minutes later, Pedro caught Batalle's arm and signaled them to take a foot trail to the right. They stepped onto the trail, walked far enough that they couldn't be seen from the road, and took off their packs to cool down.

"We'll do a little preparation over the next hour," Pedro wiped the sweat from his brow. "In an hour, after seeing the next Border Patrol vehicle, I'll get my truck and bring it back here." Pedro opened his backpack, pulled out two hatchets and two folding tree saws, and tossed them onto the ground with two pairs of gloves.

"Grab a set," Pedro nodded to Katerina. "We must cut enough cedar boughs to cover the truck. It can't be seen from the air if we camouflage it."

"Seen from the air?" Asked Katerina as she reached down to pick up the tools.

"In the late afternoon and throughout the night, the border patrol uses helicopters to locate illegals. Fresh-cut cedar boughs hide the truck from overhead." Pedro explained. "If we do it early enough, the engine cools, and it's hard to see from the air even if they're using thermal cameras. By nightfall, you and I must be hidden and out of sight. I've got a place for us, and it's near the crossing point."

## Day 26, 6:40 p.m., Ruby, Arizona

They worked through the afternoon. The Border Patrol drove past their hiding place several times. The truck was retrieved from the parking area and pulled off the trail where they walked in. They immediately covered the tire tracks and hid the truck under cedar boughs. When they were done, Pedro stored the tools inside the vehicle. He pulled out a large, camouflage wool blanket and a liter of water. He slung his backpack over a shoulder, adjusted the pistol in his waistband, and motioned to her to follow him.

They followed an old game trail into Snyder Canyon. The drainage was rocky and sometimes steep. She watched where she put every step and picked her way along after him. After forty minutes of walking, they came to a small fork and took the trail to the left, continuing downhill and edging closer to the border wall. Batalle tried to remember where they traveled in case she needed to return, but finding suitable landmarks was almost impossible. The trees looked the same everywhere, as did the rocks.

Almost an hour later, Pedro stopped. The sun was beginning to set in the western sky.

"We're staying here for now," Pedro whispered. "It will be dark in two hours. We must hide, eat, and rest for a while." He pointed to a small collection of rocks surrounded by thorny scrub bushes and told her to find a place to sit down. Katerina stepped into the small space and looked for snakes, cacti, or thorns before sitting down and looking back up at him.

Pedro unfolded the wool blanket and threw it over the hiding place. The blanket caught on the scrub bushes overhead and lay across the rocks on either side of the space. He used some heavy rocks to hold it in place. The blanket looked almost like a tent. He began to wet it with the water bottle he had brought.

"What are you doing?" Batalle asked, feeling water drip through the blanket onto her head.

"The water in the wool blanket will bring the wool to the same temperature as the surrounding air," Pedro explained, "and hide us from thermal imaging cameras they use in the helicopters."

"Does it work?"

"I've used it before. If we hear helicopters, we get under here. Keep your feet and arms under the blanket when we hear the helicopters. Got it?"

"Understood," she said. "When do I cross the border?"

"Migo is expecting you after midnight. We'll move down to the crossing point at midnight, between helicopter runs. The timing is important to get right. Relax, sleep, eat, and hydrate until about eleven o'clock. Be ready to move."

"How do you get back out?" Katerina was curious about his exit plan.

"After you're through, I return to this spot and wait until there is another gap in the border patrol flights. Then I'll take the blanket, cover myself, and walk out. It'll be cold and wet, but it'll work to camouflage me from the border patrol. I'll sleep in my truck until about mid-morning and drive out casually. I'll return to California, hopefully missing any Border Patrol stops. If anyone does stop me and ask about you, I'll tell them you caught a ride home with a friend."

# CHAPTER THIRTY-FIVE

### Day 26, 11:00 p.m., Arizona Border Wall

Almost four hours later, Pedro tapped on a sleeping Batalle's arm. She was instantly awake. "Time to go," whispered Pedro. Katerina stretched her legs as she stood outside the makeshift tent. She had several sore areas from sleeping on the rocks, and she tried to rub them away. She picked up her backpack and put it on.

"Wait a minute," Katerina said to Pedro. She walked up to him and, with a swift movement, pushed him off balance. While he flailed his arms to catch his balance, she deftly pulled the gun out of his waistband and turned it on him.

"Hey! Now, was that necessary?" He asked.

She reached into her pocket and let five hundred dollars fall to the ground between them. "I'm not stealing it from you. This is payment for the gun. I think I'll need it in Mexico more than you'll need it on this side."

Pedro looked at the money on the ground and slowly bent down to pick it up. "You could have asked." He growled.

"You would have told me no. I moved things along a little quicker."

Pedro looked at his watch as he knelt on the ground. "Well, we've got to get going if we're going to make this work and not get caught," he said.

"Lead the way. I'll be right behind you." Pedro walked down the trail, followed by Katerina, about three to four yards behind him.

Twenty minutes later, they were less than half a mile from the fence when they heard the sounds of a helicopter.

"Shit!" Pedro exclaimed. "They're not due for another hour! We've got to run!" Pedro moved fast across the rough terrain toward the border wall, with Batalle following closely behind. The sound of the helicopter grew louder as it crested the hill parallel to the border wall. It had a spotlight sweeping right and left across the border.

Pedro and Katerina were less than a quarter mile from the border when the helicopter appeared over the hill. Pedro signaled to Katerina to hide behind a scrub tree. If the spotlight hit them squarely, the tree wouldn't hide them enough. The helicopter slowed, and the spotlight began sweeping the hillside on the US side of the border, about a hundred yards from where they stood motionless.

Suddenly, the helicopter slowed to a hover and swung its spotlight toward the border wall and the Mexican side of the border. On the other side of the border stood a lonely coyote with a desert vole hanging from its mouth.

Bathed in the intense spotlight, with the loud aircraft noise, the coyote didn't know what to do. It dropped the vole and moved toward the brush, only to change its mind and run back to the vole. Picking up its dinner in its teeth, the coyote trotted back into the bushes and disappeared.

The Border Patrol helicopter kept the light on where the coyote had been moments before. Then, the aircraft moved forward and passed over the next ridge, disappearing into the night.

Pedro dropped to a knee to catch his breath. "That was close," he whispered to Katerina. "I don't know how they didn't see us."

"Come on, let's go," Katerina whispered. "Where to?"

"Follow me. We've gotta get up to the fence. It's in the low spot where the drainage is."

Katerina followed Pedro up to the border fence. They moved to a slight depression where rain, whenever it happened, would drain under the wall into Mexico.

"Here," Pedro moved some dried-out branches away from a round concrete culvert used for diverting rainwater, "this is where you go."

"I'm supposed to crawl into this and come out the other side?" Katerina was surprised.

"Yes, we use it often." He reached the top of the culvert and removed a metal clasp, securing a large iron grate to the opening. Opening the grate, he turned on a small flashlight and pointed it down into the concrete hole. It was dry and empty, at least as far as she could see.

"How do I know it's open on the other side?" Katerina asked.

"It only needs to be locked on one side to make it impassable, right?" Said Pedro. "Just trust me; I've used it before. There is nothing on the other side blocking the exit. You'll see when you get to the bottom and see out the other end. There is no grate on the outflow."

Batalle had put the gun in her waistband; now, she pulled it out and pointed it at Pedro. "You go down and show me it's open." She flipped the gun towards the opening. "You can come back after I'm through."

"Our deal doesn't have me crossing into Mexico, only you."

"I'm changing the deal." She shook the gun at Pedro. "Get in."

Pedro took off his backpack and scowled at Katerina. Holding his flashlight, he crawled into the opening and disappeared. She followed him at a safe distance.

The hole proceeded downward at a fifteen-degree angle for about twenty-five feet until it bottomed out. Pedro moved toward the outflow at the bottom of the culvert when he suddenly stopped and began backing up.

"What are you doing?" Katerina's voice echoed in the concrete tube as Pedro started to back up toward her. His arms and legs were moving fast.

"Snake!" Pedro screamed. He started throwing rocks and dirt in the direction of the snake. Batalle tried to see around Pedro with her flashlight but saw nothing.

"Stop!" Batalle yelled, "Move up against the left wall." Pedro did as she asked. Batalle played her flashlight down the culvert and trained it on the snake. It was a five-foot Western Diamondback rattlesnake moving slowly toward Pedro.

"Cover your ears and open your mouth," she told him as she pulled the gun up. She saw Pedro cover his ears. She aimed the gun at the snake and fired two quick rounds. The blasts reverberated in the concrete culvert and left her ears ringing. Pedro slowly uncovered his ears. He picked up his flashlight and trained it on the snake. Both bullets struck the snake, one almost taking its head off.

"Good shot!" Pedro called over his shoulder as he slid up to the snake and used his boot to push it ahead of him.

"What?" Batalle yelled. Her ears were still ringing from the two loud blasts.

Pedro looked back at her and motioned her forward. As they crawled to the lower opening, he dropped out the other side and waited for her to make it through. She climbed out, stretching her back and legs.

"See, as I told you, there's no grate on this side," Pedro said, picking up the dead snake by its tail and tossing it away from them a few feet.

"Good to know," Katerina grumbled, flexing her jaw to ease the ringing in her ears. "Where do I go now?"

Pedro whistled and flashed his light at the trees. A short whistle came back from the edge of the trees, and Migo stepped into the moonlight. He was smaller than Pedro but looked strong enough to hold his own in a fight.

"Hey, Migo," Pedro smiled at him. "How are you doing?"

Migo stepped closer and smiled at Pedro. He looked at Batalle, pulled his gun, and held it on her. "Who the hell was shooting at me?"

"Relax, pal, not at you, but at a big rattler inside the culvert."

"I got here only a minute or two ago," Migo said. "Otherwise, I'd have warned you about it. I always check it out before I put anyone in there. I think they go in there to cool off."

Migo kept the gun pointed at Batalle as Pedro walked over to where she stood with her hands partially raised and took back the gun she had taken from him.

"I bought that from you." Katerina nodded toward the gun.

"Sorry," Pedro smiled at her. "You almost got me killed by a snake." Turning toward Migo, Pedro said. "She's all yours, Migo, but I wouldn't trust her." He looked at his watch. "Gotta get back, brother. That last chopper came early."

As Pedro returned to the culvert, Migo motioned for Katerina to move away from the wall and into the scrub bushes. "Talk soon, brother," Migo said quietly as Pedro disappeared into the culvert. He turned to Batalle.

"We have a long night ahead of us. Can you ride?"

## Day 27, 2:00 a.m., Sonoran Desert, Mexico

It was dark. Not the 'pitch-black-can't-see-your-hands' dark, but dark with a tiny sliver of a moon reflecting light on the empty, desert landscape of saguaro cactus, thorny mesquite trees, and low hills of ancient rock outcroppings surrounded by sandy red dirt.

Batalle wasn't a rider. She knew how to ride a horse, but this was her first time on a burro. The burros they were riding were uncomfortable, by any measure, but they were much better than walking through the desert at night.

She decided the one she was riding was probably named "El Diablo" because it would intentionally walk close to the thorny mesquite branches to force its rider out of the saddle. She could feel some blood oozing from both legs where the sharp thorns had torn through her clothing and into her skin.

Migo suggested she try to rein the burro away from the trees when it headed toward them, but the burro was quite stubborn. After a few hours of fighting the burro, she gave up and would either dismount or try to balance in one stirrup as the thorns would scrape across the saddle, leaving deep scratches in the old leather. The miserable burro didn't seem bothered by the thorns.

The burro path they were taking was on the northern edge of the vast Sonoran Desert, and it seemed to Katerina that few people traveled this path either into or out of the US. Migo led the way, and she followed. As they moved away from the border, she relaxed for the first time since San Francisco.

"Why did you want to sneak into Mexico?" Asked Migo after several hours of riding.

"It was a bad situation," was all Katerina would volunteer.

"I'm taking you to Hermosillo and on to Chihuahua, is my understanding."

"If you can get me on a bus to Hermosillo, I'll be fine," she said fluently to Migo.

Migo turned around in his saddle, "You speak well. Do I detect a

Central American accent?"

"I've lived and traveled many places," Katerina said, "but I've been told before I sound like I'm from Panama or Costa Rica."

"Yes, they all have accents, like Mexicans from different parts of Mexico have different accents."

"What's your accent?" Katerina tried to keep a little discussion going.

"I sound like a kid who learned Spanish from my Mexican parents but grew up in the US. That's what my friends here in Mexico say. It's not a compliment."

The burro ride lasted most of the night. The burros followed the winding paths through gulches and ravines. By morning, they arrived at a small farm called Los Borregas. They rested, ate breakfast, and refilled water bottles. The burros were returned to the farmer with a cash payment from the money Batalle had given to Migo before they left the border.

After breakfast, Migo threw their packs into an old pickup truck. He drove south down a dusty track toward La Arizona and further to Santa Ana. He intentionally avoided areas with active Mexican Border Patrol units. They arrived in Santa Ana late in the evening.

"We'll stay here tonight. I'll help you get on a bus in the morning. There are no buses tonight," Migo said as he drove into a small farm on the outskirts of Santa Ana. He pointed toward a small house with a sign indicating it had rooms to rent. They walked up to the house, and Migo smiled at the young woman on the front porch who was washing pinto beans in a large bowl.

"Hola," the young woman smiled at Migo, "I see you've returned."

"Just for tonight, Theresa," Migo said. "Are there a couple of rooms available?" "Yes, do you have money?" Theresa asked. Migo flashed some cash, and she smiled up at him. Theresa led them into the house and pointed out a bedroom for each and a shared bathroom.

Katerina threw her backpack on her bed and headed toward the bathroom to shower with hot water. Twenty minutes later, she was out of the bathroom and heading toward her bedroom when she heard a noise from Migo's room. Stopping at the door, she could hear the sounds of the bed squeaking rhythmically and heavy breathing with controlled whispers. Batalle listened for a moment, then quietly moved along to her room.

She found a bottle of water and semi-cold beer on a small table. Reaching for the beer, she popped the top off. Closing the door, she settled into her room for the night.

The following morning, Theresa served a light breakfast of pinto beans with bacon and dark homemade sweet bread called 'conchas,' orange juice, and hot chocolate.

After they finished breakfast, Migo drove Batalle to the bus station in Santa Ana and watched as she bought a ticket for a bus to Hermosillo. He stayed in the area until the bus pulled out.

## Day 27, 10:00 a.m., Washington, DC

Mac walked into the DC office of the Secret Service. He was feeling upbeat. The Interpol DNA request took time, but it came through with a match to a hair found in a rental car that was linked to a bombing in Spain ten years ago. NSA supercomputers linked facial images taken in Dallas, Minnesota, New York, and San Francisco to the same woman using three aliases.

"Mac! Mac!" Andrea hollered at him as she came out of the elevators.

"Good morning!" Mac said, smiling at a breathless Andrea.

"I need to catch you before you meet with the director. Daniel Whitefeather has something important he wants to share with us. Can you spare a few minutes?"

Mac looked at his watch, "My meeting with the director is at 11:00 a.m. I have a few minutes for you."

"Let's go back to my office," Andrea smiled. "Daniel wanted to talk to both of us this morning, and I know it's got to be good news!"

"I'll follow you." Mac encouraged her to lead with a flourish of his hand.

In the break room near Andrea's office, Mac stopped and poured a cup of coffee from the large pot, then walked into her cubicle. Andrea was already at the computer. She sent a quick message to Daniel Whitefeather, who replied in seconds and soon was live on Andrea's screen.

"Hello, Mac, Hello, Andrea. Good to see you." Daniel smiled.

"Good to see you, Daniel. Andrea tells me you may have some news for us."

"Yes, I think I do. Let me give you the details, and you can determine for yourself."

"We're listening."

"I figured in today's world, criminals are exchanging not only cash but also cryptocurrency," said Daniel. Mac looked at Andrea and nodded at Daniel to continue.

"So, I set up a secure system and used it to jump onto the Dark Web. I searched crypto transactions from one week before the bombing until yesterday. About 200 thousand records were found, but only a few dozen from San Francisco. One transaction occurred less than twenty-four hours after the explosion."

"This is interesting," Mac said, listening intently.

"Here's what I think you'll like," Daniel smiled. "The location was an internet cafe in Redwood City. I called the cafe to see if they capture images of users. It's a security measure that some businesses do. This cafe captures a snapshot whenever a new user logs into the computer."

Daniel was busy on the other end of the video conference."Here's the image of the user who accessed their crypto wallet and converted crypto assets into about $18,000 she picked up from a crypto ATM about fifteen minutes after the transaction." Daniel shared an image of a red-haired Katerina Batalle, fresh out of the shower with still wet hair, looking concerned as she faced the screen.

"I'm not a facial expert, but I think that's her!" Mac quipped.

"Computer says it's a match." Daniel smiled.

"Excellent! Anything else?"

"One last thing: the initials on the crypto account are 'KB.' Although we don't know if it's her real name, we did find a current Spanish passport for this woman with the name 'Katerina Batalle.'" Daniel grinned on the screen.

"Wow! We have a name! We've got a new lead!" Mac whooped. "Daniel, can you flag the user and let us know if she makes another transaction?"

"It's already done," Daniel confirmed. "We should know within minutes of the transaction if it's on a busy hub. If it's on a small hub, the transaction could take longer to upload to the servers. But when it happens, we'll get an IP address and a location."

"Daniel, I know you've heard this before," Mac was serious but grinning. "But I'm happy you're on our side!"

After the goodbyes, Mac turned toward Andrea. "Katerina Batalle, if that's her real name, is in the crosshairs now. Can you update the APB with the new alias and add this photo and the Spanish passport photo?"

"I'll have it done in less than an hour, Mac."

"Thank you, Andrea, you're the best!"

# CHAPTER THIRTY-SIX

## Day 27, 2:00 p.m., Hermosillo, Mexico

Batalle made her way off of the bus when it arrived in Hermosillo. The ride had been uncomfortable, and the roads had been rough. The old bus was not air-conditioned. The people talked across the seats and shared food and drink as they traveled toward Hermosillo. She couldn't sleep.

Katerina looked at the clock inside the bus station. She had four hours before the next bus left for Chihuahua. She wanted to be better camouflaged for this next trip. She had a couple of hundred dollars left from her first crypto withdrawal. She needed makeup, a hair color change, a new change of clothes, and a new identity. The first three items could be managed with cash in hand. The last, a new identity, would take more time and money and may not be something she could do in Hermosillo. But she knew she could do it in Mexico City.

She left the bus station and flagged down a green and white Volkswagen taxi. She told the driver she needed a hairstylist and that they needed to be nearby. The driver nodded and took her to a stylist his wife recommended near the Universidad de Sonora, less than a mile from the bus station. Katerina was pleased. The distance was short, and she could walk to the bus station if needed.

The salon had sixteen chairs and was busy. Katerina figured she would soon be forgotten. She walked inside and was seated. She asked to look at the different color dyes and promptly picked a medium black dye. The stylist told her it was the most popular. Two hours later, Batalle walked out of the salon. Her red hair was gone. The length had been cut back a few inches to about an inch below her collar. The color was black. The style was short enough to hide under a wig and easy to maintain.

Batalle looked at her watch as she exited the salon. It was over an hour before she needed to be at the bus depot. Seeing a couple of students walking toward the university, Batalle asked them where the nearest internet cafe could be found. The students pointed down the street and gave her the cafe's name. On her way to the cafe, she stopped at a thrift shop, found a new outfit of gently used clothes, and changed into them.

Arriving at the internet cafe, Batalle paid for the computer time and slid behind an older desktop computer. She signed into her crypto wallet and initiated another transaction to convert a few more of her crypto assets to local currency. The local currency exchange was for Mexican pesos, equivalent to over $10,000 in US dollars. After being inside for ten minutes, she signed out of the account, rebooted the computer, and picked up her pack. She exited the cafe and walked to the assigned ATM.

The transaction was completed in a local crypto node and stayed in the node for approximately thirty-nine minutes before the blockchain transaction was added to the public database and copied, computer by computer, into the blockchain of the crypto network. Fifty minutes after it was entered, the specific transaction by the numbered crypto wallet, now known as being owned by Katerina Batalle, was flagged in Daniel Whitefeather's NSA crypto computer.

When the transaction was flagged in DC, Katerina was aboard the bus in Hermosillo wearing her new disguise. The bus exited the loading area and headed south on Highway 16 toward Chihuahua. This bus was slightly better than the last bus from Santa Ana. It was cleaner and had a swamp cooler attempting to cool the cabin. The moist air included occasional water droplets with a hint of mold within the air vents.

*Better than nothing,* Batalle thought as she settled for the long ride.

A new identity was next on Katerina's list. After ten years of this work, she was far more comfortable traveling on an alias. It had been almost four years since she had traveled through an international airport using her real name and passport.

## Day 27, 5:35 p.m., NSA Headquarters, Fort Meade, Maryland

Daniel Whitefeather's computer, cell phone, tablet computer, and pager all chirped, dinged, and tingled simultaneously. Daniel jumped into action and switched from programming to an email messaging screen. He read the notification: "POI #202345567 EVENT INDICATED 21:03:05 GMT." He clicked on the hyperlink, which took him directly to the detail, and scanned it. Dropping his pen on the desk, he called Mac Krieger's mobile phone.

"Krieger," Mac answered.

"Mac, this is Daniel Whitefeather. We've had a ping on our person of interest."

"What have you found?"

"I'm reading it now," Daniel paused. "It appears Katerina Batalle was online again. She was at a coffee shop near the University in downtown Hermosillo, Mexico, at 2130 GMT, about 3:30 p.m. in Hermosillo. She accessed the same crypto exchange as before. She probably needed to access more local currency. She wasn't online long; about ten minutes."

"Daniel, does Hermosillo have an international airport?" asked Mac.

"Let me check. Yes, Hermosillo International Airport is located there." Daniel was typing. "Give me a moment. There it is. Okay, Mac, there is one international flight to Phoenix. All the rest of the flights are within Mexico. I'd say it's not much of an international airport."

"Can you check all flights departing after her time on the computer and see if she was careless enough to use her passport in Hermosillo?" Mac asked.

"I can try Mac," Daniel said with some doubt. "However, the regional airports in Mexico are not known to be rigorous in passport documentation and routinely have internet issues. Mexico City is pretty good, but the others are not. I'll see what I can find and call you back."

"Thanks, Daniel. I appreciate the help. Can you please pass all of this information on to Andrea? You've found her twice, and we can see she's running. I think it's time to head to Mexico City and see if we can cut her off. Let us know when you find anything more."

## Day 27, 5:37 p.m., Washington, DC

Mac signed off with Daniel and turned away from the window overlooking the Washington Monument to face Robert Fitzgerald, Director of the US Secret Service, who sat behind his desk looking expectantly at Mac.

"NSA has again located Batalle's online presence, this time in Hermosillo, Mexico. She successfully crossed the border somewhere and made it to north-central Mexico."

Robert smiled at Mac, "I suggest you take a small team with you and go after her. Keep the joint task force in the loop, as you've been doing, but take the lead and track her down."

"Yes, sir," said Mac. "Although this is like chasing a ghost. We never know where she'll pop up next. She could be gone before we get to Mexico."

"You've got access to the largest database and the fastest computers on the planet with NSA. Use them." Robert encouraged. "The president wants her captured. He made it clear this morning at the daily briefing, and the security chiefs were all present. I've spoken to all of them, and you're closest to catching this terrorist. Don't stop until you do!"

"I'm taking a small team, only four or five agents with me. We'll use space at the US Embassy in Mexico City. Can you call the Ambassador to help grease the wheels?"

"I'll do one better. I'll call the Mexican Ambassador and request support from Mexican officials. I'll get someone to help you while you're in Mexico City."

"Perfect, thank you. I'll call you daily with updates." Mac turned from the window and walked to the door.

Director Fitzgerald smiled at Mac and said. "Call me before the president's briefing if you can. I like to keep him updated with the latest information before my colleagues try to steal my thunder." Mac smiled at him and nodded. He left the director's office, quietly closing the door behind him.

## Day 27, 10:05 p.m., Chihuahua, Mexico

Dust kicked up by the large tires enveloped the bus as it pulled into the parking lot of the poorly lit bus station in central Chihuahua. The dust cloud slowly disappeared into the darkness as the bus stopped and the door opened. At 10:05 p.m., the activity level in the bus station was minimal. A few old Volkswagen taxi cabs were loitering in the pickup area, awaiting folks with money for the fare and a destination. The bus riders began to exit slowly.

Batalle had been left alone by the other passengers on the bus. She sat next to a college-age girl heading home from University in Hermosillo. The girl was from Mexico City and had arranged to stay the night at a hostel in Chihuahua, not far from the bus station. Katerina bought her a sandwich at the third stop when it became apparent she didn't have enough money for food and the bus ticket.

She was one of the last people off the bus as it emptied. Before exiting, she peered through the windows on all sides of the bus, looking for signs of someone watching: a parked car, people loitering, a police car, or someone watching from a nearby window. In her heightened awareness, almost anything could have triggered her alarm. But she saw nothing to be alarmed about.

## Day 28, 9:45 a.m., Mexico City

Mac and his team were met as they departed the American Airlines flight in Mexico City by a team of five from Policía Federal Ministerial, the branch of the Mexican Federal Police primarily focused on drugs and corruption but also tasked with terrorism. Salvador Cano Garcia, the Deputy Minister, was the only welcoming committee member who had difficulty fitting into his dress uniform.

Mac was the first person to deplane. Wearing a windbreaker and carrying a small black duffle bag, he approached Cano.

"Deputy Cano?" Mac put his hand out to the sweating man in the dress uniform.

"Si, I mean, yes," Cano said. "You must be Special Agent Krieger of the US Secret Service?"

"Yes, I am. I'm pleased to meet you. Let me introduce my team: Bill Elliot, FBI; David Osrick, Secret Service; John Riccardi, FBI; and Andrea Douglas-Pfeiffer, Secret Service Intelligence Services."

"I'm pleased to meet all of you," Cano smiled. "Each man behind me has been hand-picked to help you; all have excellent English language skills. I have five vehicles outside the airport and Mexico City Police on motorcycles. Agent Krieger, you and I will ride with my driver wherever you want us to go."

"You can call me Mac, Deputy," Mac said as he and the rest picked up their bags. "Andrea needs a ride to the US Embassy to set up shop. The rest of us all have assignments to watch the four Mexico City bus terminals for arrivals from Chihuahua."

Cano nodded at Mac and directed his officers to pair up with their American counterparts. The group walked to the front of the airport passenger terminal, where the vehicles were waiting, and departed.

## Day 28, 12:00 p.m., Chihuahua

*Twenty-four hours? On a bus?* Batalle stood outside the bus terminal in Chihuahua, looking at the schedule for Mexico City. *Let's try something else.* She stepped from the bus terminal, walked to a taxi, and climbed in.

"Aeropuerto, Terminal Privada," Katerina said. The driver nodded and slowly pulled the taxi away from the curb. She wondered what she would find as the cab drove thirty minutes to the private terminal at the Chihuahua airport.

Once inside the small building adjacent to the larger commercial terminal, Batalle saw a single small counter, the Fixed Base Operations counter, known to pilots as simply the FBO. A small cafe nearby was doing a good midday business with about twenty people in the area. She walked to the restaurant and sat beside a man wearing a pilot's uniform at the counter.

She ordered a soft drink and a sandwich. The man beside her paid his bill and left his seat. A few minutes later, the chair was filled again, this time by a much younger man. Batalle guessed him to be in his late twenties. He was dressed in casual clothes with a worn pilot's cap. He was sporting a three-day beard growth. She thought he might be a candidate.

"Are you a pilot?" She asked the man in English.

"Huh?" The man looked at her.

"You American?"

"Costa Rican," Batalle said. "You American?"

The man chuckled, "No, Señorita, I'm not American. I don't think I would be here if I were."

"Problem with Chihuahua?" she asked.

"Problem with Mexico," the young man grumbled. "Businessmen want to fly in jets; cartels will fly in anything. If you have a propeller plane, the best business is flying cartel members. But I don't fly for cartels. I don't want to wind up owned by the cartel or dead."

"I take it you're a private pilot." Katerina nodded at the waitress as her sandwich arrived. "People or cargo?"

"I take both," the pilot said evenly, "as long as they're legitimate."

"Are you based out of Chihuahua?" Understanding this woman wanted to talk, the pilot removed his hat and slowly turned toward her in his chair.

"What's your game?" Katerina, sandwich in mouth, stifled a cough and held up her hand as she swallowed the bite and drank to clear her throat.

"I'm sorry, I didn't mean to ask too many questions. I'm looking for a pilot and plane to take me to southern Mexico, near Belize. I'm looking to get back home to Costa Rica."

"Plenty of commercial flights available; you could easily get one of them."

"Yes, but I don't want to fly commercial," Batalle said. "I like the adventure of flying privately. I have a pilot in Costa Rica who flies me to and from our Hacienda to the airport when needed. I love the freedom of traveling privately. I think it's the lower altitude and the better views."

"It's a much longer flight at 250 miles per hour versus 500 in commercial jets." The pilot was growing interested in the woman. "And it's more expensive."

She winked at the pilot and smiled. "What's your name?"

"Eduardo DeLay, I fly a low-wing twin-engine Beechcraft Baron. She's in excellent condition and ready to fly."

"Any plans for the next couple of days?"

"Nothing I couldn't change for the right price." Edwardo countered.

"Could you fly me into Belize?"

"Do you have a passport?"

"Yes, but one I don't want to use for this trip."

Eduardo looked at her closely. "Cartel?"

She shook her head. "No, I'm not Cartel. I want to travel home to Costa Rica without notice."

"Are you running from something? I ask because I need to know if I'm risking anything here," Eduardo was serious.

"I'm no danger to you," Katerina smiled at him. "I want to travel home quietly to see if my husband is faithful to me."

Eduardo pointed to an open table near a window. He caught the waitress's eye and signaled that he and the young lady were moving to the table. She nodded. Batalle grabbed her water glass and sandwich and walked to the window table. After they sat down, the waitress brought

Eduardo's fish tacos and set them in front of him. After she went away, he looked at Katerina and began talking.

"Are you from Mexican Customs or Immigration or any police agency? If you are, you must tell me."

"No," Katerina played with him. "Are you?"

"No, of course not," Eduardo sputtered, "I take precautions to keep my pilot's license and not become a wanted person in Mexico. It's harder than you may think."

"Look, Eduardo," Katerina said. "I'll trust you, and you can trust me. I want to make it to Costa Rica. Can you get me there? Or part of the way?"

"I can get you to Belize," Eduardo said quietly. "There are many small airports within an hour of Belize City."

"How much to get me there?"

Eduardo looked down at his fish tacos; they were getting cold. He thought for a moment as he looked at her. "I can do it for five thousand US."

"Five thousand? For a flight to Belize?" Batalle retorted, "I can buy three or four round trips commercially to Costa Rica for that amount. I'll give you two thousand cash."

"Three thousand cash," Eduardo looked around and brought his voice to almost a whisper. "I'll make sure you get into Belize quietly."

She appreciated his attempts at negotiation, but she wasn't done. "Twenty-five hundred into Belize quietly, and we leave within an hour," Batalle said with finality. "How many stops?"

"Agreed," Eduardo offered his hand to her to shake. "Cash before we leave. I expect two stops for fuel."

"Fifty percent before we leave, fifty percent when we land, and I'll pay you cash for the fuel en route." She waited until Eduardo nodded before shaking his hand.

Eduardo smiled at her and suggested she pick up some water and snacks and visit the bathroom before they left. He went to fuel his plane and scheduled a departure with the FBO. Katerina smiled to herself and walked to the bathroom to prepare for a quiet flight to Belize.

## Day 28, 4:00 p.m., Mexico City

Mac Krieger and Deputy Minister Cano stood at the Central Bus Terminal-North arrivals area for five hours. They'd seen three buses from Chihuahua arrive and watched all the passengers depart. They compared photos of Batalle and stopped anyone who remotely looked like a possible fit for questioning. Of the two women they stopped, it was apparent within moments that they were not Batalle.

# CHAPTER THIRTY-SEVEN

### Day 29, 3:00 a.m., CIA Safehouse, United Arab Emirates

The bench was small, about six inches wide, and black. It was made of hardwood and well-designed for the purpose. One end was six inches lower than the other. When an individual was laid on their back with their head on the low end of the bench and arms tied together under the bench, the feeling was more than uncomfortable; it was suffocating.

The bench was designed intentionally for interrogation, and it was effective. The bench was where the CIA interrogation specialist put Imun Zocedia. CIA operatives took him after he locked up his server farm in the small city of Annau, Turkmenistan. Someone put a hood over his head when he badged out and locked the door. He felt a pinch in his neck as someone injected him with something. Then he lost consciousness.

The specialist watched as Zocedia soon realized he couldn't move. He couldn't see much when he tried to open his eyes. Everything was a blur. The room was much too bright. He couldn't hear much beyond the blood-pumping noise in his ears. He couldn't breathe easily and didn't know where he was. His heart rate was twice his average resting rate. The CIA specialist quietly watched him from a few feet away; he judged Zocedia was ready for the interrogation to begin.

By 3:30 a.m., the CIA interrogator had the name Jahar and nationality as well as names and phone numbers for five other Russian criminal cyber attack teams sponsored by the Kremlin. By 4:00 a.m., Imun Zocedia would have given his child, if he had one, to the interrogator to stop the questioning and let him sit upright. Exhausted to the point of crying, physically weakened, and psychologically broken, Zocedia would take several weeks to recover from the past few hours.

By 5:30 a.m., Zocedia was sleeping from exhaustion and a small dose of Valium mixed into his water. He would never know if his assailants were Turkmenistani, Russian, Uzbekistani, Arabic, or Afghan; he didn't know where he was or that he had arrived by plane. The questions were asked by a native Turkmen speaker who spoke no other language in the room. Six hours from now, he would be found exhausted and sleeping in an Ashgabat park with little memory of the entire night and a splitting headache.

## Day 29, 1:00 a.m., Unmonitored rural airstrip, Belize

At twenty-five miles from the daylight-only airstrip, Eduardo called his sister's ex-husband, Zaka. The man was always open to extra-curricular activity, especially if it yielded additional money for little work.

Tonight, Zaka was parked in his truck at the end of the small, unlit runway with a box of flares. When the call came in, he took three flares and snapped off the end of each flare, igniting it. The first one, he dropped at the end of the runway, and the other two he threw, one to each side of the runway.

Climbing into his truck, Zaka started the engine and pointed it down the middle of the dark runway. Every fifty yards, he stopped, ignited two flares and threw them to either side. He continued this until he reached the far end. Looking back, he saw the lights from Eduardo's Beechcraft Baron aligning to the runway and dropping into a landing glide path.

Zaka watched as the plane settled quietly onto the runway and braked, stopping about fifty yards from the end. In the cockpit, Eduardo turned the aircraft around and shut the lights and the engines off. In the darkness of the early morning in Belize, the only lights were from the red, slowly burning flares as they illuminated the plane.

The plane door opened. Eduardo led the way down the pathway; behind him was a tall, athletic woman carrying a small bag. Zaka rolled his truck, lights off, up to the plane. He stepped out, walked to the passenger side with a small flashlight, and opened the door. Katerina Batalle climbed into the passenger seat, and Zaka closed the door behind her and turned to Eduardo.

"So, I take her to a hotel in downtown Belize City?" Zaka looked at his former brother-in-law.

"Yes, she has a reservation at the Golden Bay Hotel," Eduardo confirmed. "Give her your phone number in case she needs your help. Otherwise, after you drop her off, we're done." Eduardo handed him a wad of bills worth about two weeks' average wages for Zaka and watched him stuff them in his pocket.

"If she needs my help?" Zaka let the unfinished sentence hang in the cool night air.

"You negotiate with her for any assistance you may provide," Eduardo said. Zaka nodded.

"How about you? Where are you headed?"

"I'm going back across the border into Mexico. I picked up enough fuel at the last stop to get halfway to Mexico City tonight. I'll land in the early morning hours, refuel, and be on my way back to Chihuahua. I should arrive by midday tomorrow."

"You better get going before the flares run out." Zaka looked down the runway. The first flare he had ignited was beginning to sputter.

"Gracias, amigo! Be nice to our lady friend and get her to the hotel."

"I will," Zaka promised. After briefly embracing, Eduardo walked back to his plane and climbed the stairs into the cabin, pulling up the stairs after him.

Zaka walked to the driver's side and climbed into the pick-up beside Katerina. They quietly watched as Eduardo started the plane's engines, went through a quick preflight routine, and initiated a takeoff down the same runway he had landed on. The flares were burned out, but the embers were still bright enough to let Eduardo know the runway limits. He had the plane in the air and began a slow turn to the north in a gradual climb.

In the truck, Zaka looked over at Batalle. "My name is Zaka. I'm taking you to Belize City, the Golden Bay Hotel." She looked at him and nodded.

"I need to pick up these flares, and then we're on our way." In less than two minutes, Zaka made a round trip and picked up the extinguished flares. He put them into a bucket with some water in the back of the truck.

"Does Eduardo fly here often?" Katerina yawned as she spoke.

"A few times a year to see his sister," Zaka said. "Usually, he flies in during the day. This is the second time he's done a late-night landing that I know of."

She nodded. "Do you know any pilots who could take me to Costa Rica, Zaka?" He looked at her. "I don't know many pilots, but I do know someone who might be able to get you a new passport. Would you be interested?"

"Yes," Katerina nodded and said. "Yes, I would be interested."

"I'll leave you my phone number when I drop you off at the hotel. You can call me if you want me to set something up."

"I'm going to take a nap," Katerina yawned. "Wake me up when we're close."

"Sleep well," Zaka murmured as he pulled onto a highway.

## Day 29, 7:00 a.m., Mexico City

Mac was disappointed but not surprised. They'd been in Mexico for over twenty-four hours and had nothing to show for their efforts to find Katerina Batalle. Mexican Deputy Minister Cano was interested in helping to find the terrorists but not in chasing ghosts. The Mexican and US teams agreed to meet in Chihuahua, the last known location for the woman.

"David, please call Natalie and have her book flights to Chihuahua as soon as possible. Ask her to book hotel rooms for two nights as well. Let's take everyone except Andrea; she can head home." They were sitting in a conference room in the US Embassy.

"Yes, sir," David confirmed. "We'll catch the next available flights and try to be in Chihuahua before the state police. Do you want me to get your flight as well?"

"Yes," Mac said. "I need about an hour to call the director to update him on the plan for today. If you can leave here before me, go ahead; I'll be on the next flight."

"I'll let you know what flights we can take in about fifteen minutes," David said, exiting the room. Mac looked at the agents from the FBI and the Secret Service in the room. "Well, everyone, pack your bags and meet back here in thirty minutes."

## Day 29, 9:00 a.m., Golden Bay Hotel, Belize City, Belize

Batalle stretched out on the king-size bed and yawned. She rolled over in the bed, dialed room service, and requested coffee and breakfast be delivered. The call took less than a minute. She flung off the sheets, sat on the edge of the bed, stood, and walked naked to the bathroom, where she turned on the shower.

When she came out of the shower with towels strategically wrapped around her head and body, she immediately noticed the blinking light on the phone. She went to the door and found her breakfast outside. The food was still warm, and the coffee was hot. She picked up the tray and looked up and down the empty hallway before closing the door.

Setting the tray down on the small table, she poured a coffee and pulled apart a piece of croissant. Munching on the croissant as she drank her coffee, she realized she was still hungry from yesterday's plane flight. She picked up the piece of paper Zaka had given her the night before and decided to call and ask for his help connecting with a passport forger in Belize City.

She picked up her cell phone and dialed Zaka's number. He picked up immediately. "Hola," Zaka answered.

"Zaka?" Batalle asked in English.

"Yes, you are the lady from last night. What can I do for you today?"

"Can you introduce me to your passport person?" Katerina asked.

"For a small fee, I'll be happy to do that, five hundred US."

"Five hundred is a bit on the rich side, Zaka," Batalle scolded him, "let's make it two fifty. I think that's more realistic for providing a contact."

Zaka thought fast. "Yes, but this includes me picking you up and being your taxi for the day. Wherever you want to go in Belize." She smiled at Zaka's resourcefulness.

"All right, Zaka, five hundred for the day. Pick me up in two hours from the hotel and plan to take me to your contact. I'll meet you out front."

"I'll be there," Zaka repeated, "two hours." Katerina hung up the phone, took another long drink of coffee, and looked out the window. She was six stories above the large pool. In the distance, the sandy beach and deep blue ocean were a short walk from the hotel pool. The hotel staff was setting out chairs and umbrellas for the day. She tried a few bites of the fruit ensemble accompanying the croissants. The mango was delicious.

"I need to keep moving," she reminded herself. She stood, dropped the towels, and began to get dressed.

## Day 30, 8:00 p.m., Islamabad, Pakistan

In the private enclave of Park View City in city sector F-15 of Islamabad, Jahar P'Shari pulled up to his mansion in his Bentley Continental GT Convertible. He stepped out of the expensive car and looked around for his employee, Baji, who was supposed to take the car away, wash it, and put it in the garage. But Baji was nowhere to be seen.

Muttering to himself about where Baji could be, P'Shari was oblivious to the three CIA operatives dressed entirely in black with H&K MP5 silenced rifles pointed at his head, approaching him silently from behind. One operative stopped twelve feet from P'Shari and looked through his short-range scope at the house, looking for a guard or someone watching. The other two operatives closed the distance. Three feet from the target, the lead operative slid his rifle down and off to the side as he pulled a black bag out of a pocket. The other operative pulled a hypodermic needle filled with a fast-acting agent to render P'Shari unconscious.

P'Shari heard a slight shuffle behind him, saw the man with the bag at the last instant, and immediately inhaled to scream. The operative pulled the bag over his head and put a gloved hand over his mouth, muffling the scream. The other operative plunged the needle into P'Shari's neck, emptying the syringe into him. Leaving the syringe hanging, he held down P'Shari's plump arms. The chemical worked on P'Shari, with his arms falling to his sides and the large man falling backward into the first operative's arms. He slowly lowered the collapsed man to the ground.

The two men positioned themselves head and foot on P'Shari and lifted, both grunting under the weight of his almost three-hundred-pound body. As they moved toward the drive, the third operative slung his rifle below his armpit, grabbed P'Shari's belt, and lifted hard, taking about seventy-five pounds of weight from the other two men and enabling them to move down the drive to a waiting van. Hauling P'Shari into the van, they set him beside Baji, who was sleeping quietly. The door closed, and the van with its occupants slowly moved away from P'Shari's home.

When the guard saw the van approaching the community's entrance, he turned off the video recorder, opened the gate, and let the van pass unchallenged. After the van was gone, the guard turned the video recorder on. In the low-level light of the guard shack, he reached into his pocket and removed a heavy envelope. He bounced it in his hand, admiring the weight of the cash. Smiling, he set about counting it.

# CHAPTER THIRTY-EIGHT

### Day 30, 11:50 p.m., CIA Safe House, Islamabad, Pakistan

In the basement of the CIA safe house on the outskirts of Islamabad, Baji began to awaken from the effects of the chemicals in his neck before Jahar. Once he did, he started screaming and struggling. The screams startled Jahar into consciousness, and he looked over at Baji, who was tied to the interrogation bench. Jahar grunted when he tried to move his hands and found them cuffed to the table where he sat.

Looking around and blinking, Jahar P'Shari found himself in a dark room, poorly lit except for one lightbulb over Baji and one over the table where he sat. He saw the backside of the man sitting beside Baji. The man spoke softly to Baji and encouraged him to calm himself like a mother does to a small child.

"There, there now, calm down. You'll be fine. I have a few questions for you." The small man spoke softly.

"I can't breathe," Baji stuttered, struggling against the restraints. "Who are you?"

"You have the information I want, and I think you'll give it to me willingly. I want information on your employer, Jahar P'Shari, and his family. If you help me, it'll get no worse than this for you. If you don't help me, it'll get much worse."

"Much worse?" screamed Baji. He struggled at the restraints again.

"Yes, it will. Talk to me, and I'll help you." Said the interrogator.

"What do you want to know?" Baji cried. Across the room, P'Shari sat with the gag in his mouth and watched.

"Who does Jahar P'Shari work for?" The interrogator asked.

"I don't know for sure. I think it's a bank or something," said Baji.

"Do you know what he does?" "I don't know anything about what he does," Baji moaned, "only that he travels a lot and has a lot of money. He buys a nice car every year. His wife has fine clothes and jewelry. His children go to the best schools," Baji whined as he struggled to free his hands.

"Tell me what you know about his wife." The interrogator changed subjects.

"She's beautiful but runs the maids and cooks out of the house with her demands. She's mean and unfaithful."

"How is she unfaithful?" The small man looked over his shoulder at P'Shari to see if he was listening. P'Shari raised his eyebrows and lifted his head toward the interrogation, still feeling the effects of the drug.

"She has male visitors come to her house when Mr. P'Shari is away and when the children are in school, at least once or twice a week. One of the men might have been a cricket player; the other is a doctor." Said Baji.

"How do you know she was unfaithful?" The interrogator pressed. "She's loud in the bedroom when she's with these younger men," Baji gritted his teeth in pain. "Would you like to know the cars they drive? I can tell you."

The interrogator looked to P'Shari again. Jahar's face was getting red as he listened to Baji tell all.

"Here's something for you," Baji said as he warmed to the informant role. "Mr. P'Shari sometimes wears a jacket with the word 'SAIB' on it. I don't know what it means, but he wears it sometimes."

"SAIB," the interrogator focused. "Any idea what the initials are?"

"I've no idea," Baji said truthfully. "Would you like to know something about his daughter?"

"What would interest me?" The interrogator let Baji talk. Jahar saw him glance over his back toward him to make sure he was listening.

"She's not a virgin. I know she's had sex with two of the house staff. Joberi was one, and Doujri was the other. One is the butler for Mr. P'Shari, and the other is one of the new cooks hired this year."

Jahar P'Shari moaned and thrashed against his restraints as he heard the news about his wife and his daughter. Tears were coming from his eyes, and his face was beet red.

"Time for you to take a nap." The interrogator took a needle from his pocket, removed the protective cap, and put it into Baji's arm above the elbow. The injection was quick. The chemical took about 10 seconds to send Baji into unconsciousness.

The small man got up, slowly walked across the room, and sat opposite P'Shari.

"Do you mind me calling you Jahar?" the thin man asked. "I know your preferred language is English. I don't want to listen to your poor Urdu, the official language of our country; I'll talk to you in English."

"Mmmmfh, Mmmfta," Jahar tried to yell at him, but a red rubber ball gag in his mouth prevented him from speaking.

"Ah, I can probably remove the ball from your mouth. Promise me you'll be pleasant when I do." The small man stepped behind Jahar and removed the gag from his mouth.

"You son of a bitch!" Jahar growled when the gag was removed. "Just who the hell do you think you are?" Not waiting for a response, Jahar continued. "I'll have you ruined! I know important people! I'll make sure you and your families disappear."

"You'll do nothing of the sort." The small man walked from behind Jahar to the opposite side of the small table. He reached across the table and slapped Jahar's face with a calloused hand. It wasn't a little slap. One could have heard it from a block away on a busy street. The slap reverberated through Jahar's heavily jowled head. It left him speechless and caused more tears to well in his eyes. A small trickle of blood started down his nose into his mouth.

"You'll do nothing of the sort," repeated the small man. "If you don't understand your situation, let me explain it. Your employee Baji is currently unconscious on the bench. You'll be next. I was nice to Baji because he knows little about what I want to know from you. But it's obvious Baji knows more than you do about your own family."

P'Shari winced at the mention of his family. The small man continued, "Jahar, we know you're linked to a terrorist organization. We know you paid for the website that claimed ownership of the bombing in San Francisco. We know the organization is fake. We also know you work with South Asia Independent Banking Incorporated, also known as SAIB." Jahar blinked at the interrogator, his eyes wide.

"I want you to know how serious I am. Your wife and children may be next to lay where Baji is sleeping. And you may listen as I interrogate them. I will not be as nice to them as I was to Baji." The interrogator looked hard at Jahar. He raised his hand. "Do you understand me?"

"No, no, please," Jahar's false bravado collapsed. "Leave my wife and children out of this. They're innocents and know nothing to help you."

"You're a smart man, a man of the world. Well-educated, Oxford, I believe? Did you attend? I can find out," the small man said, nodding in the direction of the torture bench.

"Not necessary, not necessary," Jahar sobbed and shook his head from side to side.

The interrogator softened. "Or we can be civil about this, and you can tell me everything I want to know over a cup of tea."

"I'm hungry," Jahar muttered, ready to talk.

"Answer my first question, and I'll consider getting you some food."

"What's your question?" A visibly shaken Jahar asked.

"How high does this go in South Asia Independent Banking?"

"To the top. Gamir Halibid, he knows everything." Jahar confessed.

"Good," the interrogator said. "It's going to be a long night for you. What shall we eat?"

## Day 30, 5:30 a.m., Chihuahua Ramada Inn

Mac was asleep when his cell phone began to chirp. Three rings woke him up, two more helped him find the phone, and a final sixth ring focused his eyes. It was Andrea Douglas-Pfeiffer calling from Washington.

"Hello, Krieger." Mac was groggy.

"Mac! Mac! It's Andrea! Are you awake?"

"I'm waking up now, Andrea. It was a long night."

"Sorry to wake you, Mac. I took the red-eye from Mexico City; I think I had too much coffee this morning."

Mac winced at her energized voice. "What time is it anyhow? Sometime after midnight?" Mac grumbled and looked for his watch.

"It's five thirty your time, Mac, six thirty here in DC. Sorry to wake you up, but we've got a break in the case."

Mac sat up in bed, "What happened?"

"The CIA interrogated a man in Pakistan responsible for the Turkmenistan website. You remember? The website claimed responsibility for the bombing in San Francisco."

Mac could hear Andrea smiling across the phone. Mac spun around and put his feet on the floor. He was fully awake. "Somebody in Pakistan? Andrea, this is great news! What else do you know?"

"They're still trying to unravel the money side of this, but this man in Pakistan told them of a training camp in Costa Rica and specifically named Katerina Batalle and Amir Abadai as key figures." Andrea was quiet for a moment as Mac's brain caught up with the news.

"Costa Rica!" Mac exclaimed. "Do you think this woman, Batalle, is trying to get back to Costa Rica?"

"It's a good guess, Mac."

"Anything else?" Mac asked.

"I'll send you the summary from the CIA. It came across about ten minutes ago. The money man is someone named 'Gamir Halibid.' Whoever is ratting him out is unnamed at this point, apparently trying to negotiate a softer landing."

"Gamir Halibid," Mac said. "Why does the name sound familiar?"

"He owns South Asia Independent Banking Incorporated," Andrea said. "The Pakistani government will be informed soon. He may be arrested in the next day or so."

"When does the boss get in?" Mac asked.

"Usually, he arrives about now. I'm guessing any minute," said Andrea.

"Tell him I want to go after Katerina Batalle!" Mac said, now fully awake. "I want to head from here to Costa Rica. Can you ask the CIA or NSA to get us a location where she's going in Costa Rica? Tell the boss I want to use a SEAL team to go after her in Costa Rica."

Andrea looked down at her phone, which had a flashing light, and said to Mac, "Director Fitzgerald is ringing me now. I have to go. I'll do whatever I can to get you what you need." Andrea hung up without saying goodbye.

Mac stood beside his bed and knew he couldn't get back to sleep. He walked to the window and looked outside at the darkness. The sunrise was still an hour away. He reached into his backpack, pulled out his laptop, and set it on the table. He walked to the bathroom and turned on the shower.

Walking back to his computer, he turned it on, connected, and signed on. He started downloading his emails and looked over his shoulder toward the shower. Steam was rolling out of the bathroom door. Mac glanced at the emails downloading slowly through the Mexican internet system and headed for a hot shower. It was going to be a hectic day.

## Day 31, 8:45 a.m., Philip S. W. Goldson International Airport, Belize City

The tall woman with long blond hair, oversized sunglasses, and a rose-colored pantsuit with a matching rose-colored Panama hat stood out in the crowd. She carried a matching purse, a small rolling suitcase, and a small dog carrier containing a tiny and quiet Chihuahua. The woman stood in the first-class line for the flight from Belize City to San José, Costa Rica.

The woman was suntanned with the healthy tan of someone who pays money to maintain her skin and is careful where and how she gets her sun. She had a small mole on her chin—not the "look away" size, but small and interesting enough to draw the eye to it. She was engrossed with her dog, talking to it like her best friend and feeding it small sips of water to ensure it wasn't thirsty.

This woman's name on her passport was Lucia Olivia Alvarado. She was from the Dominican Republic. She had a driver's license, passport, and credit cards with matching names and an address in the better part of Santo Domingo. She had a first-class ticket on the next plane out of Belize. She didn't look like Katerina Batalle or any of her other aliases.

"First Class is now boarding," the gate agent announced. Batalle put the ticket in her jacket pocket, picked up her bags, and moved forward. As she reached the check-in agent, the young woman reached out her hand to take her ticket.

Batalle didn't move to help her; she said, "I'm sorry, my hands are full. Can you please take it from my pocket?"

Nodding, the young lady reached up, clasped the ticket, and ran it through the scanner. "Have a nice flight!"

"Thank you, I will." Katerina smiled. With matching bags and a small dog, the beautiful woman walked down the jetway toward the plane.

# CHAPTER THIRTY-NINE

## Day 31, 12:00 p.m., Chihuahua International Airport, Mexico

The silver C-20 coasted into view as it descended on a prescribed flight path into Chihuahua International Airport, coming over the desert mountains of north-central Mexico. Mac Krieger, Bill Elliot, David Osrick, and John Riccardi watched as the small jet turned on its final approach and settled onto the runway.

Three minutes later, the small troop transport was rolling up to the men as they waited by the Mexico Air National Guard building near the same FBO facility where, days earlier, Batalle had quietly departed Mexico. The four men were ready to join the SEAL squad out of Naval Air Station Key West. The SEALs were part of the US Southern Command (SOCOM) and were already aboard the jet. The squad consisted of two four-person fire teams led by US Navy Lieutenant Byron Gardner.

As the military transport rolled to a stop, the pilots shut down the twin Rolls-Royce engines and opened the aircraft door located behind the pilot. A Pemex aviation fuel truck rolled up, and a flight crew member stepped down the stairs to oversee the refueling operation. Mac walked up the stairs and ducked his head into the military version of a Gulfstream IV. The other three agents, visible through the windows, stood off the aircraft's left side.

Mac met the SEAL team as its members attempted to stand upright in the low cabin and stretch from the one-and-a-half-hour flight from Miami.

"Good afternoon, and welcome to Mexico. My name is Mac Krieger. Bill Elliot, John Riccardi, and David Osrick are waiting outside. Which one of you is Lieutenant Gardner?" Gardner raised his hand.

Mac nodded at the Lieutenant. "We plan a quick flight to Soto Cano Expeditionary Base in Honduras. Our target is in Costa Rica. We don't know what to expect in Costa Rica, although we're told there may be a group of mercenaries at the target location who may put up a fight. That's why you're here."

Mac smiled at them. "I'd recommend a quick latrine break in the building as we refuel. We've got sandwiches and drinks for you inside.

There are no weapons inside the building; we don't want to cause an international issue with Mexico. We will be 'wheels up' in twenty minutes. I recommend you don't delay."

Mac paused as the men started to move. "Lieutenant, can I talk with you on the tarmac?"

"Yes, sir," Gardner said. Mac backed out the door as the Navy SEALs followed him. The active-duty men nodded at the FBI and Secret Service agents and entered the civilian FBO building. The agents carried their bags onto the plane, found seats, and exited the plane to get lunch.

"Sir?" Gardner asked as soon as he and Mac were alone beside the jet.

"Lieutenant, what are your orders?" Mac asked.

"Assist the Joint Task Force, led by you, in the capture of a wanted terrorist as quietly as possible. Firefight if necessary to protect our team."

"Affirmative, Lieutenant, please get something to eat, and we can discuss the rest of the details when we're airborne again."

"Roger," said Gardner. He walked away to catch up with his team.

Thirty minutes later, the team was airborne and on the way to central Honduras, a little over two hours away. Mac sat in a small group with Gardner and the other agents toward the front of the plane. The SEALs were sitting in the back, quietly talking amongst themselves. Two pallets of equipment were strapped behind the men.

Mac explained the situation in Costa Rica to the men surrounding him: "The CIA interrogated one of the money men who financed these attacks. He confirmed the location of the hacienda they were on was about an hour by flight in a small Cessna aircraft from La Fortuna to somewhere near the Nicaragua border. An hour's flight in a Cessna 172 takes one close to the border if you go straight north out of La Fortuna. We're focusing satellite imagery in the area and looking for something indicating a training camp."

"Do we know anything else about the training facility?" Elliot spoke up.

"It's named 'Rancho Trevio' or something similar. Andrea's been working to get any intel we can, but we don't have much access to records in Costa Rica."

"Is there a landing strip? Could be a way to reduce the number of possibilities." Osrick volunteered.

"Good suggestion, David; unfortunately, there are dozens of grass strips in northern Costa Rica."

"We don't have permission to overfly Costa Rica. I was told we would need to find another way in." Gardner said.

"Yes, I'm aware," Mac said. "I'm hoping they're close enough to the border with Nicaragua that we can overfly Nicaragua along the border."

"SOCOM said our lowest political alignment in the area was Nicaragua," Gardner said.

"The State Department confirmed this as well." Mac agreed. "So if we're going to anger anyone, it'll probably be Nicaragua. The desire is to get in and out without alarming *any* government in the area."

Mac pulled out a map of Central America and pointed to a spot on the map in Honduras. "Soto Cano Expeditionary Base is located in Central Honduras. We're going to use Soto Cano as a transfer base. Two UH-1 helicopters are now being offloaded with pilots. Our current plan is to use Hueys because They've got the same sound as the older Hueys Nicaragua uses to patrol its borders today." Mac looked up to make sure everyone was following. "The USS *America* is returning from deployment to Asia and is on its way to San Diego for refitting. The ship will be 100 miles off the coast of northern El Salvador this evening. We're taking two extra fuel pods on the Hueys to reach the ship from central Honduras. After we get there, the ship will move south, past Nicaragua, toward the northern coast of Costa Rica overnight. The ship will stay well away from Nicaragua and Costa Rica's territorial waters." "The ship will hold off the northern coast of Costa Rica for twenty-four hours to enable our infiltration and extraction.

The USS *America* is our operational base. It's also a place we could hold enemy combatants when or if we capture them."

"The USS *America* is an amphibious assault ship, like a small aircraft carrier," Gardner added for the benefit of the group of agents. "A couple of destroyers or submarine hunters usually flank the ship. You must have some pull in DC to get this ship re-tasked."

"The president made the call." Mac smiled. "Once the final location has been approved for our action, we launch early in the morning from the ship and enter Nicaraguan airspace along the border with Costa Rica." Mac traced a line along the border for the team. "We stay below the radar, drop the teams near the target, and return for refueling. The Hueys pick the team up and pull them out after we've achieved our objective. Then we sail home to San Diego with the ship and our terrorist."

Gardner looked at the map and measured distances with his fingers. "The distances are within the helicopter's range. Having the USS *America* on standby to support any air operations is a luxury we usually don't have," Gardner smiled at the others. "The plan seems operational. We split up my teams between the two UH-1s. Assuming you can put us down in a good location, I'll work out the preliminary attack plan with my guys on the flight from Soto Cano to the USS *America*. We'll need to have good satellite photos of the property from you to work out the operational plan."

"I'm hoping to have an exact location and updated images before we get to Soto Cano," Mac said. "We have a two-hour turnaround at Soto Cano and a communications center at the base. We can talk on secure lines with SOCOM, the White House, and our analysts and researchers. We'll lock it down. I'm told we'll have satellite photos of the target area by nightfall."

## Day 31, 2:00 p.m., NSA Headquarters

Like his Creek forefathers who migrated into what is now known as Florida and rebranded themselves as Seminoles, Daniel Whitefeather enjoyed hunting. Unlike his forefathers, he hunted amid wild herds of data, looking for footprints to track the most deadly kind. Telephone intercepts, video surveillance clips, dark web sites, locked static files, encrypted dynamic files, all data sites were his hunting grounds. Gaining access to the data was the hunt. Decrypting a secure file to acquire the information was the kill. Daniel rarely met a security system he, with the help of NSA's supercomputers, couldn't overcome.

This afternoon, he was hunting for a property in Costa Rica. It wasn't going well. He looked through files from the Costa Rica Civil Aviation Authority, Dirección General de Aeronáutica Civil, or DGAC. The Costa Rican registry identified every plane with the country code TI, and all aircraft needed to be registered to land at a public airport.

Daniel knew the suspect who had been interrogated in Pakistan had divulged that he had been flown in a light aircraft from La Fortuna to a hacienda in northern Costa Rica. Therefore, Daniel looked for a Cessna 172. Unfortunately, the 172 is one of the most common light aircraft in the world.

"This is too many!" Daniel exclaimed as he looked at the three screens of data listing all the Cessna 172 planes in Costa Rica. "Maybe I could cross-reference this list with tail numbers that have flown out of La Fortuna," Daniel spoke to the screens of data. "Where would the data be?" His fingers were flying across the keys, and windows were opening one upon another.

He was deeply engaged in the hunt when his phone rang. Glancing at it while he continued typing, he saw it was Andrea Douglas-Pfeiffer. He reached over and punched the speaker phone.

"Hi, Andrea, I'm busy."

"I know," Andrea retorted. "We all are. The director asked me to call you and find out if you have any additional information."

"He doesn't think I would call immediately if I had something?" Daniel said.

"I know Daniel," said Andrea. "You know the game. He asks, I call. I tell him what you tell me. What can you tell me?"

"I'm trying to find the airplane. The land records seem to be a waste of time. I have a list of all Cessna planes in Costa Rica, and I'm trying to gain access to the La Fortuna traffic database to see if I can narrow it down to a few." Daniel said impatiently. "Departure records would give me the destination, even if it's a grass strip. Once I know, we'll have GPS coordinates for the strip. With coordinates, we can task satellites to overfly it, and our teams can plan missions based on the data."

"I love the plan. I'll let the director know." The phone clicked off.

Daniel began typing furiously.

## Day 31, 2:30 p.m., La Fortuna Airport, Costa Rica

Batalle was pulling into the La Fortuna Airport rental lot. She had rented the car in San José after arriving midmorning on the flight from Belize. The three-hour drive from San José to La Fortuna through the Costa Rican lowlands was beautiful. For the last hour, she saw the green cone of the Arenal volcano in the distance, growing ever larger as she steadily covered the miles.

On the drive, she had time to decide what to do next. She knew she needed to disappear. She reasoned the fastest way to disappear was with the false passports and cash sitting in a lockbox inside a drawer in her room in Rancho Trevio. The two passports, plus the two she had on her, and a crypto account with ten million dollars could easily allow her to disappear almost anywhere in the world for years.

After she dropped off the rental car, Batalle caught a shuttle bus that dropped her off at the La Fortuna Flight Base Operations building. This small building was where all the private pilots picked up and dropped off passengers. Walking into the FBO, she approached the single counter and looked at the young man chatting with another pilot.

"Do you know Ernesto Garcia Secico? He flies in and out of here several times a week," Batalle asked the young man.

"Oh sure," he said. "I see him almost every other day. He probably flies groceries almost as much as he does passengers."

"I need to contact him to come pick me up, but I don't have his phone number or a way to reach him. Can you help me out?" Katerina smiled at him.

"Sure, happy to help. Do you want to talk to him, or do you want me to tell him there's a passenger here to pick up?"

"How often does he have a passenger to pick up that he doesn't know about in advance?" Katerina asked.

"Not often, but it's happened twice in the last couple of weeks."

"Well, let's make it a third time," Katerina confirmed. "Just tell him he has a passenger, and she's in a hurry."

The young FBO operator on duty smiled when she mentioned she was in a hurry. "Good idea," he smiled at her. "Sometimes, he takes a while to get here."

Katerina took a few bills from her pocket and gave them to the young man. "For your time and trouble. I'm going to get something to eat at the deli."

"It's no problem, ma'am; I'll let you know when Ernesto has clearance to land."

"Thank you." Batalle smiled at him again. He smiled back before becoming self-conscious and turned to make the phone call.

*Almost there*, Katerina thought. *Can I afford to stay at Rancho Trevio for a day or two? Or should I pick up my documents and a few clothes and leave immediately?* She thought about it a little longer. *It'll be evening by the time I get there. I'll arrange with Ernesto to go early in the morning.*

# CHAPTER FORTY

## Day 31, 4:15 p.m., NSA Headquarters

Daniel sweated. It wasn't pretty. He had been on the hunt for the location of the training camp now for six hours and had not slept in over twenty-four hours. He popped the top on another can of Red Bull and stared at his screen. He was locked out of an FBO departure log at La Fortuna airport by a four-digit password, most likely numbers.

This particular PC had some rudimentary DNS blocker software. It would kick him out after four tries and block his DNS and ISP. The blocker slowed him down but didn't stop him. Daniel had to program one of the most powerful computer systems in the world to trick the other computer into thinking that a new user from a new location was requesting access every four tries. It took under three thousand variations to find the correct four digits.

Daniel smiled. He was in the file. It wasn't big, only a few kilobytes. He downloaded it and looked at it for a few moments. Flagging the key columns of data in the file, he did a quick cross-reference against the Civil Aviation database he had downloaded earlier. The computer was done almost before his finger traveled the entire distance of the key press.

"Three," Daniel muttered, "just three dinky, damn Cessnas flying north out of La Fortuna and only one doing it almost every week. Let's look at this tail number. Ernesto Garcia Secico, Cessna 172, flies to private airstrip N23 routinely. It looks like it started about two years ago but has been busier in the last six months. . . hmmm."

Daniel pulled up an NSA satellite map of Costa Rica and overlaid all identified airstrips. N23 was north, near the Nicaraguan border. Daniel then pulled up the NSA's most recent satellite image and dialed Andrea Douglas-Pfeiffer.

"Daniel?" Andrea answered the phone.

"I got it!" Daniel chuckled into the phone. "There is one Cessna 172 flying routinely from La Fortuna to a private airstrip near the Nicaraguan border." "Looks like the most recent departure was about an hour ago. It's probably landing now. I'm sending the most recent satellite image and coordinates. I looked at the images, and there has been some recent construction. Even better, the plane was there during the overflight, and the tail numbers match."

"Daniel, this is awesome news!" Andrea was excited. "What can you tell me about the location?"

"I'm not an analyst, but the location looks like some of the ISIS training camps I've seen before, no tents and no sand. It looks like gun ranges and specific building setups to practice assault operations. I think the analysts will tell you the same thing. I've asked the NRO to task a new sat flyby with operational details. They should be doing it soon." Daniel paused to study a piece of paper with a schedule and the clock on the wall. "You'll have the full operational package delivered in about two and a half hours with analyst comments."

Daniel went silent for a moment. He started again, all business. "Got a pencil? The coordinates are 11° 6' 05" north and 85° 23' 36" west. You get that?"

"11° 6' 05" north; 85° 23' 36" west," repeated Andrea, a little breathless now that they finally had a location.

"Daniel, you're a Superman," Andrea exclaimed. "I'll send on your preliminaries and let the director know. Thank you!"

"Tell them to get her," Daniel sighed. "I'm going to be here for a little longer, but after twenty-five hours, I'm burned out and gotta get home to the family and a comfortable bed. Call me if you need me."

## Day 31, 4:18 p.m., Secret Service Headquarters, Washington, DC

Andrea hung up and speed-dialed Director Robert Fitzgerald's executive assistant, Dennica.

"Director Fitzgerald's office, how can I help you?" Dennica cooed into the phone.

"Dennica? It's Andrea. Is the director in? I've got the information he'll want to hear."

"The director is in a meeting. Please come up, and I'll step into his office and advise him that you have information on this priority operation. Can I assume you have the location he's been waiting for?"

"Yes, I do, Dennica," Andrea smiled. "Yes, I do. I'll be right up."

## Day 31, 7:40 p.m., 100 nautical miles offshore Nicaragua's Pacific coast

The second UH-1 had already landed on the deck of the USS *America* when Mac Krieger, John Riccardi, and the four-person SEAL fire team climbed out of the first bird. The trip out to the ship had been uneventful. Each UH-1 was loaded with the SEAL's operations gear in the storage lockers and carried four SEALs, two special agents, and two pilots.

The fire teams hustled off the UH-1s, and the maintenance and operations teams took both UH-1s below deck for refueling and a maintenance check. They would stay below deck until the teams were ready to use them, tentatively planned for 0300 hours.

After a quick meal in the mess hall, Gardner and agents Riccardi, Elliot, Osrick, and Krieger met with the ship's commander. Captain Bryce Dixon and his special operations leader, Lieutenant Commander Peter Wiseman, met with them in the operations room. After introductions, Mac briefed them on the situation, the target, and the plan. After he finished, Captain Dixon was the first to speak.

"Special Agent Krieger, Lieutenant Gardner, I understand the NSC and your chain of command have authorized your operation. However, I'll need authorization from Admiral Dennison and General Corcoran before I can commit the resources of the USS *America*. We're here by special order of the president. The ship must be battle-ready if something happens or we get visited by Nicaragua's or Costa Rica's armed forces. I need to hear from my top brass before I can put this ship on battle alert."

"Yes, sir," Mac said. I understand your position. After this briefing, we'll have a video conference with the National Security Council. Dennison and Corcoran will attend the meeting. In the meeting, the Joint Task Force will discuss the detailed summaries of the known facts from the CIA, FBI, and Secret Service. An NSA Analyst will review the target location with the latest satellite images.

"Lieutenant Gardner will discuss the entry, operation, and exit plan he's been working through with his team. Special Agent Riccardi and I will be joining the SEALs on the operation. Our specific target is the woman suspected to be the terrorist responsible for the San Francisco bombing. The plan is to get in and arrest the targets. A firefight is the last option, but we're going into a location that may be a mercenary training camp. Batalle is a known terrorist. A firefight is a possibility."

"Agent Krieger," Dixon said. "It sounds like you've got the right people meeting with us. Do we need to have any air operations available for you?"

"I'll take the question, sir," Lt. Gardner stepped into the conversation. "Captain, we don't expect to be chased as we exit the area. But we need to be prepared to respond. We may need recovery operations and medical support depending on the opposition we face when we get there."

Commander Wiseman turned to Dixon. "Captain, we can scramble medical and recovery helicopters when we know their return. If anyone in the area asks, we'll tell them we're conducting routine recovery drills. There should be a couple of birds in the air at any time, and we can drop some buoys in the area and recover them if anyone is looking too closely."

"I'm concerned Nicaragua would scramble a squadron of Russian MIG-29s if they feel their airspace has been violated," Dixon warned. "If it happens, we'd have to scramble F-35 Bs to meet or head them off. They could be on us almost immediately at this location. We could be targeted with missiles at fifty miles."

"The CIA reports that only four of the eight MIG-29s in Nicaragua are currently airworthy. It seems they're having trouble getting spare parts from Russia," Commander Wiseman reported.

"Yeah, and the CIA's often wrong, too," Dixon growled. "I have to assume all are airworthy."

"We'll monitor all activity in Nicaragua and have a squadron of F-35 Bs on deck if we detect any movement from the MIGs, sir," Wiseman said.

Dixon nodded in agreement. "Sounds appropriate to me."

Mac looked at his watch. "Let's get on the call with the NSC and get our approvals for the operation." As Mac finished, the door to the operations center opened, and a communications officer entered. He delivered the most recent images and analysts' opinions on a thumb drive and some printed documents. Commander Wiseman received the drive, turned on a large television, and pulled up the images on the screen. The men gathered around to look at them.

"There's the airplane, and that's probably the pilot standing next to it," Riccardi volunteered.

"There is another plane there, too." "It looks like some new construction," Gardner added. "What are these buildings?" Pointing to the row of buildings almost a mile behind the main house.

"Barracks would be my guess," Wiseman countered.

"What does the analyst say?"

"The analyst agrees with you," Mac said, reading a paper copy of the analyst's notes. "The analyst says it's similar in layout and design to some of the training camps we've documented in Yemen and Saudi Arabia. Shooting ranges, assault training areas, physical fitness areas, and probably an armory are all nicely disguised and far enough away from the main house. Delivery drivers or visitors wouldn't see much unless they ventured deeper into the forest."

Gardner pulled another image, "This looks like the main farmhouse."

Mac looked up. "Hold it! Look, on the patio! There's a person. See if there is a tighter image of the person."

"Right here," Gardner said as he moved to the following image. "A nice zoomed-in picture."

"It's a woman," Mac said, looking at the image.

"Is she our target?" Riccardi asked. Mac shuffled the papers and found the analyst's opinion. "The NSA analyst says it's a strong probability, but without facial recognition, they can't be sure."

"With the NSA, that's about as good as you'll get," Dixon growled. "They can read license plates from space, but unless the target looks specifically at the bird when it goes over, you can't get facial recognition."

"So we gotta go in," Mac confirmed. "Let's call NSC and get moving."

Two large television screens flickered a few minutes later when the encrypted video conference began with a picture of National Security Council chairwoman Dr. Angela Franklin. She looked at the screen, and when the video was stable on her end, she smiled at the camera.

"Captain Dixon, it's good to see you again," Dixon nodded. Franklin continued, "Can the rest of you please identify yourselves for the NSC? I'll show the room on your second screen."

The second screen switched to a packed room with military and civilian leadership. Robert Fitzgerald was visible, and Andrea Douglas-Pfeiffer sat in a chair behind him. Fitzgerald's colleagues from the FBI, CIA, NSA, and NRO were seated beside him, and a gaggle of analysts sat behind them. Admirals and Generals with admirable lettuce leaf ribbons were seated at the table with the Secretary of State, Chief of Staff, and, for added impact, the president himself. The men and women in the war room on the ship identified themselves.

Robert Fitzgerald began, "Madam Chairman, Mr. President, distinguished members of the National Security Council..."

## Day 31, 8:30 p.m., Rancho Trevio, Costa Rica

Katerina Batalle sat at the dining room table, picking at her meal and drinking a glass of Argentinian wine. The room was quiet, and she was alone. On the table was her duffle bag packed with two sets of false identities, each complete with a driver's license, credit card, and passport. Cash in multiple currencies, primarily yen, dollar, and euro, was in the bag. She had packed two changes of clothes in the duffle, including a vacuum-packed wig and a lightweight black jacket. The late addition was a Beretta 9 mm with a screw-on suppressor built by Nasreen.

It felt good to be back in control of her situation. Running across the southwestern tip of the US and half of Mexico and cautiously making her way back to Costa Rica, all the while looking behind her, wasn't how Batalle liked to travel. She prided herself on being invisible.

She caught the news at the airport in Belize. Her friend and colleague Amir Abadai was dead, and the US was continuing its search for her. Most of her aliases were blown, and governments knew her real name. The plans for the hacienda in Costa Rica and the invisible mercenary strike team would be something she would never see. She was going to disappear for years. It was the only way forward.

She picked up her wine, carried her dinner plate and silverware to the kitchen, and put it on the counter. Strolling back into the living room, she stopped and looked at a picture on the wall outside the door to the kitchen. It was a black and white photograph in a rough-hewn frame. In the picture, two middle-aged people, a man and a woman, stood beside an old tractor amid rows and rows of cabbage. She saw a large field rising behind them. The shadows were long in the photo. The picture may have been taken in the late afternoon. *At one time,* Katerina thought, *these two were the owners of this plantation. They'd removed the trees and created the fields. They shared their farming life with their children, and their children did the same.* The two founders looked strong, determined, and happy in the picture.

Katerina studied the picture and tapped it once with her fingernail. She walked over and picked up her duffle bag from the table. She stepped toward her bedroom. Katerina was in her physical prime: tall, confident, and assertive in her black slacks and black, sleeveless, v-necked pullover. She was strong, determined, and unstoppable. Tomorrow, she will leave Costa Rica forever. She had skills certain people appreciated. She wasn't worried about her future employment prospects.

# CHAPTER FORTY-ONE

**Day 32, 2:00 a.m., USS *America*, off the coast of Southern Nicaragua**

Both SEAL fire teams were up and moving. Mac didn't know if they slept last night but knew he didn't. Gardner stood outside the Operational Readiness Room, pouring coffee at a small drink station. He smiled as Mac walked up to get his cup of coffee.

"How do you like it?" Byron nodded his head toward the coffee carafe.

"I find it's hard to screw up black," Mac said. "By the way, how do I address you on the operation?"

"Just 'LT,'" Byron confirmed, referring to the initials of his rank. "That's how my men address me on operations. How do I address you? Or Agent Riccardi?"

"In the field, we generally use last names," Mac said.

"In SEALs, we're trained to reduce names to single syllables with hard consonants. 'Mac' is good; it has a strong M and C and comes through on the radio. 'John' is less so. The J is strong, but the N is weak. We prefer something like 'Jack' with hard consonants."

"How about using 'Mac' and 'JR' for the two of us?" Mac said.

"That's easy to remember and good phonetics," Byron said. "On the radios, we'll use Team One, Alpha, Bravo, Charlie, and Delta. Team Two will be the same. You'll hear me ask 'Team One roll,' each man will confirm by saying, 'Alpha One, Bravo One' or 'Alpha Two, Bravo Two' to prove they're upright and moving in position. If one man doesn't return, the team leader will call out again for confirmation a third time, using their name to ensure we know who may be down or unable to respond. You'll be Echo One, and JR will be Echo Two. We'll need you to respond when a roll is requested. We'll practice it in the Hueys on the way over."

"Got it. I'll tell John, I mean JR." Mac grinned.

"You look to be in pretty good shape, Mac. You can probably keep up with us as we move through the jungle," Byron said. "I'm a little worried about Riccardi."

"He's a fighter," said Mac. "But he's getting older and slowing a little. We've talked, and I think mentally, he's ready. Physically, it'll be a challenge."

"Let's see what we've to work with when we land. Dry Jungle isn't bad for five or ten clicks. Wet Jungle is the most difficult. If the ground is wet, we may want him to stay with the Hueys and return for retrieval."

"I'll tell him you'll make the call when we arrive. Are you good with that?"

"Roger," Gardner said. He snapped to attention as Dixon approached the two men.

"At ease, LT," Dixon growled. "Are you men ready for the operation?"

"We're finalizing some communication protocol, sir," Gardner said.

"That's good to hear," Dixon said. "I'll be up on the bridge when you depart. The weather, with low winds and cloud cover, looks good for flying today. Mac and Byron, best of luck to you both." The captain shook their hands and saluted the Lieutenant. He left with his trailing senior officer close behind.

Mac looked at Byron, "He seemed to be in a happier mood once the president gave him permission to defend his ship in any way he saw fit."

"Wouldn't you be?" Byron smiled.

When the two men returned to the readiness room, they found the entire team up, dressed, and preparing their equipment for the operation.

## Day 32, 2:45 a.m., USS *America*, off the coast of Southern Nicaragua

The UH-1s, refueled and ready, were elevated to the LHA-6 flight deck. The two fire teams, including Krieger and Riccardi, were fully dressed in tactical black. They wore helmets, backpacks, and goggles. Each carried standard-issue sidearms and rifles. All the men bent over slightly and walked to the two UH-1s. Pilots and copilots were seated and doing final checks as the rotors began to turn.

The teams climbed in and buckled into their seats. The SEALs took positions at the doors and left the inside seats to Krieger and Riccardi. Gardner was already in one of the middle seats. Mac nodded to Gardner and turned his head to the pilots, "SEAL team ready."

The two helicopters lifted off the LHA-6 deck simultaneously. The pilots rolled back from the platform and elevated the helicopters to one hundred feet off the ocean. They turned toward the coast of Nicaragua, a little over one hundred miles away. The UH-1s leaned toward the distant shore and approached it at over 125 miles per hour.

Mac and LT put on headsets to respond to the pilots and any communication from Commander Wiseman in the Operations Room on the

USS *America.*

With over three thousand hours of flight time in a UH-1, the twenty-eight-year-old pilot clicked on the intercom switch. "LT, Agent Krieger, you copy?"

"Copy," LT said.

"Copy, and you can call me Mac."

"Roger. LT and Mac," the pilot confirmed. "Just to let you know, the weather is calm but cloudy, and the radar is clean at the landing zone. We're staying inside Nicaragua's border and tracking the border as best we can. We don't plan to exceed two hundred feet to avoid radar detection. Supposedly, Nicaragua's radar is old school, and they will not be able to track us close enough to know if we're in their airspace or Costa Rica's. We're hoping the same for Costa Rica, although they don't have any MIG-29s for us to worry about."

The pilot paused for a moment to talk with the co-pilot. Then he came back over the intercom. "I'm switching over to connect with Commander Wiseman in Special Ops. You're welcome to listen in, but I'll mute your mics for now and wave my hand if someone needs to talk to you."

Mac looked out the window for several minutes. A quarter moon tried valiantly to shine through the clouds. He could see the ocean rushing by in the blackness. It was fifteen minutes after 3:00 a.m. in Costa Rica and a little after 4:00 a.m. in New York, where he had been for the last seven years. He smiled to himself and chuckled. Gardner saw him and keyed his mic on the inside channel.

"What are you smiling about?"

"I should be doing more of this," Mac looked up at Byron. "I went to the Academy to be on the seas and in action. But I let myself get pulled into the Secret Service before I could get my boots wet. I didn't know what I was missing. Now I spend too much time pushing paper."

"You're too smart," Gardner needled him. "You needed to be dumber, like me." He smiled at Mac. "To be truthful, you might make a good Navy SEAL. We may find out this morning."

Twenty minutes later, the pilot waved his hand, and LT and Mac switched to the communication channel with Commander Wiseman. The pilot reported, "Commander Wiseman, LT, and Mac are on the radio."

Wiseman boomed, "LT, you should be crossing onto land about now, according to my radar." Mac looked out, and sure enough, they were crossing the beach and over a forest as they climbed away from the beach.

"Roger, Commander, we see the beach," LT said.

"Our radar and satellite peeks at the MIG bases don't show any lights on or movement. Looks like they're still sleeping. Radar shows no aircraft in your area or along your intended approach."

"Commander," Mac spoke up. "Any updates from DC?"

"Yes," Wiseman confirmed. "New satellite images with infrared show only one person in the house, probably the female suspect. However, there appear to be ten to twelve sleeping bodies in the barracks and one in what we assume is an armory or warehouse. There is one or two at the house by the gate. I'm sending the images to LT's phone now."

Gardner checked his sat phone and gave Mac the thumbs up.

"Confirmed." Said Mac. "We have the images."

"DC also reminded me to tell you all of the personnel at the target location may not, repeat, may not be enemy combatants. There may be civilian workers such as cooks and farm workers; even the pilot may be a noncombatant." Wiseman advised.

LT and Mac looked at each other. Mac said, "If they don't shoot at us, we won't shoot at them." He glanced questioningly at LT, who gave him a thumbs-up.

"Roger," Wiseman confirmed. "I told DC I would pass it along."

"Ops" LT looked at Mac as he keyed his mic. "Any update on conditions?"

"Yes," said Wiseman. "I know you were concerned about whether the ground was dry or wet at your entry point. I asked the NSA to give me a moisture reading from the satellite. The ground is dry."

LT smiled at Mac, "Roger, sir, thank you."

"I'm doing my job. We'll monitor your COMMS link. Let us know if you need anything. My radar shows you about thirty minutes from LZ."

"Roger, Ops, thank you," LT said.

The trees flew by fifty to one hundred feet below the speeding UH-1s. At the assigned coordinates, the UH-1s swung south and crossed into Costa Rican airspace. The distance was short, and the two aircraft began to slow down immediately. The pilot and copilot talked on their headsets as they watched the GPS read off the distance to the LZ. The copilot pointed at a small clearing less than a mile ahead. The two UH-1s descended into the clearing and hovered about two feet off the ground.

The four-person fire teams jumped out of both sides of the helicopter. All wore night vision goggles. They continually scanned the area through their ACOG 4x32 rifle scopes for movement. Krieger and Riccardi followed them out. LT gave the pilots a thumbs up, and both Hueys lifted off the ground and cleared the trees. They headed north to cross into Nicaragua's air space and head back to the USS *America* the same way they'd come in.

The fire teams moved into the trees on either side of the clearing. They stopped momentarily to put the COMMS link in their ears, do a quick radio check, and adjust the night vision goggles on their helmets.

LT addressed the men through the radio.

"Fire teams One and Two, we're heading straight south, but we want to maintain operational safety and remain more than three hundred feet apart. We're moving, but I want to remind everyone that this is an active terrorist training camp. We don't know what type of welcome we may find. KEEP YOUR EYES OPEN!"

"Team Two, Roger," said the team leader, a large man named Carl.

"Team One, Roger." LT's second in command, a wiry man named TJ, responded for Team One.

"Okay, Let's roll. We want to be on top of the guys in the barracks before they get out of bed."

# CHAPTER FORTY-TWO

**Day 32, 3:55 a.m., Inside the northern border of Costa Rica**

It was almost 4:00 a.m. when the helicopters left the two teams on the ground in a foreign country. A country that would be angry if they knew the United States military was conducting a covert incursion into their sovereign territory without permission. Better to ask forgiveness than be denied authorization to chase a terrorist who murdered hundreds were the final comments of the President.

The weather was cooperating. There were clouds, but no rain. A partial moon filled the forest with scattered moon beams hitting the ground as it filtered through the canopy—the rain forecast to begin in a few hours. Throughout the year, dry and wet times were loosely linked to the calendar. This month was traditionally wet. The forest smelled of green growth and moist soil. Downed trees were growing green, fluffy moss as they lay decaying on the forest floor in an endless cycle of life and death. The two fire teams skirted around and sometimes over the trees as they weaved through the forest, moving fast and silently.

Mac watched the backs of the other men as they moved south. The SEALs led the way, with the experienced members alternating to take the lead or to follow. Mac was always at the rear of the unit, and he was happy to watch the professional team do what it did best. LT would conduct a roll call every ten minutes to ensure everyone was keeping up. Thirty minutes in and over a mile completed, everyone was keeping up, even Riccardi.

The pace was fast but cautious. The SEALs were conditioned and trained every day for this type of activity. Krieger and Riccardi were not. They were used to coffee breaks, sidewalks, sit-down meetings, and a more leisurely pace. Typical days for the FBI and Secret Service didn't include ten pounds of rifle and ammo, fifteen pounds of a tactical backpack with a medical kit, a four-pound bulletproof ceramic vest, and a two-pound ceramic helmet. Mac sweated profusely. He wondered if Riccardi was as well. It reminded him of his training days at Quantico and some of the training he did at the Naval Academy over ten years ago.

241

After two miles of a fast-paced double time, they neared a clearing in the trees. Mac watched as LT raised his hand and halted his team. At the same time, he told team two to hold via the radio.

"Operations, do you have a visual on our location?" LT asked.

"Roger," said Wiseman. "SOCOM tasked a U2 Dragon Lady to provide recon for the operation late last night. She's up there at 70,000 feet, circling your location with eyes on. Since it's still dark, we're watching you with infrared. You're approaching a large clearing that appears to be a shooting range. We don't see any hostile signatures in your immediate vicinity."

"Roger, Ops," said LT. "Fire teams stay in the trees along the edges. Use infrared and night vision to scan ahead. Let's make sure we don't miss anyone waiting for us. Let's go."

Both teams moved forward along the edge of the clearing, scanning ahead. Fire team two was moving along the right side of the clearing, about four hundred yards away from team one, when team leader two, Carl, held up his hand and halted his team in place.

"LT," Carl growled in a low voice, "we have a problem."

"Roger, Carl," LT said as he held up his hand and halted his team. "What's up?"

"There's a camera mounted on a tree ahead of us. It's pointing away from us and not moving. It may be stationary. Appears to be pointed over the clearing."

"Roger," LT confirmed. "There is probably one on this side, too. We should find it. Carl, can you take yours out?"

"Roger," Carl growled again in his low voice. "It's not too high to reach. But it may trigger an alarm or something when it goes offline."

"We're within a mile of the target and can't risk anyone getting a headcount or our exact location. There may also be other cameras. Stay in the trees. Let's continue to move forward and take them out as we find them. Everyone stays on alert. It could get hot."

Three hundred yards later, both teams reached the end of the first open space with one camera found. The range was well designed, with five different berms bulldozed into the landscape at 40, 110, 220, and 330 yards. Wooden racks were in front of the berms to hold a variety of target shapes, mostly human outlines.

"LT, this is Ops," broke in Wiseman. "We're seeing some movement in the bunkhouses. It's almost 5:00 a.m. Maybe it's normal. We'll let you know if we see an all-out scramble."

Mac looked at LT. "We've got another click to go before the barracks. Let's get there while they're still in their stocking feet."

LT nodded in agreement. "Team one and two, let's keep moving south. There should be another clearing coming up within half a click."

"LT, this is Ops," Wiseman broke in again. "We've got a hostile departing the barracks and moving in your direction along a road. It appears to be alone and moving, like a runner. Team Two is in the best position to intercept."

"Roger, Ops. Team Two, get in position to intercept potential hostile."

"Team Two, Roger," Carl said.

Team Two split the men into two on the right and three on the left side of the road. They waited for the runner to come to them. In the pre-morning darkness, the runner was easy to hear coming toward them from the rhythmic steps and fast breathing. The runner was a male of average height and build and was moving.

As soon as the runner passed the first two men, the second group of men stepped out from the sides of the road. The runner saw them and slid to a stop. He smartly decided to retreat versus taking on the two men with guns. The runner reversed direction and looked up in time to be smacked in the face with the butt-end of an M4a1 assault rifle.

"LT," said Carl, "we have a hostile down."

"Still alive?" "Yes, but he'll have a headache."

"Roger," LT confirmed. "Immobilize and move on."

Team Two put the unconscious mercenary in zip ties and left him slightly off the side of the path but visible. They would pick him up on the return trip. Both teams moved forward into the second clearing. Several training structures were at various levels of completion. Most were a mix of exterior and interior walls and doors, but no roof. Several targets were set up inside the building for small arms training. It was apparent they were used.

"LT, this is OPs," broke in Wiseman. "We're seeing more movement in the bunkhouse."

"Roger, Ops." Said LT. "Let's move teams. We're within five hundred yards of the bunkhouses. Stay in the trees and stay spread out. Fire if fired upon, and don't give them a clear target."

Mac tensed up as they moved forward as a unit. He was aware this was a life-or-death situation. He carried no fear, sense of foreboding, or concerns for his own life, only complete mental and physical engagement with this team. His mind didn't stop to recall where he was a month ago, sailing on the sunny Caribbean Seas off the coast of St. John.

Mac held onto a single focus: the here and now. He was with a team of America's military elite, taking on a dozen trained mercenaries in the jungles of Costa Rica. This was putting one's life on the line for a higher cause. It felt right. Mac checked on Riccardi.

"Echo Two, you okay?"

"I'm good, Mac," said Riccardi. "Let's finish this."

# CHAPTER FORTY-THREE

### Day 32, 5:15 a.m., Rancho Trevio, Costa Rica

The teams proceeded through the trees. Ahead of them, the day was beginning to take over the night as the sun approached sunrise. Visibility was increasing as the teams approached the clearing and bunkhouses. They could see commotion in the bunkhouses and watched as several men broke out of one of the barracks and ran a hundred yards from the barracks to the outfitting building. Mac could hear them pounding on the door and yelling, "Nasreen! Nasreen!"

As the fire teams approached the edge of the clearing, LT raised his hand and whispered into the mic, "Team one, team two, we need to clear these buildings as fast as possible. Put down any resistance we meet and restrain the others."

"LT, I want to get to the house," Mac said. "If she's there, we must hit all three simultaneously."

"Can you and Echo Two take the main house?" LT asked.

"Affirmative," came the reply from both Mac and JR almost at the same time.

"You need to skirt the barracks," LT told Mac. "Go around the barracks on the east side. Stay in the trees on the edge until you hear us enter the barracks, then you go hard and fast to the main building."

"Roger," Mac said, looking around for Riccardi to see if he was coming. "East side, wait until you hit the barracks."

"LT, this is Ops," Wiseman broke in. "We see movement in the main house too. The subject seems to be looking out the windows. Can't tell if the subject is armed."

"Roger, Ops." LT Looked directly at Mac, "We will assume the subject is armed."

Mac nodded at LT as he heard Riccardi huffing and puffing his way up to Mac's position. Mac motioned Riccardi to follow him as he moved away from the team to position them for a run to the main house. Mac hoped they'd have a few seconds for Riccardi to catch his breath. They didn't.

When the first shot rang out, Mac and Riccardi had almost gotten into position. It came from the outfitting building. One of the men who had scrambled out of the barracks to wake up Nasreen walked back outside with a loaded AK-47 and fired a volley into the air to get everyone's attention. LT's second in command, a stout soldier nicknamed TJ, saw the man come out of the outfitting building with the rifle and trained his M4a1 on the man. The moment he pulled the trigger and the first shot went off, TJ dropped him with a headshot. A dead finger pulled the two other rounds in the volley.

"Team One, Team Two, move!" LT yelled. Within seconds, both teams were out of the trees and into the barracks, leaving a man outside to watch for hostiles.

Krieger and Riccardi broke from the trees and sprinted toward the farmhouse. Behind them, they heard 'POP!' 'POP, POP!' As they ran, Mac saw a man's head peer out of the outfitting building and duck back in.

"Hostiles in the armory!" Mac hollered as he ran. The man looked out of the outfitting building again and then suddenly raised a rifle at the two federal agents as they sprinted toward the farmhouse.

"Gun!" Mac yelled as he dived for cover. The AK-47 opened up in full auto mode on the two of them as they both rolled behind a truck about fifty yards from the house.

A dozen bullets ripped through the light metal and pinged off of the engine. Ten more ripped through the passenger compartment, exiting the far door, leaving one-inch holes in the metal. One tire was punctured, and several bullets whizzed by Mac and JR's heads as they ducked behind the wheel wells of the truck.

Mac switched his M4a1 to full auto and waited. The shots from the outfitting building paused slightly. Mac stood and fired a volley of shots into the building's door. He kneeled and looked over at Riccardi, who tried to keep his head below the top of the wheel.

"I always wanted to do that." Mac grinned at him.

"You're nuts," Riccardi shot back.

He keyed his mic and hollered, "Team Two, can you help us with the shots from the outfitting building?"

"On it," Carl said. "Delta Two, can you assist?"

Delta Two, the man outside the barracks, ran to the unoccupied third barrack and looked around the corner of the building. The location gave him an angle to the front of the door. He saw the rifle come back out, and shots began again. Through his scope, the young man named 'DJ' from Colorado moved his crosshairs from the gun to the door frame and back along the wall about six inches, then fired two quick rounds. The rifle dropped, and a moment later, the man behind the gun rolled forward and out the door, dead.

"Hostile down," DJ whispered calmly into the mic.

Mac and Riccardi bolted from behind the truck when they heard. Both were running hard for the main house, and they covered the distance in a sprint. Mac used a hand gesture to signal JR to go around the house and look for a back door. JR nodded and moved away. Mac looked around the corner to the front of the house and saw the large patio. He saw no one outside. He glanced around the corner again and saw a large expanse of glass doors and windows with little cover.

"Hey! Hey you!" came a call from the direction of the airstrip. Mac looked up and saw an unarmed man walking in the direction of the house. He was a small, older man with a graying, thin mustache and wearing a cap with "Cessna" in white letters on a red background. His arms were spread to either side. Mac looked at him and waved him away from the house. In the background, another 'POP!' 'POP!' at the outfitting building as Delta Two cleared the armory of its combatants.

Hearing the gunshots for the first time, Ernesto ducked low and turned back toward the airstrip, keeping much lower than he did when he walked toward Mac. He scrambled back to the plane and hunkered beside it to wait. Mac watched him go.

Triggering his mic, Mac reported, "LT, there is a pilot by the plane; he appears unarmed and may not be a threat."

"Roger," LT confirmed. "Have you cleared the house?"

"Working on it," Mac mumbled. Mac eased around the side of the house again, this time trying the front door. It was locked. He stepped away from the doorway and took two steps toward the sliding glass doors. He squatted behind a wall when three shots came from inside the house and punctured the center of the door, exactly where Mac had stood seconds before. One shot was head height, and two were center mass. Mac dropped to his knees and put his back against the house wall.

"Echo two; we've shots fired from inside the main house." Mac spoke quietly, "JR, where are you?"

"Outside the back door," JR whispered. "I've looked in a few empty rooms. The suspect must be by the front door. The back door is unlocked. I'm going in."

LT broke in hurriedly, "Echo One and Echo Two, hold positions; Calvary is coming." Three more shots rang out from inside the house, this time narrowly missing Mac's head with the first shot, but a second and third shot caught him in the back, knocking him flat onto the patio. "OOFF," Mac woofed as the impacts knocked the wind out of him. The sound was audible on the radio.

"Echo roll call, please," LT demanded.

"Echo Two," said JR.

Mac tried to catch his breath but struggled.

"Echo One, respond," LT's voice sounded urgent. "Mac, you okay?"

"Echo One," Mac said breathlessly. "I'm hit."

"Roger, Echo One," LT confirmed. "We're on the way."

Mac rolled over onto his back and looked at the bullet holes in the wall where he had been crouching when the bullets hit him. He saw movement in the glass and looked up to see Katerina Batalle looking out at him with a cold stare. Mac reached his hand out for his rifle and found the blow had knocked it a few feet away. He saw her leveling her Beretta at his head through the glass doors. Mac reached for his pistol and attempted to rake it from its holster on his hip.

John 'JR' Riccardi kicked the rear door open. The noise caused Batalle to pause and turn her head toward the noise. The split-second interruption enabled Mac to get his pistol and bring it to bear. She saw Mac's gun motion upward and jumped out of his sight line at the last second as Mac's 9 mm barked and the large glass pane shattered.

JR hollered, "Mac!"

Mac yelled, "She's in the front room!" JR positioned himself inside the kitchen door and glanced around the corner as a bullet embedded itself three inches above his head in the door molding.

"Jesus!" JR murmured under his breath.

"Katerina Batalle!" Mac yelled, pistol pointing at the shattered window. He scrambled to the wall to find some cover.

"Katerina! You've nowhere to run." Batalle alternately pointed toward the front door where Mac was and toward the kitchen door where Riccardi waited to take a shot.

"Katerina Batalle," Mac bellowed again, "there is nowhere for you to run. We know you, your disguises, and even your crypto account. There is nowhere you can run where we can't find you."

"It's a temporary setback," hollered Batalle. "With the two of you dead, I start over."

"If it were only the two of us, maybe you'd have a chance," Mac said. "But we're not going anywhere, and neither is the SEAL team that took out your mercenaries. Look out the window, Katerina; you can see them."

Riccardi chanced another look out of the kitchen. Another shot splintered the wood above his head.

"Jesus Christ!" Riccardi hissed.

"Katerina, please," Mac hollered. "This doesn't have to end with any more dead." Katerina paused as she considered her options.

Mac tried again. "Katerina, put down your weapon. There's nowhere to hide. No one else needs to die."

"Only one," Batalle sighed. She leveled the Beretta under her chin and tensed her finger on the trigger. Mac glanced around the broken window frame and saw Katerina.

"NO!" He yelled. Katerina saw Mac looking at her. She quickly aimed and fired two shots at Mac, striking the window frame as Mac ducked behind it.

Riccardi, hearing the shots toward Mac's location, leaned out of the doorway and into the hall and fired three shots at Katerina before she could turn toward him.

The .40 caliber shots lifted her off the floor and threw her body against the wall. Blood and brain matter hit the wall behind her, and her body slumped to the floor. Mac and JR didn't move after the shots. The sound of the body falling was muted by the gun blasts ringing in their ears.

Gardner and fire team Alpha ran up to the house as the shots were fired and positioned themselves on the side of the house next to Mac.

Mac called out, "JR!"

"I'm here, Mac," said JR. He stood up and walked to where Batalle lay on the floor. The top half of her scalp was missing. A pool of blood surrounded her head.

"Suspect is down," JR spoke into the microphone. He leaned back on the door jamb and kept his gun trained on her motionless body. He muttered to himself, "And I'm tired."

"Bravo One, clear the room," LT commanded. He stood at the corner of the house with Mac. "Delta One and Charlie One, clear the rest of the house."

The fire team went from room to room, verifying that the house was empty. LT dropped to a knee to tend to Mac, who was still trying to catch his breath.

"Where did you take it?" Asked LT.

"In the back, the hits knocked me flat on my face and took the wind out of me."

"It must not be too bad," LT said. "You're not spitting up blood, and I could hear you yelling fifty yards away. Roll over, let me take a look."

Mac rolled to his side, and LT looked at his backpack and vest.

"You took two shots in the back. They went right through the backpack and into your vest. It appears the vest stopped the bullets. The ceramic inserts are still in place." LT was clinical in his description.

"Well, it hurts like hell anyhow," Mac said, as he tried to smile but could manage only a pained grin. "Let's take off the vest to be sure. I've never been shot before."

Inside the farmhouse, Riccardi was up and searching for the one bedroom that appeared to have been used recently. He found Batalle's duffle bag inside and brought it out to the main room.

"LT, is he finished whining?" Riccardi shouted. "Because, if he is, I've found something he would want to see."

"I'm coming." Mac struggled to his feet with the help of LT. He had taken his vest and shirt off. His back was already showing signs of significant bruising at the impact points.

Mac limped slowly into the house through the frame of the sliding glass door he had shot out. He approached Riccardi and asked, "What did you find?"

"Just the evidence we needed to assure everyone this is our terrorist," Riccardi smiled at Mac. He lifted the bag slightly off the table, spread the duffle bag apart, and tipped it forward. Multiple passports, money, and an additional magazine for her Beretta spilled out onto the table.

"One of these passports is her real name," Riccardi commented as he spread the Spanish passport with Katerina Batalle's name and photo.

"Zip it up and bring it with us," said Mac.

He looked at LT and quipped, "Hey LT, are the Hueys on their way? It looks like we're about done here. If we don't want to start an international issue, we should be going."

Ten minutes later, the sound of two UH-1 helicopters and one Sikorsky HH-60-M MEDEVAC helicopter coming in fast over the treetops began to drown out any conversation. Lt. Gardner took charge as the helicopters flew directly up to the house and landed in the open area between the main house, the barracks, and the airstrip, next to the bullet-riddled truck that saved Krieger and Riccardi's lives.

Mac watched as the crews ferried the dead terrorist and several mercenaries to the MEDEVAC helicopter. The shackled mercenaries were split among the three helicopters. The SEAL fire teams were split up to keep an eye on the mercenaries.

As the UH-1 lifted off the ground, Mac looked down at the receding compound. He saw the pilot of the Cessna aircraft, whose tail number had helped them track down Batalle, standing by his plane, watching the helicopters lift off and head north. Within seconds, the helicopters had disappeared over the trees.

Mac settled back in his seat and felt a pain in his back. He grimaced and leaned forward again, wondering how long it would be before the bruises healed. A calm overcame him, and he felt the weariness enter his body. The helos moved into Nicaraguan airspace and headed west toward the waiting USS *America*.

Mac looked over at Lt. Gardner and smiled at him. "Thanks, LT. We got her. She's not alive, but we got her. We couldn't have done it without you and your team."

LT reached over and fist-bumped Mac. "I'll work with you anytime, Mac. You pulled your weight back there. Your intel was solid, and you kept up with us. The same goes for JR."

They both glanced over at JR; he was fast asleep, leaning his head against the helicopter's window. Mac and LT grinned at each other.

"Thanks, LT. Let's not take on a group of mercenaries next time. We got lucky," Mac said.

"Roger, Mac. We caught them in their stockings."

# CHAPTER FORTY-FOUR

## Almost a year later, 7:00 a.m., the Caribbean Sea, near St. Kitts and Nevis

The sun shone brightly, and the sea swells were light as the sailboat cut across the light green water on close reach. It had been a year since Mac's last sailing adventure had been cut short, but here he was again.

A Presidential Medal of Freedom sat quietly in a display case on his new desk in Washington, DC. Mac was guaranteed by his boss, Robert Fitzgerald, the new director of Homeland Security, that he wouldn't be interrupted for two weeks.

The recovery in San Francisco was progressing as the people of California and the rest of the nation pulled together to rebuild the city and the downtown. Mac was on hand to dedicate a new memorial site for the victims.

The US confiscated funds from SAIB facilities in Puerto Rico, Guam, the US Virgin Islands, and American Samoa. The amount recoverable was measured in billions of dollars, and all the money recovered by the US was placed into a trust for San Francisco residents and businesses impacted by the bombing. Local governments were recovering millions of other dollars from other parts of the globe. The current ruling party of Pakistan was contesting the ownership of the money.

Gamir Halibid was in the wind. Pakistani army forces had surrounded and breached his compound a day after the body of Katerina Batalle was returned to the US. Halibid and his family were gone when they arrived. An INTERPOL arrest warrant was issued on the same day. The CIA felt it was a matter of time before he surfaced. No one knew his whereabouts, how long he could disappear, or how many millions he had stashed away.

Jahar P'Shari and his family were secretly moved to the United States by the CIA and entered into supervised witness protection under new names. P'Shari was helping the US recover assets outside of Pakistan for the US and key partner countries in exchange for leniency. It was expected to take several years to recover all the funds. The president told the justice department to hold off on prosecuting the charges against P'Shari while they recovered the funds. Pakistan's worldwide search and arrest warrant for P'Shari was yielding no results.

Mac was wearing a white polo shirt, dark blue shorts, and deck shoes without socks as he scrambled over the cabin of *Mary's Baby* to untangle a jib sheet caught up around a turnbuckle. Today was the third day of an intended ten-day cruise. Mac had started planning the cruise a month after he returned to New York from Costa Rica. The boat was heading west-northwest, moving into the wind at an angle that would bring him to the US Virgin Islands in about two days' sail. It was early, and the wind was light. He settled into the cockpit, adjusted the trim on the mainsail, and checked the autopilot.

He saw movement in the cabin as Rae climbed the steps up to the cockpit, holding two cups of coffee. Her hair bobbed up and down as she struggled to find her balance and footing on the steps. Mac saw the movement and smiled.

He moved to the edge of the door, "Good morning! Let me help you." He reached and took Rae's two mugs filled with steaming coffee in one hand. With his other hand, he helped her up the steps and into the cockpit, sitting next to him.

"Thank you, and good morning to you as well." She smiled, leaned over, and kissed him. Rae wore a short white crop top and shorts she had slept in. Her hair was mussed, but her eyes were alive with anticipation. Her smile was beaming at Mac.

"Slept well, I hope?" Mac smiled at her.

"I always sleep well after, you know, a little hanky-panky," said Rae, smiling.

Mac laughed, "Me too. A little exercise is good for the heart."

"Where are we going today?" Rae slid closer to Mac and put a hand on his leg.

"We've got a long day of sailing today, and the same is true for tomorrow." Mac watched the large mainsail. "We're heading toward the Virgin Islands, but it'll take two days to sail there, sailing ten hours a day. We can get to Gallows Bay by tomorrow night if the winds hold."

"When we get there, will we stay at the docks?" Rae looked at Mac as she asked.

"Sure, if you want to. Or we could even spend a night or two in a hotel," said Mac.

"We must stay at least one night at the docks," said Rae, smiling deviously at Mac. "I consider it returning to where we met."

"I thought we met in a bar," Mac teased. He squeezed Rae's shoulder against his chest.

"When are you going to teach me how to sail? You've shown me how to make coffee in the kitchen; I mean galley," she corrected herself, "and how to mess up the sheets on the bed." Rae winked at Mac as she asked the question.

"Right now," Mac said. "We're about to pop the jib. That's the big sail in front. It'll help us go a little faster. You get to hold the starboard jib sheet as I send the jib sail up and lock it in."

"Let me put the coffee cups away first." Rae stood on the tilted deck and collected the two coffee cups in one hand. "I'll put them in the sink and come back up." Rae climbed down the stairs as Mac watched her go.

Mac looked out across the ocean. He saw no ships on the horizon. He looked at the sails and the autopilot settings and then toward the cabin where Rae had disappeared. Mac stood and walked to the cabin steps. As Rae returned from the galley to the topside, he walked down the steps. She smiled as she met him at the bottom of the stairs.

"Change of plans," Mac whispered playfully. "I'm sorry, but I can't seem to leave you alone." He reached for her and kissed her on the lips. He slowly slid Rae's shirt over her head. "What got you going?" Rae lifted Mac's shirt over his head and pulled it away. She wrapped her arms around his waist.

"Just seeing you is enough to get me going," Mac whispered. "Being here, alone with you, is better than I ever could have imagined. Even better than long weekends in Denver or New York." Mac paused, "I take that last part back. The first weekend we got together in Denver was pretty special, too. I wouldn't change that."

"What about the sailboat? Don't you need to be up there watching?" Asked Rae as she pulled Mac toward her.

"We're good for about twenty minutes. Then, I'll have to check again to ensure no other ships are on an intercept line. The radar will also let us know if something is in our way."

"We can do a lot in twenty minutes," Rae cooed in his ear.

"I know; I'm dreaming about it already."

"Time to stop daydreaming," Rae pulled Mac toward the master stateroom. "Are you sure the boat's okay?"

Mac smiled, "The boat's fine, the weather's perfect, and the company is beautiful, smart, and sexy. It doesn't get much better than this. How often have I mentioned that the autopilot is pretty cool, too?"

"Too many," Rae laughed. "Let me take your mind off of the autopilot."

The End

# ACKNOWLEDGMENTS

Many people have read this book from its rough first draft to its final result. Some have even read it multiple times, pen in hand, to circle errors or omissions or point out areas that needed more work. The author highly valued our discussions in each instance.

Thank you to my lovingly patient wife, Mary, who painstakingly waded through the first, third, and almost-final revisions. My thanks to Mike Wiseman, a man who loved his editing. He dived into the novel with enthusiasm and a red pen more than once. Thanks to Buck and Jeanette Attaway, who provided real-life feedback on sailing the Caribbean Sea. Buck helped determine where the seal team should be based and several other technical details.

Thanks to Bill and Jane Casper, good friends my wife and I met years ago. They gave great feedback on the characters, helping me to create a stronger story. Thanks to Art Pellenberg, a native New Yorker, who straightened me out on the boroughs of Queens and Brooklyn! Art used to deliver meat for his grandfather in those boroughs. David Wolf, a friend since high school, and his wife Pam gave excellent feedback and encouragement.

I would be amiss if I didn't thank the "real" John Riccardi who gifted his name for one of the characters in the book. Yes, John, you are much better looking than JR!

Many others deserve mentioning for their input: Jeff Melson, Alicia McNamara, Charlie Sherrod, Andrew Bergum, Geoffrey Becker, Steve and Linda Becker. All provided unique and valuable feedback and encouragement. Finally, thanks to the "Word Warriors" critique group of the San Gabriel Writers League for their insights, recommendations, and encouragement. It's an honor to work with these accomplished people. To anyone else I may have missed, my apologies.

T.L Becker
March 2025

www.ingramcontent.com/pod-product-compliance
Lightning Source LLC
Chambersburg PA
CBHW060541260626
47161CB00003B/1007